Bitter Passage

An Allegheny Beckham Novel

Geoffrey Bates

Norumbega Press

Norumbega Press

NorumbegaPress.com

Jacket Design: David Prendergast

ISBN: 979-8-9904260-0-9

E-Book ISBN: 979-8-9904260-1-6

For Ann and Jean, the Barrows sisters,
and for Susan, who has been very, very patient.

Bitter Passage

One

I switched on my lightbar's red and blue strobe. Diminishing snow flurries shifted briefly to patriotic confetti, then mixed informally with the yellow caution flashers of the Chamberlain County snowplow that sat idling in front of me. Beyond our lightshow, the morning was still black.

"Deputy Beckham responding to the 10, uh, 10-52 at 65 Merry Hill Rd., Huntley."

"10-4 Beckham," the dispatcher responded.

I climbed out of my Explorer. Waist-high mounds at either side defined the open road. *Jesus, who the hell comes out in this shit?* We'd been pounded for a day and a half by a late winter nor'easter. Downed trees had cut power to much of southern Maine and side roads were generally impassable. Merry Hill Rd. is inland but the elevation would probably get you a glimpse of Muscongus Bay on a clear morning.

"What'cha got?" I called as the driver climbed down from the cab. Diesel exhaust sullied the frigid air.

"Jeez, Deputy umm . . . Hey, you're tall for a girl," he said, angling his head and doing the once-over.

"It's Beckham. Deputy Beckham."

"You play basketball?"

I ignored the question.

He moved on. "It was you, took Sam's job? Too bad about Sam. Boy, was that bad luck? A Vet like him and all."

"It's always the unloaded gun that kills," I deadpanned. "So, what'cha got?" I repeated.

"I come up this hill and everything's goin' fine," he began. His mouth turned down. He waited a beat, raised his head and cleared his throat. "I didn't see no cars from the village all the way out here. Hell, you know they closed Route 1 for the first time I can remember? Had to double back twice 'cause of trees and lines. Been doing this for fifteen years. I seen all sorts. Helped deliver a baby once. Never nothing bad. Now, this." He gestured toward the front of the plow.

"So, what's the issue?" *I don't need a Goddamn resume, just tell me why the hell I'm out here.*

"C'mon up," and he signaled to follow.

He'd backed his truck to give a better view and the issue was clear as we moved into the headlights. The plow had cleared its usual nine-foot swath. The white body-paint of a high-end SUV effectively blended into the snow. It was halfway pulled off the road and cut open like Boy Scout's can of Dinty Moore stew. The SUV was still heaped, the open metal gash a jagged contrast to the smooth lines of the car. Looking back at the plow, it was plain how the raised corner matched the slice.

"Shit! See what I mean?" He was looking anxious now. He shuffled in his Carhart coveralls. "I been out here for eighteen hours straight. Once I was done with Merry Hill I was going back to the shed." Gray stubble hinted at his age. He squinted, "Jesus, this is a freakin' 'Rover, too."

"Okay, look. I've gotta fill out a report." The guy started wringing his hands. I tried to assure him, "It's a good thing you called it in. You know it's standard procedure. Don't worry, you're covered by county insurance—you'll be fine."

While examining the car, I ran my gloved hand along the sharp rip, then drew my citation pad from my hip pocket and paused. There was something curious about the scene. I looked to the eastern horizon—it was brightening, but there was no sun, yet, so there was no source for color except the strobes and the light of our headlights. I looked back at the car. The passenger and driver's windows were down. The interior was full of snow. And it was pink. I pulled my flashlight and tried to get a better look, holding it at arm's length and at an angle so the beam's reflection wouldn't blind me. The snow's color shifted from a rosy hue to deeper crimson and, finally, to a man's face in three-quarter profile, veiled in icy crystals.

"What's your name?" I'd been with the sheriff less than two weeks.

"Larsson. Lars Larsson."

"Lars, we've got an issue here."

"You mean I'm getting written up?"

"No. Hell, no. You don't have to worry about that now. Do me a favor. I'm gonna back up some and I want you to just back up a little more, too."

Larsson adjusted his knit cap and reviewed the situation. He climbed back into the cab, keeping his eyes on the SUV.

Departing clouds on the southern horizon were beginning to show faint signs of gold as I slipped back into the warmth of my cruiser.

"Deputy Beckham here. Uhh, we've got a situation. Ummm, lemme see, I think we have a 10-49 . . . It's probably a 10-49 . . . I've got a dead body out here on Merry Hill Rd."

Two

I'd come back to Chamberlain County because it was home, and I figured it would be quiet. After five years patrolling South Chicago's Auburn Gresham district, I was exhausted and desperate for a change, tired of rolling up and finding kids shot to death.

So I knew the drill, even though the circumstances were new. I pulled a mini-snow shovel from the shotgun clip and dug carefully through the drift at the rear of the Rover, searching for the license plate. Like in Chicago, my cruiser was equipped with the Automated License Plate Recognition system. The car-mounted cameras deliver automatic alerts to the officer's dash computer when they "see" a plate from the state's Hot List of stolen or otherwise flagged vehicles. And, like in Chicago, frozen schmutz fouled the lens and made the cameras pretty much worthless during snow season. Back in the SUV, I held my hands to the dash vent and let my fingers warm a moment—this guy wasn't going anywhere—before I did it the old-fashioned way and keyed in WHITE, LAND ROVER, VELAR, PLATE I/D NCLY-K9.

The car was clean and registered to a Major and Honor Fielding in South Prescott. Number One Fielding's Landing. I rolled it around a couple of times *. . . 1 Fielding's Landing . . .* couldn't place it. When I pulled up the Google map, the area shown on the screen looked more like a district of the village than a street address.

Contacting the dispatcher again, I confirmed the 10-96, summoning the Sheriff to the scene and started the paperwork for a homicide. Larsson was sleeping in his cab. About a half an hour later, Sheriff Latch arrived. Lars climbed down and we waited while he called in.

I'd had a phone interview with Latch as part of the hiring process and, of course, had met with him once I started with the department. He had the height and had maintained the build of the standout basketball star he'd been at Madison Academy, well before my time. He straightened and reviewed the situation while Larsson and I stood at our vehicles.

"You touch anything, Beckham?"

"Nossir. Just dug out the license plate. I've been waiting for you or Maine State Patrol or the examiner to arrive."

"Well, let's get to it. Gimme that shovel." He began to clear a path while Lars pushed snow from the hood with a broom he had pulled from the side of the plow.

"Car's been sitting open since, probably Friday night. Never seen anything like this before," the sheriff said, standing back for a moment.

"Shouldn't we be taking photographs or something?" Larsson asked.

"Hell no, there's nothing on the outside of this car that's going to help with the investigation." Latch replied. "C'mon, let's get this thing cleared off so we can see what we're dealing with." The roof was cleared and revealed a ski rack with three sets of skis and an open moonroof filled with dusty-pink snow. This was a remote road. We'd had warnings for almost a week about the blizzard so the car wasn't here by accident.

The sheriff declined my offer to help and they continued while I watched. Latch was intent on getting the job done himself. Larsson was breathing hard, but the sheriff was hardly winded by the time they'd cleared a walking space around the vehicle. We'd heard a car approaching and the two of them stood back as an old Jeep Wrangler with a light flashing on the dash pulled in behind me. Latch looked away and his expression shifted while the occupant prepared for the cold. The door opened and I tried to conceal my surprise. You still don't see many black folks in the Maine woods.

"Bon jour, LuLu," said the sheriff. He seemed a little cool.

"Bon jour," she replied with an accent that couldn't be faked and then, looking at me, "Bon jour, Miss . . . ?"

"Beckham. Deputy Beckham"

"Ahhh. Deputy Beckham. So, you must be the replacement for Sam," she said absently as her focus shifted to Fielding's vehicle. She ignored Larsson. "Sheriff, why have you cleared the car? The Maine State Patrol, they will be in charge of this investigation, *non*? It is a murder? Yes?"

"Deputy Beckham, this is Chamberlain County's Medical Examiner, Dr. Lucienne Charlevoix," he said, ignoring the M.E.'s question. "And no, we don't know it's a murder. Maybe it's just a cherry snow cone in a Land Rover."

Charlevoix smiled without humor. I wasn't going to say anything. "But, James," she insisted with a familiarity that seemed unwarranted, "We really should wait. The State Patrol, they will be here in a moment or two." The distant whoop of a siren seemed to confirm her speculation.

I expected the sheriff to back off, but he turned from the car and forced a broad smile, perfect teeth flashing a boyish grin.

The authority.

"This is my damn crime scene, LuLu," he said affably, but assertively. "We'll get it started for our friends from Augusta."

Three

"HERE BECKHAM, TAKE THIS." Latch handed me the shovel and then he and Larsson opened the front doors and began to pull handfuls of snow from each side of the car. I stood back with the examiner, shocked at the difference between here and Chicago. There would've been 25 cops and detectives blocking off the space, doing witness interviews, keeping angry and grieving neighbors at bay, wrangling the media, laying out evidence blocks. Light towers, if needed. My gaze shifted west, down the road. A line of white birch stood, highlighted and erect. Gentle hills rolled into the distance, where the deep sapphire of night remained. A waxing moon was a tipped-up bowl on the horizon. Not Chicago. Except for our little party, there was no activity. Another *whoop*, louder now, broke the moment as a car crossed onto Merry Hill Rd. The sheriff stopped, waved off Larsson, and signaled me to stand behind him. I stepped between him and the Rover, using the shovel to balance. Flashes of blue occasionally twinkled off the frozen surface, hinting at the car's progress. The headlights of a Maine State Patrol cruiser finally appeared down the hill and we braced ourselves for its arrival.

A heavy-set guy sort-of leapt from the passenger's side as the car slid to a stop. "What the hell are you *doing,* Latch?" he shouted, coming around the front and using the hood to balance. He slipped once or twice on the ice in his hurry, but caught himself before he went down. "This is an MSP investigation. Now, get the hell away from our scene!"

"Back off, Hodgkins." Latch stood firm, arms akimbo, in a theatrical pose. "This is in Chamberlain County and, as such, it's our crime scene. You're just here to make everything official."

Hodgkins pulled up and got his balance. Squinty eyes glared at the sheriff. He chewed for a moment on a thick salt-and-pepper moustache.

"Look here, Sheriff, you know the protocol. You know the Goddamn *law*. You're not supposed to make a move until the Maine State Patrol arrives. That'd be me. And yet . . . and yet . . . *Jeeezus*, you've completely compromised this . . . this . . ." he hissed, opening his arms and embracing the site dramatically. "How the hell are we going to get anything from this piece of shit?" By now, his partner was standing next to him, equally put-out.

Latch stepped aside. "I have to apologize for my rookie deputy."

"Deputy Beckham here got over-excited. After she called it in, she went at it with her shovel. When I arrived, it was already compromised. I figured we'd just keep going. There probably won't be any evidence lost in this snow."

Hodgkins turned. I stood with the shovel in hand, blindsided. "All due respect Sheriff, but . . ." I stammered.

"Save it for later, Beckham. Sam would've known to keep his hands off. You'll learn."

"This will appear in my report." Hodgkins said, his eyes shifting back and forth between the Sheriff and me. "Expect a reprimand from the AG, Beckham. If you don't know what to do, then don't do a Goddamn thing." My fist tightened on the shovel. I'd already dealt with a lifetime's share of murders but, clearly, I was going to be the fall girl here. *Suck it up, Beckham, you need this job.*

"Yes, sir." I replied.

Latch stepped to the pair of men and put a hand on Hodgkins's shoulder. "Let's get 'er done," he said amiably, looking directly at me. The three chuckled and moved to the open SUV. They'd circled the wagons. They relaxed a little, knowing they had a scapegoat.

I started for my car.

"Hey Beckham, gimme that," Latch said, pointing to the shovel. "We might as well put it to some good use." I tossed it over the hood. He caught it by the shaft and turned to give Larsson some instructions. "The bottom's supposed to drop out. We need to get this cleaned up before it freezes solid. And—hey Beckham," he called, dismissing Lars and looking over the roof of the SUV. "See if you can get someone to deliver some coffee, donuts, and sandwiches, okay? Captain Hodgkins, if I remember right, you like the chicken salad sandwiches from Donna's and you drink your coffee black?"

Hodgkins was surprised. "Yeah, that's right."

"Right. Beckham, call Donna's Diner, we've got an account there. She lives above the store so she'll answer. Get me a ham and swiss, order for yourself, Hodgkins and his partner Gerrity, Larsson here, and LuLu. And get a couple dozen other assorted sandwiches and some doughnuts. Tell 'em we need, like, four gallons of coffee—they have some insulated urns. Tell the dispatcher that Junior McCann should pick 'em up on the way out. We don't know how many officers we'll have here or how long we'll be—it's gonna get colder'n a penguin's pecker."

I looked to the M.E., who stood back during this exchange. She gave nothing away as she turned to the scene.

"Veggie wrap," she said over her shoulder as she approached the Land Rover.

Four

MORE COUNTY PERSONNEL AND the MSP Emergency Response Team eventually arrived. Pretty soon after that, the place began to look like a crime scene. Hodgkins told Larsson to leave the plow-load of snow that was sitting in front of the machine when I arrived. The driver plowed the space fore-and-aft of the scene for about a quarter-mile as best as he could, given Merry Hill's slim dimensions. A hodge-podge of official vehicles now filled the narrow road, made to feel even tighter with the ancient stone walls that lined both sides. The M.E. was told to back off for a while as Hodgkins "assessed this piece of shit," and bustled around directing his team. Latch ordered the section of Merry Hill closed and posted cruisers at each end as a matter of procedure. It wasn't really necessary. Even though Merry Hill was known locally as a 'cut through' between Wooster and the way north, no one was traveling. He had me string police tape well away from the situation, giving folks some room to move. I expected to be directing traffic, but he told me to assist the M.E. *Yeah, that's about right, the girls can work together.* Reporters from WLHS-TV and the Portland Free Press showed up and stood outside the tape eavesdropping and angling for interviews. The Sheriff emphasized he was the only one to talk to the media, and he wasn't ready. Hodgkins had been cowed into silence.

I needed to pee. By this time, I was ten-and-a-half hours into an eight-hour shift. I hadn't gone since I'd stopped around 2 a.m. at a quickie mart whose owner had kept up with the snow, using a little A.T.V. to plow every hour. I looked around for some cover, then down the hill to the southeast. The sun revealed a pair of soft white rectangles with roof lines exposed from the wind and a Dish TV antenna. Trailer homesteaders. Other mounds of snow blossomed where

I guessed junked cars, boats, and decrepit outbuildings settled quietly into the landscape. A flat parking circle was pierced by a dead white pine tree that had been stripped of its limbs and turned into a flagpole. A Confederate battle flag moved listlessly. Amber glow snapped on under the snow at one end of the nearest box as I watched. *Nope. Not going there.*

I approached the sheriff.

"Beckham, where the hell's our coffee and doughnuts?" He was standing with another deputy and a statie. They smiled.

"Gee whiz, Sheriff, you might have heard we had a storm last night." I tried to keep my voice light. "It might take a while." His buddies drew their breath and looked expectantly at him.

"Lighten up, deputy." The universal brush-off. "You need something?"

"You mind if I take a short walk?"

"Whassamatta, ya gotta pee?" The three smiled at one-another.

"As a matter of fact, I do. May I take a short walk, *sir*?"

"Sure, but don't be lookin' for us if you fall into a drift." Smiles all around.

I stopped at my car, pulled my go kit, and searched the perimeter of the scene. The wind had scoured the base of a pair of balsam firs, just off the road in the direction of the trailers. As I walked, I could feel men watching. I found a place that was reasonably concealed and, on my way back, everyone was back at work. Maybe I was being oversensitive.

Was I wrong to come home to Maine? When I interviewed over the phone, the Sheriff sounded like a decent guy. Sure, I'd be the only female deputy patrol officer, but that was because Bertie Smalls had retired last summer after a 45-year career of writing parking tickets. It hadn't been perfect in Chicago. There were plenty of jerks. Latch said he was looking for 'fresh blood' on the force and told me that, with the combination of my work in Chicago and being a native, I would be the perfect hire. Okay, maybe I *was* being oversensitive.

My path had taken me past the front of Fielding's SUV. Snowbanks reached over 6 feet high in places along the downhill shoulder after Larsson's plow job, but I'd found a convenient break in the wall where I'd been able to access the trees. As I dipped back under the police tape, I decided to check in with the M.E. She was still waiting for Hodgkins to complete his site investigation. Turning toward her Jeep, something out of place caught my eye.

"Be completely present to whatever speaks to you at an investigation," Lieutenant Torres had always counseled, "no matter how insignificant." Her advice was more memorable than the shouted "Keep yer fuckin' eyes open, probie!" I'd hear from the guys regularly.

I looked again, but there was nothing. I stepped back under the tape and tried to mimic my earlier movement. Nothing. I tried again, and as I stood, the plow's yellow strobe flashed true from the jagged mound. Standing, nodding my head, bobbing and concentrating with the light's rhythm, I was able to fix the reflection and cautiously approach its source. A tiny corner of laminated paper poked out, about waist-high and 15 feet from the front of the SUV.

I called Hodgkins over.

"Well, Beckham. *Beckham, Beckham, Beckham.*" Hands on hips. He sighed to himself as he knelt to inspect the area. It was a wall of packed icy sludge shot through with sticks, shredded leaves, the occasional half-empty Coors Light can, a faded McDonald's bag, bits of loose pavement picked up by the plow, and stones. "I was watching you do your little dance over here. That how they solve crimes in Chicago, doin' a little do-si-do?" He stood and did a little step and smiled, hands outstretched in the standard *"Ta-Da!"* position, expectant of applause.

I pointed to the plastic corner. He sighed and pulled a pair of tweezers out of the tool vest he was wearing and gently teased out a four by six-inch piece of laminated card stock.

"If you hadn't trashed the site before we arrived, this might actually have been a clue." He stood and held it up for me to see. "It's a kid's lift ticket for The Mountain. But, of course, there's the distinct possibility it's just part of all the other shit people have dumped along here. We'll never know. We'll bag it and set it aside. Thanks, Beckham—and let the M.E. know I'm done with the scene for the moment." He walked back to his partner, who was melting and straining the snow from Larsson's plowload, searching for shell casings or any other clue.

Charlevoix had her eyes closed as I approached the jeep. By now I was cold and hungry and wondering when the hell McCann, Jr. was going to show up with the food. I tapped on the window. She opened her eyes and gestured to join her.

"Thanks," I said, stepping in and enjoying the warmth.

"Certa," she replied, closing her eyes again.

I looked across at her. She had taken off her hat and scarf in the car. There was an air of efficiency: closely cropped hair would be easy to maintain. I got it. I'd considered getting a bob before I'd left Chicago but couldn't afford it and hadn't had the time since I started with the sheriff. Simple but well-chosen makeup; her amber eyes complemented deep, bittersweet chocolate skin. Knee-high Grundens boots nodded to the fishing industry and were effective, not flashy. She was trim; perhaps she worked out? My first encounter had left an impression of youth, but sitting here, close to her, I could see laugh lines and the hint of age. At a glance she could pass for mid-thirties but she was probably closer to late-forties. She had the look of tired experience.

"Hodgkins said he's done with the scene work for now and that you're welcome to begin with the body."

"It can wait a moment or two. You can sit for a minute, yes? You must be freezing."

"Yes, I am. Thanks." We sat for a moment with our eyes closed. I realized I was falling asleep.

"Okay, I'm good," I said, reaching for the door. I didn't want to get called out as a wimp.

"Very good, suit yourself," she replied, grabbing a clipboard as she stepped out of the car. "Here, put these on," she said, pulling a wad of latex gloves from her pocket and singling out a pair for me, "in case you need to touch something. The sheriff said you've got some familiarity with murder scenes? Let's see what this gentleman has to say to us."

Five

ALL FOUR DOORS AND the hatchback were open as we approached the Land Rover. Snow had been removed from well around the car and messy slush was evident where Hodgkins and others had been working. Major Fielding was still sitting in the driver's seat. Someone had unclipped his seatbelt. His chin rested on his chest. Hodgkins had used a soft brush to remove most of the loose snow that had encased the corpse. Flakes had melted with his waning body heat and then refrozen as the temperature continued to fall. A crystal sheath on his exposed skin made him look artificial.

There were two bullet holes in his head. Blood and goopy brain matter had soaked, then frozen into the headrest and stained the shoulders of his white Patagonia ski jacket. A thin wire looped through a zipper on the left arm near his shoulder. The jacket was unzipped and open. Deep crimson surrounded a matted hole in his chest and faded to pale pink as it moved to the outer edges of a white cashmere turtleneck. *Expensive.* One hand rested comfortably on the seat, the other on his leg. The left hand was shot through with a single bullet hole where it made sense to think he had reacted, trying instinctively to block the gunshots. I stood outside the door, looking over the doctor's shoulder while she reviewed the setting.

"Well, we can be reasonably certain of the cause of death." The M.E.'s mouth was tight and she focused on the scene in front of her. She laid her clipboard on the hood.

She turned and called out, "Officer Gerrity, have you found any brass?"

"Not yet," he replied as he tossed a five-gallon bucket of water across the drainage ditch.

"My guess is 9mm but we'll know when we find the slugs," she mused. She cocked her head to the left, then to the right, analyzing. She crouched and leaned into the cabin to see the front of the headrest better. "It appears he saw what was going to happen and tried to dodge the first shot," she said, as much to herself as to me. She stood and pointed to his palm and then to a grazed area at his hairline where it looked like something had removed the hair down to the bone. "His skull, it was snapped back by the first. The second shot was to the forehead. A third to the heart to make sure." She reached across and moved her gloved hands gently down Fielding's jacketed arms. She pulled an expensive pen from inside her jacket and bounced it lightly on his knuckles. It made a *'dink-dink'* sound. She did it again on what should have been a softer place on his arm. *Dink-dink.*

"Frozen solid."

"Dr. Charlevoix, is that a mark on his arm?" I asked, pointing. From where I stood, there seemed to be a shift in color near Fielding's wrist that she might have missed. I couldn't tell if it was post-mortem discoloration or something else.

"Call me LuLu, please," she answered. "Good eyes, Deputy Beckham."

She called to the Sheriff, "James, Deputy Beckham noticed he may be missing a watch. Have you noted that?"

He stepped over. "Yeah, we saw the tan line. Wallet's gone, too. Hodgkins said his name is Fielding. That right, Beckham?"

"Yes sir. Major Fielding."

"Is that a title, Beckham—he in the military?"

"No sir, seems to be his given name." Maybe Latch was reaching out. "I pulled up a map of his place in South Prescott, it's huge—takes up a big chunk of Wey's Island."

"It looks pretty simple to me, LuLu," Latch turned, ignoring me. "His watch is missing—probably a Rolex or better—his wallet's gone . . . the guy stops at a convenience store, gas station, I don't know. Some junkie's there trying to keep warm, sees the watch, sees him flash a wad of cash, follows him until they're in the middle of boofu, pulls ahead and blocks the car, gets out and shoots him. Boom. Robbery for drug money. You're done." His lips were pressed firmly together.

Certain.

"Perhaps," LuLu replied. "But, it seems if that were the case, the robber would have shot him through the window and there would have been glass littering the site. There's none. The shooter appears to have been much more efficient than just a random murderer . . . to me, at least. Three shots, all of them hit the target. It looks—again, to me—as if Fielding rolled down his window to talk to the killer. He wouldn't do that if he thought he was going to be robbed, *non*? And from the look of the car and his clothes, he would know enough not to trust anyone who pulled in front of him the way you are suggesting."

"Okay . . . we can agree that it was a robbery, right?" Latch countered.

"That will be for you and your detectives to determine. My job is to see what this Mr. Major Fielding can tell us about his demise." She raised his sweater to examine his stomach and shined a mini-light she'd pulled from her jacket on the skin. It looked pretty good. There was no staining or change in color that I could see. She pressed his abdomen. It didn't spring back. "Frozen, Sheriff. Even if we could get a probe in, it wouldn't tell us anything. You believe that he has been here since late Friday afternoon, yes?"

"Yeah, that'd be my guess. I figure the car was here and he was dead just as the storm started ramping up." The Sheriff was talking to her from across the car's interior. "That's the only way it could have filled with as much snow as we found."

"So, it's Sunday morning. That would mean he died 36-40 hours ago." She straightened and looked over the SUV's roof at Latch, who was now leaning against the open passenger door. "Yes, I think I can agree with that assessment. That should at least provide you with a reasonable time for the crime, Sheriff. There's really nothing else I can do here."

"Okay, we'll book that time and proceed on that assumption," he said, and walked back to a group of deputies who were gathered at my cruiser. The food had arrived and they'd set up a winter picnic on the hood and were busy wolfing sandwiches and drinking coffee. The Sheriff spoke a few words to the crew, grabbed a sandwich, and walked to his vehicle. The food looked pretty good—I hadn't eaten since breakfast the day before.

Charlevoix broke in. "Deputy Beckham, would you please help me move Mr. Fielding?"

I nodded, then called the guy from Lentz's funeral home over. I was already learning stuff. Evidently, Maine relies on a rotating roster of funeral homes to transport bodies to Augusta. He pulled a gurney from the hearse and rolled it to the rear of Fielding's SUV. He introduced himself as Kurt Lentz and we shook hands.

"Man, that's a stiff stiff," Lentz said, smiling at LuLu. They knew each other from previous encounters. She acknowledged him as she considered the situation.

"Yes, Kurt," LuLu replied as she placed her hands on the roofline and leaned in. "Tell you what, why don't you go around to the opposite side . . ." He left the gurney, made his way to the far door, and peered through the interior. "Good. Now, reach across and catch his feet. If you can do that and pull and swivel Fielding on his butt, Deputy Beckham and I will twist and lower him to the seat, yes?"

"Sure," he said. "Would it be okay to slide these back to give us more room?"

"Of course," Charlevoix replied. "MSP is done with the car—except for finding the slugs—and I expect they'll be in the upright cushion."

I'd already knelt to grab the bar under Fielding's chair to slide it. There wasn't one. *It's a Rover, Beckham. There's no bar.*

"Can you flip the keys, Dr. Charle – LuLu?" I said, over my shoulder, "It's got electric seats."

Lentz had made the same discovery. I stood as she reached through the wheel. "It's keyless," she said, fumbling her hand along the steering column. Lentz, who must have been a little more familiar with upscale starting systems than LuLu or me, leaned in and, using the empty chair to balance, reached for the dash. He pressed the ignition button.

Nothing.

The M.E. straightened and turned, searching. She found Hodgkins with the brunch crew. "Captain Hodgkins!" she called and motioned for him to come over. I heard a door slam somewhere.

Hodgkins took his time finishing the final bite of his sandwich and wiping his mustache clean. He excused himself from the group.

"Yes, Doctor?"

"Did you remove one of those 'fob' things from the car?"

"Yeah, it was laying in the console. We bagged it and tagged it."

"Can you please bring it so we can move the seats and get our victim on his way to—"

"GERRITY!" Hodgkins yelled, startling us as much as it did Gerrity, who had taken a break from melting snow to replace Hodgkins at the meal. "The good doctor wants the key fob for the Rover."

Gerrity reluctantly gave up his place to look for the fob. LuLu busied herself with examining the rear of Fielding's seat for any sign of exit holes. Lentz pulled his phone and checked his Facebook feed.

There was movement at my cruiser as a guy appeared in snowshoes from the trailer encampment below. A couple of the deputies seemed to know him. He declined a sandwich after jamming his poles into the embankment outside the tape. He looked like he might be more interested in the vic than socializing.

Gerrity ambled over with the bagged fob and LuLu nodded to him as he raised it to the car. She reached for the ignition button.

Nothing.

"Just a sec," I said, kneeling again and pushing the brake pedal with the heel of my hand. She pressed the button again and the engine began to hum. Notification bells chimed and video imagery spread across the built-in screen announcing that this Land Rover Velar was ready to conquer mountains, rivers—any driving obstacle the owner might encounter, except, perhaps, a shooter on a rural road.

"Thank you, Officer Gerrity," LuLu said. "We can manage from here." I heard Hodgkins scold the kid for breaking from the water detail as they retreated to the sandwich group. "Kurt, let's try this again."

Lentz and I reached for the chair controls on our respective sides and both slid back noiselessly, giving us a little room to maneuver.

"We're in business," said Lulu.

Lentz climbed on to the passenger seat and positioned himself facing us with one foot on the floor to give some leverage. He leaned forward to grab Fielding's knees.

"Deputy Beckham, please guide Mr. Fielding's hands past the steering wheel, if you can, as we tilt the body. I'll get the head," the doctor instructed. She and I were shoulder-to-shoulder in the open door and I leaned in. "Good. Okay everyone, now, gently."

Lentz grasped the vic's knees and gave a steady pull. LuLu pulled from the shoulders in the opposite direction. Nothing. He was frozen to the leather.

"Okay." She took a breath.

I reached in front of her, being careful not to touch the vic, and clicked the seat warmer buttons on the center console. *"'Voila!',"* I offered.

Charlevoix turned full face to me and smiled at my attempt at French. *"Oui! Voila—bonne idee—Merci!"*

We waited a moment or two in awkward silence. Lentz checked Facebook again. LuLu busied herself checking boxes on the clipboard's forms.

Finally, LuLu slid her hand under Fielding's butt to see if he was ready.

"Kurt, Deputy, let's try this once more."

We positioned ourselves and began to move in concert when she gave the signal. The body shifted, but remained insistently seated, reminding me of an Egyptian statue. LuLu cradled his head and we laid him, flat on his back, bent legs and feet in the air.

"Very good." She stood back, appraising, hands clasped as if in prayer, while Lentz and I steadied Fielding, looking to her for the next step. His shoulders were past the edge of the seat, his chin was still on his chest and the head hung, frozen and unsupported, past the door's rocker panel. His handsome face caught the sunlight. Something there attracted LuLu's attention. She bent at the waist and caressed the sides of his head, her face almost touching his.

"Hey, what the FUCK?"

The area was silent for a long beat. Torn yellow police tape fluttered uselessly to the ground and snowshoes clacked on the sloppy pavement. I looked to the klatsch of eaters. Nothing.

Stepping around LuLu, I raised my left hand: Police Academy 101.

The visitor came with unexpected speed across the narrow expanse, brandishing one of his poles like a baseball bat.

"Hey pal, where ya going?" *Officer Friendly.*

No one else moved.

He paused and jabbed the air in the direction of LuLu with his pole.

"What the fuck is she doing? Respect, man!" he called to the picnic group for solidarity.

My right hand reached for my baton. It wasn't there.

"Go fuck yourself, Eddie." I heard LuLu say behind me, loud enough for everyone to hear. I was stunned. These two had history.

The effect was electric. His camo field jacket was thrown tight against his chest and then he leaned into his snowshoes and started to make a run at us.

By now, I was at the rear of Fielding's car and put up both my hands.

"Hold on."

Firm.

The kid twisted sideways and put on the brakes, sliding as he started a windup with the pole.

I sensed the empty gurney at my thigh and shoved it, hard. It didn't make as much progress in the slush as I hoped, but at least it sort-of rolled broadside to him. I ducked as he swung for the fences and missed. He should have fallen with the follow-through, but he caught himself on the rail.

We were close now, diagonally across the empty red pleather pad. I could see he was older than just a teen. He smiled without warmth. I caught a whiff of chaw just before he spit a huge wad of tobacco juice. The mucous-y gob caught me full-face. I gagged reflexively and caught sight of LuLu moving fast at my right as I smeared the muck away.

She grabbed my jacket by the collar and pulled me back as Eddie used the pole to slash the air in a backhanded arc. I cleared my eyes in time to see him take a lunging jab at LuLu. She was fearless, catching and yanking the pole free and throwing it across the snowbank.

"Espèce de maudit osti de colon!" she shouted. "Get the hell away from my crime-scene!"

Incensed, he started to crawl up and over the gurney but thought the better of it, recognizing too late that it was impossible with snowshoes. With that effort, his mitten hooked between the rail and the bed. He was jammed up and desperately tried to free himself. The gurney swiveled wildly. I seized the moment, scooting in front of LuLu and catching the corner of the cart with my hip. With both hands firmly on the rail, I put everything behind it and pushed hard once more, but this time, stepping through. The semi-frozen slop was working in my favor now. His snowshoes got caught up in the wheels and he stumbled. He tried to catch himself on the rail again but this time it slid from his grip and he lost his balance and collapsed to the pavement. When he hit, rank nicotine smell exploded from his jacket. I moved quickly into his space.

Taking advantage of his surprise, I pinned his upper right arm to the pavement which put him face down.

I straddled his body and reached left.

"How 'bout some help here!" I called, forcing his wrists together and cuffing him.

No one came to my rescue.

"You fucking nigger-loving bitch," the kid hissed under his breath. "I will gut you for this." *The friendly faces of Vacationland.*

"Hey, what do I have to do to get a hand here, Sheriff?" I called in Latch's direction. I started to pull him up.

The picknickers began to turn back to their conversation.

"McCann! Kennedy!" Latch called from his cruiser and motioned two deputies in our direction. He walked over to me and the kid. I didn't know if this was a catch-and-release situation or if we were going to take him in. LuLu was back in her Jeep, composing herself. The Sheriff stood a moment, assessing.

"What the hell, Eddie? You gotta learn to control yourself."

"You saw her, Sheriff. She was gonna kiss that man . . . a dead white man—"

"Shut up, Eddie. She's doing her j— "

" —and you heard her, too! She's a fucking racist. Who knows what kinda names she was calling me with that Frenchie mouth of hers? I'm gonna file a hate-crime report against her and your dyke deputy . . ."

"You do that, Eddie," Latch said. McCann and Kennedy had arrived and seemed amused at the exchange.

"Take him home," the Sheriff said to the two deputies. He returned his attention to the kid. "Stay the hell away." He started to head back to his car.

"But, Sheriff," Eddie was winding up again. "You know what she did—"

"Shut the fuck up." Latch had been somewhat accommodating. Now he was getting angry. He gestured at McCann and Kennedy. "Get him out of here!"

The two deputies wrested the kid away, thoughtfully collected his pole from across the snowbank before they snagged a sandwich for him and grabbed his other pole. They moved him through the torn tape and started down the hill, trying to follow his earlier trail and taking exaggerated steps through the drifts. The Sheriff went to finish up with Hodgkins. Lentz was still in the Velar and looking uncomfortable. He was holding onto Fielding's ankles and sort-of balancing the stiff on the seat. I walked over to get the gurney. LuLu joined me and helped me lift it upright.

"Thanks, Beckham," she said.

"Yeah. Sure. Anytime." The cold shot through me as I started to relax. I shuddered.

"You okay?" she said, reaching across the cart and helping me back it to the edge of Fielding's car.

"Are you?" I replied.

"I suppose." She looked tired. "I apologize. My guess would be that you didn't expect that," she said to Lentz and me as we wrangled the corpse onto the bed. We laid him, flat, on his side so he looked curled up for sleep as opposed to a cartoon dead-person. It was clear to me she didn't want to go any deeper.

"There are assholes everywhere, every color, every age, everywhere," I said, looking to Lentz for approval of my tie-downs. He responded with a rueful smile and took over rolling the body to the hearse.

"Yes." She reviewed the scene: groups of men huddled together talking shop, Maine State Police officers busying themselves with final measurements, the Sheriff working the press. "Thanks again . . . "

"Allie," I offered.

"Thanks again, Allie. Hope to see you here and there."

Latch appeared.

"Beckham, you've had a long day," he said. "Nice job with the kid. We're winding down here. When's your next shift?"

"Tomorrow morning for the day shift. Today I was supposed to be off." It came out sounding more like whining than explanation. *Shit.* My first ten days had been all-nighters. I was beat.

"Take a couple of sandwiches and go home."

"Thanks," I replied. He'd already turned back to his buddies.

"Thanks, one more time," LuLu said, shaking her head as she watched Latch retreat to the klatsch and extending her hand. "I enjoyed working with you this morning,"

"Thank you." We shook hands. I smiled at LuLu, then realized I'd need to break up the picnic before I headed out.

Six

KENNEDY AND MCCANN HAD given the final sandwich to Eddie and by now the coffee was tepid. Things were winding down. One of the deputies gathered the garbage and urns from the hood of my Explorer and I started for Folkestone.

After navigating icy roads in the Huntley hills, the village streets were a piece of cake—300 years of northern New England winters gives you a lot of practice with snow removal. I pulled into a spot directly in front of 144 Cushing St., the rooming house where I rented. I found my key, entered, and nodded to two other tenants who were sitting in the kitchen. They started to say something, but I waved them off, too tired to be friendly. *That's right, Beckham, Miss Congeniality!* Climbing three flights to my space, I made certain I didn't hit my head on the ceiling as I turned on the final landing and unlocked the narrow door. I hung my coat and flak vest on the rolling coatrack and took stock of the simple furnishings. The bed and dresser came with the place. I had added a chair and a desk I picked up at the hospital guild's thrift store. It wasn't much, but it was all I needed for the time being. I peeled my clothes, shook out my hair, and stood at the south window, eyes closed, luxuriating in a sun whose winter angle slanted warmth directly onto my skin. Hanna and I would do this when we were girls in South Prescott. She called it "sunny dipping." The cool of my sheets felt welcome as I dove into bed, pulled the covers up and over, and slept for 15 hours.

◆

"H EY B ECKHAM , S HERIFF SAID he wanted to see you as soon as you arrive," the dispatcher called through bulletproof glass. She buzzed me into the secured office area.

"Thanks . . . ," I looked at her name badge, "Officer diSimone . . ."

It was my first time on day duty and I was early for my shift. A cluster of cubicles were arranged in a large room—the bullpen. A couple of other deputies were at their desks, doing paperwork. They kept working as I stepped to my space. *Welcome to the team, Allie!*

I'd seen the sheriff on the morning news where I'd grabbed breakfast. Local stories were sandwiched in-between national feed pieces that focused on Chinese guys wearing surgical masks. The reporter from WLHS had finally gotten Latch to make a statement about Merry Hill. He was comfortable in front of the camera but terse, saying he'd taken charge of the investigation and wasn't releasing the name of the victim, pending notification of next-of-kin, which surprised me since they had an entire day and night to locate someone.

The buzzer sounded again and a guy about my age entered. Buttoned-down. Sports-jacket, tie. He assessed the room, shared a nod of recognition with one of the desk-bound deputies, and looked my way.

"Beckham?" He held out his hand. "Jack Gill. I heard about Merry Hill. Congratulations on catching your first case." The other deputies looked up.

"Yeah. Allie Beckham. Thanks, I guess."

"Welcome back to Chamberlain County." We shook hands. "S'great to have a woman on the team."

Latch had told me a little about Gill. Decorated veteran, Criminal Investigation degree, he'd taken a bullet in the vest a couple of years before. He'd risen quickly and was already a lieutenant overseeing three longtime detectives in the department—the fair-haired boy—although truthfully, his hair was jet black and he had a look that wasn't quite "Maine." Latch must have let Gill know a little about me, too.

"Thank you," I said, smiling. "I'm happy to be back, despite the circumstances," I continued, acknowledging what everyone in the room already knew.

"Yeah, tough break about Sam." Gill's brow furrowed. "He and I worked together, as your new colleagues will attest," he said, nodding at the deputies. "DiSimone says Sheriff wants to see you ASAP."

"Right," I said, moving to the stairs. "I better get going. Thanks for saying hello." The other deputies were back to their paperwork.

"You bet. And Allie, if you need anything, let me know. I'm here to help." I paused as he dug out a business card, took the two steps across and handed it to me.

"Thanks, Jack," I said, taking the card. "I will."

Finally, a friendly face.

Latch's office was up three stairs and down a corridor. The county had used Homeland Security grants to renovate and add on to the 19th century courthouse. I passed the armory and a corridor that led to holding cells and the jail. The sheriff had been able to get his office moved to the front of the building during the renovations. I knocked and entered.

"Morning, Beckham. You're early. You get some sleep?"

"Yes sir, thank you." The sheriff's space was immaculate, unlike the deputy cubicles which, like the Chicago PD, were cluttered with case files and paperwork. Select mementos from high school, UMaine Orono, and the Marines—an MVP Madison Academy 1988 basketball trophy, some photos from one of the Gulf Wars, Rotary recognition—were on one wall. Family photos occupied the windowsill behind him that fronted the Gainsborough Village Common. The view east over his shoulder was pure New England. In the early morning light, the Coaticook River showcased its golden sparkle, while steepled white clapboard churches, capes, saltbox homes, and brick and cut-stone storefronts were nestled among grand oaks. A maze of snowy corridors hinted at the presence of sidewalks.

"Good." He got right to business. "You know the Merry Hill victim's spouse is Honor Fielding. Turns out she's the owner/manager of The Chamberlain Brewing Co. You been there yet?"

"No sir, haven't had the opportunity." The Chamberlain Brewing Co. had opened a couple of years before, below the Common, next to the river. It fit my dad's description of a "fern bar"—catering to summer visitors but making efforts to appeal to the locals.

"They make a good porter and a great Imperial Stout, if you like dark beers."

I nodded. *If I need beer ratings, I'll go online.*

"Anyway, we talked to her people at the pub and she's been out west at a conference and is in transit. We tried to get the Vegas PD to catch up to her but . . . it's Vegas and what happens . . ."

"Yes sir. They didn't find her."

"Right." He paused. "She and her husband must use one of those private jet services—"

"Sure, JetSuite or FlexJet. We used to see that a lot in Chicago."

"Of course." He paused again. "Beckham, skip roll call today. I'll let Chuckles know. I want you to go down to South Prescott to notify and interview Mrs. Fielding. The gal at the pub said she's supposed to be returning sometime this morning."

"But sir, I caught your interview on the TV. You said you're taking personal charge of the investigation."

"I am, but I can't get down there today. Once you've completed your interview, you will call me directly, do you understand? Here's my private cell number," he wrote it on a business card and handed it to me. "Tell diSimone you're heading back up to Huntley."

I took the card and considered before replying. Huntley is north. South Prescott is, well, south. *Go along to get along. Another reason I left the CPD.*

"Yes, sir. Is there anything in particular you want me to ask Ms. Fielding?"

"No—I'm sure you had plenty of interviews like this in Chicago. Have you been to South Prescott since you got back?"

"No sir. Haven't had a chance."

"Not much has changed."

" 'Never does . . . "

Seven

Life was returning to coastal Maine as I left Gainsborough. I passed back through Folkestone, where merchants tidied sidewalks and streams of snow arced white, like fountains, from driveway blowers. I turned onto Rte. 145 and headed south. The drive to South Prescott runs along the spine of one of midcoast Maine's many peninsulas. The road offered teasing glimpses of the Mackinnock River through stands of evergreens laden in white, and across the occasional drifted field as it wound its way up and down. Even after seven years, everything was familiar.

I reviewed the case so far. Major Fielding, a man of means, was found shot to death on a remote Maine road. As far as we could tell, all that was missing was his wallet and a watch. I re-imagined the scene. People in the northeast drive all winter with skis on their car top, so that might or might not mean anything. The wire on his left arm . . . that could have been from a lift tag, but a guy like Fielding wouldn't leave it half-removed. And then there was the kid's lift tag I found from The Mountain—while somewhat remote, Merry Hill was the most direct route from The Mountain to South Prescott. It wouldn't have been an easy drive in a blizzard, but folks like Fielding figured they were invincible in their expensive four-wheelers.

I crested Falk's Hill and slowed to drink in the view. The deep azure horizon of the Gulf of Maine was broken by the islands of Franklin Bay. A mile-wide pool of brilliant sunlight shifted reflection with the breeze in the middle ground. The business district of South Prescott: two stores, a fisherman's co-op, and the post office, lay below me. The two-lane road led steeply downhill. Modest clapboard homes of fishermen and stately vacation retreats were stacked somewhat uncomfortably as the land slid to two distinct bodies of water that flanked the state route. In the summer, West Harbor held sail and pleasure boats of all types. East Harbor was reserved for lobster and deep-water fishing boats because of its ease of access to the bay and then, further out, the Gulf of Maine. I made room for a kid delivering a stack of newspapers to Pierce's Supply as I crossed "The Neck," a natural causeway created by a narrow granite dike that joins what would otherwise be an island to the village proper. The road's path resumed its game of peekaboo with ocean views as it moved into dense wood and then opened along jagged coastal outcroppings with million-dollar views. I continued on.

Wey's Island was permanently linked to the mainland by a drawbridge in the early 50s when the Feds established a Cold War Naval listening post on its southernmost tip. From what I could tell looking at the Google map, it seemed that Fielding must have bought the entire installation during the recent draw-down. As a kid, Hanna and I rode our bikes out to the island and Janie Pierce's house. The three of us would be out all day sailing, fishing, exploring, defending "Fort Beckham" from the Bucklin boys, meeting new summer arrivals, and reuniting with other seasonal friends. I smiled to myself.

I arrived. Here were some changes. The ten-foot chain-link fence that used to surround the installation was gone. The institutional gatehouse had been removed and replaced by a structure clad in cedar shakes. The stone wall had been repaired in places but the dense stand of fir and white pine continued to block any view of the interior of the compound. The drive was plowed. I pulled slowly to the bar and punched "Call" on the keypad.

"May I help you?" A woman's voice.

"Yes, thank you. This is Deputy Beckham from the Chamberlain County Sheriff's office." I said, smiling at an invisible video camera I knew must be broadcasting my image. "I'd like to speak to Mrs. Fielding. Is she in?" *Miss Manners.*

"No. May I ask what this is about?"

"It's a personal matter and I need to speak directly to Mrs. Fielding. May I come in, please?"

"Certainly," the voice replied as the gate swung up and I pulled through.

Thick forest continued on either side as the pavement began a slight incline. A 19th century family cemetery appeared on the left just before the road moved down and between two gigantic granite outcroppings. The woods thinned and opened to a wide meadow that glittered under the snow in the low south light. Off to the right, a stand of arbor-vitae obscured an extensive solar array. The drive ended as a circle at a three-story contemporary Queen Anne-style shingled mansion. Multiple porches and catwalks joined different sections, unified by white trim. A more modest cape stood to the left, separate, but by the look of its design, clearly built at the same time as the main home. The caretaker's house. Other outbuildings were placed with an eye toward aesthetics, not happenstance. As I pulled up to the front door, an older woman emerged.

"Good morning," the voice from the gate said brightly as I walked toward her. "Your timing is excellent, Deputy Beckham. Honor should be—Here she is!"

I followed her gaze over my shoulder and an SUV appeared from the wood—a white Land Rover Velar that matched the car on Merry Hill. License plate SNOWBNY. *Cute.* It pulled to a stop behind my cruiser.

"Mom, what's going on?" Honor Fielding stepped quickly out of the vehicle. "Is there something wrong?" She was younger than I expected. Petite. She wore a practical, but not particularly flattering, long quilted coat and had a large floral-patterned bag slung over her shoulder. Naturally curly blonde hair spilled out of a knit cap. She looked better than I would have after a red-eye flight from Vegas. But then again, she flew in on a private jet.

"I don't know. Deputy Beckham, here, just arrived. She said that she needs to speak to you," the mother replied.

As I moved to introduce myself, a John Deere utility vehicle with a plow attachment pulled around the house and into the turnaround. I presumed the driver was Honor's father. He cut the engine.

"Hey I saw the sheriff—what's up Honor?" He smiled, "You been speedin' again?"

Nobody else smiled. I reached out to Honor Fielding. "Mrs. Fielding? Deputy Allegheny Beckham, ma'am. Can we go inside?"

"Sure, but what's this about?" she replied. "Where's Major, mom? Where are Trevor and Celeste?" she said, taking charge now and moving to the door. The three of us followed.

We passed through an entry area and into the warmth of a coffered foyer. I could see into a kitchen that would have filled one of the floors of the rooming house. In the other direction, light streamed from floor-to-ceiling windows along what I imagined was a living room that opened to the water. We were still in our coats.

"Frank, what's the matter with you?" It was Fielding's mother. "Get Deputy . . . Deputy Beckham's coat. Here, Honor, let me help you. How was your flight from Las Vegas, dear?"

Frank moved to help me, but his daughter turned and waved him off. "No. We'll do this right here. Right now. What is going on? Is this about Major? What has happened?"

"Mrs. Fielding. I'm very sorry to inform you that your husband— "

"Oh no! Is he hurt? Was there an accident?" she grabbed reflexively for her mother's arm.

"Mr. Fielding was found dead yesterday morning in Huntley." *No way to sugarcoat information like this.*

"Oh my God NO!" Her eyes were wide. She was clutching her mother's arm now with both hands. "But Trevor and Celeste—Trevor and Celeste were with him! Oh God, they weren't hurt, were they? They're here, right, Mom? Why didn't you call me?" She looked accusingly at her mother.

"But Honor, I thought they got stuck at The Mountain with the storm and all and they'd be home today . . . "

"Mrs. Fielding—," I began to ask who Trevor and Celeste were.

"The twins . . . Are they in the hospital? You took them to the hospital, yes? They must be in the hospital, right? Were they hurt in the wreck? What happened—did someone hit them? Was it a truck?"

I felt like I'd been sucker-punched.

Twins.

"No ma'am. There was no one else in the car."

Twins. Missing.

"*What!?*" The three of them reacted.

"No. Oh no, *that can **NOT** be!*" Honor Fielding reached and caught my jacket, her jaw clenched tight. Her eyes flashed an anger that was simultaneously desperate and focused. "My daughter and son were with Major. They *must* have been there."

"Honor, let's get these coats off and go to the living room so you can sit down," her mother said as she gently pulled the daughter's hand from my sleeve, then took the bag and began to pull the large coat from her shoulders. I kept my jacket, but her father collected the other two and moved to the closet. Honor Fielding wandered toward the living room. Her mother guided her to a seat on a long sectional. Dad came in and walked over to a bar. He poured glasses for his wife, daughter, and himself. He looked at me while his wife was settling Mrs. Fielding. I shook my head and he delivered the whiskey to the women. Honor Fielding was sobbing.

"Maybe," she said, "Maybe . . . Maybe he left them on the mountain. But they're so young—and we've talked about that . . ."

Her mother looked up. "I apologize, Deputy Beckham. I haven't introduced myself—Mary Chapman. This is Frank. We're Honor's parents." I nodded. "Tell us what happened."

"This is going to be difficult. I need to let you know there was not a wreck. Mr. Fielding was murdered. There was no indication that there was anyone else in the car with him."

"Sonuvabitch," Frank Chapman said under his breath.

"Murdered? How, why? Why would someone want to kill Major? But the twins—they spent the week skiing . . . " Honor Fielding was confused. She wasn't alone.

"He was shot while sitting in his car."

We needed to move on. Missing twins. I knew we were already behind.

"Trevor and Celeste," I said, trying to ground Honor and myself, "They were twins? How old? We'll send someone up to The Mountain. I'll need a description and a photo."

"They'd just turned fourteen."
The same age as Hanna and me.

Eight

The first 24 hours of a missing persons case is considered the most critical. It's why you have Amber and Silver alerts—to mobilize the public to action as soon as possible after a report. Honor Fielding was telling me there were two children missing for what—two-and-a-half *days*? But they might not be missing? They might have stayed on the mountain?

"Do the kids have cell phones?" I asked the group.

Honor was in a different world.

"Yes, of course, Deputy. Honor, we'll call the twins and get this all cleared up." Mary Chapman was trying to be helpful.

Her daughter's gaze locked on something outside, then softened as tears came again. Mary handed her a tissue and she blew her nose loudly.

"Where's your phone, dear? In the car? In your bag?"

"In my bag."

Frank Chapman rummaged through the quilted bag until he came up with the phone. "Here you go, Hon."

Honor looked at the screen and it opened up. "Call Celeste."

No ringtone. It went directly to voicemail and a young woman's friendly voice filled the room.

"Hey you reached Celeste—leave a message or call me back when I can talk!"

Honor Fielding cleared her throat, "Celeste! Oh, Celeste honey." She smiled an *"It's-going-to-be-okay."* smile at the three of us. "Please call me back as soon as you get this message. It's very . . ." And here, her voice began to break. She paused, looking at her mother who nodded encouragingly and reached to touch her knee, "Very important. Please, please call." She closed the call and was sobbing again.

"You did great. That was perfect." I was the professional in the room. I hoped it showed. "Can you please call Trevor? Maybe his phone is working." I knew it wouldn't be but, due diligence and all . . .

Honor wiped her cheeks and blew her nose again. She held the phone in both hands, like a talisman, and told it to call Trevor. Straight to voicemail.

"Hello. This is Trevor Fielding taking your call for . . . Trevor Fielding. Please leave a message for Trevor Fielding. Thanks! Trevor Fielding."

Frank Chapman smiled at his grandson's cheeky message. This time Honor was a little more in control.

"Trevor, this is mom. You need to call me as soon as you hear this message. As *soon* as you get this message. I love you—talk to you soon!" She got through it this time without breaking up.

We needed to keep checking off boxes. I knew the phones would be a dead-end from here on out. "Does the family have a place at the resort?" I asked Frank Chapman. His wife was trying to comfort Honor. She was shaking now and had already gone through her whiskey.

"No, they just stay at the Inn. They have a place in Vail but decided that the snow's been so good they'd ski local. The kids were on break from The Barton School." *Vail, The Barton School. Of course, only the best.*

"Okay." I looked past Honor and Mrs. Chapman to the bar and noticed an 8x10 close-up snapshot of two kids who had to be Trevor and Celeste. They were sitting in a sailboat. He wore a South Prescott Yacht Club t-shirt and swimming trunks. She was in a competition swimsuit and baggy shorts. They looked older than 14. Smiling, completely comfortable with each other. Colorful spinnaker sails of other boats were frozen in full bloom in the background. They had each inherited their mother's naturally curly blonde hair, freckles, and All-American look. They were clearly twins, yet distinctly boy and girl, the essence of Anglicized ideal beauty.

"Mrs. Fielding, is that a recent photo? Can I pull it from the frame? I want to get an image to our dispatcher as soon as possible in order to establish an alert." Honor Fielding looked through me, processing my request.

"Sure, Deputy Beckham. Anything you need," her father said, moving to the bar and beginning to remove the picture.

"But why? Why? Why? ***Why?***" Honor said as her mother hugged her. "He can't be dead. Not murdered. Not Major." She began sobbing again. Her mother handed the empty glass to Mr. Chapman, who handed me the photo and then poured another for his daughter.

"Mrs. Fielding," I prompted. "Mrs. Fielding."

Her mother looked at me and then turned her daughter's face to hers. "Honor, Deputy Beckham needs to ask you some questions. Come on, now. Focus."

"Mrs. Fielding," I held up the photo of the kids for her to see, "I'm going to shoot this with my phone and send it to our dispatcher so we can begin the process of setting up an alert." I sensed a shift as she turned to face me.

"Yes . . . yes, of course." Her eyes narrowed and I could tell she was with me. "Whatever you need."

"Great." I reached out and touched her shoulder. "We will find Trevor and Celeste and we will find whoever's done this to your husband and we will make them pay for it. We just need to get going on it." I stood. "Why don't you take a moment to gather yourselves while I step outside and let the department know about the twins? Once I've done that, we can talk in some more detail about Mr. Fielding. I will need you to answer some questions." *"Give them an itinerary, it'll help them," Lieutenant Torres would say.*

Honor Fielding looked up and tried to smile. "Yes . . . Okay . . . Good." She looked at her mother and then outside. I followed her gaze. Six-foot rollers swelled to their crest and crashed against ragged shoreline sending spray that built into lumpy ice-glob sculptures that glistened in the sun. A momentary surge of grief threatened to overcome her, but this time she rode it out.

"Dad, call the pub. Tell them I won't be in today and I'm not sure when I'll be able to stop by. Let Billie know she can take whatever overtime she needs and that she's in charge. James wanted to start a trial batch of a spring I.P.A. and tell her to approve whatever he needs."

"Sure thing, Honor," Frank responded to her assertive tone and he moved to the kitchen. "What should I tell them about Major and the twins?"

I jumped in. "Let's not tell them anything right now. We don't know where this is going or if the kids are truly missing yet . . ."

"Tell 'em I caught a bug out in Vegas," Honor interrupted me. She drank some whiskey and continued to stare at the water.

Frank moved on to make the phone call.

"Okay," I said, directing my attention more to Mary Chapman than her daughter, "This may take a few minutes. I need you to get some paper and write down the names, and if you have phone numbers that would be great, but the names of: A.) Anyone you know and trust at The Mountain who might be able to quickly find, check in on, or otherwise confirm that Trevor and Celeste are currently there. And then, and this is a tougher assignment . . ."

Honor turned to me.

"B.) We'll need a list of anyone who might have had an issue with Major—people he crossed in business—What *was* his business?" I asked, looking around.

"He's a . . . he *was* a financial planner. He has clients but they're all very happy with his performance . . ."

"Yes. Of course. We'll need a list of his clients but I want you to also think of anyone—*anyone*, who Major might have crossed in any way, no matter how trivial. Anyone he mentioned, even in passing, that he might have angered. Anyone from South Prescott? Anyone, anywhere at all."

Mary was looking in a drawer for some paper and something to write with. Honor's eyes met mine.

"Find my twins," she said.

I nodded and walked out the door.

◆

I sat in the Explorer, gathering myself. This wasn't Chicago, where I'd learned to trust my investigative instincts. This was home. South Prescott, home to the Beckham twins, Allegheny and Susquehanna. I tried to put that away and address the issue at hand. The Sheriff told me to interview Honor Fielding and report directly to him. But this was before I knew there were children missing.

I took a picture of the photo with my phone. I pulled the two business cards I had collected that morning and punched Latch's number into my cellphone. It went straight to voicemail. *Shit.* We needed to move and move now on this missing person report and I was handcuffed by the Sheriff's directive. I tried again. Nothing. I left a message, "This is Beckham. Call me at this number. We have possible missing persons."

I looked at the other card. Lt. Jack Gill. Criminal Investigation Department. If the twins were truly gone, we needed to move immediately. If they were still at The Mountain, well, I'd get another reprimand but that part of the case would be solved. *Great start, Beckham. How many reprimands can you rack up in a week?* I didn't remember Gill putting his cell number on the back, but was happy to have it. Maybe he could at least begin the paperwork.

"Yeah, Gill here."

"Lt. Gill? Deputy Beckham."

"Oh—Beckham! Hey, just a second." I could hear him moving and a door closing.

"Okay Allie, what's up?"

I explained that I needed some help. I told him I'd send him the photos of the twins and asked him to tee up the report so as soon as I heard from Latch we'd be ready to go. I also told him Latch asked me to keep this on the QT.

"Oh, okay . . . Yeah, sure, Allie. No problem. Let me know when you need it and I'll make sure it goes out."

"Thanks, Jack." I didn't like asking favors like this—*"The helpless girl."*—but finding the kids was paramount.

❖

I RE-ENTERED THE HOUSE. Mary and Honor had moved to the kitchen and were sitting at a counter the size of Long Island. Frank Chapman was making them sandwiches. "Deputy Beckham, you want one of my famous ham and egg sandwiches? McMuffin's got nothing on me." he asked as I entered.

"Please call me Allie. And yes, that would be great, thank you." I didn't know when I was going to have the chance to eat again. I turned to the women who were concentrating on a pad. Honor looked up. Her nose was red from blowing but she had washed her face and tried to smile. She still had a glass in front of her but looked much better. I looked at the pad on the counter. "So what do you have for me?"

"We have some close friends at The Mountain, the Kringles," she began. "The kids are close. Major said he was going to ski with Kris on what . . . maybe Thursday? He might have said something to him about any plans he had for the kids."

"So, this guy's name is . . . Kris Kringle?" I asked.

"Yes." She smiled at the thought, "He's the farthest thing from Santa Claus you can imagine, thin and very intense. He and Major worked at Bertram & Cohen before the crash. We've known them for years. The twins might even be staying with the Kringles." Her face brightened. "Maybe I could call them and find out if the kids are there?"

I was conflicted. On the one hand, if she called and the kids were there, well, we might be able to clear everything up here and now. On the other, with the sheriff wanting to keep everything going through him . . .

"We'll make a visit to The Mountain to interview anyone who might have seen Major or the twins before Friday," I replied. "I'm sure Sheriff Latch will send someone up today and they can check in with Kringle. Anyone else you can think of up there, anyone in management at the resort?" I might have been a little brusque, but it seemed to move the conversation along.

"No, not really." Honor looked a little disappointed, but she continued, "There was this one guy—whatshisname? I'm sure it's in my book. I think staff is pretty fluid from one year to the next so I'm not sure he'll be there. . . ," her voice trailed off.

"Okay. We'll get in touch with Kringle—is he married?" I asked.

"Yes, Fran—Francesca—is his wife's name. They have a daughter, Justine—she and Celeste are very close. She goes to The Barton School, too."

"Super. We'll run this down." Frank delivered my sandwich. It seemed like a good time to shift gears. "Now we need to talk about anyone who might have had a grudge against your husband. Anyone in business, any past associates, men or women, *anyone* you can think of. Was he involved in drugs—now or at any time in his life? Gambling? We want to look at anyone who might have an interest in seeing him dead."

Honor considered for a long moment. "Major tried to be up front with people in business. Sure, there were some folks along the way who lost money, but mostly when the Dot Com bubble burst and that was, what? over twenty years ago. As far as drugs are concerned, yeah, he smoked some dope in college and we've bought stuff in Colorado and have it around to party once-in-awhile," she looked at her mother, "But he's never been into anything hard. Never."

"If you don't mind me saying so, you seem, well, a little younger than I expected. Was this his first marriage?"

"No. No, he was married to Liz," she said. She looked at her mother. The two of them stiffened. "They had a boy named Stephen. He's an only child." Mary looked at the floor and shook her head almost imperceptibly. Frank looked out the window.

"Okay. Let's begin with Liz and Stephen. Are they around here?"

"No, they're still in New York," she began.

"Stephen. What an imbecile," Frank said to no one in particular.

Through occasional tears and brief editorial comments from her parents, Honor Fielding related Major's story. How he was born on a tobacco farm in North Carolina, earned his MBA at Duke and started with Lehman Brothers in 1983. How he met Liz Keating during a takeover negotiation in New York. She was an attorney on the opposite side. "He always said they kept that adversarial competition as part of their relationship."

"Yeah. For two people who supposedly understand business, they sure as hell didn't understand that marriage is a partnership, not just a relationship," her father interjected.

"Frank . . ." Mary Chapman said, reproaching her husband.

"No, it's okay, Mom. Dad's right. I think there was maybe a level of destructive competition there . . . maybe even on his part."

Honor's voice drifted off as she considered the implication of her comment. Frank turned and began tidying the stove top. Honor sighed and then faced the task at hand. *This girl might be tougher than she looks.*

"They lived in Manhattan and went through au pairs like they were changing socks," she began again. "Liz was always suspicious of him but he never played around. He was such a good man," Tears again.

Keating divorced him in 2002 after the DotCom crash. They had lost big-time. Nonetheless, she had gotten a big settlement.

"He was such a hard worker—he had to be with Liz breathing down his neck all the time. We met in 2004. I was crewing that summer on the Fair Isle and he was up with some clients." Her parents smiled at one another. "That's a windjammer— "

"Sure, I know her . . .," I interrupted.

"Oh, are you from around here?" Mary asked.

"Yeah, around here. But go on—you met in 2004?"

"So, we met on the cruise and then I visited him in Manhattan. Omigod, it was magical. We fell in love and married in 2005. Trevor and Celeste were born in February of 2006. Mom and Dad were a little worried—"

"Well, sure we were," Frank broke in, "I mean c'mon Honor, you were literally half his age. But we quickly realized that Major was the right guy for you and—"

"We grew to love him as if he were our son," Mary finished his sentence. The three were quiet for a moment.

"Tell me about Stephen," I said. "He's got to be, what, like in his mid-30s?"

"Stephen." Honor sighed.

She explained there was little time for Major and Stephen to get together in the early days. Liz intentionally maintained a busy schedule for their son, while Fielding's work obligations, including child support, alimony payments, and the exorbitant cost of living in Manhattan, left him with little to no free time. It had all taken a toll on their relationship.

"By the time I met Major, Stephen was 20, only three years younger than me. That didn't help, for sure, but I tried to relate to him. Not as a mother, but not as a peer, either. It was a little weird."

"Anyway, he had already flunked out of Rutgers and was working on flunking out of Manhattan Community College. Talk about drug issues . . . Liz never set any boundaries. He's like a kid with no direction whatsoever. He doesn't get in touch with us very often but when he does it's almost always about money. But, I don't think he could have come up here?" she said, questioning herself. "I don't think he has enough initiative."

"We don't know that," I said and continued, "How did you end up here, with all this, if Major was so strapped for cash?" I was trying to reconcile the story she was telling with what I was seeing and hearing. "I mean, hard work will get you so far but . . ."

"Don't use that tone with my daughter. What the hell are you implying?" Frank placed his hands flat on the island.

"It's okay, Dad," Honor responded gently. "Yes, we've been very fortunate."

She explained how Major had left Lehman in 2005 and started with Bertram & Cohen. "He saw some stuff going on he didn't like at Lehman's and decided he needed a new start when we got together. God, those first few years were tough. We lived in Manhattan and we had almost no money. I couldn't even afford to visit Mom and Dad." Fielding had caught a glimmer of the real estate situation in '05 and had gotten a number of his investors to bet against the market. When everything went to hell in 2008 they were sitting pretty. He made tens of millions, started his own firm and took his clients with him. "We bought the naval installation in 2010— Dad was in real estate and had an inside line." Frank brightened. "The twins and I live here. Major does business . . ."

She stopped.

"It's okay, hon," Mary Chapman offered.

"Oh mom, what will I do?" She looked at her mother and then finished her glass and handed it to her dad. She sighed and breathed deeply as he went to replenish her drink. She forced a smile as she looked at me.

". . . Major *did* business in Manhattan a couple of days a month. We still have a place there. We have a house in Kiawah, South Carolina, too."

I continued to write as we sat in silence.

"I know it sounds too unbelievably perfect. But, it was."

Nine

"Contact me if anything comes to you, no matter how insignificant, anything that might help us either find Major's killer or locate the twins. Thank you for the sandwich, Mr. Chapman."

Mary and Honor spontaneously hugged me as I stood. *So much for professional distance.*

Honor continued holding my hand. Her face brightened. "Of course, you're going to do some sort of Amber Alert, right? My twins need to know we're looking for them."

I had no clue what the hell the Maine law was on Amber Alerts, but I understood what we had in Illinois and I presumed—hoped—it was close enough.

"Mrs. Fielding. I'm sorry, but Amber Alerts don't work that way. The first step we need to take is to confirm they're not staying with anyone you're familiar with. Amber Alerts are really for super emergency situations where lives are at stake." Her grip tightened. I continued, using my open hand to loosen her grasp and then took both her hands in mine. "They're tricky and they can go both ways," I said with care. "Sheriff Latch will need to approve it and he's the next call on my list. We'll keep you informed, I'm sure."

She wasn't happy but Mary Chapman pulled her away.

Her dad stepped in. "It's a tough time. Honor will get through this. We believe in you, Allie."

I replied with a smile that I hoped displayed confidence, left my card, and started back to Gainsborough.

◆

I WAS CONFUSED. I was just a patrol officer—*One of your friendly Chamberlain County sheriff's deputies.* Everything so far made me the lead. Sure, I'd done some investigating in Chicago but I was the rookie here. I tried Latch's cell again.

"Latch here."

"Sheriff Latch, Deputy Beckham."

"Beckham. How'd it go? You learn anything?"

Yeah, I learned I'm not priority number one on your call-back list.

I summarized the morning's conversations. Latch didn't sound too surprised when I told him that twins might be missing. "It's likely they'll turn up somewhere on the slopes. These people have so much money they have no idea, or even care about, what the hell their kids are doing."

I voiced concern about the case. "Shouldn't I have a detective working with me? Maybe Jack Gill?"

"Look, don't worry, Beckham. I'm the lead." Latch responded. "You told me you were up for Detective in Chicago, right? Well, let's see what you learned. You're the legs. I don't want Gill or any other Detective involved in this. Here are your orders: Go up to The Mountain this afternoon. I'll contact Sheriff Poole and let him know you're going to be asking some questions. As far as an Amber Alert is concerned, we need to hold off. There's no need to alarm the entire state if these kids are bunking with a family friend."

"What am I looking for?" I wanted to avoid another Latch blindsiding.

"What the hell do you *suppose* you're looking for? Find the kids. And if you can't find the kids, then Goddammit, get me some information I can use to figure out why Fielding was murdered. MSP and LuLu haven't given me anything. Someone needs to start earning their keep."

"Yessir," I said, cutting the call.

I started for The Mountain. There's no easy way to get from South Prescott to Oxford County so I took the route Fielding had intended—back through Folkestone, up along Merry Hill, through Huntley and the Conklin Preserve. After I passed through the murder scene and moved deeper inland, the dramatic results of the coastal blizzard diminished somewhat. Hills became mountains and farms gave way to rustic cabins tucked into the woods.

I found the resort and wound my way up to The Mountain's Grenoble development. The entry at Killy Drive was gated and pass-card protected, of course. A FedEx van was leaving as I pulled up and I slipped through before the gates swung shut. I continued on to the address Honor Fielding had given me.

The scale of the homes in the Grenoble section ranged from somewhere between a cozy cottage and Valhalla. They were all placed discretely off Killy Drive, which wound its way along a natural ridge. Dramatic vistas up and down the valley were accentuated by dappled sunlight as it splashed along the silver line of the Androscoggin River. A ski lift platform rose above the tree-tops and was located so residents and their guests didn't have to mix with the rabble of weekend skiers at the Inn.

If the Kringles weren't here, I'd move on to the resort. I knocked on the door. I wasn't looking forward to another notification.

There was movement inside. A petite woman, just on the wrong side of pleasantly plump peeked out a window. She disappeared and a moment later, the lock clicked. The door swung open and I was surprised to see Kris Kringle, tall—lanky in a good way—Nordic sweater, tousled hair and two days' worth of blonde stubble.

"Can I help you?"

"Mr. Kringle? I'm Deputy Allegheny Beckham with the Chamberlain County sheriff's department."

"Okay." He looked at my cruiser. "May I see some I.D.?"

I pulled my badge and ID. He examined it.

"What's the problem, officer?"

"Honor Fielding provided me with your name and address. You're a friend of the Fieldings?"

"Sure. Major and I were skiing last Thursday." He got serious. "What's this about?"

"May I come in?"

A high-pitched voice came from inside. "Kris, what's going on?" Fran Kringle joined us at the door.

"Mr. and Mrs. Kringle, I'm sorry to inform you that Major Fielding was murdered last Friday night on his way from here to South Prescott. If you don't mind, I have some questions I would like to ask you."

Kringle instinctively wrapped his wife in his arm. "Major. Murdered? How? Why?"

Fran Kringle buried her face in her husband's side, who pulled her closer. She looked up at him, then at me. "My God, it can't be. Honor must be . . ." She stepped away from him. "Of course, come in, come in," she said and led us through an entry space that opened into a two-story living area. A fire in a stone hearth threw heat into the Great Room. Nothing was out of place. Cathedral windows ran floor to ceiling, flanking the chimney and highlighting views of The Mountain's peaks and runs. The design was rustic-contemporary, but the feel was sterile. She wore a fine woolen turtleneck in a deep mahogany red. Her chirpy voice and quick movements created the impression of a plump spring robin.

"Please have a seat, umm—," she said, gesturing toward a trestle table as she gathered a stack of folders and papers and moved them to the counter to make room. She angled her head and looked expectantly at me.

"Beckham, ma'am. Deputy Beckham."

"Sometimes my husband forgets his manners," she said, admonishing him with a look.

"Deputy Beckham," she said as she gestured toward the long table, "This is certainly terrible news, but can I get you some coffee? Anything?"

"No, thank you, ma'am." We found our place at the long table. Kris Kringle dithered a moment before choosing to settle next to his wife. He seemed a little detached, almost lost. "Do you mind if I take some notes?" I said, opening my notebook and clicking my pen.

"No, no. Not at all. How did this happen?" Fran Kringle took her husband's hand, but he continued to be elsewhere.

I explained what we knew.

When I got to the part about the twins, her hands instinctively covered her mouth and she exclaimed, "Oh my! Oh no. They're so young, and what . . . why would someone take them? I'm sure they must be terrified." She glanced at her husband. "No, no, they're not here with us," she said, anticipating my question.

"Thank you for confirming that. Mrs. Kringle . . .," I began.

"Please—it's just Fran and Kris," Fran said, gesturing to herself and her husband. "But, my God. Major. Dead."

"Fran," I nodded. "Yes. I'm sorry. When I spoke with Mrs. Fielding this morning, I had the impression the kids might sometimes stay with you. Is that right? If they're not with you, is there anyone else up here who knows the family well enough to let the kids bunk with them? Someone you could easily call to check and see? When was the last time you saw them?"

Kris Kringle was still MIA.

"We—the kids spent some time together last week and Kris skied with Major," Fran said. "But, as far as someone else at The Mountain, not really, no, I don't believe so—no, I don't think they have another close friend up here."

"Okay," I said, writing. When I finished, I looked up and Fran Kringle was waiting for my next question. "Well, if you don't mind, would you talk a little about your relationship with the Fieldings?" I was trying to understand the dynamic, since the two of them looked closer to Honor's age than Major's. "How did you become friends?"

Fran looked expectantly at her husband. She touched his hand and he finally turned his attention to the conversation. He took a deep breath.

"Major needed someone who could help him establish a beachhead at B&C—Bertram & Cohen," Kringle explained. "I had been there about ten years when he started and we both had wives who hailed from Maine." I looked at Fran Kringle. She was no Honor Fielding. "He'd just come off the divorce and the twins were new. Fran had only recently had Justine—she's our daughter. There was a lot going on and we all . . ." They exchanged a look. "Somehow, we connected."

"It was a different time," Fran said, almost wistful. "Justine, well, of course Honor had both twins actually, but Justine and Celeste were babies. We were all in Manhattan. Honor and I spent a lot of time together."

"So, are you here full time now?"

"Oh, goodness no!"

I thought I saw a shadow cross Mr. Kringle's brow. Then it was gone and he was back in the conversation.

"No, not now."

I moved on and asked Kringle if he might be aware of anyone or any reason someone would want to do this.

"He was completely committed. I've done okay but I didn't have the vision or the guts that Major had. He had one guy—a client—while we were at B&C who was sentenced to jail for tax evasion. Swore it was Major's fault. Let me see . . . Ben . . . Benjamin Locke was the guy's name. He's probably done with jail by now, but I can't see how he would blame Major for that."

"You never know. We'll check out Locke," I said, writing. "What about him and Honor? What was their relationship like?"

"I was so jealous of them," Fran looked down, appraisingly. Her husband was distant. "She's beautiful and he worshipped her."

"Are you and Honor still close friends?" I asked.

"We're friends—I mean, Kris and Major are close," Fran said, looking at Kringle for approval, then, frowning, "*were* really close," when she realized her *faux pas*. "The girls are fast friends. Justine, our daughter, goes to The Barton School with Celeste."

"Yes, Honor told me."

"The kids were all off for winter break."

"Major said he was looking forward to getting back to The Landing and seeing Honor." Kringle said, looking up the mountain. A pair of skiers schussed past, "Celeste has stayed with us—,"

"*Both* twins have stayed with us, *many* times," Fran interrupted. "Kris, you weren't paying attention. Especially when they were a little younger. We've been to their place in Vail," she continued. She rolled her eyes and smiled knowingly. She straightened her turtleneck and placed her hands in her lap. She paused, considering. She pursed her lips. "But lately, Trevor hasn't been as sociable." She paused again. "You know, he'd stay with us, but kept to himself in the bedroom glued to his I-Pad. They're getting to be teenagers, you know, and boys . . ."

"Major didn't say anything about them staying this weekend," Kringle asserted. "And he wouldn't have left them alone at the Inn."

I heard a door open at the back of the house, followed by loud clumping and stomping.

"Hey Mom," called a girl's voice, "There's a cop car in the driveway!"

"Justine, Becca, take off your jackets and hang them neatly, shake out your snow pants, stack your boots, put your gloves in the dryer, then come to the kitchen, please," Fran Kringle replied. "Teens." She smiled at me.

"Yes, ma'am," came the weary reply.

Fran explained that Justine was with her friend Rebecca Thompson and confided, "She actually lives year 'round at The Mountain!" as if it was some sort of hardship. "Becca's an only child, like Justine. Celeste has a brother so when the three girls get together, it's like they're sisters."

Finally, the sound of a dryer tumbling heavy clothes kicked in and two girls appeared.

"Whassup?" Their smiles disappeared when they saw me. *Must be the stylish uniform.*

Fran introduced us. I explained why I was there. The girls quieted.

"Was there anything Celeste said that gave you the impression they might be staying here for the weekend?" Fran prompted.

"No, not really," Justine said, looking at Becca. The alpha girl. She straightened in her chair and deliberately pushed hair away from her face. Self-conscious. Practiced. She leaned back a little and pulled her phone from her waistband. "Maybe I could text Celeste? She might answer and then everything would be okay?" This was pointless, but in the interest of keeping the girls engaged, I agreed. She banged out a quick message, "I'm saying *Hey C, let me know when you'll be back at school.*'"

"That's fine, Justine, go ahead." I didn't want any references to "Where are you?" included. I circled back to Fran's question. "Was there anything you heard from either Celeste or Trevor that led you to believe they might be on The Mountain for the weekend?"

The two of them looked at one another. Justine answered for them both.

"I mean, yeah, she actually said she was going to ask her dad if she could stay and have us take her back to school tomorrow."

"So, if that happened, what would Trevor do?" I asked.

"I dunno. He'd probably just go home with his dad," she replied simply.

Did I see something shift in Becca's face? She started playing with a spoon that was on the counter.

"Did you guys hang with Trevor much?"

Becca drew a breath but Justine cut in, "Naw. He was into snowboarding and video stuff."

"Becca, is there something you want to say?" *The gentle therapist.*

She shifted in her seat, "We were in Loon Lodge Friday. . ." Becca began slowly. Justine's expression tried to wave her off.

"Trevor was with this guy named Breezy."

"Who's Breezy?" Kringle looked sharply at his daughter.

"Relax, Dad. Just some guy, somebody he met at the lodge."

"How old was Breezy—your age? Younger? Older?" I asked.

"I dunno. Yeah, probably older." Becca replied.

"How much older? You think he could drive? Was he in college?" I might have been coming on a little strong.

By now Justine was looking hard at Becca, who was unsure of exactly where to go.

"Becca," I said, looking at Justine, "You need to realize that Celeste's father has been shot dead in his car and she and Trevor are missing. She could be dead or she could be alive but if you want to help Celeste, it's critical you disclose any information you have about Trevor and this Breezy guy and you need to tell me **now**."

Forceful.

"He was nice. You know, friendly." Becca was trying. Her eyes glassed up. "He looked like he could be in high school. Maybe college. He and Trevor seemed like pretty good friends, like Trevor knew him better than just meeting him Friday." She reflected for a moment. "He really liked Celeste."

Justine was silent.

"Jus-*tine*," Becca began, with the emphasis on the last syllable. She was trying to engage her friend. "I got the feeling he was only visiting—like he didn't fit. Like he wasn't here to ski. You know, he was wearing jeans and . . ."

Justine was having none of it and was shut down completely.

". . . an alpaca sweater and a T-shirt," Becca said, completing the thought and looking up at me. She felt like she was helping. She was. "The sweater was bright, like, a robin's egg blue. V-neck. And dress shoes—like you'd see in a fashion shoot."

Teenage girls. Ya gotta love 'em.

This was actually beginning to feel like a direction. "What else about him? What was his hair like—long, short, dark?"

"It was blonde—bleached blonde and not too long. He had one of those . . . not a goatee beard but one of those . . ,"

"A soul-patch? Like a mini beard just below the lower lip?" I offered.

"Yeah. And three earrings in his left ear. He offered to buy us lunch—he was buying lunch for Trevor. He had a huge wad of cash—but Celeste was like, *"No way!"* She didn't want to have anything to do with him." Becca looked at me. "Do you think Celeste is okay?"

"I don't know. This is helpful." *Don't build their hopes up.*

I looked at Justine. "How about you, Justine. Does this sound about right? Is there anything you want to add?"

Justine looked at Becca and then at her parents. She took a deep breath.

"Trevor's into porn."

"What?!" the Kringles erupted simultaneously. Becca stared at Justine, horrified.

"C'mon, mom and dad," Justine leaned into them. "Grow up." Her eyes shifted to Becca. "He had a crush on you, right?" Becca's face shot through with red.

"Justine!" Becca pleaded.

"The deputy wants to know *every*thing," Justine continued, in control again. She went on. "He was always trying to get us to be in videos. You know, boobs and panties and stuff."

"Justine!" Fran squeaked as her hand slapped flat against the table.

I reassessed these two. Both girls were wearing leggings and close-fitting tops. They were past the "awkward" stage of puberty and moving into young woman-hood.

Justine dismissed her mother with a look, "So we did, a couple of times," she said, defiant.

"Oh Justine!" Fran swung her head and fixed her husband in an angry glare, "*This* is what I've been dealing with!"

"Okay," I needed to snag this thread and keep the girls on track before everything went to hell. "What did Trevor do with the videos?" I asked, trying to be the clinician, "Did he post them online?"

"I don't think so. I never saw them online. We did it just for fun." Justine was matter-of-fact. "It was just, like, peekaboo stuff, Dad. But, then . . ."

"Please, Justine, don't!" Becca started crying.

". . . he started sexting pictures of his junk, all hard and everything, to Becca until she told him she was going to tell his parents."

"Jesus Christ," whispered Kris Kringle. Fran shaded her eyes.

I stepped in. "Becca, is this true?"

She nodded. Fran handed her a tissue.

"So, where was Celeste in all this?" I asked.

"She knew. She was worried." Justine looked serious for the first time. "She had an idea he was spending most of his allowance on chat rooms. She didn't know what to do."

Chat rooms. That stuff isn't cheap. I looked at her father. "You were close to Major. Did he express any worry about Trevor or money or anything?"

Kringle weighed the question. "No, not really. One thing that Major did, and I thought this was a mistake, was to give the twins complete discretion on how they spent their money. They had private accounts and neither he nor Honor had access to them. He said he wanted them to learn how to manage their money 'like they're in the real world' but it was a lot of cash. A couple thousand bucks a month. They had to pay their own tuition, buy clothes, everything out of that money."

"Back to Breezy." The group was quiet. "Was there anything he or Trevor said about their plans for the rest of the day? Did you see Trevor on the slope at all Friday afternoon?"

Becca rejoined the conversation. "Once we said we weren't going to have lunch with them, they sort-of ignored us, but—"

"But what?" I probed.

"But . . . I overheard something about tricks so maybe Trevor was going to show him some snowboarding stuff. I don't know. He kept looking at Celeste."

"Who, Trevor or Breezy?"

"Breezy. I looked over while we were eating and he was like, laser-focused on Celeste."

Ten

I WASN'T GOING TO get much more from the Kringles or Becca. I asked the girls about social media. They said after the sexting they had unfriended Trevor from all their apps and Becca had blocked his phone number. She was terrified her dad would find out about the video. Her parents were divorced and her mom wasn't on the scene.

"That's between you and him but I can't guarantee it won't come out sometime."

Delivering happiness everywhere . . .

Fran was lecturing the girls on the dangers of the internet as her husband began to escort me to the front door. I expected some commentary about, "Let us know if there's anything we can do to help," but he was quiet.

"So, Mr. Kringle. Are you commuting to New York from here? Or does B&C let you work remotely?" I was looking for a little clarification on how much face time the Kringles had with one another.

The shadow again. "Um. No, not commuting to New York. My bet was with the real estate market."

A downbeat pause.

"I left B&C and opened a retail financial planning office in Portland after the crash. We have a small condo in Portland . . . So I run back and forth from there to here during the winter."

Tight smile. His gaze moved over my shoulder, toward the Clubhouse complex.

"Oh. Okay," I pulled my notebook.

I wrote for a moment. He was ready to get back inside. "Just one more thing, Mr. Kringle." *Friendly. You-can-tell-me-anything.*

He looked down at me and smiled again. His face was all, *"How can I help, officer?"*

"Where were you Friday night?"

Shadow.

"I . . . I . . . ," he stammered.

"It's a standard question."

Matter-of-fact.

"I was . . . on the mountain skiing. They light some runs and offer night skiing most Friday nights."

Off balance.

"During the blizzard? Was your wife with you? Justine?"

"No, I, uh, the storm . . . it went south of here. And. Um. I like to go alone."

"What time did you come home?"

"I don't remember. They run the lights all night. Maybe two, two-thirty . . ."

Focusing.

"Anyone at the Inn be able to verify this? Did you stop at the lodge for a drink? Meet any friends?"

"No."

Harder now.

"I was alone."

I let that hang for a moment.

"Okay. Thank you. And thank you for your time this morning." I left him with my card and started for The Mountain Inn to do my due diligence. I knew the twins weren't there.

◆

THE GUESTS WAITING FOR check-in at The Mountain Resort Inn were not thrilled to see me. I felt like Moses parting the waters as I entered the lobby and walked to the desk. I showed my badge. Honor Fielding had found her contact's name and I asked the clerk whether Barry Daniels, the day manager, was on duty. She disappeared into the mystery room that seems to be located behind every hotel front desk. A moment later she reappeared with Daniels.

"Officer . . ."

"Beckham," the clerk supplied.

"Officer Beckham." Barry was in his late twenties. Black jeans, hiking boots, black turtleneck under black fleece pullover, two day's stubble and lightweight down vest, black.

"Mr. Daniels, can we talk in your office?"

He looked relieved. "Of course," he said, leading me back through the mystery room. Brochures spilled out of broken corrugated cardboard boxes; a printer/scanner/fax machine overflowed with cheap cruise offers; a message board was crowded with too many notes. "Ski The Mountain" posters with twisted frames were stacked loosely in a corner.

Mystery solved. Whatta detective!

We entered his office and he offered me the stackable plastic chair. A crack ran through the back.

"No thanks, I'll stand."

He got comfortable behind a heavy metal desk. Relative to the mystery room, his workspace was neat, with several stacks of paper and a laptop computer. "What's this about? You're a little far from home, aren't you, Deputy . . . ?" he said, fishing for my name as he checked out my shoulder patch.

Well then, Barry, you're observant.

"Correct. Deputy Beckham, Chamberlain County Sheriff's office."

"And...?" his face seemed to be asking.

"I'm looking into a murder in Huntley last Friday night," I began. "Our understanding is that the victim and his children had been lodging here and checked out that afternoon. There's a question as to whether or not the kids were with him when he left."

"Yeah, I saw something about the murder on the news," he said and placed his hands expectantly on the keyboard. "Normally, we don't provide information about our guests but . . . ," covering his ass, he continued, smiling. "We'll call these 'extenuating circumstances,' right, officer? I can check if they were here. What's the name?"

"Major Fielding was the dad."

"Oh. Oh, Jeez, he's not the one who was killed, was he?" Barry turned from the computer screen. He wasn't smiling.

"Yes. Did you know him?"

"Well, no, I didn't *know-know* him, like a friend or anything, but he and his wife . . . Honor?"

I nodded. This guy was good.

"Honor always handles the reservations. She asks for me," he said, confirming his authority. "I guess they have a tradition of coming here for the kids' winter break. There's a particular suite . . . 503, that looks out toward Grenoble and up the valley. Once, when it wasn't available, I gave 'em a major upgrade." I nodded. "They were a pair."

"How so?"

"Well, . . . ," he began.

"Well, . . . what? Tell me."

"Well, we get a lot of couples like them. He's the older guy and she's real young. They were one of the couples who actually seemed like a good match, you know, he kept himself in shape. They seemed pretty happy most of the time. Some of them, Jesus, the guys dress for the slope but wouldn't know what to do if you put a pair of skis on their feet. It can get a little weird."

"Did it ever "get a little weird" with the Fieldings?" Maybe their relationship wasn't so perfect.

"Mostly, I'm stuck here," he said, looking around the windowless room, "or at the front desk. But we're always short-staffed so sometimes I end up getting into the halls, bars, or restaurants to help out. Occasionally, you see stuff. I remember, I don't know; I think it was last year . . . I saw Mrs. Fielding at the Brew-Ski Pub with Kris Kringle a couple of times."

The name just rolled off his tongue. "You must be friends with the Kringles then?"

"Everybody knows Kris and yeah, I know Fran and Justine. I'll see him on the slopes and we'll ski a couple of runs now and then. He's on the Board here. Nice guy."

"Mrs. Fielding and Kringle; they were alone?"

"Seemed to be. I've been working with Honor for awhile," he reflected. "Major is one of those guys who's never on vacation. He's always connected to work and sometimes he'd need to leave for a quick trip back to South Prescott or even New York. He must have had a million miles on that Rover." Barry was leaning back in his chair, legs crossed. "Anyway, it might have been during one of those trips."

"You said you saw them a couple of times. Was it just once, or a couple of times?"

"More than once. Yeah, for sure."

"How friendly were they? I mean, there's sitting at the bar and then there's . . ."

"After a couple of drinks, most people look like they're with their best friend. Or like they'd rather be somewhere else. They weren't canoodling or anything, but yeah, they were friendly."

"Okay. So, about the twins." I knew the answer to this question. "Did Major leave them here for the weekend?"

He shook his head. "I actually caught sight of them on their way out Friday after dinner." He was sitting up now. "The twins weren't happy about leaving; from what little I could gather they wanted to stay with the Kringles, but Major was pretty amped to get back to South Prescott to beat the storm and all. He was pissed at Trevor about something. It seemed a little late to me but . . . "

"About what time was that?"

"Let's see . . . I was off duty and heading for the Brew-Ski so it would have been, like, six-thirty, seven o'clock."

It was time to move on. "You ever heard of a guy named Breezy?"

"Breezy?" He said it with a lopsided smile that answered my question.

"I noticed there are cameras in the lobby. Do you have cameras anywhere else up here? Loon Lodge Café?"

"Short answer is no. Some of the outbuildings have cameras—all the stores do but each has their own system. The lobby is the only space with working surveilllance—digital with a week's recording. It rolls over on Sunday. Loon Lodge Café? There's a camera but it hasn't worked for years. Kris has been pushing to get everything updated—I've seen guys, even a few gals, skiing with a gun on their hip and, well, it seems to me that anything could happen these days—but Management won't spring for it."

We sat for a moment. No twins. No security cameras. A kid who shot racy videos of his sister's BFFs. A guy who may or may not have a thing for his friend's wife. And Breezy. *A productive afternoon.* I pulled out a card and handed it to Barry, who stood.

"Well, thank you for your time Mr. Daniels. Please contact me if you think of anything else that might help the investigation."

He looked at the card. "Wow. Allegheny. That's some handle." He smiled. A little too friendly.

"It's Deputy Beckham."

He ignored my tone. "You ski?" He opened a drawer and pulled out a couple of lift passes. "Here ya go. I'd like to buy you a drink sometime, you know, when you're off duty."

I turned for the door. "Sorry, I can't accept gifts."

Eleven

Late afternoon sun slanting through acres of barren winter forest lit the road in staccato bursts as I started south for Gainsborough. The Fielding case, my return to South Prescott, being upstate—it all took me back to losing Hanna.

❖

The family had spent MLK weekend in Solon, north of Bangor, with Grampa Beckham. Grandma had died at Christmas. The loss was still raw, but we'd had a good visit. Gramps was getting along okay. There were court-dates for Mom to get back to and Hanna and I had school the next day. We left for South Prescott after dinner. Dad stayed. He and Grampa needed to do some ice fishing and Dad had a client upstate he'd meet later in the week.

When night falls in rural Maine, even designated state routes become tree-lined solitary tunnels of darkness. Small towns flash by in silence, marked by signs that say "Welcome to Fill-in-the-Blank, founded in Fill-in-the-Blank." A brief January thaw had come to a hard end and the snowmelt that flowed across asphalt during the day created rivers of black ice. Mom braked gently to a four-way stop that was North Sourton. Clapboarding on a Congregational Church reflected peach in the light of a single streetlamp.

An air horn blasted in the darkness to our left and then began repeating over and over. What I remember seeing was the yellow cab-lights of a tractor-trailer and high-beams blinking violently.

"Mom, back up!" Hanna shouted from the backseat.

The Freightliner careened into the intersection and began a slow, sliding jack-knife, pulling a trailer overloaded with raw timber broadside to us. Mom slammed the SUV into reverse but when she hit the gas we went nowhere. There was a piercing whine as the tires burned through ice. A pyramid of rough-cut pine logs tipped our way when the trailer's wheels dipped into a deeper-than-necessary drainage ditch that edged the asphalt. Bang! . . . bang-bang! *Restraining chains snapped. Vertical posts created a chute and the horizontal forest tumbled and bounced like bowling pins in pursuit of our car.*

Our tires reached pavement and the car jumped and then slid erratically. Hanna and I were screaming.

In an instant, logs danced and bounced the ten yards that separated us. "Get down girls!" Mom shouted. I dove for the seat. Airbags misfired as the first log rumbled through the windshield, curling the driver's side roof back and crushing mom's skull. That log skipped over Hanna's seat, but a second one came across the car like a rolling pin, missing me and flattening Hanna. She hung on for two days. I was scratched and bruised. Dad, Gramps, and I were with her when she died.

Dad was devastated. I was beyond grief.

◆

DAY WAS FADING AS the sun dropped behind the line of mountains to the west, its final beam flashing silver off the reverse side of a YIELD sign in the opposite lane. I shook off the memory and called the sheriff.

"Latch here."

"Sheriff, it's Deputy Beckham."

"Just a minute." *Always the top priority.* I could hear muted talk and a door close as he returned.

"What the hell, Beckham? I thought I told you to keep this investigation strictly between you and me."

"Yessir." *Where is this coming from?* "I'm calling with an update."

"Jack Gill came to me this afternoon. You asked him to tee up the Amber Alert for the twins? Can't you follow even the simplest directions?"

Shit.

"Sir, I'm sorry sir but when I couldn't get in touch with you—"

"But you *talked* to me, remember? We talked, what, three hours ago? I said we'd hold off on the alert, didn't I?"

"Yessir, but this was *before* we talked."

"Beckham." Controlled anger. "When I tell you not to discuss a case with anyone but me, you don't mention it to anyone but me—not Jack Gill, not your mother, nobody. I'm disappointed. You can't let your emotions run this investigation."

"Yes, sir. I won't sir." *Women. Ya just can't trust 'em to do anything without getting all gooey.* "But, sir, all due respect, sir; why the secrecy? Don't we need to go public with this?"

"No, Goddammit. And, it turns out, Gill confirmed my opinion," Latch said, triumphant. "He agreed we should hold off on the alert. With any luck, the killer doesn't know who these kids are and is looking for a place to dump them. If it's a ransom kidnapping, we want to keep it between the three of us and on the down-low until we hear from them."

I came around a corner and hit the brakes. A freelance plow-guy was methodically dropping the blade on his F-150 and back-pulling drifts into the public way. Both lanes were essentially blocked. I flipped on my lightbar and gave him a *'whoop.'* That got his attention.

"What's going on?" Latch said, hearing the siren.

"Some guy with a plow—seems to be trying to block the road with snow. What's 'New Albion?'" The pickup's headlights lit up a warped 4x8 sheet of plywood. It was spray-painted with red fluorescent letters and leaned up against a decrepit wooden gateway that stood at the treeline and marked the entry to an unpaved roadway.

"You in Huntley? The old Camp Miq-Maq? Bunch of self-proclaimed guardians of our right-to-bear-arms rented the place. Been fixing it up to be the "New Albion National Armory" or some-such. They call themselves the Lincoln Brigade of New Albion—you know, Lincoln Rockwell, Mr. American Nazi, Maine's pride and joy."

"But the Lincoln Brigade, they fought in the Spanish Civil War, didn't they?—on the Communist side?"

"You can't confuse these guys with facts, Beckham. They're proud to be our Maine Militia."

I waited in the roadway with my lights flashing while the plow-guy cleaned up the road. We were alone. I waved a 'Thanks' at the driver when I crawled past. He gave me the finger.

"Back to the Fielding case." Latch had cooled to a business-tone. "So, the kids were not at The Mountain?"

I outlined the results of my interviews and suggested we take a look at Kris Kringle. He and Honor could be having an affair. He could have hired someone to kill Fielding.

"I don't know, Beckham," his voice laced with disdain. "It's just not plausible, given that they were business buddies and all. And if Kringle wanted Fielding dead, don't you think he could have figured out a time when he didn't have the kids with him? It's too messy. Too many moving parts. Come back to Gainsborough. I want you to get together with Gill and see if he can find some real direction."

Twelve

I called the Fielding compound to update Honor on my progress. Frank Chapman answered, saying that Honor was in Augusta with Mary identifying Major's body. We chatted for a moment and then I moved on, letting him know I'd check in the next morning. My stomach was rumbling. I stopped at The Taj Mahal, an Indian place I had seen outside of Twin Rivers on my way up to The Mountain, and picked up a box to go. Gill was expecting me when I got back to the station and he invited me into his office.

"Mind if I eat?" His space was small, but neat. Homemade handbills with pictures of missing girls and a few boys covered most of a bulletin board mounted on one wall—there were more than I would expect in a jurisdiction the size of Chamberlain County.

"No, go ahead. You get that from The Taj? Malik's lamb tikka is as good as you'd get in Kandahar and if you make friends with Nadia, she might put together some *mantu* dumplings for you . . . *Khoraak akhla!*

"Enjoy your meal!" he said, translating. "Yeah, you spend a couple of years in a place, you can't help but pick up some of the language."

Gill reclined in his chair and responded confidently as I asked questions about his service while balancing the clamshell box on my lap. He'd done two tours in Afghanistan with Army Intelligence and picked up a lot of internet skills. He was right, the food from The Taj was good. I'd offered to share, but he wasn't hungry.

"Yeah, I was lucky. I transitioned pretty smoothly from Army to here. How 'bout you?"

I kept it brief: raised in South Prescott, out to Chicago, a few years with CPD, back home to Maine.

We confirmed we were the same age. "Didn't you have a sister?" he asked casually. "Maybe I remember something about an accident?"

"Hanna." It had been a long time since I'd said her name out loud. It still hurt. I shifted gears a little.

"Jack," I began, shutting the clamshell and making an effort to maintain a nonchalant tone, "Why did you inform Latch about the Amber Alert? We were gonna keep it quiet, right?"

"I probably should've let you know that the Sheriff and I don't keep secrets. It's one reason he and I work so well together. Besides, once he heard, he thought it was a good idea that I give you a little back-up on this as it develops. He hasn't shared with me why he wants to play it so close to the vest, but I'm sure there's a good explanation."

"Okay . . . Then tell me about Sam. I'd like to get an idea of who I'm replacing."

"Sam Martin." Gill focused in the distance. "Let's see . . . what can I tell you about Sam? He and I worked closely for the past two years, really since I came on board. He was a good cop. From Lewiston originally. Dad worked in the mills—youngest of seven kids. Married, there's a daughter. And Kourtney, his wife . . ." He exhaled. "She's a piece of work."

"Oh yeah? How so?" This was the first I'd heard of Mrs. Martin.

"Kourtney wants more of everything. Man, she is one high-maintenance girl. Bigger house, better car, newest clothes. We'd hang out and she always looked as if she had just walked out of a magazine. Tabitha was the same way."

"Tabitha's the daughter?"

"Yeah. Sometimes I thought they were in competition with eachother. Tabby left home, what? Like in November. It kind of busted Sam up." He stood and began pulling the Missing posters down and making a neat stack on his desk. "We'll use this for a case board."

"Those kids, they're mostly from away?"

He glanced at the pile of informal portraits. "Yeah. Since I'm the primary on the sex trafficking, I get posters from across New England. A lot of them—what's the statistic? Like, 94% show up eventually but with the Fielding case," he said, pinning a photo from the crime scene onto the board, "With the Fielding case, we can *confirm* that kids are missing. Twins, in fact." He looked at me. "Here's our victim, Major Fielding. Tell me what you know."

I related the information I'd discovered. Gill took a few notes, put up the photo of the twins I had texted to diSimone with a note they were missing, and then just slips of paper with handwritten names of the other players as I mentioned them, including Mr. and Mrs. Chapman, Fielding's Ex and their kid, the Kringles, and Daniels and Breezy from The Mountain.

"This is our universe," he said simply when we were done. "Unless there are individuals we don't know about, yet. Latch said he heard from LuLu and it was a nine-millimeter pistol that capped Fielding. No surprise there."

"What do you think of this Breezy guy? He seems to be the only thing out of place."

"Well, from your description of what the girls said, he might be a friend of Trevor's from Barton. Sounds young. Did you ask Justine if she knew him from school? Kids with this kind of money get around a lot. Maybe Breezy's from St. Mary's or some other hoity-toity prep school. It seems like he was really into Celeste and my guess is he wanted to use Trevor as an avenue to get close to her." Gill paused, thinking. "Obviously, we're still missing information. We need to look at Locke," he said, pointing to Benjamin Locke's name, "and Stephen Fielding."

"Yeah, Locke sort-of makes sense. Except the impression I got from Kringle wasn't that Mr. Fielding put this guy into prison as much as he was this guy's broker when he was arrested."

"C'mon, Allie, ten years in the slammer will fuck with your head. He's not thinking rationally." Gill was tapping his magic marker against Locke's name and smiling. "Can't you see him spending that time being pissed off at Fielding?"

He continued, "Planning, planning, planning and then *BOOM!* He gets out, tracks and kills him. He gets a bonus by taking the kids and driving the wife crazy. It makes sense. It'll be easy enough to find out if Locke's been released."

Gill seemed to be making some broad assumptions, but we needed to get off the dime, so I didn't object. "Okay, I'll look into Fielding and see what's there," I offered. "I can do a phone notification of his Ex and see what she says. I've got a friend at NYPD who might be able to check into the kid."

"Excellent. I'll check out Locke and let the Sheriff know we've got a plan. As far as the kids are concerned, it's important that we wait at least one more day before we open this up to the public. Once that happens, the place will go ape-shit"

◆

I WALKED TO MY desk and checked the time. 8:05. The dispatcher's voice carried a monologue from the next room. I dialed the number that Honor Fielding had given me for Fielding's ex.

"My I speak with Elizabeth Keating, please?"

"This is she."

Unsure.

I identified myself. "Ms. Keating, I'm sorry but I have some news about your ex-husband, Major Fielding."

"Okay."

Cold.

"Ms. Keating, Mr. Fielding was found murdered in his car last Friday night."

Silence.

"Okay."

"May I ask you some questions? Please understand this conversation is being recorded."

"Okay, go ahead."

I went through the basics—

Last time she saw the victim: "It's been, what? Twelve years?"

Characterize their relationship: "He's my ex. He married a bimbo. What do you think?"

Where was she last Friday?

"Look, Deputy . . ." she said, taking a deep breath when I asked about her whereabouts. "I know you have a job to do. Trust me, I didn't kill that redneck son-of-a-bitch, no matter how much I might have wanted to at one time. He left me to raise his son by myself. He made his millions. He got his missy and their Bobbsey-twins. *He* found some happiness."

"I'm sorry you feel that way Ms. Keating, but—Can you tell me where you were last Friday night?"

"Goddammit! I was . . . I was here—in my condo—by myself, watching television."

"Thank you. One last question . . . ," I knew where this was going, but figured *'What the hell'*, "Can you please tell me how I might get in touch with Stephen?"

"No. Leave my son alone. This conversation is over. Goodbye."

Guess I'll need to do some detecting. I switched to my cell and phoned my friend at NYPD.

"You've reached Tommy DelVecchio, please leave a message."

"Tommy, this is Allie Beckham. S' been awhile but I need a favor. I'll text you the details. Thanks for any help you can provide."

I put together a text message that included a brief synopsis of the case and a street address for Stephen that Honor had dug up from her husband's papers and sent it to DelVecchio. That was it for tonight. I stopped to check out with Dina Garrett, the dispatcher. We'd had a chance to chat a couple of times during my first week of night shift duty.

"Hey Allie, I heard you're working with Gill. That right?" She was holding her hand over her headset mic.

"Yeah, we're on this murder case together. Why?"

A deputy entered the building guiding a middle-aged woman who was stumble-down drunk. Dina's attention abruptly shifted to the surface of her desk, then to the deputy and his dance partner.

"Hey Kimball. Mrs. Preston again?"

"How 'bout giving me a hand here?" Kimball demanded as he wrestled a rubbery figure through the door.

"What about Gill?" I asked Dina as I reached to help Kimball with Mrs. Preston.

"We got this!" he barked and yanked her away from me as Dina stepped through.

"Yeah, we got this Beckham!" Dina said brusquely and pushed me aside, catching the drunk as she slumped to the floor. "We'll put her in three, Kimball." She gave me a *"We'll talk later"* look as she passed. Kimball pushed by, pointedly ignoring me.

"Sonuvabitch!" he shouted as Mrs. Preston puked all over his shirt.

I started for Folkestone and home. *What about Gill?*

◆

THE RHYME ABOUT CATS and wives was running through my head as I crossed the bridge from St. Ives to Folkestone when my cell startled me. I hit speaker without looking at the ID. "Beckham here."

"Allegheny Beckham. What happened to your manners? You were such a polite little girl. Then you start at CPD—they don't have phones in Chicago?" It was DelVecchio. "Seven years. Seven *years* I don't hear from you. And then you call from Maine wanting me to do *your* job?"

"Quit busting my chops, Tommy. You always told me if I needed anything to call—so here I am." Coastal life hadn't suited Thomas DelVecchio. He left after high school and headed for The Big Apple to be a cop and worked his way up to Chief of Detectives on the Upper East Side. He and my father were besties back in the day and he was one reason I considered joining the CPD. I never figured out how he knew to send me an oversized bouquet of flowers my first day on the force. It made me cry.

"Okay, okay," he replied, "So now you're a hotshot Deputy Sheriff. We'll get to that in a minute. What about your dad? You two patched things up?"

I knew this was coming. I hadn't contacted my father since I came home. Hell, I hadn't spoken to him since I'd left Maine.

"I haven't been back for two weeks yet, DelVecchio. Don't worry, I'll get around to it."

He was quiet for a moment. "So, I took a moment to read your text and made a couple of phone calls."

"Wow, that was quick."

"The NYPD, *ever at the service* of the Chamberlain County Sheriff's Department.

"Anyway, Fielding's in the system . . . some petty theft, shoplifting, and other minor stuff but everything dismissed. He was arrested for a stabbing a couple of years ago—the guy survived. Someone paid for a hotshot lawyer and he was released on a technicality. Dude's got an apartment in Williamsburg so he can't be doing too bad."

"I'll bet that's Mom . . . Tommy, can you arrange an interview? There's a lobster dinner in it for you."

"Oh, you planning a trip to Manhattan soon? Or you talkin' kitchen table at *Chez Beckham?*"

"Well, I *am* on a budget, Detective DelVecchio."

He chuckled. "Okay, Allie. I'll carve out some time tomorrow and take a trip across the river. I'll let you know what I find out. In the meantime, think about getting in touch with your Dad. Life's short."

I pulled up to 144 Cushing, "Thanks for the favor, Tommy." I cut the call and walked inside.

Thirteen

SOUNDTRACKS FROM CONFLICTING TVs came through two doors flanking the entry. I made my way up the broad staircase to the second floor. Four of the seven rental rooms in the house are arranged around the landing. Bright light spilled from Room 5. There was the sound of a metallic *slap-slap*, pause, *slap-slap*, pause and I looked in as I passed. Clip-on floods threw bright halos of light straight-up. A well-used drop cloth covered the floor. Jesse Thorne, my landlord, was working from a stepladder and patching the ten-foot ceiling. He moved like an artist, balancing midway and gathering compound from an aluminum drywall hawk he held in one hand—his palette—onto a broadknife scraper with his other. He cleaned the side of the knife using the edge of the hawk, then distributed the mud firmly in a line and smoothed the surface. *Slap-slap,* pause. He was good at it. He stopped briefly to assess his progress. I knocked lightly so as not to startle him.

"Hey there, Jesse."

He twisted on the ladder, squinting in the light. "Hey there, Allie. Everything okay?"

"Yeah, everything's okay. Someone move out?"

He cleaned his knife and stepped down, missing the bottom rung of the ladder, losing his balance and nicking the heel of his hand with the broadknife when he stumbled, *"Scheisse!"*

"Are *you* okay?"

"Yeah," he said, examining the scratch, then licking it. He looked up at his work. "It's always something."

Jesse was a local guy who'd built a successful real estate business, eventually selling it to one of the big chains. He was proud of what he'd accomplished with this former 19th century inn. The brick exterior was what had saved it from ruin. He had an eye for preservation *and* a conscience. Buying the place, he put on a new roof and rehabbed it room by room. Nothing fancy, but clean and done right. You'd never think it was Section 8 from the outside. Sometimes the more affluent neighbors grumbled about 'low-income renters' but, as Jesse noted, *"Everyone needs a place to live. As long as you pay your rent and stay clean, you're welcome."* It didn't hurt that I was a cop.

"But yeah, Jo Baskin moved out. Did you have a chance to meet her? She got a job in Portland. Thought I'd take the moment to tidy a couple of cracks here. How're you doing? Everything going okay with re-entry?"

As Miss Congeniality, I hadn't taken the time to introduce myself to any of my fellow residents.

" 'bout as well as can be expected, I suppose. You sure that's okay?" I said, pointing to his hand. Each slap of the knife honed the blade and Jesse's hand looked worse than he let on. *Nurse Beckham, that's me!*

"It'll be fine," he said, wiping red onto his paint-stained pants. He stepped back to the ladder and I sensed we were done. I heard the *slap-slap,* pause resume as I climbed to my attic home.

Jesse had done a good job fixing up the place but, in the end, the building was almost 175 years old. The attic had no dedicated heat source so on a night like this, with outdoor temperatures expected to drop below zero, my room was frigid. Sure, the heat from two other floors rose, but that only went so far. Goose flesh coursed up and down my body as I climbed under the covers. Yeah, I could probably afford a better place. But not only did I owe Lt. Torres my life, I owed her some major cash. And I couldn't let that go. I fell asleep to the rhythmic *slap-slap-pause* of Jesse Thorne's broadknife on the ceiling below my bed.

◆

DURING THE NIGHT, I'D gotten a text from Gill saying to meet him and the Sheriff before roll call.

"Come," Latch called when I knocked.

"Coffee, Beckham?" he asked as I entered. The view over his shoulder to the outside revealed mounds of snow losing their once pristine charm. The river flowed in a broken, pale line behind the buildings that marched to its bank. The clarity of Monday's sky was gone. Fat snowflakes floated and bobbed, animating the scene.

The sheriff had his own Nespresso coffee machine in the office. It was probably better than the swill in the patrolmen's space.

"No thanks, I'm good."

He offered me a seat. I told him about my phone calls with Fielding's Ex and DelVecchio and that I didn't see them as leads. Gill knocked.

"Yeah, come in Jack. Coffee?"

"I got it, thanks." They were comfortable with each other. "Hey Allie."

Gill looked a little ragged this morning. Not the picture-perfect blazer/tie of yesterday. Hip-length leather jacket, fitted. Open collar, silver chain and some sort of medallion at the throat. Fashionable stubble. "Good morning, Jack."

He got his coffee. We looked expectantly at the sheriff.

"You get any video hits?" It was a general question.

My blank look answered. Latch sighed.

Gill stepped in. "I'm surprised you didn't think to check in with the gas stations when you were up there, Allie. I got Hank Petrillo, Adams County's IT guy, to look into it." Then, to Latch, "There're only three places and only one has a camera."

Latch was looking hard at me as Gill continued. "Hank said the vic filled the SUV about 13:30 at a Maritime—sounds like a real OCD-type. I haven't seen the tape yet. He said he'd forward it sometime this morning. Hodgkins ever find any brass on site?"

"Nope. Nothing. Whoever capped Fielding took it with them," Latch said.

Their back-and-forth made me feel like a third-wheel.

I cleared my throat as unobtrusively as possible. I wasn't successful. They both looked at me and, in concert, took a sip of their coffees.

"Okay," the sheriff started again, "Beckham updated me on DelVecchio."

"Who's DelVecchio?" Gill asked, pausing in mid-sip and pointedly looking over his cup at me.

"He's the guy, the friend—he's a Detective in Manhattan. I told you I'd contact him about Stephen Fielding."

"Oh, right." He was standing and had parked himself next to Latch's desk. *The power couple.*

"I should hear from him sometime today," I continued. "The Ex isn't involved and I told the Sheriff I'd be surprised if her kid did it. Just doesn't sound like he's got his shit together enough to pull something like this off."

"Well then, what do you think, Allie? Maybe the twins offed their dad and waltzed into the Maine woods on their own? They're looking for the gingerbread house? That makes sense." Gill was asserting his authority. *Okay, you're my boss.*

I started to answer and my cell buzzed. I looked and mouthed *"Honor Fielding"* to Gill and Latch. They nodded. I pushed the button for speaker phone.

"Beckham here."

"Oh thank God! Allie, I got an email this morning. They've taken my children. Oh my God, they sent a photo—they've got them blindfolded and naked. They said not to contact the police but Allie, they want fifteen million dollars."

"Fucking morons," I heard Gill say under his breath.

"What am I going to do? I don't know where to go. I can't raise that kind of money."

"Honor, take a deep breath." I looked at Latch. He nodded. "Honor, I'm here with Sheriff Latch and Lieutenant Gill, head of the Criminal Investigation Department. You're doing the right thing." I placed the cellphone on Latch's desk. "You're on speaker. Can you read us the note?"

She began, her voice quavering:

"Your banker's dead. We know you opened this message. If you want to see the brats whole again, you will wire $15,000,000 to a specified account no later than 5 p.m. this Friday. You have the resources. Do not involve the police or FBI. If you agree to this, post "Spring is just around the corner—join us for free beer this Saturday!" on the brewery's Facebook page. We will contact you with further instructions."

"Whole again" What does that mean?" she asked.

I didn't want to address that, yet. I checked with Latch and Gill. They looked grim. The term 'these brats' caught my attention. It sounded personal. "Honor, have you ever heard anyone refer to Trevor or Celeste as a 'brat?'

"Oh Allie. Oh God, no. I can't imagine Stephen would have killed his father . . . but I . . . Major told me . . . Stephen called the twins the 'Brady Brats'. It's one of the reasons Major cut his ties with him—he was just so incredibly bitter."

Gill smiled the *"What the fuck do you know?"* smile as he looked at me. I nodded to him with the go-ahead. "Mrs. Fielding, this is Jack Gill. We're doing everything we can to find the twins and your husband's killer. Deputy Beckham will be following up with a contact she has in the NYPD about Stephen Fielding and I am looking into Ben Locke in case he's been released from prison. Can you forward the note and photo to Deputy Beckham? Once we have a chance to review that material, she and I will come down to South Prescott and see if we can trace the message back to the IP address."

"Yes, yes, of course. But Allie, what do they mean, "whole again?"

My throat was dry and I could feel my jaw tighten. "It means they might hurt the twins. But we won't let that happen."

Gill and Latch glanced at each other and Latch jumped in. "This is Sheriff Latch, Mrs. Fielding." He gestured with a hand at his neck, signaling me to silence. "What Deputy Beckham meant to say is that we are doing everything we can to return your children safe and sound. Lt. Gill and the deputy will process this information and be in touch about a visit later this morning. Thank you for contacting us."

Honor was sobbing. "Oh dear God. Yes, Sheriff. Please find my children."

Latch reached over and cut the call. "What the hell are you doing, Beckham? We can't guarantee these kids will get home whole."

"And this is why we waited on the Amber alert." Now Gill was in *I-told-you-so* mode. "If we'd gone with it, as you suggested yesterday, they'd probably be dead."

I was quiet.

Latch's cell began a sing-song alarm. "Okay you two. You know what needs to happen. Let's get down to roll call. By the time that's done Beckham should have the materials on her laptop." Gill deferred to the Sheriff as he stood and moved to the door. "Mrs. Fielding's got it tough enough with the husband gone. We need to make sure she sees her kids again."

We filed out of Latch's office and started for the armory with me in the rear. Lawyers entered the main hall of the Courthouse with large case folders. They knocked gray, sludgy snow-mess from their boots onto absorbent mats and their foot-stomping echoed in the cavernous space. A deputy waited expectantly at a walk-through metal detector.

"McCann!" Gill's voice reverberated in the marble and tile room. The deputy turned. "You getting any ice fishing in?"

"Gill! You so-and-so! Yeah, Patsy and I were out over the weekend." He smiled at Gill and pointed to the conveyor belt for a woman attorney. She returned his smile and dumped her files, briefcase, and purse into plastic bins.

Everyone knew everyone. I was the odd-man-out. McCann's smile broadened as we walked past. "Sheriff, you need to come out again—" he nodded absently to the attorney as she walked through the gate that remained silent. She collected her materials.

"Yeah, that was a good day," Latch agreed.

"Never hurts to send the boss away happy! Jack—c'mon out Saturday, 'supposed to be super cold," McCann offered.

"Thanks, Chaz, but I've got something going," he responded quickly.

"Your loss—not too many more winter weekends this year . . . ," the deputy called as I followed them down a couple of stairs and we continued to the morning ritual.

Personnel gathered in the hallway that joined the bullpen and public areas of the Department with the courthouse entry and Latch's office. Deputies coming on looked crisp and alert, the ones finishing up were less so. The group opened as our trio approached and the sheriff made some small talk, working the group like a politician. We took a left into the narrow corridor that led to the armory. I was ahead of Gill but behind some of the other guys as the sheriff passed into the brightly lit room. Several men stepped in front of me and hesitated, blocking the door for a moment. *Okay, I get it, I'm new.* I rocked back to catch my balance and felt a hand rest lightly on my right hip. It moved quickly down my ass and cupped the inside of my butt-cheek. I felt a finger probing. I moved to grab it, but it disappeared as quickly as it had come and the suddenness of my action disturbed the flow into the room. Gill came around me with Deputy Taylor saying something about the Bruins' goalie. The guys who were off-duty drifted back down the corridor, heading home. I gathered myself and was the last person in.

I'd visited the armory with Lt. Match when he'd issued my duty weapon and then daily at afternoon roll call for the past week and a half. The large room was in the center of the building and had no windows. A heavy steel-screen wall separated the rear third into a storage area, where the firepower of the Chamberlain County Sheriff Department was housed. The weaponry was pretty dated. In Chicago, we'd had access to snub-nosed Kel-Tec shotguns; futuristic bullpups that made me feel like Lara Croft every time I picked one up. Here, a dozen Remington 870 pump-action shotguns, six Savage long rifles, some miscellaneous other rifles and a couple of government-issue surplus RPGs were racked and ready. When I'd asked about modernizing, Match smiled. "We don't expect ISIS to be storming the courthouse," he confided with a grin. "And one of these will stop a bad-guy just as fast as a Bushmaster," he finished, patting a Remington lovingly.

Benches were pushed to the edges of the open section. I found my place in line and stood at attention with the four other officers from my shift. Latch, Gill, and Hank Holby, another detective, were off to the side. Roll call was pretty much like Chicago, just smaller in scale: a review of and schedule for the day, with assignments.

"Thanks for making time to join us, Deputy Beckham." Sergeant Charles "Chuckles" McCann said flatly. The resemblance to the deputy in the foyer was obvious. "Sheriff Latch will update you all on the Fielding murder investigation."

Latch stepped to the front. "Thank you, Sgt. McCann. I've asked Lt. Gill and Deputy Beckham to work together on this case. They are pursuing leads related to Fielding's son by a first marriage and a former business partner. If you have a question, come to me. If you hear something, anything, that you think might help us, please relay that promptly to Lt. Gill. Any questions?

It was quiet. "Okay, thanks for the work you do on behalf of the citizens of Chamberlain County. Be safe out there." The sheriff strode out of the room.

Chuckles stepped up. "You heard the sheriff." He took a step toward me and got close. I caught a whiff of the coffee, bacon, and homefries from his breakfast. "Beckham, here, will be pulled out of rotation to work on this murder investigation." He moved down the line of deputies. "That means that you, Taylor, and you, Farber, will need to pick up her slack. There are a number of papers she would be serving—I'll get them to you. McCann, Jr. is on lobby duty." He mentioned Mrs. Preston from the night before and a kid who was in custody for jacking a car, then the meeting was over.

We fell out of line. Other officers were talking to one another and I stood alone. I was just about to tell Gill I'd be in his office when a deputy walked up to me. I recognized him as the guy who, with McCann Jr., had returned "Eddie" to his trailer park. He looked young.

"Beckham—Kyle Kennedy," he said, reaching out and smiling. We shook hands. "So, how do you get to play Detective after being here only a couple of weeks?" he asked, holding my hand a little too long.

"Maybe it's because I passed the Detective exam before I left Chicago," I replied, a little too loud.

The room went dead. I smiled. He didn't. He dropped my hand, turned, and walked out. I looked at Gill, who came over as the final officer shifted out. We were alone. "Jeez Allie. You're making friends left and right."

"Ya know, Jack, I'm just trying to keep my nose clean. It's not my fault Sam Martin died and I got hired to fill in as his replacement." My frustration echoed in the room. I took a breath. "I'm as surprised as anyone that Latch wants me on this case but, here I am."

"Yeah. Okay. Just lucky, I suppose." Gill looked around, emphasizing the fact that we were alone. It made the space uncomfortable. "So, you didn't mention that last night—You passed the Detective Exam?"

Was there a hint of an edge?

"Why'd you leave?"

Were you listening last night?

"I think I told you, I was tired of Chicago and wanted to come home," I said, moving away from him and half-expecting him to yank my arm and turn me back.

"Oh. Okay," he said easily and followed me. "It's just that, Allie," he caught up and crowded my space in the narrow corridor, "As partners, we need to build trust. And part of that trust-building is sharing. That's all."

"Here's some sharing," I said, stopping and turning. "I want to clear this fucking case so I can go back to patrol, okay?"

"Yeah, sure. You don't have to be so sensitive," Gill had his hands up in mock protest. "I get it—you're back home and just want to do your job. So, let's get to it."

We found our way to the bullpen without talking. I picked up my laptop, went to Gill's office and fired it up. We stood in silence as I entered my password and opened my Chamberlain County email account.

I hadn't developed much traffic yet and Honor Fielding's forwarded message was at the top of the list. The subject was "Trevor and Celeste".

I clicked on the heading.

Fourteen

THE TEXT OF THE message was just as Honor had read it. The images were a little different from what she described. There were two photos, black and white, inserted into the message, one of each twin. And they weren't naked but were wearing underwear and were each laying on a single bed: metal frame, bare mattress.

Gill reached in. "Allie, let me play with that." I stepped aside and he began to show his skill, deftly creating new folders, saving the photos to a separate file, and sending the package to his computer. He sat and got comfortable with his keyboard, then worked some digital magic and, in a moment, enlarged images opened on his oversized desktop screen. The pictures appeared pixelated and fuzzy.

"Smarter than I thought," he said, partly to himself. "They've sent small files so we can't enlarge them too much for detail. But . . . ," I walked around the desk and stood behind him. The photos disappeared into a file at the bottom of the monitor then reappeared in another program he started. He highlighted Celeste's photo and clicked on several slider bars, making adjustments back and forth. It clarified a good bit and elements appeared that weren't visible in the originals.

"Is that a bruise on her left cheek?" I pointed to the area.

"Looks like it. Jesus. Deleting the color was smart. If I enlarge it more, it just dissolves." he said, demonstrating. "That's about all the resolution I can squeeze out of these," he added, adjusting Trevor's and enhancing the focus.

We examined the images in silence. They were pretty clinical looking. The kids seemed posed. The two were splayed on the beds with their arms at their sides and legs apart. They might have been awake, but with duct tape covering their eyes we couldn't tell one way or another. It's possible their wrists and ankles were discolored but, again, with the black and white, the color definition just wasn't there and it was tough to see exactly what was going on. Trevor was wearing boxers, Celeste, a bra and cotton panties. Their bodies revealed the kids' athleticism. Faded tan lines attested to their love of the outdoors. Trevor had the beginnings of six-pack abs. Celeste was lithe and muscular. Her naturally blonde hair was pulled back into French braids that peeked out from behind her head. They looked more physically mature than their 14 years.

"Allie, is it me or is this the same mattress, shot twice? I mean, they're not on different beds, right? Gill indicated a tag and handle on the corner of Trevor's mattress. It was the same in both photos.

"Yeah, check this out," I took my pen, leaned over his shoulder, and made a circling motion around an area of the metal frame where it looked like paint was missing and there was a pear-shaped discoloration, most likely rust. I found the same thing in the picture of Celeste. "I think that matches up in both images."

We both straightened. "So, they were each moved separately and laid on this bed for the photo. Which means they were probably drugged. My bet would be roofies. Their bodies are super relaxed. And they're trying hard to control exactly what we see," he observed. Then, "These were shot with a phone, for what that's worth. Digital phones are tremendously forgiving. Compare the detail on the floor to Trevor's face."

His comment shifted my attention to the space. The background revealed the prominent grain of aged pine boards, worn and darkened by time and use, and emphasized the black and white format. Classic Maine camp cabin. I squinted at the boy. Freckles bridged his nose and cheeks despite the low resolution of the image file. Everything from floor to face was in focus, relatively speaking.

"With a higher quality lens in SLRs that shoot video, there'd be a shift as the focal length moved from one area to another. Not with a phone camera."

"Okay. But what does that tell us?" I noticed the wall behind the bed for the first time. Unfinished sheetrock. That's different from a Maine cabin.

"It tells us that one of the five billion cell phones on the planet was used to shoot these." *Mr. Cocksure.*

"Thanks for narrowing it down, Jack. What's this?" I pointed to a black blob that appeared on the floor near the head of the bed in Celeste's photo.

He tried to enlarge it, but the resolution shifted to a series of black and gray blocks as it filled the screen. "Whatever it is, it's black. There's no light reflection, no definition of form."

My cell went off. I didn't recognize the number, but it had a 207 area code. I walked to the opposite side of Gill's desk. He looked at me quizzically and I shrugged.

"Beckham here."

"Deputy Beckham?" The voice was female, insistent, and afraid.

"Yes. Who's this?" The background filled with the sound of pounding and a man speaking loudly.

"Deputy Beckham, this is Becca Thompson."

"Yes Becca, what's going on?" I hit the speaker button and laid the phone on Gill's desk. "Are you okay?"

"My father," and in Gill's office the garbled shouting coalesced into *"Becca Thompson, you fucking little slut, you let me into this room!"*

"Somebody called my dad. They said they saw the video with Justine and me online. Omigod he's going to kill me!"

Gill responded.

"Becca this is Jack Gill. I'm calling the Adams County Sheriff. You need to stay on the phone with Deputy Beckham. Do not hang up." He punched the numbers into his desk phone.

"Deputy Beck—"

"It's Allie, call me Allie, Becca. Do you think your dad might hurt you?"

Scrambling sounds.

"Please Allie, help! Oh shit! He's trying to beat the door down!"

A pause, and then a booming, *"Who are you talking to?"* came through loud and clear.

Fist pounding.

"Becca, is there anything you can move in front of the door?" I called to the desk.

"Maybe the bed . . ." The tone shifted. She was further away from the phone's mic. Now the door-pounding was with something hard, not a fist. We heard scraping against wood.

"Becca! Becca! Are you still there?"

She was back. "Oh Allie I'm so scared. I'm soooo sorry. I made a mistake . . ."

Gill leaned in. "Adams Sheriff Deputies are on their way, Becca. Hang on."

Another call was coming into my phone. It was Becca, requesting Facetime. Smart kid.

I accepted and Becca Thompson's tear-streaked face filled the screen. Gill and I hovered over the desk from either side. She was hysterical.

"Can you stop him, Allie? I am so scared."

From what I could make out in the video, Becca's house was probably not located in the Grenoble development.

Wood splintering.

"Omigod, Allie, he's breaking the door!"

She flipped the image. The latch was loose in the jamb. I could see the tops of her toes up against the frame of the twin-sized bed. She must have been on the floor with her back against the wall and pushing it hard up against the door. Her feet bounced with her father's pounding.

"Let me in Goddammit!" her father called between blows.

"Dad, please, I'm sorry!"

"You don't know sorry!" The door was free of the jamb.

"Daddy—Allie! Help! Please stop him!"

"Mr. Thompson! Deputy Allie Beckham here—Stop what you are doing. *NOW!*" I shouted ineffectually as I turned the phone so I'd fill the frame. Like that was going to make the difference. He'd pushed the door wide enough to get his body into the opening. He was a big guy; his face and fists were red with exertion.

He moved into the room and was trying to figure out what to do next. The video gave me the feeling she was holding her cell at arm's length, like a shield.

Gill snatched my phone, "Thompson! This is Lieutenant Jack Gill of the Chamberlain Sheriff's Department. Do not touch your daughter!—Stop now!"

he demanded. "Adams County officers are on the way to your house. You do not want to do anything you will regret." He put the smartphone back on his desk.

"You fucking called the *police?*" Thompson tipped the bed up and the inexpensive mattress fell on Becca. The video image scrambled and tumbled as Becca held it back with her elbow. Gill and I were both shouting, "Thompson leave her alone!"

She surrendered to the mattress and scuttled across the floor to the corner and hugged her legs tight to her chest, camera focused out. Her father had heaved the bedframe to the side and stacked it vertically against the wall. He waded over the floppy pad and we could see him reach for the phone.

His footing wasn't good, but he caught her hand and yanked it away. As he did, he must have held his finger on the flip button because the image shifted back and forth from the pink-orange of his hand to Becca cowering in the corner. He tossed it aside where it settled on the floor. We stared at the ceiling and heard repeated slapping as her terrified shrieks turned to wails of pain.

The beating stopped. Becca whimpered. When Thompson stood up, the camera frame caught the top half of his torso and head. From our vantage point, he looked down at the corner where his daughter cowered as he towered over us.

"Have I made myself clear, Becca? If you even think of doing something like this again . . . Stay the hell away from Justine Kringle."

Gill moved away from my shoulder, where he'd parked himself, and the motion must have caught Thompson's eye. He reached down and the image disappeared.

Gill called the Adams County Sheriff again. They were just arriving on the scene. He summarized the situation for the dispatcher who said she would pass it along to the responding Deputy.

We looked at eachother.

"We should alert the Kringles," I finally said. "We need to make them aware this is being circulated, and not just at The Mountain."

"No, that's not a good idea."

"Jack. Don't you think if someone posted a porno with your daughter—if you had one—don't you think you'd want a heads-up?"

"My daughter wouldn't be making pornos."

He considered for a moment. "But, fine," he agreed, then continued, "Consider this, though, Allie . . . maybe we should find this mysterious video, see what it's all about, before we get our panties in a twist? It may not be that bad . . ."

"Right. As if we'd be able to find a video of two fourteen-year-old girls in millions upon millions of clips."

"Sounds to me like someone has done some porn searches . . ." Gill replied, arching his eyebrow. I didn't take the bait. "Sometimes ya just gotta know where to look," he said, sitting again. "Pull up a chair. I'm the head of the county's Sex Crimes Task Force, after all."

I was skeptical but curious. And jaded enough to continue.

"First, we need to narrow our search field. Someone undoubtedly ran across this on one of the main supply sites. We'll start with SkinFlix."

My time in Chicago exposed me to some sex work, but I hadn't heard of SkinFlix.

"Yeah, it's a new-ish site. Yet another Grand Central for porn. Everybody wants in 'cuz the money these guys make is so unbelievable—" He pulled up the homepage. It looked somewhat different from sites I'd seen before. Brighter, neutral pastel horizontal bands gave it a more female-friendly feel instead of the usual black background and lurid text. It had a "design-ey" vibe. Smooth jazz supplied the mood. As he began to scroll down, though, there was the standard catalogue of thumbnail images categorized by hair color, body type, and nationality with banner ads shouting "POV blowjobs" that featured repeating video gif closeups of girls struggling to manage huge erections. *Right, female friendly.*

"So, how are you going to find Trevor's video with all this shit floating around?"

He directed his cursor to a dialog box with a sunrise logo and the title "Daily Diet."

"This is where they showcase new talent." At the top was a video of a guy pushing his fist into a woman's vagina. Her face grimaced in the background while he licked his lips in tight closeup. The Daily Diet piece was below. Sure enough, Justine and Becca were pictured on a couch. I recognized the fabric from the Kringle's great room. *Fran's gonna be thrilled to see that.* Both girls wore top-of-the-line form-fitting black leggings. Justine had on a pink sports bra. Becca's long-sleeved teal-colored top was scoop-necked.

"Okay, here goes." Gill hit the triangle play button and the screen transitioned to black. "Tiny Titty Teens Find Love" scrolled across the panel and faded into the two girls sitting close on the sofa, a bowl of popcorn between them. The camera panned to reveal the Kringles' 75" TV where an old "Girls Gone Wild" video was playing silently. You could tell Justine was waiting for the camera and direction as the image panned back.

"I'm thirsty, how 'bout you?" she said stiffly to Becca.

"Um-hmm." Becca replied, looking straight into the lens.

Justine reached off-screen. The long neck of an open Grey Goose vodka bottle came into view. She raised it and put it to her lips and took a hefty pull and swallowed. Her eyes widened as the vodka passed into her tummy and she coughed lightly. "Ohhhh. That's warm. Here ya go."

Becca moved the bowl of popcorn to the floor and leaned in as Justine delivered the bottle to her open mouth. She caught the neck with her tongue, pulled it in, and drank. She seemed more expert. Justine began to lower it but Becca drew the long-neck back with her hand and took another draught, licking the mouth of the bottle with her tongue and looking deeply into Justine's eyes as she swallowed. This time she coughed and spilled some onto her chest. She looked down as the liquid marked her budding cleavage and then smiled at the camera.

We continued to watch as one long take occasionally zoomed in and out and went on for about ten minutes. The two girls fumbled around: kissing, fondling, and doing what 14-year-olds thought might be sexy. It didn't seem erotic to me but I could tell Gill was trying to cover a shortness of breath. The piece closed with Becca dozing off, wrapped in Justine's arms. They had stripped down to their panties.

"I don't think Trevor's going to win an Academy Award for camera work," Gill said as he created a new folder and saved the location to his toolbar.

"Do you think he posted this?" I couldn't see Trevor having that much savvy, but I could have been wrong.

"Probably. Even though . . . the guys that run these sites—SkinFlix, Pretty Kitties—they're careful about what they put up. They really try to steer clear of any kid younger than 18—especially U.S. citizens—because they know they can get hammered by the Feds—so we might have some leverage. But with the open access stuff—kids like Trevor who upload directly to the site—they don't need to worry, *"We didn't produce it. We can't be responsible for the entire world's behavior."* Believe it or not, I've developed a few relationships in the industry. As disgusted as most of the world may be, they try to keep it legal, or . . . just on the inside edge of legal. I've always figured live and let live . . ." I raised my eyebrows as he added, ". . . within the boundaries of the law, of course."

"No concern about the exploitation of women, then? That the women—girls really—that even if they *do* participate consensually, they're not reaping any financial benefit from their performance? Not to mention they're being sexually debased by guys who could care less about their future or well-being?"

"C'mon Allie, don't get all Hillary on me." He put his hands together, swung his chair around, and leaned back. "This industry rakes in billions, with a "B", of dollars. A lot of the girls are paid, and if not, they're getting some benefit along the way. And we're a tiny sheriff's department in boo-foo Maine. Just after I got here, Sam and I busted up a prostitution ring that had been going for like, five years. I do what I can do. All this—the Fielding kidnapping, this video—it's not like I could see it coming."

I looked at the final, frozen image of the two girls. For them, it was probably just a lark.

I pushed on. "Okay. We have an idea of what we're dealing with. We need to call the Kringles. Fran's wound pretty tight and I'm not sure how she's gonna react to the news that her daughter's an internet sensation."

"Feel free, Allie. You can handle that."

"You don't know Fran. I could really use your gravitas and credentials. You're the lead Detective on the county's Sex Crimes Task Force, after all." *Taking on the role of the considerate partner here, Jack.*

"Okay. Sure. Go ahead and call the Kringles."

Fran Kringle picked up on the second ring.

"Hello?" Her answer was harder than I expected.

"Hello, Mrs. Kringle?" I figured I better keep it formal. "This is Deputy Beckham from the Chamberlain County Sheriff's Department. We met yesterday."

"Oh! Oh. Hello, Allie." She sounded a little confused, then, "The caller ID said it was Jack Gill. I wasn't expecting your voice. I don't think I know a 'Jack Gill'."

"Sorry for the confusion Mrs. Kringle. I'm calling from Lt. Gill's office. He's the lead Detective for our Sex Crimes Task Force and he's here with me. Do you mind if I put you on speaker phone?"

"Oh. Oh no, go right ahead," Fran said. She was happy to help. Then, "Sex Crimes Task Force? What's this about?" she asked with some apprehension.

I turned on the speaker.

"Good morning Mrs. Kringle," Jack said. "This is Lt. Gill. May we call you Fran?"

"Yes, yes of course. But, what's this about, Deputy Beckham?" she chirped, ignoring Gill. "I don't understand. Sex Crimes?"

"Is Mr. Kringle with you?" I asked.

"No, he took Justine back to school yesterday and had appointments in Portland this morning." Her tone was more urgent. "What's this about?"

"Fran, we had a call from Becca Thompson earlier." I said. "It seems that the video she and Justine shot has been uploaded to a server and is being shared on the web."

"What? What do you mean?"

"Fran," it was Gill speaking, "Someone got ahold of a video file and either sold it or simply loaded it to SkinFlix, an internet pornography site. It must be the one Trevor Fielding shot of Becca and Justine." *Boy-oh-boy, no sugarcoating there.* "We're calling to give you and Mr. Kringle a heads-up. Becca's father received an anonymous call about it. He was pretty upset." Gill looked across the desk with a *"That's an understatement"* expression.

Fran blew up.

"Sex crimes? But she hasn't . . . But she's . . . ! Omigod Kris will . . ." She made some unidentifiable noises. "It's just that, my God, these girls are so young and I just can't believe Justine would do this and, but . . ."

"We all do stupid stuff when we're kids." Gill interjected. "Fran, have you seen the video?"

"Me? Oh God no. I couldn't . . . I'm just . . . I . . . I understand that some people like it but I have no interest in that kind of filth."

"Yes, of course. I understand your reluctance." His mock sincerity overcoming the sarcastic tone. "We are working on getting the post removed," he said. *Reassuring. That's our Jack!*

"Well, you've got to make it go away, Lt. Gill! Kris will be so angry—I don't know what he might do." A loud noise flooded Gill's office as she blew her nose.

"Fran." Gill was assertive. "Fran, we will do what we can. I can't promise that we can make this go away anytime soon but we will do our best."

My turn. "We're thinking this could help in our investigation of Major Fielding's murder. Presuming Trevor, in fact, shot the video, we might be able to trace this back in some way and come up with a connection to his and Celeste's disappearance . . ."

"Trevor and Celeste? *Trevor and Celeste?*" Fran cut me off and her voice, transformed, was guttural, almost animal. "I don't give a god – ," she started, then stopped. She took a long breath. A little more composed. "Yes, of course you're concerned about Trevor and Celeste. But this is my Justine—my beautiful Justine . . ."

Gill signaled me with his hand. "Do you think Justine knows about this being online?"

"I don't know. She never mentioned it but, then again, I mean, it's clear she wouldn't tell me something like this. I try to be a good mother, and, well, this is just so upsetting—Now I'm scared to death—You don't think Terry Thompson will come over here, do you?" She was winding herself up again. "And Kris doesn't know yet—How am I going to . . . how can I tell him?"

"Mr. Thompson won't bother you," Gill confirmed. "We're pretty sure he's talking to the Adams County Sheriff's Department as we speak." *Omitting a detail or two, eh, compadre?* "Mr. Kringle may be upset, but I'm certain you'll be able to work this out. It feels like the end of the world at this moment but Justine isn't hurt or missing . . . you will all get through this." She settled a bit. "We'll make sure we give this our full attention. It wouldn't hurt to check and see that your doors are locked. And don't answer the phone if you don't recognize the phone number."

"Thank you, Lt. Gill. But, you don't think . . ."

"You know, Fran, we don't know what to think."

"Please do as Lt. Gill has requested," I said, stepping in. Woman to woman. Gill smiled.

"Yes. I will."

Deep sigh. She blew her nose again.

"Thank you, Allie. And thank you, Lt. Gill." He tipped an imaginary hat to the phone on the desk. "Please make this horrible thing go away. Oh my goodness. The world has changed and we all need computers in our lives but it's terrible . . . just horrible that young people have easy access to such perverted wickedness."

"Yes, Fran. The world has changed." My turn to be reassuring. "We will do everything we can to make this go away. In the meantime, don't be to be too hard on Justine. She will need your support. As Lt. Gill said, we all do foolish things when we're young." I was well aware this could be a much bigger deal than Justine ever bargained for. My phone was off before she could respond.

"Perverted wickedness?" Gill said. "Welcome to the 21st Century Mrs. Kringle! Has she turned on her TV lately? Jeez. Besides, this isn't our priority. I'll check in with my guys in the biz and see if they can give us a lead. We need to stay focused on the Fielding kids," Gill said, standing. "Let's get going."

Fifteen

Gill was pre-occupied as we traveled from Gainsborough, through St. Ives and Folkestone, and on to the peninsula. The flurries from early morning had intensified into real snow and were accumulating in abstract patterns on black mud flats exposed at low tide. It was still weeks before temps would be above freezing. As soon as that happened, there'd be clammers in hip-waders dragging mud-sledges and digging the flats with three-pronged claws, searching for delicately flavored steamers. Maine is a great place to live but a tough place to make a living. Snowflakes came at us in a mesmerizing pattern. My mind drifted. Seeing the video of Justine and Becca took me back to my first encounter with real sex, before Google and the explosion of the information revolution.

◆

Hanna and I were walking in the woods down near "Fort Beckham," an informal scattering of massive glacial boulders at the edge of our property bordering the ocean. I couldn't recall which summer Hanna christened the space and laid claim: "For all time, until the ends of the earth should crumble, for the Beckham twins, Susquehanna and Allegheny."

It was autumn, and the light was crystalline in its clarity. The stones encircle an ancient sugar maple that was spared when the original settlers cleared the land. Its broad canopy towers over the open space. The south side of the tree is hollowed and warm tan heartwood delivers life to its upper reaches.

We came upon a couple taking full advantage of the solitude which post-Labor Day September-in-Maine offers. Against the bright red leaf litter, I noticed a woman's hiking shorts and turquoise underwear. His pants were crumpled at his feet, half on and half off. We peeked over one of the boulders and eavesdropped from over his shoulder. Her legs wrapped tightly around his waist. His ass flexed and released as he pushed her into the soft interior of the magnificent maple.

Since Hanna and I had gotten our periods and were "young women" as mom called us—little mini boobs and all—she had hosted a series of "Ladies' Teas" where we'd discuss sex. We kind-of had a handle on the idea of procreation, but when Hanna asked whether it was true some men like to kiss a woman's 'ta-ta' and Mom said yes, and some women actually enjoyed it, we looked at each other and Hanna gave the "Look out—Could be trouble ahead." signal we'd developed for silent communication.

It was a lot for a couple of 12-year old girls to take in. Hanna would have none of it and tugged on my arm. I was transfixed.

Hanna was shocked. She was the alpha twin. "This isn't right," she whispered, then gave me the secret hand signal. She moved away, heading toward home.

The woman brushed her hair from her face and in doing so, saw me. We shared something in that moment. Her chin dropped. She smiled at me and we connected.

She urged him on and she watched me as I watched her. With each powerful thrust, she closed her eyes and shivered with delight.

She giggled gently.

She opened her eyes and looked through me.

She smiled.

"So, this is the Glory Train that Mom talked about."

Drained, I quietly headed home. I knew I wanted a ticket for that ride.

◆

"ALLIE—HEY *ALLIE!*" GILL REACHED from the wheel and pushed my shoulder. "You with me?"

I shook off the hypnotic effect of the snow and took a sip of coffee. "Yeah, uh, sure, Jack."

"So, what's our play in South Prescott? You've met these people." Gill pulled his cup from the holder drank as he drove. His Charger felt like more car than you'd ever need on these roads.

"There's no 'play.' Mr. and Mrs. Chapman—Honor's parents—are mostly bystanders. They might be able to fill in a little information here and there about the family's history but I don't think they can contribute too much." Gill slowed to pass a parked box truck. A guy in coveralls was unloading stock for the Winkleigh General Store. He nodded in appreciation as he placed cases of canned goods onto a two-wheeled hand truck. Gill sped up as we passed and the boxes toppled to the ground. The Winkleigh post office flashed by and we were on to South Prescott.

"There's always a play. Stuff like a kidnapping and murder don't just happen. You know *"There's no such thing as coincidence."* We've got a guy who's murdered and his kids are taken. Tell me what you know about Honor Fielding."

I related my impressions and re-iterated the story of Honor and Major's relationship. Gill was looking for an angle of approach. He asked a couple of questions, but mostly listened. We arrived at Fielding's Landing and were buzzed through the gate by Frank Chapman.

Snow fell, disappearing into the ocean as we arrived. It nearly covered the gravel turnaround area that Frank had cleared the day before as we pulled up to the main house. We approached the entry steps and Gill looked around, assessing the layout.

"Always gotta go big, don't they?"

I started to explain about Honor and that she was local. He waved me off and Mary Chapman opened the door before I could ring.

"Good morning, Allie!" Gill looked surprised at her familiarity. Frank was in the foyer and Honor busied herself in the kitchen. The smell of coffee and baking wafted through. "How can we help you?"

"Mrs. Chapman, this is Lt. Gill. We spoke with Honor earlier this morning and we've come to take a look at the message about the twins. Lt. Gill will need to collect Mr. Fielding's computer." *Formal, simple.*

"Oh. Oh dear. Well, yes, of course. Come in, please come in." She led the way and introduced Frank as he offered to take our coats. Gill hung on to his laptop case and Honor came to greet us.

"Boy, it smells great in here," Gill said as he stuffed his scarf into his coat sleeve and handed it off. "So, Mrs. Chapman, are you the baker or is it Mrs. Fielding?"

"Oh, thank you. Lt. Gill," Mary Chapman said, implicitly accepting the compliment. She wiped her hands on the apron that hung from her ample waist and turned to her daughter. "Honor, this is Lt. Gill and you know Allie."

"Please call me Jack," Gill said, offering his hand.

"Mom's the baker, Lt. Gill," Honor said, smiling and looking at her mother as she shook Gill's hand. "Have you eaten at The Chamberlain Brewing Co.? If you've had any of the desserts . . . the recipes come from Mom's kitchen." Honor looked better than when I last saw her. She was comfortable in a royal blue silk top and skinny jeans, heavy socks, and fluffy slippers. Her eyes were still a little puffy and her nose was red from blowing but she seemed more together.

"I haven't been able to get past the gingerbread with toffee sauce," he replied, charming Mary Chapman as she beamed. "It's so good I haven't seen the need to try anything else."

"The coffee's fresh and the scones are hot from the oven, Lieutenant. I'll put something together while you settle in Honor's office." Mary Chapman bustled into the kitchen and Honor led the way to the living room. Frank got comfortable in front of the TV.

"Mom and Dad have always been so helpful but with this . . . with Major's death and the twins . . . Well, at least I don't feel *completely* alone," Honor said as we passed out of the living room, through a formal dining room and then up a wide set of stairs. "It kicked Mom's baking-genes into overdrive." We met ourselves in a full-length mirror at the landing on the second floor. Gill was watching Honor Fielding move, comfortable amid affluence. I compared myself to these two as we moved through the space: taller than both, my standard-issue uniform shirt and sweater weren't as complementary as Honor's silk blouse, but at least I could acknowledge some real shape there. Slowing, I glanced up a narrower set of stairs which continued up to the third floor and what I presumed were sleeping quarters. I paused at an open doorway, anticipating.

"That's Major's office. Or, was . . . well, it still is, I suppose. He was so good to me." She gathered herself, then continued down the hallway, "We hadn't even thought of the brewery when we built The Landing but he told me he knew I'd need my own space for "the big things" in my future. So, we took the area above the living room and dining room and split it in half," she said, opening the door to her workspace. It sure beat the hell out of my cubicle in Gainsborough.

Being on the second floor broadened our view of the ocean, whose ceaseless roll filled a bank of tall, double-hung windows. Treble Island, one of "The Triplets"—three small islands topped by pine scrub that marched up the coast about 400 yards from shore—appeared translucent in the snowy light. Her sister islands were shrouded in squalls. Inside the room, contemporary furniture rested comfortably on antique silk rugs. A wide desk with an oversized, gently-curved computer monitor looked toward the ocean. Love seats placed between the fireplace and the windows subtly echoed the cherry hue of the desk in their nubbly pattern and faced eachother, flanking a mid-century Noguchi coffee table. Large-format black-and-white portrait photographs of the twins and Major Fielding separated bookcases and file cabinets on the long wall facing the water. The dominant hue was a pale dusky-rose. *Warm. Discrete. Tasteful.*

"Here you go, Lt. Gill," Honor said, offering her chair. "The message should be up."

"That's some view," Gill said, settling in and finding the mouse. "How do you get any work done?"

"Surround yourself with beauty and beauty will come to you." Major used to say . . ." Honor turned to me, then looked out at the water. Gill took the unguarded moment to assess her profile. "It's never the same. Always changing. After a while, it recedes into the background but . . ." She turned to him. A picture of the family appeared as the screen saver when he moved the mouse.

"I'll need your PIN to get in."

"9615," Honor replied. Then, to me, "That was the street number of Major's apartment in Manhattan when we met."

The message she had forwarded appeared on the screen. She reached for my hand when Gill scrolled down and the photos of the twins surfaced. I held it for a moment, gave it a reassuring squeeze, then stepped behind Gill, who was working on tracing its source. We'd agreed that it would be better for him to do the search with Honor present.

He'd already pulled up a second window with several pages of back-door computer gobbledey-gook. He keyed "Received: from" into a dialogue box and waited. A highlighted IP address appeared in the maze of numbers and letters. Copying that, he hit a few more keys and pulled up a search engine. He entered the IP address. Various identifying markers were listed. He chuckled, " 'Figures . . ." and jumped to Google maps and submitted the latitude and longitude supplied with the IP. A map of Bukhara, Uzbekistan was outlined with red pin. He shifted to satellite mode and enlarged the image, then went to street view. We saw a single-story concrete slab building. He moved the mouse cursor in a circle around a tiny sign that read "Hotel Rumi."

"They're spoofing," he said, his smile indicating some admiration.

"This isn't funny, Lt. Gill," Honor said.

"Sorry, Mrs. Fielding. You're right and I didn't mean to sound flip." He adjusted his position so he could look directly at Honor. " 'Spoofing' is an IT term. The IP address—Internet Protocol—the IP address has been set up to appear as though the public access computer at the Hotel Rumi sent the message," and here he turned back to the screen and pointed with his free hand at the image, "from Bukhara, Uzbekistan. They've used a VPN—virtual private network— to mask their true location. It's pretty standard stuff but clearly whoever has the kids isn't a newbie to the 'net."

"That's it?" Honor looked at me, then the lieutenant. "That's it, Lt. Gill? You can't get any closer than Uzbekistan?"

He stood. "Mrs. Fielding . . ." I sensed a shift in his tone.

There was a light knock at the door and Mary Chapman appeared with coffee and the promised scones. "Here you go," she said brightly, walking to the coffee table. She laid the tray of goodies and stepped back. "We know you'll find Trevor and Celeste and bring them safely home, don't we, Honor?" She looked at her daughter, then Gill and me. The mood lightened a bit and she walked out.

Honor sighed heavily. "I'm sorry. It's just that I just . . . . I, my God, Mom and I drove up to Augusta to identify Major yesterday afternoon. They told me to prepare myself but he was still frozen, laying on his side and . . .," her head dropped and the blonde curls fell forward. She looked like a lost child. "He looked *so* cold. They said it would be a day or two, yet, before he was completely thawed and they could complete their work . . .

"Christ, I'm talking about my dead husband as if he was a steak." A hand covered her face. She used the other to pull a drawer and a tissue from it and wiped her eyes. "I . . . He was such a loving, warm person and I, I just can't believe he's gone. And then with the twins—it's like someone pulled the plug on my life and everything that means anything to me ceased being, yesterday morning."

I wanted to comfort her, to say something, but Gill moved to the loveseats. "May we sit?" he asked, getting comfortable before Honor could reply. I found a place next to him and she sat across from us.

"So, tell me about the twins," Gill said matter-of-factly as he dug into the scones.

Honor looked at me, and I nodded, encouraging her. "What do you want to know, Lt. Gill?"

"How 'bout we start with their friends?" he replied, pouring himself a cup. "Who were they close to? Did Trevor have friends at school? Were they involved in activities? What was their relationship to their father?" He sat back and followed a bite of scone with a sip from his cup. "Great coffee."

Honor glanced my way and her jaw set. "Who *are* they close to? *Does* Trevor have friends at school? *Are* they involved in activities? Trevor and Celeste *are* twins, Lt. Gill. They are still alive."

"Of course. Sorry— ," he said through a mouthful of scone. "I was saying it in the sense of before-and-after they disappeared. I apologize. Of course they're alive. And, call me Jack, please."

"Trevor and Celeste are twins, Jack, and because of that, they're extremely close to one another. They don't really need outside friends—their best friend is their twin. However, Celeste makes friends outside the relationship very easily. She has a generous, open spirit about her. It's a little different with our two, because they're boy and girl. Trevor is not as social. I'm not sure whether it's being a 'tween boy but . . . Well, he's always kept more to himself." She had poured herself some coffee after I declined. She was looking down at her cup. "Celeste is involved in a number of school clubs, she's on the equestrian team. For her Service Hours she chose to learn American Sign Language so she could help with a pair of deaf twins at Barton's elementary day-school. Those girls love being with her." She paused again. "But, you know they're in boarding school so, well, I'm not as aware of absolutely everything they do—not like if they lived at home."

"How about Trevor?" I asked. "What are his interests? Is he in clubs? Who are his friends?" *Probing.*

"Like I said, he's not as social." She sounded a little apologetic. "Trevor, especially lately, has gotten involved with computers. I suppose all the kids are . . . but his interest seems to go deeper. He belongs to the computer club at school and he's been very active there."

"That's for sure," Gill said, covering a smirk as he wiped his mouth with a napkin.

Jesus, he's angling for a blindside.

"Excuse me?" Honor sat up straight and placed her cup on the tray with exaggerated care.

"We have some information you may not be aware of," I said, hoping to short-circuit or at least cushion the revelation. Gill turned his head toward me in an overly casual manner. "It appears that Trevor may have had—may *have*—an interest in . . . pornography. We've seen a risqué video of Justine Kringle and her friend Rebecca Thompson. It's been posted to SkinFlix, a commercial porn site."

Honor sat looking at me. "I'm sorry. What did you say?"

"We think Trevor has been using his video skills to dabble in pornography." I tried to soften the revelation by employing the word "dabble." I wasn't successful.

"Oh my *GOD!* You have *got* to be kidding me!" Honor exploded as the pain and frustration of the past two days erupted. The faintest smile passed across Gill's face. "My husband is killed—gunned down in his car, my children are *taken* for ransom and you are accusing my son of being a *pornographer!?*" She was standing. "Get the hell out of my house!"

"Mrs. Fielding," Gill sat calmly. "Honor, please sit down."

I stood. "Honor, we're not making a judgement here. And we don't know if this has anything to do with the disappearance of the twins. But we saw a video this morning. I met Rebecca and Justine yesterday. For better or worse, they told me Trevor was into porn, that he was sexting Becca until she put a stop to it. There's no mistaking who's performing. And everything points to your son being the cameraman."

"But it can't be Trevor! He's only fourteen, you know." She looked at his photo across the room. "He's made some family videos that Major thought showed promise—he made one of the regatta last summer we all loved. But," she turned to me and something flashed in her eyes, "Oh my God! Fran and Kris . . . but if they think that Trevor did this. Omigod! You've met Fran. And Kris . . . Kris will be . . ."

"Can we set aside the pornography issue for a moment?" Gill said, taking charge and emphasizing the topic while dropping it. "We need to talk about the ransom note and our strategy for getting Trevor and Celeste home safely." He looked around the room, appraising. "Fifteen million dollars is an opening gambit. Nobody can raise that kind of money in a few days. We need a figure you can manage. Is five million more realistic?"

Honor leaned on the desk. I sat down again. She crossed her arms and looked out the window for a long time.

"Five million dollars?" She sighed. "I suppose so. But, four days? I mean . . . of course. I would pay anything—*anything* to get Trevor and Celeste home safely and if we have to, well, we'll make it happen. But realistically, it takes some time to put that kind of cash together, even if we're going to wire it somewhere. But how do we even let them know we can't make the fifteen million in four days?"

"We'll figure that out. The thing is, we want to control the schedule and draw it out as long as possible. Depending on what sort of pros these guys are, we might be able to gain as much as a week or so. Obviously, the longer we can delay them, the better the chances are of getting the twins home safely simply because we'll have more time to gather information." Gill's tone was softer. "So, you think you could do five million if you needed to?"

"Yes. Yes, of course. I just don't know if I can do it in four days." Gill and I let her think.

"I can talk to Kris," she said after awhile, but then, in a rush, "Oh, but how can I call him now? He . . . Fran . . . They will hate me."

"My mother always said it's better to tear-off the Band-Aid and get it over with than to prolong the agony with a slow pull," I offered, not sure if the metaphor worked or not. "It sounded like you were all good friends when I visited the Kringles yesterday. You'll all move past this. You're adults. All of you understand what's most important here."

"We've known the Kringles for a long time but it was the kids that provided the thread . . . well, the kids and Major and Kris's friendship. Fran can be . . . well, you know." She paused. "I would trust Kris to look at our positions and make recommendations about what should be liquidated. But, it all needs to be done so fast."

"That's okay." *Gentle Jack.* "The main thing is, they need to believe you're working on it."

"Have you posted the message on the brewery's Facebook page?" I asked.

"No, no, I wanted to talk to you first. I simply want to bring them home . . ." She took her seat across from me, signaling she was back on board for the moment.

"Great. Then, this is what I want you to do." Gill took charge. "Post a message that says *"Spring is just around the corner—Free beer next Saturday."* One way or the other, they'll respond."

"But . . . But look," she said, pointing to the computer screen, "They said if we wanted to see the children 'whole again.' My God, I don't want them to—,"

"No. Trust me. They won't harm the kids." His tone was positive. "The message uses "We" to describe whoever has them. That's good news. It means we're probably not dealing with some psychopath who'd just as soon cut them up as return them." *Thanks, Jack, that'll make her feel better.* "If it's two or more people that have them, it raises the possibility of putting a wedge between them, appealing to one over the other. The first thing we need to do is try to buy some time."

"Jack's right. We took a close look at the photos and we're pretty sure they're being held locally—probably in Maine and certainly somewhere in New England." I didn't have any real reason to say this other than a hunch, but I figured it might settle her and give Gill and me a chance to get out of the house on our own terms. "Let us do our job. Go ahead and do as Jack suggests, make the post on Facebook and we'll see what happens. They won't hurt the kids—they're an insurance policy worth at least five million dollars at this point in time."

Honor was desperate. "How long do you think it will be? It's just killing me. They won't let me bring my Major home and . . . and I feel so . . . powerless."

"We recognize you're in an impossible situation." Jack was encouraging. "But try to be positive. The kids are alive and we are going to get them back. Can you post your response from here? The sooner we respond, the sooner they'll react and, in their reaction, we may be able to find a clue about where they have the twins."

"Sure." She went to the desk and swiveled the monitor so we could see it from where we were sitting. She pulled up the brewery's Facebook page, then went to another program where she laid out the announcement and saved it. The message had the wording Gill suggested, and we approved it. She returned to Facebook and copied, then posted the graphic. *Professional.* She sighed again. "Okay. That's done." She looked to Gill and me. "What next?"

"You said you wanted to talk to Kris Kringle about raising the money?" he volunteered.

"Yes, I think that would be best. Major and I share ownership of the accounts. I have a pretty good idea of what's there but . . . but I'm not tuned into the stock market like those guys are and . . . if we're liquidating five million dollars in securities I want them to be the right ones. And, then, there are the tax implications . . ." She hesitated, then, questioning her decision, "That's not being selfish, is it?"

"Of course not," I replied.

Gill stood. "Honor, I have a subpoena for Major's computer," he said stiffly, pulling the warrant from his jacket and tossing it onto the table.

C'mon, Jack. What's with the power-plays?

She looked at it, then at me questioningly, then at him. "Okay. But, how are Kris and I supposed to review our portfolio if I don't have Major's computer?"

Gill pulled a thumbdrive from his coat pocket. "I'm guessing a guy like Major was pretty organized. I'll copy and paste the financials from his machine to yours. Not a problem," he said, standing and moving to the door. "Can you get me into his computer?"

Honor took a small book from her desk.

"Here." She gave the book to Gill. "The pin and password are listed under "L" for The Landing."

We moved to Major's office. It was a mirror layout of Honor's, but in harvest tones with nautical charts and photos of the family sailing. Gill moved efficiently, scanning through the husband's files and copying what he needed to the thumbdrive. Honor pulled me away and asked about the video. I told her it was really pretty innocent, that she should remain focused on helping the twins, and that Kringle would probably help her with stocks. What I didn't mention is that if Trevor was convicted, he could be registered as a Sex Offender for life because the girls were underage. But that would be if, and when, we got the kids home.

We moved back to her office and he copied the information to his laptop and her computer. He collected various passwords and pin numbers from Honor and let her know that he would be remotely monitoring traffic on her machine.

"So, what happens next?" she asked.

"We wait for their reply," Gill said simply. "And, Allie and I are following up on leads. She should hear more about Stephen today," he said, looking at me, "and I'm going to nail down Locke's status."

"Thank you. I apologize for earlier," said Honor as Gill packed his laptop. "I know you're doing your job but, my God. Trevor. It's so different now, even from when we were kids, you know? I'm not a prude but for a fourteen year-old to be able to access this stuff. And then you and Lt. Gill coming into the house . . . it feels so invasive . . ."

"I know. But this is how we can best help the twins." I said.

"Let me walk you to the door."

I took a final look out the window as Honor and Jack moved to the hall. The snow had strengthened and with it, the wind. A large black seabird, a great cormorant, fought to make way just inches above the heaving waters. Hanna and I would watch cormorants on summer afternoons while they dried their wings, bat-like, on sunny tidal ledges. We'd marvel at their ability to dive and swim for minutes, not seconds, underwater, then bob to the surface and work their wriggling catch down their gullets. *Good times.* This one disappeared, still fighting for progress in the air, into the curtains of white that advanced on the shore.

I heard Frank Chapman call to Mary as we landed in the dining room. "Gotta hand it to the Quakers. They're not giving these fucking Nazis an inch."

Mary saw us approaching as she moved from the kitchen to behind the sofa to see what he was watching. "Oh dear! Please pardon Frank's French." He turned in our direction.

"Goddammit, Mary! Lt. Gill, you know anything about history?"

"Yes sir, some." We stopped to look at the TV. A noon news show was on and the reporter was live, covering a protest somewhere.

" 'know what the Battle of the Bulge was?"

"Yes sir. W-W-2. Germans tried to break through the Allied lines. It was winter. Christmas, I think .. "

"Very good! Most kids don't know shit about history these days. My dad spent the winter of '44 in a foxhole so assholes like this can play Nazi?"

I recognized the reporter from Major Fielding's crime scene. Over her shoulder, a line of three women was bookended by two men. Heavily bundled against the cold, they stood on a dirt road that disappeared into thick woods. Behind them was the broken-down gate that I realized was the entrance to Camp Miq-Maq. Someone had replaced the plywood "New Albion" lean-to sign. "Nation of New Albion" was neatly lettered in black on a white ground. The new sign was 4 x 8, but not plywood, maybe MDF, and mounted on a pair of 4 x 4s braced by angled posts. Much more formal. The reporter was explaining that the Midcoast

Friends Meeting had committed to protesting the presence of Nazism in the state and would continue until the organization disbanded. This was the first day.

The group was holding hands and blocking the entrance to the camp. The men at each end held the corners of a long sign made of lightweight luan plywood that bore the message "Hate has no home in Maine." It rested in the snow, leaning against them.

"They must be freezing." Mary Chapman commented. At that moment, the protesters' attention moved off-camera and they began to chant, "Two-Four-Six-Eight—Mainers have no place for hate!"

From over the shoulder of the cameraman, the hood of a white box truck nudged its way into the video frame and toward the group as they chanted. The Quakers held their ground and continued.

Without warning, a pickup truck appeared on the wooded road from behind the protesters, charging into view and coming to a sliding stop a scant five feet from the group. Four young men leapt from the bed and surrounded the line. They each held a sturdy section of white birch about the length of a baseball bat.

"Oh my goodness—what is going on?" Mary echoed everyone's thinking. We stood quietly as the reporter urged her cameraman to get a better angle.

As the toughs advanced, the driver of the pickup truck got out and walked purposely to the Quakers. He placed himself between the reporter and the line. He was young-ish, probably early thirties and he pulled a sheet of paper from inside his jacket. The camera zoomed in. He addressed his video audience directly and declared in a clear voice, reading from the sheet:

"Native Americans have stolen the land the Lord saw fit to give white men through discovery and deliberate conquest. They fleece unsuspecting whites with their games of chance." Judging by his look, someone else had prepared the statement he was reading from. He continued, clear and well-rehearsed, "African-Americans have seized our cities. Latinos continue their wholesale invasion from the south. Asians have taken control of our internet and Jews continue to bankrupt society. In the name of the Great Jehovah, we are exercising our birthright as Native Mainers to establish the Nation of New Albion, a Nation of Purity. You are trespassing on a Sovereign District. Leave immediately or suffer the consequences."

One woman replied in a clear voice, "We turn our backs on your racism." The Quakers locked arms.

The spokesman for New Albion nodded and two of the thugs set-to with their clubs, swinging them against the sign, splitting it and knocking it face-down in the snow. The Quakers remained with their arms locked for a beat or two and then the men were on them, first going for their legs and then pounding them as they fell to the ground, men trying to cover the women with their bodies. The spokesman joined in the beating while the others advanced on the camera crew, who stood fast. Screams from protesters mixed with sickening thuds as the clubs came down hard against thick down jackets. Red began to spatter the pristine snow. There was confusion in the news crew and the reporter urged her cameraman to continue to roll as they began a strategic retreat. The frame opened up and the box truck pulled slowly into the melee. It was unmarked. The driver moved forward in his seat, craning his neck.

By now, the pair of toughs assigned to the news crew was on them. Video was rolling but the image was swinging wildly, swooping back and forth and around the scene as the cameraman tried to protect himself from the coming blows. The haphazard view zoomed in and caught a tight close-up of the box truck's cab. It had drawn parallel to the fight, and the driver turned full-face to the lens as he looked down to try to make his way. Finally, he saw an opening, checked the way ahead, swung his head forward, hit the gas and the TV screen went black.

Sixteen

WE WERE STUNNED AT the savagery. No one spoke.

"Jesus," Frank slumped in the chair.

"We'll try to reestablish contact with Sarah," the talking head in the studio said, obviously shaken. The station went to commercial.

Mary was sobbing, "What is happening in this world? This is Maine, not Baghdad for God's sake."

"Beckham, that's the old Camp Miq-Maq in Huntley. State Route 115. Call it in and get someone there immediately."

I clicked my shoulder phone and DiSimone answered, "Go ahead."

"Deputy Beckham. Lt. Gill and I just witnessed a beating on TV. We need a . . . um, uh–"

"*10-57!* Ambulance is 10-57, Beckham," Gill interjected.

"Yeah, we need a 10-57 with supporting officers dispatched immediately to Huntley to the entrance to the Old Camp Miq-Maq, State Route 115. They will find multiple injuries."

"10-4 Beckham. 10-57 with officers in support to Camp Miq-Maq, Rte. 115, Huntley."

Frank turned off the TV.

Quiet.

Honor moved to get our coats. We put them on and said a subdued good-bye to Frank and Mary who retreated to the kitchen. Honor went to get the door, but Gill placed his hand on hers as she reached for the knob. She looked up at him, surprised.

"How long have you and Kris Kringle been having an affair?" he said, directing his full attention to her reaction.

She stood for a moment while she processed the question. Then she pulled her hand carefully from under his and took a step back. She looked at me with loathing and then shifted her attention to Gill and said carefully and quietly, "Get. Out."

"C'mon, Honor. Major was what, thirty years older? And we all know what Fran can be like," Gill said, glancing my way. "You're a young woman. You've got needs. We get it."

"I opened my house to you because I trusted you," she said deliberately and looking directly at me. "You accuse my son of being a pornographer and me of . . . what?" Her attention moved to Gill and her eyes narrowed, "Fucking my husband's close fr - . . . my dead husband's . . . my murdered . . ," tears started down her cheeks but resolve came to her and she swung the door open. "Get the hell out of here," she said to Gill and then, shifting back to me, "Do not come back until you have my children." She held the door wide and stood resolute as snow blew into the foyer. Tears darkened her blouse. Gill stepped through the door. I hesitated for a moment as he walked to the Charger.

"Get out."

"Honor, I will fix this. I—."

"Get. *Out.*"

The door closed hard in my face. Gill tossed me a snow broom as I approached the car.

"What the hell, Jack? What was that?"

"Shut-up and sweep the car," he said, working the rear section while billows of exhaust mixed with whirling snow.

We finished and got in without speaking. He shifted into drive and gunned the engine. Tires spun as the back-end fishtailed, spraying gravel until it gained traction and we roared back through the woods and onto the main road.

Gill broke the uneasy silence. "Get with the program, Allie." He threaded his way through pick-up trucks that were parked on both sides of The Neck in South Prescott. It was lunchtime at Pierce's. "I needed to get that on the table. We've gotta move if we're gonna get the kids back and we can't tiptoe around wondering about this or that. Kringle doesn't have an alibi for Friday night. Who was the first person Honor thought of when we talked about the cash for the kids? We know they were getting together on the sly up at The Mountain. I've only heard Fran Kringle's voice on the phone but, from your description . . . I mean, c'mon, Allie. Sex is "perverted wickedness?" Honor versus Fran . . . think about it. And this would be the perfect way for Kringle to pimp the guy he had helped get back on his feet, showing him the ropes at B&C—the guy who then went on to make a boatload of money in the crash . . . the crash that Fielding saw coming and Kringle didn't, leaving the Kringles high and dry.."

It was a new way of looking at the situation and made a certain sense when I heard him say it out loud. But did it justify alienating Honor? "But what about the twins? If you're going to kill your lover's husband, why do you need to kidnap her kids? And where does he have them? And who'd you get to do it, anyway? The kids would recognize Kringle."

"If you're banking $15 million—or even $5 million—tax free—you can afford a pretty damn-good babysitter."

"But, there's Fran."

"Fran is incidental. Once everything settles out, Kringle divorces Fran and moves in with Honor. Money and sex. It's not exactly the first time they've been a motive for murder. Besides, Fran's got it good with Kringle for the moment. I mean, c'mon—it's Fran," he said, almost as though he'd met her. "I don't see her divorcing him—let's face it, they may not have the Fielding fortune, but they're not exactly in the poorhouse."

Gill's logic had a sick plausibility. If Kringle and Honor were having an affair and he got rid of Major, then he'd be able to step into Major's role. If he divorced Fran, with a $5 million dollar nest-egg set up somewhere secret, he could afford whatever alimony she'd hit him for and besides, he'd be sitting pretty in Fielding's Landing managing Fielding's fortune. And, by helping Honor out in her time of need, he'd be the White Knight, riding in to save his damsel in distress.

"Okay. Let's assume this pans out. Where do we go from here? Do we drop the other leads?" I wanted a concrete plan.

"No, even though I think we both know they're probably dead-ends. No, we spend some time following up and even maybe tease it out a little so Kringle's feeling comfortable. I don't think Honor's part of it . . . She's near out of control because her kids are gone. We need to follow up on the leads so we have some information to feed her, which, I'm guessing will get back to Kringle and make him feel more comfy."

He slowed as we pulled up behind a plow that was clearing snow and laying sand. "Let's keep this piece between you and me. Once we get some more of the puzzle, we'll let Latch in on it. He wants us to handle everything anyway. Honor gave us permission to tap her phone. We'll monitor everything in and out. I'll tell Latch it's for the kidnappers . . . and it is, in a way."

We followed the plow into Folkestone. The downtown—three blocks of retail and restaurants arranged along Business 1—was busy for late February and we crawled through, stopping for pedestrians at every crosswalk. My gaze fell on a mother shepherding her two daughters across. She waved in appreciation as they walked in front of Gill's car. I smiled and waved and followed them to the opposite sidewalk. Gill sat, lost in thought. We moved slowly to the next crossing.

"So, Jack, tell me about the medallion," I said, making conversation. What looked like a coin hung at his neck. I'd noticed it again when he was working at Major Fielding's computer.

Several trim older women waved thankfully as they began to cross with their yoga mats slung over their shoulders. *Namaste!*

"This?" he touched the coin lightly. "This, Allie, is a seventeenth-century Portuguese *Real*," he replied then paused, reflecting.

"'*Native*' Mainers . . . ," taking his hands off the wheel to supply air quotes, "They all talk about how many generations their people have been here, like it gives them sort of special primacy, legitimacy. *This*," he was holding the coin away from his neck between his thumb and forefinger, "This *Real* came down through the family from my I-don't-know-how-many 'greats' grandfather, Santiago." I raised an eyebrow and nodded at the empty crosswalk. He edged forward.

"The family story is that this was all he had in his pocket when he crawled up onto the rocks after his fishing fleet foundered in a storm."

A mixed group of five teens paused at the next walk. Steam from coffee cups wafted as they looked for permission to step into the street. Gill waved them across. They took their time.

"It was, like, 1697 or something. Everyone else drowned. He was able to use this coin as collateral, and then through hard work and some luck, he built a new life. The Gills have been here ever since. Gills fought in the Revolution, worked as shipwrights for the blockade in the Civil War. We've been here since Maine was Norumbega. Everyone else is a Johnny-come-lately."

I thought of the Wabanaki—"Children of the Dawn"— who'd been stewarding Maine for thousands of years before the European arrival. They might have something to say about that. My family, farmers from Norfolk, England, had arrived just in time for the Civil War—maybe seven generations.

"So Jack, is there a Gill family property somewhere?"

"C'mon Allie. He was a fisherman, not a stockbroker and we were Portuguese, not Anglo." The Charger was coming up to speed as it merged onto the through section of Rte.1 and the plow started throwing sand again.

"Jesus Christ!" Gill exclaimed as the grit peppered the front of the car. He tapped his brakes to put some distance between us and the truck. "Naw, the original Gill place, it was on the coast. It was never big but at least it was home to the family fishing business. But, ya know, my people had to fight history across different nations, states, you name it. Finally, folks from away arrived in the 40s looking for a view and my great-grandpa decided cash out. He sold the place and bought a house in Portland."

"You have sisters, brothers?"

"Nope. Last of the line. But in the interest of building trust, here's a secret: my given name is Joaquim. Yeah, with an "m" at the end – the Portuguese version of Joaquin," he replied to my unstated question. "School was brutal. I couldn't stand the way kids butchered it—called me Wack'em-Smack'em. When I joined the army, Jack was a whole lot easier."

We came around a curve and entered a long straightaway. He goosed the Charger, jumped into the passing lane, and sped by the plow, leaving it and a line of other, more timid drivers in our wake.

◆

LATCH WAS GONE WHEN we arrived at the station. He and two other deputies had responded to the call in Huntley. DiSimone said the Quakers were beaten-up pretty good. Ambulances removed three to Folkestone and one needed LifeFlight to Portland. The New Albion recruits, who held long rifles and blocked entry to the property, outnumbered Latch and his men. Their leader, who they called "The Professor," was "not available at this time." Gill asked DiSimone to keep him apprised of any developments.

Gill and I agreed to follow-up our individual leads during the afternoon. We'd meet later and catch up. I went to my desk for some quiet. I couldn't get the images of Trevor and Celeste out of my head. For me, it didn't matter who killed Major Fielding—he was dead and someone would figure it out. I needed to find the kids.

◆

THERE WAS SOMETHING ABOUT the fight scene at Miq-Maq that kept gnawing at me. I called WLHS and asked that Sarah Loundsberry or her cameraman contact me when she returned to the station. I figured being a Deputy at the Chamberlain County Sheriff's Department would get a pretty quick response.

I called DelVecchio, who answered this time.

"Hello Tommy, Allie Beckham. Have you got anything more for me on Stephen Fielding?"

"Allie. Hang on a minute." His hand brushed across the mouthpiece and I could hear some indistinct speech and a door close. He came back. "Sorry 'bout that. Yeah, I talked to some folks in his condo. He seems to be regular enough. Comes and goes—not so much that he keeps to himself but, you know, he's a New Yorker so nobody talks that much to their neighbors. Doorman—"

"Doorman? His condo's got a doorman?" I interrupted.

"Yeah," he chuckled, "Like you said, I think Momma's footin' the bill. I talked to the doorman and he let it drop that he works at Charles Hutchins."

"You say that like I should know what it is."

"Well, don't you, *dahling*? Everybody who's *anybody* shops there," DelVecchio said, his voice dripping in friendly condescension. "Anyway, I needed a new tie so I went down and asked around. Seems he took last week off and called in yesterday asking for an extension. He sells shoes—he must be pretty good at it because his manager said it was okay for him to take a couple more days—said he was up in New Hampshire skiing."

Shit, he's in the neighborhood. That complicates things.

I thought for a moment. "Did he say where in New Hampshire?" I wasn't looking forward to contacting ski resorts about whether Stephen Fielding had registered in the past ten days. "Was he traveling alone?"

"No, he just said New Hampshire. I tried to make out like I was an old friend of the family, you know, *"Gosh, I was hoping we could get together for lunch and catch up on old times."* The guy referred me to a sales associate who seemed to know him a little."

"Okay . . . ," I said.

"Some kid—probably mid-twenties—they'd dated a couple of times . . ." This was news—no one said Fielding was gay. Maybe they didn't know. "You know, dinner, a movie. Pretty basic and the kid said it was Dutch Treat so Fielding wasn't flashing cash. They'd gone back to his condo one night but the kid declined to stay. Said Fielding's a nice enough guy "but a little too old for me." So I guess it doesn't matter what your orientation is, old is old . . . I pushed him a little, asked whether he thought Stephen was traveling with anyone. Kid said Fielding told him he was hoping to meet someone on the slopes. Impression I got was that they're still friends. I'll be honest with you, Allie, it sounds like Fielding may have turned the corner. Obviously, you can't afford a condo in Washington Heights on a shoe salesman's salary, no matter how upscale the store. But other than that, he seems pretty clean."

"Did you mention his dad to the kid? You know, "Hey, Stephen's Dad told me to look him up when I was in town." or something like that?"

"Jeez, you oughta be a detective," he said, chuckling. "I tried an angle and the kid acknowledged that he knew Fielding was from Maine, but it was more like they'd talked in a general way about their families. You know, stuff like where they were from. I don't think they discussed Fielding Sr. in particular."

"Okay. Well, thanks, Tommy. This is helpful."

"You betcha. I'll keep digging and if I get something, I'll let you know."

"Hey Tommy—"

"Yeah?"

"Did you get your tie?"

"Deputy Beckham, you know I like a new tie. But, no, I can't let myself fork over $250 for a tie, no matter how gorgeous it might be. I got no Momma payin' *my* bills."

I smiled. If anything, it was probably the other way around. Tommy was a great cop but his domestic life was a shambles. "You and Jenette still together?"

"In the words of the immortal Freddie Mercury—"

And I finished the line, "*Another one bites the dust.* Oh, Tommy, what's that make it now . . . ?"

"Allie, after three, I stopped counting."

Seventeen

So Stephen Fielding was in New England over the weekend. Would he tell his boyfriend he was planning to kill his dad? On the other hand, if it was Stephen who stepped in front of the car, well, Fielding Sr. would certainly stop for his son and at least roll down the window. And maybe little Stephen *had* gotten greedy. He already had his mom supporting him, but he saw what his father had put together and wanted everything.

My desk phone rang. "Beckham."

"Hello, Deputy Beckham?" It was a man's voice. I checked the caller i/d. WLHS.

"Yes, who is this?"

"Rich Claiborne, Station Manager at WLHS."

"Mr. Claiborne, thanks for returning my call. Is Sarah Loundsberry okay?"

"Sarah's okay. Mike Delavan, her cameraman, he got whacked and his camera is demolished but they'll survive. We had no idea these guys were going to explode like that."

I knew a Mike Delavan back at Madison Academy—part of the A/V crew. But this wasn't the time for reminiscing. "Yeah, I think it surprised everyone . . . Perhaps, even themselves."

"Sarah's pretty shaken up but she'll be fine. I told her to go home. What can I do for you?"

"It's my understanding that you're able to pull a frame or two out of a video, right?"

"Sure, we do it all the time. What are you looking for?"

"At the very end of Sarah's report, at the moment just before the transmission crashed, there was an image of the driver of the box truck. I need a picture of that driver—something that shows as much as possible of his face and anything else that might help identify him—clothes, hands on steering wheel, anything."

"We can do that. We'll probably adjust it for exposure and tighten the focus—Mike was trying to protect himself at the end. But yeah, I'll get it to you this afternoon if that would be okay?" *Surprising how cooperative the media can be when it's one of their own.*

"Perfect. And Mr. Claiborne—," I figured I was on a roll . . .

"Yes?"

"Before the fight started, Delavan got some close-ups of some of the other men. There was at least one tight shot of a Quaker and, at least as I remember, a few solo pics of the Nazis. Would it be possible for you to send individual portrait jpegs of those to me, too? Everything in the same format?"

"Yeah, I'll see what I can do."

I gave him my email address and told him the Sheriff was on site. He let me know the station had sent another crew and their coverage would resume on the six o'clock news. We said goodbye.

The clash at Miq-Maq, combined with Gill's and my commitment to the Fielding investigation, stretched the personnel resources of the County. Latch continued to be adamant about keeping everything under his control. He'd brought in a couple of part-timers to cover for the guys he wanted out at the camp. "Red" Richmond, the late-shift sergeant in charge of the station-house while Latch was on site, had outlined the situation during an informal gathering and guys were in and out of the Armory. Dina Garrett arrived early for her shift. I was still curious about her take on Jack Gill and stepped into the Dispatcher's room after diSimone left for a quick lunch.

Garrett was just getting settled and looked up as I entered. "You saw the fight at Wiki?" she asked.

"You mean Camp Miq-Maq?"

"Oh, yeah. Sorry." She turned and scanned the computer screen for messages, adjusted her headpiece, then looked back at me and smiled. It was friendly. "I still call it Camp Wiki . . . You know how people call stuff by its original name for years, even after the name's changed?"

For a moment, I was back in Chicago where the Sears Tower—once the world's tallest building—had been sold and renamed "Willis Tower." Nope. It would always be "the Sears" to folks in Chicagoland.

"Well, most people around here still call it Camp Miq-Maq but for me, it's Camp *Wiki* because Chelsea, she's my daughter and . . . well, she's eighteen now but it was called Camp Wiki when she attended for a few summers."

Sorting through this, I had a vague memory of some friends going to Camp Miq-Maq. Hanna and I were never sent to camp—we had each other and kept ourselves plenty busy. I nodded, but my face must have betrayed some confusion because Garrett continued.

"Miq-Maq was in trouble. It was, like, fifty years old and everything needed work. A couple from away bought the place. Traditional camps are having such a tough time making it these days, which I don't understand because I loved camp when I was a kid. Didn't you?"

I smiled.

"This couple from away, they put a bunch of cash into it and changed it to a co-ed computer camp," she continued. "You know, trying to cater to kids these days. At least they had the good sense to change the name . . . Wiki still sounds kind-of, well, sort-of Native American-y don't you think? They had programming, and social media stuff, and even some video production. We weren't sure about sending Chelsea to an overnight co-ed camp." She gave me the *"You're a parent, you understand."* look. My face was blank, but she persisted in her genuine, if over-sharing, kind of way. She'd already delivered more personal information than anyone in the county had volunteered in ten days. I wanted to circle back to her and Gill, but in the interest of getting along, I let her continue.

"Afterall, she is, well, she *was* fourteen and it was *co-ed* but they were good about, well, *you* know . . ."

She trailed off, checking her screen. I was ready to ask about Gill when she started again.

"They installed high-speed fiber optic cable, the best. This was before most folks had—well, most folks in rural Maine *still* don't have any decent internet service. We—Scott, my husband and I—We think they put way too much money in. Sort of a typical thing for away folks, ya know? Can't judge the Maine economy for anything. They advertised in the New York Times and stuff. We were able to send her for the three years it was going. But that was it. BOOM! They went belly-up." My eyebrows must have raised in a question and she continued. "She made some good friends, though." Garrett nodded, mostly to herself, "Yeah, it was a stretch for us but Chelsea loved it. She picked up a lot about programming and even has an internship lined up for this summer. So, you saw it happen?"

It took a moment for me to realize she was done.

"Yeah, Gill and I were in South Prescott with Honor Fielding when it went down. We saw it on the TV. Hey, if you don't mind, I wanted to follow up on what you started to say about him last night."

Garrett's eyes flashed first to the reception area and then back over my shoulder into the Deputies' section. I followed the glance. Gill came into the room to catch up with a few of the guys who were going on patrol.

"Unh-unh, not here." She shook her head slightly and then smiled an *"Isn't everything wonderful in Gainsborough, Maine?"* smile and said through her teeth, "Stop over for lunch sometime. We can talk." She put on her headset as Gill cracked the door and poked his head in.

"Hey Dina."

She swiveled around in her chair, nodded and smiled brightly. "Hey Lt. Gill!" *Perky.* She threw her full attention to the screen.

Gill turned to me. "Allie—you got a moment?"

Garrett spoke into her mic. "Go ahead, Marston."

"Sure." I looked at Dina. She was in the zone. I stepped out and closed the door behind me.

Gill was wearing a flak vest. "What's up, Jack?"

"Latch wants me up at Miq-Maq," he said, signaling me to the hallway where we'd be alone. "He told me he wants you to take over recovery of the twins *and* the Fielding investigation on your own. Make sure you keep me aware of what's going on."

"What the fuck, Jack? I'm the only person working on it?" This was not okay.

"Latch doesn't want the Miq-Maq situation to blow-up. I'm supposed to try to arrange a meeting with this "Professor" guy," he said, gesturing air-quotes. "He's concerned one of these kids is gonna get excited and shoot somebody. If that happens, we're all fucked."

"I don't get it."

I was feeling whiplashed by the changes in direction. First it was going to be Latch in charge, then Gill. Now me. I was getting ready to say this when Lt. Match came around the corner from the armory with one of the Remington shotguns. We were quiet.

As soon as Match had moved to the other room, Gill began, "Look, I'm just the messenger." He lowered his voice. "You've probably figured it out—Latch is a control freak. Everything is about the public's perception and who gets the headlines. The national media will be all over this because a couple of their own were roughed up—it's what he lives for."

We were both leaning against the wall. "No one knows about the twins' disappearance and the murder is . . . literally yesterday's news. You heard Honor give me permission for the wiretap. Rest assured . . . I'll keep you updated on the details.

I interrupted.

"I want in on the 'tap. Everything you've got set up."

"Well, Allie, I'm not so sure . . ."

"Jack, if you and Latch are punting, I've gotta know what the hell is happening and you've made it clear you won't have the chance to keep me informed. Cut me in on the tap," I said as he looked away. I grabbed his sleeve and pulled it to get his attention. "I want to watch you set it up on my laptop," I declared and continued, "And you need to make sure I have access to Honor's home phone, her cell, her computer feed, and it wouldn't hurt if I had access to Kringle's, too."

He was looking at me again. "Fine," he said. "Jesus Christ, you're an insistent one, you know that?"

"Yeah. I've heard it put other ways."

He smiled, sharing what he thought was a joke. "Sure. Okay. The wiretaps are in place. I'll see any conversations between the lovebirds and keep an eye out for the kidnappers' response to her Facebook posting. But, sure, I'll set up your laptop so you can see it all, too. I've got your back, Allie. When something develops, tell me. I'll be there for you."

"Whatever." I didn't like it, but at least I'd have access to the players' status in real time. "Show me where to find the email and Facebook stuff on my laptop. And update me on Locke's status."

Gill grinned, "That's my girl! Bring your machine and come to my office," he said, guiding me with a light touch on my arm.

"Sure thing, Jack. Just let me freshen up a bit!" I replied. He didn't pick up on it.

Gill and I exchanged information during our meeting. He added an app to my laptop, so I'd be able to access the wiretaps and he was thorough in his instructions. He told me that Locke was on parole, but had relocated to California and couldn't have been in New England the previous Friday. I updated him about Stephen Fielding's trip to New Hampshire.

Jack thought. "Okay. So maybe this wasn't a planned hit. Maybe Stephen actually drove to New Hampshire to ski and look for love. But things didn't go well . . . he didn't meet anyone. He got depressed; he thought of his Dad and then . . ."

We were quiet. I thought of the gun. Gill anticipated my question.

"He could walk into any gun store in Massachusetts, New Hampshire, Vermont, or Maine and leave an hour later with a weapon. Sure, he's got an arrest record but no convictions for anything—and given this scenario he wants to show Major how strong he is, so he buys a little friend to back himself up."

"But how would he know Major and the twins were at The Mountain? And how would he know to intercept them on the way to South Prescott?"

"It was you that said they had a tradition of skiing there over winter break. He knows they have friends at The Mountain. Maybe Stephen just followed his nose. He was depressed. He wanted some of his father's attention. Destination: The Mountain, because he wanted to see what the Twins were getting. It's all about comparing his story to that of the kids. He was so full of self-pity that he drives to The Mountain. He catches sight of them. They're happy. He's not. He dithers and suddenly they're gone. But, he knows the way to South Prescott and intercepts them. Thirty-plus years of frustration boils over and then everything goes to hell."

He looked at his watch. "Hey, I gotta get going. Latch wanted me in Huntley twenty minutes ago. Here are your marching orders: Check up on Fielding and find out where he is—maybe you'll find the twins and him together. I have a strong hunch this is our guy. Watch the phone and email traffic between Kringle and Honor Fielding and I'll do the same as time permits. You have full rein as far as advising Honor what to do. Simply keep me in the loop—I'm not looking to approve action, I just need to know what's going down. Feel free to work out of my space if it will help. You can do this, Allie – You passed the CPD Detective test."

It was tough to tell whether this was sarcasm or encouragement.

"Okay. Be careful up there."

"Yeah, thanks." Gill left me in his office.

Eighteen

I sat in Jack's office. The activity surrounding the marshalling of the troops had died down and the department was quiet. Dina Garrett was afraid of Gill. But why? I could walk back and put the screws to her and get her to talk to me but I felt like I needed to respect her fear. And what did that have to do with the investigation of the Fielding murder/kidnapping? I reviewed the photos and names Gill had posted on the board with lines connecting relationships. Sure, Stephen Fielding was a wild-card. But something told me he was just a lost soul trying to find his place in this world. He'd been an asshole as a kid and young man but maybe, just maybe, he was finally coming to terms with that. I could relate. Somehow, I didn't see him as the killer type. Besides, he'd have to have found his dad in a raging blizzard and then had the balls to kill him and, on top of that, kidnap his siblings.

No. Breezy was the name that didn't fit into this galaxy. I returned to my desk. Gill and Latch wanted me to check into Fielding. That could wait. I pulled up the NCIC database and keyed in my CPD id and entered my password. Okay—I was in. Not surprisingly, no one at CPD had taken me off their rolls. They had other things to worry about. My search wouldn't be traceable back to the county. I entered Breezy in the "Known Alias" line. Two names popped up. One poor schmuck from the mid-90's who got three strikes for what looked like a little pot entrepreneurship and was still in the slammer. *Boy, times do change.* And some guy out west who'd been convicted on a Murder Two case fifteen years ago. Okay, maybe I was wrong.

What was with Garrett's fear of Jack? I switched to Google and entered Jack Gill. The top eleven responses had to do with his stopping a bullet during a domestic dispute. He stepped between a meth-head lunatic and his son. The Bangor Independent said he'd graduated from Bainbridge University in four years with a BS *and* a Master's in Criminal Investigation. It mentioned his decorated service record. Nothing there to create Garrett's reaction. My thoughts drifted to the guy I was replacing—Gill's partner—Sam Martin. I hadn't gotten the sense that Sam was a go-getter.

The first 23 hits about Sam Martin dealt with an NFL punter and a pop singer. *Jeez, I gotta update my playlist . . .* I scanned halfway down the second page of hits to an article from the Portland Free Press about Chamberlain County's Sam Martin and his accidental death and clicked. There were statements by Latch and Gill about the department's "tragic loss," what a great cop he'd been, and his "exceptional record of service to the county." It mentioned his youth in Lewiston and the fact that he was an All-State Tackle in 2000. Also that he had joined the Army just before 9/11 and did two tours of Afghanistan. A couple of the more local obits mentioned his wife, Kourtney, and several had photos. DelVecchio would have charitably termed her a "tart." I compared her to Sam's service photos that accompanied the articles—he was no hunk. The other thing that caught my eye was that Kourtney had kept her maiden name, Considine. I set that aside for a moment.

After the articles about Sam's death there were a few more about his work with Jack Gill on breaking up a prostitution ring. That happened shortly after Gill joined the Sheriff's department. There were some arrests and a conviction of a pimp on a bunch of counts of sex and drug trafficking. The guy had been running the ring out of a rest stop in Yarmouth. A couple of older gents who'd been working for the Maine Office of Tourism got fired for assisting him. They were getting blow jobs as a perk—*"The way life should be . . ."* Yeah, except for the underage girls who were swept up in the arrests.

There were three final pieces with headlines about my Sam Martin before hits concerning real estate agents, dental groups, and ancient obits began to appear. All three hits were from the Lewiston Courier-Herald.

Number one was located on page two of the Sports section from a March 2001 edition and featured two photos of Martin: the first was three columns wide; he was nailing a running back from Fairfield High School with a crushing tackle during the 2000 State Championship game. The other photo was a senior class portrait. *Okay, he was pretty hunky in 2001.* The headline read "Lewiston High's Martin Gets Full Ride" and reported on his scholarship to U Maine Orono. Article number two, dated July 28, featured a wedding announcement for Samuel MacKenzie Martin and Kourtney Cloutier Considine. They were married at the 2nd Congregational Church in Lewiston but only Sam's parents were listed as participating. No mention of Kourtney's mother or father, where they were from, or what they did.

The third was a short piece in late August that featured the coach at U Maine Orono. He expressed his admiration for Sam's dedication to duty and admitted the Black Bears would miss his presence that fall. Sam had given up his scholarship to enlist in the Army and was looking forward to training as a helicopter pilot.

My next search was easy. I checked birth announcements for the same paper beginning in September and got a hit in the Sunday, November 4th edition. Sam and Kourtney had welcomed Tabitha into their happy home the day before. Or Kourtney had. By that time, Sam was headed for Afghanistan, sucked into the post-9/11 response.

I got a ping from my email. It was Claiborne, who'd sent five grainy photo portraits from the riot at Miq-Maq. *Now we're getting somewhere.* One image, the one of the driver, showed a soul patch below his lower lip. Two earrings glinted under the edge of a black watch-cap. I called on my limited skills in digital design and put together a photo array in a Word doc, saved it as a pdf and sent it to the Manager-guy at The Mountain. I asked him to take a look and let me know whether he'd seen any of these guys in the past week or two. Maybe I'd get lucky.

◈

I STOOD TO STRETCH and looked out the window. Days were getting longer, but it was already dark. Courthouse security lights illuminated light flurries—the sort of gentle snowfall that in November and December feels romantic but by late

February is just a pain-in-the-ass. I needed some warmth. I decided to visit the Chamberlain Brewing Co. and use it as an excuse to splurge a little.

Technically, I was off the clock, so I gathered my laptop, waved to Garrett as I left, and dropped the computer at my cruiser. I'd walk to the brew-pub. Coming around the building, I stopped for a moment as Gainsborough spread before me. I looked to the river. The snow had one redeeming feature: it had freshened the view a bit. Summer's unbroken line of cars that would snake through the town, slowed to a crawl by tourists exercising their right to wander back and forth in traffic and choke the single lane, was months away. A solitary VW bus puttered by. I turned and started toward the water.

The gentle flurries had decided they were done. A biting wind—they called it "The Hawk" in Chicago—swept in and cutting snowflakes bit into my eyes. Winter's final statement. I picked my way along the cobbled sidewalk. Humpy, bumpy clumps of thawed and re-frozen ice made the footing tricky in front of shops and galleries that wouldn't open again for another six weeks. The brew-pub stood alone in what had been a 19th century shipping chandlery, next to the river.

"Welcome, officer!" A woman about my age smiled from the greeter's podium. She wore a vintage cowl-neck sweater in a becoming shade of mauve. Awards for historic preservation hung discretely behind her.

"Where would you like to sit?" she asked, offering anywhere in the vast, almost empty room.

The former marine warehouse was divided from front to back by a series of rough Roman arches, notable in their scale and proportion. I could see Honor Fielding's hand in decorating the place. Whitewashed, pickled-pine trestle tables were foregrounded by walls of reconditioned brick and field-stone. Loops of massive iron chain hung on one wall and complemented the expansive dimensions of the dining area. Thoughtfully curated maritime artifacts conveyed a sense of history without being kitschy. A line of windows had been punched through the brick exterior along the river and would flood the space with light during the day. The original walk-through fireplace was heaped with flaming logs and separated the dining room from the bar.

"Someplace close to the fire," I replied.

"Of course." She led me to a table which caught the gentle warmth of the blaze and looked into the long bar. "Enjoy," she said, leaving a menu as I hung my jacket on the Windsor chair and sat, luxuriating in the heat. I reviewed the "Bill of Fare"—well, I wouldn't be eating here often.

"Good evening and welcome to the Chamberlain Brewing Co. My name is Chelsea and I'll be your server tonight." I looked up and was surprised to see a younger version of Dina Garrett. Where Dina's naturally red hair was short and sensible, Chelsea's was long, luxuriant and had a beautiful wave. The deep ginger color, combined with the knobby nose and the rounded, freckled face made an instant connection. I put on my Detective cap.

"So, I have to ask . . . Are you Dina Garrett's daughter?"

She blushed and looked down for a moment. "Yes, ma'am."

"I'm Allie Beckham, I work with your mom. But I guess that's obvious," I said. We laughed together.

"Yes, ma'am. You're new, right?"

"Well, I'm new to the sheriff's department but I grew up in South Prescott." *Establishing my bona fides.*

"My Dad's from—well, we live in South Prescott!"

South Prescott's a small town. Even with the annual influx of summer people, folks who grow up there pretty much know everyone. My mental contact list couldn't locate a Garrett family.

She read my face and explained. "Oh right, the last name. Well, Mom's from away and she wanted to keep her maiden name when they got married. My dad's Chet Carpenter. Yeah, so I'm Chelsea Carpenter," she said, nodding her head.

"Carpenter. Okay. The Carpenter place . . . along Mussel Cove? Where The Ridge Road "T's" into it, right?"

"Exactly."

"Wraparound porch, hill that goes up in the back? Your Gramma would hang her clothes out in the summer?"

"That's it. Nana was none too happy with me when I'd run through her sheets!" Chelsea smiled at the memory.

"My sister and I used to ride our bikes over The Ridge Road and down to the Pierce's place. It was great going down but that hill coming back is killer. Is your Nana still there?"

Her expression shifted and I knew the answer, "Naw, she passed awhile ago. We—Mom, Dad, and me—we moved to South Prescott before I started high school."

"So, what does your dad do?" I asked.

"He's a plumber. Yeah, a Carpenter that's a plumber. Go figure," she replied, smiling, and then continued with the specials for the evening.

I ordered the seafood chowder and hot tea and turned to watch the fire. Chelsea delivered a basket of fresh rolls and offered a selection of teas. I selected Black Gunpowder and began assembling the teapot, thinking of Chelsea's comments about her father and my thoughts drifted to my dad.

We hadn't spoken for at least seven years. I'd heard he'd tried to reach me in Chicago a couple of times when I was on the street. I keyed in his number once or twice after I started at CPD but never hit *"Call."*

Lt. Torres, *"Mama T,"* told me I needed reach out. To make me whole again. She'd been right about so much but this was something I simply couldn't do. And yet, here I was, back in Maine. By choice, not circumstance. Maybe Mama T was right. Maybe, I was edging closer and just waiting for the right moment.

The chowder arrived, laden with haddock, clams, and bits of sweet lobster with potatoes and onion to give it heft. I tried not to devour it and was mostly unsuccessful. It was no wonder the place did good business year-round. Chelsea offered dessert, but I declined.

"Your mom told me you're a senior at Madison. So, do you have plans for next year?" I asked as she placed a padded folder on the table.

"I'm really interested in video production. Not so much the shooting but the editing and sound and stuff," She was more like her mother than she would want to admit, open and willing to offer information. "It's sort of a puzzle that you need to put together, and if you do it right, there's your story. So yeah, I'm looking at some colleges that have good video programs."

"Yeah, your mom told me you liked video stuff. She said you were at Camp . . . Wiki, right? That's where you first did it?"

She brightened. "For sure. That was a lot of fun and looking back, they had some really good equipment and two decent studios—I mean, for a kid's camp and all. I went there three summers. It was great but . . . it went out of business."

"That's what your mom said." She didn't seem to know who'd taken it over and I wasn't going to be the one to screw her memories. We were quiet.

"Well, it was nice to meet you, Officer . . ."

"Beckham. But, please, call me Allie."

"Nice to meet you, Allie," she said, smiling, and then moved on.

I began to pull my phone but thought the better of it. I sat for a few more minutes trying to suck up the heat and atmosphere of the Chamberlain Brewing Co. before I left enough cash to cover a generous tip and headed back into the night.

◆

THE WARMTH I HAD stockpiled was gone by the time I reached the courthouse, which was thrown into deep silhouette by bright tower lights on the far side of the building. Probably remote TV vans. My pace quickened as I took the long way around to my Explorer. I rounded the final corner and my suspicions were confirmed when I almost ran into a camera man who was shooting some establishing footage of the scene. Print and video reporters with their tech crews were preparing for something big and were scattered across this side of the building, ignoring barricades and police tape. Several approached me, but I waved them off and climbed into my cruiser, started the engine, and turned up the heat. I flipped the radio on and checked my computer. A series of short email messages between Latch, Gill, and Garrett revealed what was going on.

Apparently, Gill had managed to get in and make a deal with The Professor, who revealed the names of the four guys who did the beating. The crew was coming to Gainsborough for a night in jail and Latch expected them to be bailed the next morning. The Professor had promised the sheriff he could manage his people in the future. Gill remained in Huntley with a couple of deputies, just in case. It sounded like everyone was standing down. Latch was choreographing a perp walk. That explained the TV vans.

I turned on my phone. There was a text message and an email from Honor Fielding.

The text was terse. She had received a reply to her counter-offer and had forwarded the email message to me and Gill for direction. I figured Gill had been busy in Huntley and was leaving the reply to me.

I opened her email as the car warmed. She'd simply forwarded the kidnappers' latest communication with no commentary. They'd agreed to the $5 million, but they still wanted it transferred by Friday. That was three days away. There were two video pieces queued up, one with each of the twins. I clicked on the "Play" triangle for the Trevor piece.

He was on the bed again but conscious this time, sitting up, with his back against the metal railing at the head, legs straight out in front. He was blindfolded with the tape, hands and feet bound with zip ties. He was dressed. He sat stiffly, and as the piece began he spoke from a simple script he must have been told to memorize. Occasionally, he would pause. What I could see of his face communicated panic and concentration simultaneously:

"Hello Mom and Dad."

What the hell? He'd seen his father killed. What were these people doing?

"I am fine. They are feeding me. I had a shower. I miss you. Please cooperate. They say they will . . . ," and here his voice began to shake. A tear escaped the tape where it had loosened at his temple. "They say they will cut off one finger every day you delay payment." Trevor dissolved. He went off script and blurted, "Please Dad, please get us out of here!" The screen went black.

It was effective. It showed the boy was alive and his terror was palpable.

I clicked on the image of Celeste. She sat in the same bed and wore leggings, socks, and a long-sleeved ski top. She seemed more composed. Her jaw had the same set as Honor's when she was angry.

The *whoop-whoop* of a distant siren caught my ear and Latch's voice filled the Explorer's cab.

"100 to Base."

"Go ahead, 100."

"Approaching with suspects, Code Three. Everything in place?"

"Affirmative, 100."

The video continued as Celeste delivered the same speech as Trevor, clearly but very slowly, on the verge of parody, but with expression. There were no tears. She was bound in the same way as Trevor.

"100—Be advised we have media present."

"Roger that, Base. Absolutely no media inside. Break."

"Copy that, 100. Go ahead."

"We need all base officers for assistance in the walk."

"Copy that, 100. Richmond has it covered."

"10-4 Base. 100 out.

A nervous tick caught my eye where Celeste's mouth would go up on the right side and her right hand would slide slightly to the right and her fist jabbed forward. It wasn't pronounced but she repeated it a couple times during the 30 seconds she was on screen. She was clearly stressed, but I was relieved to see the twins alive. Maybe not well, but alive.

Garrett's voice interrupted my concentration again. "All available officers to the West Entry, five units arriving with suspects in custody." I closed my laptop and zipped my jacket, waving to the security camera on the corner of the building as my feet hit the ground.

"33 on site. 10-4," I replied into my shoulder radio.

"Red" Richmond and Lt. Match met me at the door. It looked like "all available officers" meant the three of us. Media flooded the parking area, ignoring the barriers and tape. The scream of sirens announced the suspects' imminent arrival. Richmond moved quickly to control the situation. He ordered me to direct the reporters off the asphalt and onto the sidewalk that led to the department's door.

Snowbanks lining the walk meant everything was going to be tight.

"Listen up, everyone!" I called. Heads turned toward me. "I need each one of you to line up, single file, along this walkway, and NOW! You can roll cameras but there will be no questions while the individuals are delivered." I drew an imaginary line on the walk with my baton, stationing them so that even though my back would be to the prisoners I could still see the lot. They were generally cooperative—this vantage point would supply them with an intimate view of the walk.

"No questions please. Sheriff Latch will make a statement," I kept repeating to their continuous requests for comment.

A syncopated cacophony of siren and light filled the air as five cruisers entered single-file and came to a stop in formation. On-air personnel gave last-minute instructions to their cameramen as Latch organized his men. I held my baton at the ready, all business. Richmond and Match were on either side of the door, ready to repulse any last-minute media assault. Finally, the procession began.

The senior McMann pulled his charge roughly from his cruiser and shoved him in the direction of the courthouse. His hands were cuffed behind his back. The guy stumbled but caught his balance and straightened, throwing his shoulders back. Defiant. With one hand on his suspect's arm and holding his baton in his back, McCann navigated the gauntlet and entered the building without incident.

Deputy Kimball followed McCann. His guy was looking sheepish. He wore a black, quilted hip-length ski jacket and expensive sun glasses—trying to be incognito. He turned his head down and away from the cameras as reporters ignored my instructions and called questions. They passed behind me.

The third guy gave a violent shrug as Deputy Doug Franklin tried to guide him to the walk. His eyes narrowed when he saw me and a sick, thin smile illuminated his face. I recognized him from Merry Hill. Eddie.

"Well, well. You're the bitch who found the dead rich guy," he said as he stepped to the curb. My disgust was clear.

"Shut-up." Franklin called, jerking one arm.

They came closer. "What's the problem?" Eddie's faux concern was evident to all. "Don't you like the looks of a real man? A white man who can give you everyth— " emphasizing the "ev" but not finishing the word. He shut-up when Franklin's open hand moved in a flash to whack him upside the head but, catching the glare of the light towers, thought the better of it and drove the flat of his palm deep into the perp's shoulder blade. The kid almost went down but Franklin caught his jacket and held him up while he regained his step. Eddie tried to turn and look back after he passed. A sharp poke in the ribs straightened him out. They followed the skier inside.

The final guy wore a government-issued fatigue jacket, the kind with a digital, blocky-tan camo pattern. There was a private's stripe on the sleeve and the name "Miller" over the left chest pocket. His escort was Kennedy, who stood a full head shorter than the perp. Kennedy didn't seem to be taking the walk too seriously.

"Uhm-Uhm—look at that ass," Miller said loudly, approaching me. "Eddie told me about you. You ever seen an ass like that on a cop?" he said, glancing over his shoulder at the deputy.

"Keep moving," I replied. *C'mon Kennedy, shut this guy up.*

"I bet you'd like that—jus' keep moving," he stopped short and shot a hip thrust toward me.

I swiveled hard to my left, swinging my right leg between Kennedy and his suspect and grabbing the fatigue jacket at the shoulder with my left hand. The baton in my right broke Kennedy's grip and rolled down Miller's spine and over his cuffed hands until it found the soft spot between his butt cheeks. I yanked hard at the jacket while I stepped into his back and pushed the baton down and forward keeping it between me and his body.

Both Miller and Kennedy were completely surprised by my speed and I pressed my advantage home. Taking him by the collar, I controlled his stride. My face went to the back of his neck where the stink would have made me puke if I hadn't been so angry. I got as close to his right ear as possible and whispered, *"Listen up, you motherfucking cocksucker! You say another word before we're inside and I'll shove this stick so hard up your ass it'll give you a permanent woodie."* I jabbed the stick home. That got his attention.

We left Kennedy in our wake. He tried to cover by holding the media at bay in a rear-guard action, mostly unsuccessfully, finally entering the station before Richmond and Match. I threw Miller to McCann.

"Take care of this bag of shit, willya? And tell Kennedy to do his fucking job."

"Hey Beckham!"

Richmond called me back to reality. He stood at the open door where the parade had finished entering. "Beckham! Get inside!"

I shook off my anger and focused on the scene. Media was regrouping around the sheriff. I went inside and headed for the ladies' room. As I emerged, I noticed that deputies and other officials were focused on the bullpen's TV. The live delay showed Latch standing comfortably at the edge of the parking lot. A sign reading "Chamberlain County Courthouse, James A. Latch, Sheriff" was over his shoulder.

". . . 'ouncing the arrest of four suspects in the beating of five protestors in Huntley this afternoon." He was in his element, having engineered the event for the 11 o'clock news and early enough for the newspapers to get an article into the morning edition. "Lieutenant Jack Gill was able to gain access to the former Camp Miq-Maq and successfully negotiated the surrender of these individuals who will be held in custody until a bail hearing. Let me make this clear: We will not tolerate this sort of viciousness—or any violence—directed at people who are peacefully gathered to assert their First Amendment right of free speech. As the brave individuals who were beaten so savagely asserted, 'Hate has no place in Maine.' Thank you."

The reporters were dismissed. Latch had already turned for the courthouse when Sarah Loundsberry called out, "Sheriff, can you give us an update on the Fielding murder?"

He stopped and carefully turned back to the group. "I'm sorry. I can't comment on an ongoing investigation," then strode confidently to the entry, through the security door, and into our space to applause.

"Thank you," he said, gesturing for quiet. "But the credit for this resides not with me, but with you—you, Jack Gill, and the officers still in Huntley who put themselves in harm's way each and every day. You have all conducted yourselves in an exceptionally professional manner as this incident has unfolded. We still have lots to do—let's get back to business." He shook hands with a couple of officers as the scene evolved into one of controlled chaos.

The militiamen from Miq-Maq had been placed in a holding cell and began to be processed one-by-one. An attorney arrived, saying he represented the four suspects for New Albion. He was present "to make sure his clients weren't mistreated" and wanted to talk to each of them after they were officially processed. Latch stationed him at the booking desk and once everything seemed to be moving smoothly, signaled to me to follow him. We found a place out of the way as other personnel moved back and forth through the room.

"Where are we with the Fielding kids?"

"Well, Gill and I are following up some leads."

"You got names? Status? Information? You're in charge now, Beckham," Latch looked around, impatient. "What about the half-brother? Stephen? What's the story there?"

I let him know I didn't think it was Fielding and that I had someone I was following up on.

He looked away and reviewed the activity in the room for a long moment and then turned back. "You, me, and Gill agreed that you would research Fielding. Yes?" He paused for dramatic effect. "Am I wrong?" He paused again. "Did you hear something else?" One more time. "We've got to get these kids back to their mother and you're wasting time dicking around with some long-shot hunch?"

I started to respond, but he cut me off.

"No." He waved his hand in dismissal.

"I don't want to hear it. I'm giving you a chance here, Beckham. You wanted back into Maine. Okay, you're here. I don't know, maybe I was wrong. Maybe you've been away too long. Quit acting like you know better than all of us. Get with the program and be part of the team." He narrowed his eyes and moved closer. "Here are your orders: you will follow up on Fielding, even if you need to spend the entire night waking up every hotel, motel, B&B, and Goddamn Airbnb clerk in New Hampshire and Maine to get a fix on his most recent location. You will deliver a report by tomorrow morning that firmly establishes his whereabouts as of last Thursday, if not tonight. If I don't have something concrete on my desk by 8 a.m., you can pack your bags and get the hell out my department. Do I make myself clear?"

The action in the room had come to a standstill. Sgt. McCann was on the way with Franklin to get Eddie Miller. Richmond and Kennedy had been moving the elder brother, Willy-Willy, back to his cell after being photographed and printed. Everyone stopped and looked at the two of us, expectant.

"Awww, little Missy's in trouble," Willy-Willy said. "What's wrong, Sheriff, your hot bitch not working out like you hoped?"

"Get him the hell out of here!" Latch exploded. Everyone started moving again. He looked back at me. "Beckham, have I made myself clear?"

"Crystal," I replied, meeting his glare. He walked out of the room toward his office and I went to my cruiser for my laptop.

Nineteen

I NEEDED QUIET. I wasn't going to find it at my cubicle. Gill's office wouldn't work either. I turned into the hall for the Armory. Match was done with distributing weaponry, the cage was locked, and he'd left the light on. I set up on one of the benches.

Thirty-plus ski resorts. Innumerable hotels, motels, B&Bs. And then there were the Airbnbs. The toughest part of the assignment was figuring out where to start. I reconsidered Fielding and whether he planned to kill his father, or not? My gut kept telling me, "No." So that meant his criteria for a weekend wouldn't depend on his proximity to The Mountain, but on price, or conditions, or other, more typical skiing parameters.

I opened the laptop and keyed in "New Hampshire Skiing" and got over 7,000,000 results. *Jeez, it might be a long night.* The New Hampshire Ski Association website seemed to be a possibility. It was a clearinghouse that correlated resorts, lodging, and other amenities with live links to websites. Fantastic, I had a fallback source. I reviewed my conversation with DelVecchio. I searched "New Hampshire Skiing LGBTQ"—98,000 hits. *Homing in like a laser.* One listing on the second page caught my eye: Board Buddies, a club for LGBTQ folks that sponsored winter activities, tours, and meet-ups throughout New England. Their calendar appeared to be current, but no events or activities were listed for the dates I'd entered. A tab headed "Lodging" seemed promising.

Seventeen hotels and inns were listed.

Stephen Fielding took some time-off to ski. He was looking for love, or at least companionship. He extended his vacay—maybe he'd found someone. DelVecchio made it sound like he was attempting to be responsible. If he was trying to live within a budget, well, he'd choose a less expensive place and not go deluxe.

I moved back to the New Hampshire Ski Association site and pulled up its massive spreadsheet. *Jesus, I'll need a CPA or a 16-year-old to navigate this monster.* I played around and figured out how to search for lodging only, then highlighted the 17 listed on the Board Buddies site. I got them to come up by themselves and sorted from least- to most-expensive. The cheapest rates were located in the southern part of the state where the skiing and the mountains were less challenging. How would I know whether he was a hot-shot skier? I decided to start with sites that indicated moderate prices. The skill levels would resolve themselves.

It was obvious I had awakened the clerk at Cass Mountain, who wasn't thrilled about a phone call from Maine law enforcement. He looked for Stephen Fielding in his database and found nothing. Nada at Pine Tree Gorge and Nolton Notch. I tried eight more sites. One had a Stephen Fielding in the system but the last time he visited was winter, 2015.

I punched in the number for Chimney Peak resort. It was further north than most of the places I'd contacted. The snow conditions were listed as excellent. The clerk answered, "Good evening, Chimney Peak Resort, Anna Pistoia speaking."

I identified myself and my purpose for calling. Anna was cooperative.

"Let me see . . . dut-dut-dut . . . Okay. Yes. A Stephen Fielding registered Sunday a week ago and stayed with us until this morning. It looks like . . . yes, Mr. Fielding was scheduled to leave Sunday but extended his reservation. Oh yeah, I remember this guy. I was on duty when he came to the desk and wanted to stay over. His room had been booked by one of our regulars so we needed to move him down the hall. He seemed okay with that."

"Was he alone? Did he have any kids with him?"

"Um, no. No kids," Pistoia responded, surprised at the question. "It looked like maybe there was a boyfriend but, no kids."

"And this was Stephen Fielding, who resides at 420 Kent Ave, Brooklyn, New York?"

"Just a moment, Officer." I could hear her keyboard clicking. "I'm looking at a copy of Mr. Fielding's driver's license. Yes, it lists 420 Kent Ave, Brooklyn, as his address."

"Thank you, Ms. Pistoia, you've been very helpful. Would it be possible for you to email me a copy of his registration, his final bill, and his driver's license, please?" *There must have been a reason I passed the CPD Detective test.* I gave her my email address and thanked her.

Maybe Stephen *had* traveled to Chimney Peak but, thinking ahead, had also rented a separate place nearby, driven to Merry Hill Rd., survived killing his father in a blizzard, kidnapped his siblings, returned to New Hampshire—during the height of the snowfall—stashed them in his extra space, photographed and produced video of the twins along with three messages routed through Uzbekistan, then returned to Chimney Peak resort where he extended his stay with a new boyfriend. *Yeah, maybe he's our guy.*

I transcribed my conversation with Anna Pistoia, then downloaded the materials she sent, and emailed my report to Latch and Gill. It was getting late.

I turned my attention to Honor and the twins. I pulled up the phone and computer's tap site. There were text messages between Honor and staff at the Brewing Co. and a phone call Mary Chapman had made. There was a text message time-stamped 1:35 pm:

Honor: Where are you?

Kringle: Mountain

Honor: I need to talk to you.

Kringle: Not now. F is on the warpath.

Honor: I don't care. I need to talk to you NOW.

Kringle: 20 minutes. I will call. DO NOT CALL ME.

She hadn't mentioned Kringle in her most recent message to me and Gill. And he'd high-tailed it back to the Mountain from Portland. I cued the phone call.

"Kris! Oh thank God you called." Honor was sounding desperate again—the anger was gone from her voice.

"Hey, you're gonna have to make this quick. What the hell is going on? I've never seen Fran like this. She made me pull Justine out of school," Kringle's voice was furtive but earnest.

Honor ignored the question. *"The kidnappers want $5 million. I need you here. I don't know what to do."*

"Shit. $5 million? How long do you have?"

"Friday."

"That's three days. Honor, I don't know how I can get away. She's locked Justine in her room and won't talk to me."

"Goddammit, I need you here now. What's happening Kris? What is happening to our world? Please, you've got to find a way to get down here. That deputy was here with her partner . . . "

"Hey, gotta go." Kringle hung up.

There was one other, brief, text session between the two of them:

> **Kringle:** OK. Tmw morning.

> **Honor:** Thank God. CU then.

I stood and stretched, then squatted to loosen up, straightened, then sat again. There wasn't much new in front of me. The fact that Fran hadn't told Kris about the SkinFlix posting was a bit of a surprise, but, maybe it wasn't. Fran seemed to have difficulty even thinking about that stuff. Honor and Kris sounded more businesslike than lovey-dovey, although they might have closed their conversation differently if they'd had more time. Honor needed cash and Kringle was traveling to South Prescott. Kringle's trip was about the only thing new there.

My butt was killing me. I got up and started for the bullpen. As I passed Gill's office, I paused, then entered and took a seat in his chair again, searching the cast of characters he'd posted. I closed my eyes. I was beat. The past two weeks' events—starting the job, the death of Fielding, interviews, meetings, research—swirled. I tried to still my thoughts and allow stuff to surface.

Something Gill said about Sam Martin's daughter floated by. Tabitha disappeared in November and he was pretty torn up about it. And his lovely bride Kourtney. Martin's marriage hadn't been great. And then he had an accident while cleaning his gun.

I opened my eyes to see Kennedy in the doorway. He was geared up, ready to take the graveyard shift at Miq-Maq. He looked both ways before he spat, "So, newbie's tryin' on Gill's office for size? Good luck, bitch." He moved on.

Nothing but good times.

The bullpen got quiet once the crew checked out and left for Huntley. It was empty, save Randall, who was the lone deputy on duty in case some other emergency came up. He was playing computer solitaire and nodded as I found my desk and sat.

My eyes closed involuntarily, but I fought it and tried to find my way back to Tabitha Martin. I had no idea where we were going, but she was tugging me along. Tabitha's birth announcement had listed her parents: Samuel MacKenzie Martin and Kourtney Cloutier Considine. There was a mental 'ping' on Cloutier. I riffed through the last three days and found myself at the Kringles' place on The Mountain. Fran Kringle moved a group of papers and a portfolio folder labelled Cloutier. The cover was illustrated with a photo of her standing next to an 18-wheeler emblazoned with the word.

I Googled Cloutier Trucking on my laptop. None of the local trucking companies that came up, including Cloutier, maintained formal websites, but BizWiz provided a snapshot of the business: Regional company; grossed about $250K in its most recent year of record; seven employees; Fran Kringle, CEO.

Okay, sure. The Kringles never said anything about Fran and a trucking business. But then again, I hadn't asked. I'd gotten too focused on Kringle, his money, and his connection to Honor to see it. I searched Fran Cloutier.

Whoa. Court papers filed in Penobscot County revealed our Francesca Bianchi Kringle was, in fact, Francine Cloutier Considine and that she inherited the company in 2009 from her father, Alain, who'd died without a will. Further, sixteen-year-old Francine Cloutier Considine had been acquitted of murdering 45-year-old Hank Considine, her husband, in 1988. Self-defense. Lurid coverage of a brief trial in the Lewiston Courier-Herald mentioned she'd been sold by her mother to Considine at fourteen. Mom OD'd on crack. Francesca, née Francine, along with her infant daughter, Kourtney Cloutier Considine, were placed in child protective services. Francine Cloutier Considine ceased to exist from 1988 – 2009, only to reappear when a diligent Penobscot deputy tracked her down.

I tried to set some priorities on my drive home. Getting the twins home alive was paramount and, yeah, the information about Fran was interesting, but what bearing did it have on Major Fielding's murder and his kids' disappearance? On the other hand, child-bride Francine Cloutier stabbed her husband to death. That didn't jibe with the person I'd met at The Mountain. The rooming house was quiet as I climbed the stairs.

Sleep came quickly.

Twenty

Sunlight splashed the opposite wall as I rolled to turn off my alarm. What little sleep I'd had was sound. I dressed and found my way to the kitchen. A young man, wrapped in a pastel chenille housecoat, sat on one of two stools at the counter. His eyes were closed. An untouched mug of coffee cooled as he self-consciously raised his hand and took a pull from an e-cigarette. The WLHS morning news team gestured silently from the flat-screen TV over his shoulder and he exhaled the vapor. He opened his eyes as I clattered pans.

"Whooo . . . are you?"

I stopped. A cosmetic headband pulled closely cropped hair away from his forehead and helped open a face with delicate features and a mouth with full, pouting lips.

"Allie Beckham. And you would be . . . ?"

"It depends."

I wasn't sure I had the patience for this game.

"Depends on what?"

"I was born Kingsford LaCasse. You may call me . . . King." He smiled a beneficent smile.

"Nice to meet you, King." I continued my clatter for a clean skillet.

"Jesse told us there would be a deputy moving into the house and it's so nice to finally meet you," he said with dramatic emphasis on the "so nice." He offered his hand.

I placed a worn non-stick pan onto the electric range and shook his hand lightly. I needed a decent breakfast and fished out a couple of eggs and some butter from my section of the fridge. King continued to sit with his eyes closed.

Sarah Loundsberry's name popped-up on the TV and the scene switched to a live-feed of the entrance to the camp in Huntley.

"Hey, King! Where's the remote?"

He turned slowly and reached behind the monitor, returning with the controller.

I yanked it out of his hand and hit the Mute button.

" . . . 'elf-declared President of New Albion, William Miller IV, called The Professor by his followers, is holding a press conference this morning regarding yesterday's altercation involving four of his men and a group of Quaker protestors."

The Professor had a sense of drama and understood the news-cycle. An old card table sat with three microphones at the intersection of the camp road and 115. The entry section was plowed and shoveled, creating two walls of snow that helped frame the view. Six big guys bundled in matching camo field jackets and wearing sidearms flanked it, three to a side. As an old Jeep appeared from the road and pulled to a stop, the platoon snapped to a ragged attention and saluted. It would have been comical, but they were deadly serious. Miller strode from the vehicle to the table. Returning the salute, he waited for one of the men to hold his chair and then sat comfortably. The 'soldiers' stood at-ease. Miller read from a prepared statement:

"Thank you for this opportunity. As you may already know, four of our brave recruits voluntarily gave themselves up and agreed to cooperate with Sheriff Jim Latch yesterday evening," he began. "I want to emphasize that these men went *voluntarily* with the sheriff. I gave permission for two of my begotten sons, William Miller the Fifth, a veteran of the crusade in Afghanistan, and Edmund, to submit to humiliation as a demonstration of good faith. Until our citizenry comes to its senses and rallies to the cause of New Albion, we will abide by and take full advantage of the laws of the United States. We hope to have all of our prisoners of war returned to us this morning."

I beat the eggs a little harder than I might have on a regular day.

"Further, and in recognition of the fact that our land is currently under the jurisdiction of the United States of America and its Constitution, we declare our right, provided by the First Amendment of that Constitution, to free expression, including expressing our anger in a physical manner if we believe we have been threatened in any way. Yesterday's interlopers were insinuating themselves onto our sacred territory. We will have none of it."

"Unbelievable," King said under his breath. His eyes were open.

The Professor thanked the audience, stood, and drove back into the camp as his men saluted and then climbed into yesterday's troop-carrier pickup that had been out of frame. Sarah Loundsberry closed the piece and the morning team dove into weather and more happy talk. I muted the control.

King looked directly at me for the first time.

"Tell me about yourself," I encouraged, as I sat down with my breakfast.

He took a deep pull on the e-cigarette and exhaled. His pretension dissolved with the steam and as I ate he told me about growing up in The County, leaving at 16 to find work in Folkestone, and breaking into performance at Portland's back bay Sea Shanty, where he was part of a gay revue four nights a week. Our landlord had been a regular at the Periscope Subshop where King was making sandwiches after he arrived in town. The kid heard Jesse mention 144 Cushing and they'd gotten to talking. Jesse'd offered him a room, rent-free for six months a year in exchange for mowing, yard work, and keeping the walk shoveled. "This winter, that's been a kicker, 'specially last weekend," he said with a genuine smile. "It ain't the Ritz, but it's clean and the people aren't *too* crazy," he finished with a dramatic flourish. "How 'bout you? How'd you end up here?"

I looked at the kitchen clock. Our conversation had made me late. "Me? Nothing special. I grew up in South Prescott, moved to Chicago, came back." I rinsed my pan and dishes and put them in the drainer. "Nice to meet you, King. We'll talk more later. Gotta go."

My plan was to surprise Honor and sit in on her meeting with Kris Kringle. I sent an email to diSimone telling her that I wasn't going to make roll-call. Lazy plumes of smoke cast lavender-tinted shadows across the snowpack as I drove to South Prescott. The Alberta Clipper that had arrived overnight delivered stunning cold to the region.

I dropped down Falk's Hill and into the village and was happy no one recognized me when I stopped at Pierce's for coffee and a fresh doughnut. Back in the cruiser, I noted the neap tide that exposed the totality of Connor's Point as I passed over the swing bridge onto Wey's Island. The point acted as the unofficial terminus of the Mackinnock River where it finally emptied into Franklin Bay and hence, the Gulf of Maine. It began as a granite table at the shore, then narrowed suddenly and stabbed into the open water like a Damascus steel dagger.

I reached the gatehouse. It was Honor's voice when I signaled for entry, "Yes?" Cool.

"Honor, this is Allie Beckham. May I come in?"

"I'm sorry Deputy Beckham. It's not a good time."

This was unexpected. "Honor, we should talk about how you're moving forward with the ransom."

"I don't need your help. Kris is here and we are taking care of it."

Shit. We couldn't monitor their face-to-face communication if she wouldn't let me in.

"Besides," she continued. "I sent you the most recent message last night. Nobody at the Sheriff's office took the time to respond. We'll manage this and get my children home safely. I don't need your help."

"Honor, I know you're still angry," I began. Honor wasn't there.

It wouldn't do to bust through the gate and roll in with all guns blazing. At least not yet.

I backtracked to an informal pull-off at Connor's Point. The natural jetty is known to mariners for its boiling currents during tidal shifts. When the tide is low, the rocky dagger stretches nearly 150 yards, accompanied by a Red Nun buoy that marks a navigable channel. Back in the day, before the green crabs invaded, Janie Pierce, Hanna, and I could slither across tawny rockweed that attached itself to the granite and pluck a bucket's worth of mussels in no time from under the seaweed's slippery fronds.

◆

One of the first things I'd learned to cook was mussels steamed in wine and garlic. Dad guided the three of us through the recipe one Saturday afternoon, cracking us up with his falsetto Julia Child voice and letting us all know that we were allowed to have a sip of wine "to make sure it's worth cooking with" as we worked.

◆

I smiled at the memory and let the engine idle. Clouds of vapor, "sea smoke," pulled from the ocean's warmth by the intense cold, hovered beyond massive shards of aqua-tinted ice that rested like a cubist-inspired seascape on the jagged promontory. Pale wraiths folded and opened on themselves as they drifted quietly south above the moving water. I reported my location, turned off the dispatcher, and pulled out my coffee and doughnut.

◆

Tourists probably see the Midcoast as expansive—broad stretches of open water and rolling green fields whose emptiness is emphasized by dense forests teeming with songbirds and other wildlife. Summer folks swell the population of South Prescott by thousands from May through September. The ebb and flow of weekly visitors combine with social and cultural events to create a dizzying calendar of activity. But during winter, the year 'round community—natives, retirees, and others—is relatively intimate, and by February it's only the most committed. Each peninsula and island possesses its own distinctive personality and cast of characters. There was a void and soul-crushing sorrow as Dad and I navigated the months after Mom and Hanna's accident. Everyone living in South Prescott knew our situation. After a few weeks' worth of casseroles and caring, they moved on. We were alone, together. This is New England, after all.

I buckled down and tried to make up for Hanna's absence by becoming the star scholar. She'd had the brains and I'd never been able to rival her academic performance. Without her as a foil, I dove into school and activities. I surprised myself and excelled. My friends dropped away and I didn't date. Dad worried and expressed his concern in awkward hems and haws. I was the teenaged girl; he was at sea with his loss.

He'd taken it hard. In the beginning we talked a little but then he hit stretches of depression where he wouldn't say a word for days. I was dedicated to making something of myself; eventually, he simply dropped out.

The law practice he and mom had worked so hard to build began to falter. She had carried the firm with her specialty in divorce and family law. Dad's area of interest, the environment, made it hard to make a living, even in Maine. He tried to diversify but couldn't commit. He started to depend on a meager annuity that came from a class-action mercury settlement he'd engineered. He let Pamela, their longtime legal assistant, go. She'd seen the potential of the internet early on. With her gone, he didn't keep up with developments in computer technology as the 'net bloomed. His client base dwindled. I was keeping house, cooking, and when I got my driver's license, I was doing the shopping. He was drinking heavily. Not violent. Not manic. Not productive.

My focus on school paid off. I earned a full scholarship to the University of Chicago and left my dad, our decaying house, and South Prescott.

◆

Looking back at the mainland, a flash of light from across the water reflected just-so from a set of windows that caught the angle of the sun. Mussel Cove opened to Connor's Point.

Dina Garrett.

She'd be at home. This was my chance to get the low-down on Jack Gill. I wiped my hands, placed the empty cup into the grease-stained paper bag, did a three-point turn, and followed the light.

Twenty-one

Chet Carpenter opened the door.

I'd driven past the house before I realized my mistake and had to back up to the driveway. I didn't recognize the place. The new cedar-shake siding was a different look from the barn-red clapboarding of my girlhood memory. *I guess a good plumber can always find work.*

The land rises sharply from the water in this section of South Prescott. The saltbox sat at the bottom of a steep hill, but above the road. Uninterrupted snowdrifts reached back in a gentle slope, then up, almost vertically, 50 or 60 feet to an exposed rock ridge that was emphasized by tree-tops silhouetted against the sky. From experience, I knew the ridge was topped by a tennis court-sized slab of weathered basalt, offering sweeping views of the Mackinnock and south to Wey's Island for anyone energetic enough to hike the Conservancy holdings that abutted the property. The Carpenter house looked across the road and over several summer cottages that had been squeezed in on the shore and the panorama promoted a feeling of layered space toward Mussel Cove, the river, and Connor's Point. The fact that the Carpenter family still owned the house and hadn't sold it to summer people offered me a sense of continuity.

"Yes, officer? What can I do for you?"

Carpenter was older and taller than I expected. Piercing hazel eyes caught my attention.

I hesitated. "Is Dina available? I work with her and wanted to follow up on something she said during a conversation last night."

"Gee." He looked at my cruiser and back at me. The eyes bored in. "Can't it wait? She's asleep—her shift goes 'til three, you know."

I could see Chelsea move into the kitchen behind her father. She did a double-take, and walked up behind him.

"Hey, Deputy . . ."

"Beckham, Allie Beckham."

"Hi." She touched her father lightly, "Dad—it was Deputy Beckham at the restaurant last night."

"Okay," Carpenter said, softening a little.

"Mr. Carpenter," I began.

"Chet," he suggested.

"Chet, Dina asked me to stop by sometime to discuss a case I'm working. I realize it's early but I was in South Prescott for another meeting and I thought I might be able to catch her."

He looked at Chelsea who shrugged and said, "S'up to you, Dad. I've gotta get to school. But you oughta invite her in 'cuz it's freezing out there." She pulled a backpack from the kitchen table. " 'Scuse me, please," she said, moving past her dad and me. "Thanks for the great tip, Allie," she called back as she walked to a blue Buick Ciera that had pulled up and was idling.

"Chelsea—who's that driving?" Chet called when she was halfway to the sedan.

"It's Emily, Dad. Don't worry, she's been approved," Chelsea replied as the passenger door opened.

"Buckle-up!" Carpenter called after her. The car didn't move until his daughter had buckled her seatbelt and he had given the thumbs-up.

Chelsea's blessing made the difference. "Sure, come on in. I'll see about Dina." He walked to the back of the house where he disappeared up a stairwell. I looked around.

All the stuff that families put away "when company comes" was strewn comfortably about. Sweaters lay on backs of chairs, a casual throw lounged across a sofa arm, peanuts sat next to a bowl of empty shells on a coffee table. There were family photographs here and there. I remained at the door, not wanting to presume Dina would be available.

Chet returned. The edge was gone. "Deputy Beckham . . . Allie . . . Dina's awake. She'll be down in a few minutes. She asked me to offer you some coffee," he said, moving to where the Mr. Coffee stood, half full and hot. "Sorry, but there are a couple of frozen pipes I've gotta deal with so I need to blast outta here pretty quick."

I declined but asked if I could sit in the living room. "Oh, sure. Go right ahead," Carpenter said as he zipped up insulated coveralls. "Make yourself at home." He walked to the door, called, "Nice to meet you!" and was gone.

Moving to the living room gave me a chance to get a closer look at the snapshots. One caught my eye and I leaned over for a better look. A much younger Chet Carpenter cradled a tiny child who was bundled in a pink snow-suit while he balanced a classic wooden toboggan with his free hand. Infant Chelsea. Dina knelt in the snow next to him, looking up, smiling and pointing at the photographer with one arm while she held a little boy close with the other. He looked about six years old. He was freckle-faced with a bright, open smile and a shock of copper hair that resisted containment under his knit hat. He balanced a softball-sized snowball, ready to throw. I heard Dina's tread on the stairs. She stepped into the room dressed in a sweater, jeans, and socks.

"Allie. Wow. Uhhh—," she brushed hair back with one hand and sort-of stared at me, still waking up. "I asked Chet to offer you coffee. Didn't he do that?" she said with the caring exasperation that comes from living with a person for a long time. "Can I get you some?" She walked to the kitchen.

"He was in a hurry so I declined. But sure, that would be great." *Two girls sharin' a cup o' Joe.* I straightened and followed her.

"Great. Chel told me you grew up in South Precott. You remember the Dyer family?"

"Sure, Lenny Dyer was one of, like, seven or eight kids. He was in our . . . my class."

"Okay, sure. Well, Lenny moved away, along with all his siblings. Old man Dyer is alone and his place . . . You take cream or sugar?"

"Black, thanks."

"His place is one of the old houses on Muskwajo Lane. His wife is gone and the property needs work."

I thought of my dad.

"Chet told me the old man woke up this morning and there was no water. And that can only mean one thing . . . ," She handed me the coffee and gestured to the living room.

"I didn't know Chelsea had a brother," I said, nodding in the direction of the winter photo as we passed. "Cute kid!"

Dina's mouth turned down and she stopped dead and gazed for a moment at the photo. I realized, too late, there were no football photos, no senior prom, no growing up. *Some detective I am.*

"That's Charlie. He was six years older than Chelsea. We lost him at nine."

"Oh, I'm so sorry."

"It's okay. Well, it's not okay. I mean, it's okay that you asked but, it still hurts. Have a seat," she said, motioning to the sofa. She sat in an overstuffed recliner and held her coffee with two hands. I waited.

She sighed deeply. "Charlie was such a light," she said and then continued quickly, as if apologizing, "I mean, we had him and then Chelsea and we were set—a boy and a girl."

I nodded.

"The hardest thing about letting go of Charlie was that we never had a real cause for his death." My eyes questioned her. "It was a Saturday . . . it was Saturday, October 22, one of those autumn days when the sky's blue, the sun is still warm, and the light through the empty trees creates magic." This was a story she had told many times before but it didn't sound rehearsed. It was her strategy for getting through it. "The four of us had been walking in the woods and came home. I made his favorite dinner—hot dogs and macaroni and cheese. Thank God Chet had been able to spend the afternoon with us and wasn't on a job."

She paused, gathering herself.

"Chet and I had hit a rough patch after Chelsea's birth," she said.

I must have looked concerned because when she continued, she sounded defensive, "Nothing dramatic, but we were trying to make some time to be alone, you know … with each other. We had scheduled a date night for that Saturday and Nana, Chet's mother, joined us for dinner. She was going to babysit."

"Chelsea mentioned running through her Nana's laundry last night," I offered, hoping to lighten the moment, if only marginally.

Dina's brow furrowed as she smiled. "Yeah. Chel loved her Nana."

Her eyes were glassy. She breathed deeply and continued.

"Nana settled Chelsea and then read a chapter from Charlie's favorite book while he lay in bed. She said goodnight, turned off his light, and came downstairs. When Chet and I got home, of course we checked on the children."

"Of course."

"Charlie wasn't breathing. He was already gone. Chet called 911, I did CPR until they arrived but he had simply passed from this world."

I handed her a tissue from the box on the coffee table.

"It was so hard," she began, and paused to blow her nose, "Then, of course there was an autopsy. I mean, how many nine-year-olds die in their sleep? It happens though. Something like four-hundred kids die *every year* this way in the U.S. Oh yes, I know *that* statistic. Sudden Unexplained Death in Children."

I was speechless.

"There were a couple of articles in the county paper," she began again, her voice harder. "At one point, before the autopsy was confirmed, we thought they were going to take Chelsea away. But South Prescott was solid. The village was with us every step of the way. Chet's family is seven generations here—there have been Carpenters on the peninsula since Maine became a state," she responded to my surprised look. "This house was built on top of Eli Carpenter's cabin foundation after it burned in 1885."

"It must have been a difficult time," I said as she drank some coffee.

"Yes, it was. But it didn't end there. Nana, bless her soul . . ."

She looked up to the ceiling, then continued after regaining her composure. "Nana blamed herself. She was certain there might have been something she could have done, that maybe if she'd checked on Charlie before we came home . . . She was crushed. I'm certain it contributed to her untimely death. She tried to put it behind her but she passed less than two years later. No real cause. She was only 62." Dina blew her nose and wiped her eyes.

"I'm so very sorry," I said. I felt helpless.

She uncrossed her legs and leaned forward. "So, you can see how precious Chelsea is to Chet and me."

"Yes, of course."

We were quiet. I wanted to ask about Gill but the timing felt lousy.

She broke the ice. "So, what's up?"

"Jack Gill."

"Oh." She was uneasy, even here in her own home. "Okay." Then cautiously, "What about him?"

I liked Dina, but it almost felt like she was stonewalling me.

"Why are you afraid of talking about him, even in your own home." *A little too hard?*

She turned away.

"Dina," I prompted. She looked back. "You know I'm working the Fielding murder with Gill. Have you heard their two kids—the twins—are missing?"

"Missing? The Fielding twins?" She pulled her mug close and sat back, into the cushion, weighing this news.

"Latch wants it kept quiet. We haven't been routing any of that information through dispatch. Kidnappers want $5 million by Friday." Her focus shifted to me. "From my perspective? In Latch's eyes, Gill can do no wrong."

A hint of a smile. But not a happy one. I pursued it.

"If you think there's something hinky with Gill, you need to tell me. We have kids' lives on the line."

I waited. *C'mon Dina!*

I leaned in, laying it out for her. "Latch threw Gill at the New Albion thing and now I'm working the murder/kidnapping—alone." She paused her sip. "You're not comfortable even hearing the guy's name . . . So, Dina, I need to know, and I need to know now: Is there anything up with Gill or do you just not like him?"

"I've been with the Department since 2009. Sam Martin already had four years in."

Why was I not surprised that she started her story with Martin?

"He made Detective that year. You've figured out there are only four detectives in the department, right?"

"Sure." Latch hired me when Bradstreet got bumped to take Martin's place.

"So that was a pretty big deal for Sam. His wife Kourtney . . ."

"From what I understand, she's a piece of work."

"Yeah. And that's an understatement. If they ever shoot a "Real Housewives of Gainsborough" she'll be the over-dressed, social-climbing, back-stabbing bitch character everybody loves to hate. Except it's for real."

"Okay. But how does this relate to Gill?"

"I heard you passed the Detective test in Chicago. Is that true?"

"Yes."

"Then you know that sometimes you put two and two together and 'just know' stuff. As a dispatcher, I hear most all the communication in the department. I see people come and go—literally. A while back, it came to me that Martin—a patrol officer at the time—was on site almost every time something was going down in Vice. He got himself appointed to the Drug Task Force. And then he made Detective."

"So, maybe Sam's motivation wasn't only just eradicating the illicit drug-trade for the benefit of the good citizens of the county?"

"Well, that's the thing. Sam worked hard, sure. And everyone loved him, he truly was a nice guy. But Allie, this isn't the private sector. You don't get end-of-year bonuses for successfully riding herd on crime. Sam and Kourtney were living way beyond their means. Well, Kourtney was. She was driving a new 600 series Beamer, her clothes weren't knock-off fashion, they were the real deal. She walked in one day with some Jimmy Choo pumps—I remember because she took them off to show me the label, right in the dispatcher space—I looked 'em up. $575. For a pair of shoes. On a detective's salary. Allie, there was something wrong."

"Okay. So Gill and Martin became partners," I offered, getting her back on track.

"Yeah. Gill rolls in, what? Five years ago? The two immediately become best buddies. Gill takes the bullet during the domestic. They bust that ring down in Yarmouth. Lots of publicity for the Department. Latch is thrilled. These two are pure gold."

"But then, they started getting sloppy and showing up places where they haven't been called. One day, like," she thought a moment, "I'm sure it was last year, Martin calls in a trip to a traffic stop in Port Isaac. This was *before* the deputy on site called it in. Turns out, it was a van with two keys of heroin. How did he know to get over there? The bust was thrown out because of," she inserted air quotes here, 'police tampering.' The deputy got hell for screwing it up and the grapevine said it was Martin that compromised the product."

"But how does Gill figure into this?"

"After that bust, I went to Gill, thinking I'd give him a heads-up so maybe he could talk to Sam and get it straightened out. We all make mistakes, you know?"

"Sure. Taking care of your fellow cop."

"Yeah, right? I'm sure this stuff happened in Chicago?" I smiled in affirmation. "So, I go to Gill and make like he's the guy in charge and I lay it out, sort-of like I've told you. That I see stuff and I don't want anything to happen to Sam and that maybe Gill should say something."

"Okay."

"So this was in Gill's office. I'm standing there and he's at his desk. When I've finished, he stands, closes the door, gets all in my face. He takes a deep breath. I'll never forget what he said:

"Thank you for your concern, Deputy Garrett. I deeply appreciate you bringing this to my attention. I will mention something to Detective Martin. Drugs and prostitution and their impact on our youth are real issues here in Chamberlain County. You have a teenaged daughter, don't you, Deputy? We are trying to make sure girls like Chelsea don't fall in with the wrong crowd. Please keep me apprised of any other concerns you may have."

"Shit."

"Allie, I was stunned. I threw-up in the bathroom. Chelsea is everything to Chet and me. And, literally, every time I see Gill now, he's super nice, asks about

Chelsea. Makes reference to her after-school activities and stuff. Jesus, it scares the hell out of me." I nodded. "Yeah. So that was about a year ago. They seemed a little more careful, because at least the communication part got to be standard. But then Tabitha, Sam's daughter, disappeared in November."

"Yeah. Tell me about that. How old was she? Gill said Sam was pretty torn up."

"Just turned eighteen, and it wasn't like he couldn't have seen it coming. But that was the thing about Sam. He had tunnel vision with his girls. Tabitha came out of the same mold as Kourtney, except dark." She shook her head. "Kourtney—have you seen her?"

"Only a picture."

"Well, Kourtney is all about glamour and Hollywood. Warm. Trashy, but in an upbeat way."

"So, was Tabitha, like, Goth? Black eye shadow, lipstick, nail polish and on and on?"

"No. But you get it. There are Preppies and then there are Goths and most of the time they're just kids who are looking for their tribe. Tabby moved with a crowd outside of all that. She hung out with older kids—guys well into their twenties. Keep in mind she had only just turned 18. Beautiful, in a tall, willowy sort of way. She could probably have been a model. I think Kourtney felt threatened by her."

"So what happened, exactly?"

"You want more coffee?" Dina asked, getting up and walking to the kitchen.

"No thanks. Three's my limit." I felt my phone buzz with an incoming text. It could wait.

Dina finished the carafe, added her cream and sugar, and sat again.

"It was . . . November . . . 23rd. Right before Thanksgiving. The word was that Sam and Kourtney had separated and Sam was living with Gill until he could find his own place. He wanted to get the family together for the holiday. Kourtney called him and asked if Tabby was staying with him. Said she hadn't seen her for two days. I know because she called his cell and I saw him take it in the Deputies' space. He went off on her and then he and Gill headed out. They rousted some kids she hung out with, looked in all her usual hangouts, traced her last known location. Sam told Latch he'd take care of the investigation—not to get the whole department involved. Latch gave him the time. Sam was in a frenzy. And then, about nine days after she disappeared, he got a call from a detective in Montreal. Tabby was dead."

I drew a breath. "Dead? As in, dead?" No one, not Gill, not Latch, no one had ever said Martin's daughter was dead. I said this to Dina.

She nodded. "Yeah. It wasn't a masterclass in parenting. Or policing, for that matter . . .," She shook her head, dismissing the thought with a slight frown. "Sam drove to Montreal to bring her home. He and Kourtney kept it quiet, had a private service. It was the end of their marriage."

"And then Sam dies in a gun accident on New Year's Day."

"Yeah. Well, I mean, he'd been depressed. Alone at the holidays and Tabby's disappearance and death and all. Jack told me the McManns invited him and Sam to Christmas Dinner but only Jack went. Then Jack had a date for New Year's Eve and came home and found Sam."

My eyebrows lifted.

"Yeah. It happened at Jack's place."

"Who made the call on the cause of death? Nobody suspected suicide?"

"Everyone liked Sam. Latch didn't want the negative publicity that might accompany a suicide investigation."

That sounded right. She sipped her coffee.

"I think Latch leaned on Charlevoix and she called it an accidental death," Dina finally said. "It was going to help with the insurance and stuff. As much as folks don't like Kourtney, they didn't want her to lose everything."

We were quiet.

Follow the money, they always say. "So, you think Gill and Martin were on the take? C'mon, Dina, this is Maine, not Chicago."

"Yeah, Allie. Chamberlain County, Maine. A county which doubles in population between May and September. And folks who visit are looking for a good time. And they have money. And Sam needed money. It isn't Times Square, but people are people. They want to get high. And sex sells." She shifted in her chair. "Tell me about the Fielding twins—"

She'd answered my question and was done talking about Gill. I gave her the highlights of the investigation and wondered aloud if there was anything she'd picked up from radio traffic that would help. She said no, but asked to see the videos. She joined me on the sofa and sat close with her legs drawn up under her as I took out my phone and queued-up Trevor's most recent message. She watched, silent.

"That's tough. And Latch won't go public with this?"

I shook my head and started the piece with Celeste. She sat and delivered, blindfolded and twitching. Dina raised a hand to her mouth, shifted her feet to the floor and sat upright.

"Oh, Allie. Oh my God." She placed her hand on my knee for stability.

"What? What, Dina?"

"Play it again."

I pushed the triangle and Celeste talked and twitched.

"Leave tomorrow. I'm sure she's saying "Leave tomorrow," she insisted.

"What do you mean?"

"Awhile back, Latch brought in a consultant from Boston to have the department take a three-day introduction to ASL. In case we had to deal with a deaf guy."

"American Sign Language. Wow. That was forward-thinking."

"Yeah, go figure. Most of the office didn't take it too seriously but I thought it was pretty cool. O'course, it's like any language thing—use it or lose it. But I do remember some of it—Play it again."

I queued it up.

"See? Especially the first time. She moves both hands the first time up and to the right. She's trying to sign "Leave". The fist-forward thing—there! That's tomorrow. I'm 99% sure she's signing "Leave tomorrow.""

My stomach began to turn over. Tomorrow was today.

An incoming e-mail notification jumped to the screen. Barry Daniels. I'd check in with him later and cleared it. I punched the triangle one more time and we watched Celeste in silence.

"Looks like I need to find the Fielding twins."

As we stood, she reached over and hugged me. It was awkward. She stepped back and held me at arm's length.

"What's next?"

"I'm not sure, yet," I replied and walked to the kitchen and placed my mug on the counter.

Dina stood, alone, in the living room. I caught her glancing at the snapshot of Charlie. I had some insight into her loss.

"Allie, be careful. If I hear anything I'll text you."

"Thanks."

I drove back to Connor's Point and parked. There was no need to return to Fielding's Landing. I checked my phone. The text message was from Latch saying to contact him immediately. I didn't have any new information for him. I deleted it.

Barry Daniels' email message was interesting. He started by saying how much he enjoyed meeting me and that he appreciated being included in the investigation. Yes, he had seen one of the five men whose photos I had attached to my email. He saw this guy with Trevor outside Loon Lodge and then again when Fielding was checking out. He said the guy was hanging back at one end of the lobby and that he noticed him because, from Daniels' experience, people are either waiting in line for something at the desk or they're on their way from one place to another, transiting the lobby. I thought back to the space. He was probably right. There weren't lounge chairs and conversation nooks. It was bare bones. If someone was just waiting around, they'd stick out. Especially if they weren't dressed for the slopes. It was a thorough message with some real observations. He'd even marked my photo line-up, scanned and sent it along with the message. Maybe Mr. Manager was good for a date, after all. The face he circled in red was the truck driver from Miq-Maq.

Breezy.

I considered. So now I had Becca describing a guy named Breezy hanging with Trevor at The Mountain, Daniels identifying someone who met the description, and a photo of this guy entering Camp Miq-Maq/Wiki/New Albion, whatever. It was reasonable to assume Breezy might be involved in some way with Major

Fielding's murder and the disappearance of his twins. I just needed to find him or the kids.

The sun, low in the February sky, warmed my cheek through the cruiser's window. The rising tide lifted jigsaw-chunks of ice the size of beds that groaned in protest as they began to bob and creak with the movement. I turned my full face to the south where the Gulf of Maine's horizon cut a hard blue line against the clear sky.

Latch wasn't going to be any help. He'd be consumed with controlling the New Albion story and countering the professor's narrative. He told me I was on my own. *Okay, Jimbo, gonna take you at your word.* Dina's comments about Gill were disturbing.

The Nation of New Albion seemed the likely place to find Breezy, but entering was risky due to unfriendly natives and my deputy-buddies camped outside. Searching Google Earth, Camp Wiki popped-up immediately. Funny thing about that—Cupertino was unaware of The Nation of New Albion's sovereignty. The camp had a long access road, ball fields, cabins, and a lake. In short—a summer camp. But, with more than 27 buildings, I needed someone to help narrow my search. I checked my rearview mirror, backed onto 145, and headed for Folkestone and Madison Academy.

Twenty-two

"ALLIE?" DINA GARRETT ANSWERED my call on the first ring.

"Dina, I need to talk to Chelsea about Camp Wiki. Would you be willing to call Madison Academy and let them know I'm on my way to chat with her?"

"Sure, but this will be off the record, right? I don't want Chel involved in anything that Gill's mixed up with."

"Absolutely—off the record." *Off the record? Sure, Dina. Whatever it takes.*

I pulled into the academy's lot. Mountains of snow were pushed to the edges. 'Live dividers' that would be green and dappled with leafy shade in the summer formed a maze of mounded, sooty-white snow punctuated by barren tree trunks. I found a space. Visitors' parking was visible from the administrative offices and the exterior door was buzzing for my entry before I reached it. The principal's administrative area was in an addition that had been constructed after I graduated. The style was pretty non-descript. After Modern, but not Post-Modern. Just sort-of a tacked-on Secondary School Brutalism. *Hmm, maybe I actually learned something in Hyde Park.*

A woman wearing slacks that were a little too tight and a bright pink blouse that was a little too hot stepped into the lobby and closed the office door behind her. She moved between me and a set of double doors that led into the older section of the building. "What can I do for you, Deputy? Is there a problem?"

"Good morning, I'm here to chat with Chelsea Carpenter. I believe her mother, Dina Garrett called." *Official.*

"Certainly, but may I ask what this is about? Is she in trouble?"

"No, no trouble." *Keep it simple.*

"May I see some identification?"

I unzipped my jacket and showed her my badge. I gave her my best, *"Yes, I'm a Deputy on official business."* look.

"Okay, Deputy Beckham. But this is *quite* irregular. Please come into the office while I see what class Chelsea's in," she said, as she opened the door to the administrative area. Another woman and a young man glanced up from their computers as she walked around the long, high counter that is the standard demarcation line between administrators and students. She stood and looked at me for a long moment. Her colleagues got quiet.

"Tim, would you please see where Chelsea Carpenter is?"

"Sure. What's up?" Tim looked at me while his fingers flew across the keyboard.

Administrator One moved to her desk. A brightly painted, jig-sawed shop-class name-puzzle sat on the corner of the desk and was visible from the counter to anyone who had business: "June Winsockie."

"Deputy Beckham needs to talk to her about . . . a case?" Winsockie confided to Tim.

"I'm hoping she might be able to provide some clarification." *Vague but official sounding.*

"Let's see," Tim said, examining the schedule. "Today's Wednesday. 10:25. She should be in . . . Frank Whitton's English class. Room 207, Hutton Hall."

"I think it would be best if I went to get Chelsea," June said. "I don't want to alarm the students and there will be fewer questions if it's me and not you who pulls her from class. Please wait here."

"Certainly." I found a seat on a Windsor-style bench that filled a short wall. Tim and Administrator Two returned to their screens but glanced surreptitiously at me as they clicked away. From my bench, I could see into the lobby. The Lady Mariners were on their way to the state basketball finals and there were posters with loopy text cheering them on. A bell rang and suddenly the empty space was flooded with kids passing from one class to another. June and Chelsea emerged at the opposite end and I watched them cross as other students surged comfortably around them, saying hello and getting smiles from Winsockie. Chelsea clutched her books to her chest and flashed an uneasy smile when she saw me stand through the window.

"Good morning, again," I said as cheerfully as possible when they entered.

"Uh, good morning," Chelsea replied. "Is everything okay at home?"

Ms. Winsockie was monitoring.

"Yes, your mom and I had a nice chat this morning after you left." *I'm a close friend of the family, June.* "Is there somewhere we can talk privately?" I asked, directing my question at Winsockie.

"Of course," she said in a way that meant "Is this really necessary?" She motioned to a glassed-in conference room at the back of the office. "I don't think there's anything scheduled for 102 until just before Noon, right, Tim?"

"Nope. It's free until 11:30. You won't need it more than an hour, will you Deputy?" Tim asked.

"Oh no, this shouldn't take long at all," I replied, looking at Chelsea, then June, and trying to communicate, *"Don't worry, it'll be easy."*

Twelve padded chairs surrounded a long desk that was flanked by a pair of flip charts and a white board along the brick wall.

"What's going on?" Chelsea asked when we were alone. She was sitting upright, hands clasped in her lap. I sat at one end of the long table and she was to my right and positioned so no one could see the laptop screen when I opened it.

"It's okay, Chelsea, you're not in any trouble of any kind," I said. "You remember last night, when we were talking in the restaurant about Camp Wiki?"

"Sure." It was more of a question than an affirmation. Like, "Yeah, but why do you need to pull me out of class to talk about camp?"

"Do you know who's running it now?"

"Not really. I've heard some guys go out there on weekends and shoot guns and stuff . . ."

"Chelsea, have you ever met Trevor or Celeste Fielding?" I didn't want to get into the politics. We had a limited window.

"No. I mean, I know who they are and maybe I might have seen them around town but I think they're younger than me and, well, I think they go to private school and . . ." She was searching for the right answer.

"That's okay." I paused her. "Trevor and Celeste are in trouble." Her eyes questioned me.

"They've been kidnapped." She drew a short breath.

"And I'm supposed to find them and I think they might be at Camp Wiki. And I need your help."

"What can I do?" Confused. "I don't think my mom and dad will let me . . ." She shifted away from me in her chair.

"No, I don't want you to help me like that. I'm going to show you a couple of short videos and I need you to tell me if there's anything about either one that might give you a clue that it was shot at the camp. But first—you need to know these video clips are frightening and we can't let on to Ms. Winsockie. Can you do this?"

"Okay, I . . . I suppose . . . ," she said as I queued Trevor's message.

Her eyes narrowed to the screen as the video played.

"Anything?" I asked.

"No. Nothing. I mean, it looked like he might be on a camp bed, but it might not be."

"Okay. Here's Celeste."

Celeste began to deliver her message.

"Oh, it's Piglet! In Wren's Nest!"

"You're gonna have to help me here, Chelsea. Piglet in Wren's Nest?"

"You know, Piglet, from Winnie-the-Pooh. My friend Abby and I were making this zombie film for one of the projects. It was my last summer; I guess it was the last summer they were open—and Wren's Nest—that's the name of the cabin we wanted to use for one of the scenes. It was perfect, we were going to have Jake Mullaney, our head zombie—he was going to be climbing in a window that you can't see here. There was construction stuff laying around because they were working on it. And that was okay. But when we started to set up the shot, there was a patch on the wall that looked like Piglet from Winnie-the-Pooh. And we couldn't have that, I mean, you know, Piglet doesn't fit with zombies."

I started the video over.

"See? See right there?" Chelsea was pointing to an area just behind Celeste's right shoulder that hadn't been visible in Trevor's. When she moved her arm, she leaned forward a little and revealed a smear that looked just like Piglet's head.

"Chelsea, this is great. Do you think you could show me where Wren's Nest is located on a map? And anything else you can remember?" I said as I closed the video and opened Google Earth to the bookmarked Camp Wiki.

It took a moment for her to get oriented. She pointed to an "L" shaped building.

"This is Wren's Nest." She was definitive. "I heard it was used for arts and crafts before Camp Wiki. My counselor said they were in the middle of changing it over to run gaming sessions year 'round. They divided the the two sides so teams couldn't hear or see eachother, but they'd be close for critique, you know, after the sessions."

Wren's Nest was at the perimeter of an expansive space that Chelsea called The Commons. There was a large building across a wide access path from it.

"What was this building used for?" I asked. A red lightning bolt emblazoned a broad satellite dish mounted above the corner. It was significantly bigger than something you'd have on a house.

"We called that 30 Rock. It's where the editing rooms were. There were two tiny rooms for editing and three studios." I raised my eyebrows and she responded. "Yeah, I know. There was even a green room studio where you could shoot special effects. It was cool."

"I'm guessing that was winterized, too? You know, finished walls and insulation and stuff?" I was trying to get an idea of how many buildings might currently be in use by the good citizens of New Albion.

"Yeah. Well, sort-of. The main dining area—actually, the building was the kitchen and dining hall for camp a long time ago, but then they built a new one . . . But the main room in the large section here," she motioned at a long, rectangular roof with her finger, "This was the place where the tables were and people ate. It wasn't insulated. But, the studios," and she pointed to the rear section that showed a different roofline, "They were. They were, like, super insulated and had soundproofing and everything, you know, I mean they were pretty good studios. And there were four other buildings that were winterized, as far as I know." Chelsea looked carefully at the screen. "This one—the Office—and . . . the Bunkhouse, here," she pointed to a square cabin perched on the edge of the hill that sloped to the waterfront, " . . . the new Dining Hall and," she traced a path that went from the new Dining Hall back to Wren's Nest and then rested on a small square, ". . . Angel Falls."

"Angel Falls?"

"Yeah, the showers and bathrooms. Angel Falls is one of the girls' bathrooms. The boys used Moxie Falls. I'm pretty sure they fixed Angel Falls for winter use. They were really planning on having people go year 'round. But Moxie wasn't fixed up or heated, for sure."

"You said there was a window that Jake was going to use to climb into Wren's Nest." I needed more details. "Can you show me on the map where the windows are . . . was there more than one door? And where are the doors located?"

"Are you going out there? By yourself?" Chelsea placed her hand on mine. A lot like her mom.

"We'll see. First, I need to know as much as you can remember about Wren's Nest and any of the other buildings you think might be in use now."

We went structure by structure, discussing the doors and windows and any other access or issues that came up about the six buildings she thought were winterized. Miller's group might have improved more of them, but I thought it was unlikely since they didn't seem to be a big budget organization. She confirmed that all the access roads and paths were unpaved, something I had presumed but was good to know for sure. We came to a stopping point.

"Chelsea, this has been super helpful. Thanks so much." I said. "I have one more request of you." I needed someone I could trust. She had relaxed by now and looked me directly in the eye.

"Okay. What?"

"You absolutely cannot tell any of your friends about our conversation but please let your mom know that I may be going out to Camp Wiki tonight and that she needs to tell Sheriff Latch, but _only_ if she doesn't hear from me by 9 a.m. tomorrow morning."

"That's two things," Chelsea said as she gave me a lopsided grin.

"Okay, two things." I replied.

"You got it."

Winsockie poked her head in the door. We were nearly at our one-hour limit. "Is everything okay?" she asked Chelsea.

"Yeah, fine," Chelsea replied, turning to me with a smile. "Deputy Beckham had some questions about video production for something they're doing at the Sheriff's office, and my mom suggested she talk to me."

"Yes, everything's good. Thank you for letting me chat with Chelsea, Ms. Winsockie," I added, returning the young girl's smile. Always good to have a little truth in a lie.

Twenty-three

AFTER SAYING GOODBYE TO Chelsea and June Winsockie, I returned to my Explorer and called Latch. He didn't pick up. I checked e-mail.

I'd been cc'd on a string of messages about the department's drone being shot down a little earlier. Apparently, McMann Junior was the go-to guy for drones in the county. Footage circulated began with him concentrating on a control-box and Gill and the other deputies assigned to Wiki craning their necks as the machine took off. McMann knew what he was doing. The silent image showed the group grow small, then enlarge a little as he adjusted the altitude to something about 75 feet up—just above tree-top level. The landscape began to move slowly as the drone followed the winding road into camp. The path appeared and disappeared as the terrain changed elevation or opened to a small clearing or the occasional snow-covered meadow. McMann retraced his steps once or twice, finding his way. The movement hesitated where the road narrowed in a hairpin turn. I sensed a rustling within the tree cover, and soon after, two militiamen emerged wearing snow-camouflage gear. They carefully stepped out of the trees and took up position on a raised granite outcropping, using their long guns to balance. One of them gestured in a silent call across the gorge. Another pair appeared on a similar ledge. It was an eminently defensible position. One of the second pair got excited and started to aim his rifle. The image went to a wider view and the gunman quickly diminished in size as McMann took evasive action by sending his vehicle higher. You could just make out a guy pushing his buddy's barrel aside. They seemed to argue as the drone descended slowly and one of the first pair of sentinels put a mobile phone to his ear. The drone moved on.

Gill was probably giving McMann direction. He'd been inside so maybe he was telling the kid what he was looking for. The video moved over a small pond I recognized from Google Earth. The drone hesitated and then, instead of proceeding to the main section of the camp, it moved a lot higher and traveled at a dizzying rate to the wide end of the lake. It paused for awhile and tilted this way and that, surveying the scene. Gill probably wanted an overview.

This looked familiar. In the summer, a sandy shore invited folks from across the region to enjoy the refreshing waters of Powderhorn Lake. The beach, formed by a terminal moraine, was a remnant of the last Ice Age when the mile-high glacier retreated. From the broad swimming area, the lake formed an almost perfectly tapered arc that extended north and west for most of a mile. The powderhorn. Before the accident, Dad would set aside a summer weekend to visit Huntley and his closest friend Scott, who taught art in Georgia and had bought a place to escape the south's brutal heat and humidity. We'd visit, swim, hike, and then have some of the tangy BBQ that Scotty had been prepping all day. I smiled.

McMann's wide view included most of the lake's perimeter. On the west bank was New Albion, née Camp Wiki, which showed up as organized space on a wooded bluff that sloped steeply to the water. The village of Huntley owned most of Two Spring Mountain, which rose from the opposite shore. At this altitude, trees read as masses of gray, patched with pine-green. An organic web of snow-white lines that mostly followed elevation contours indicated old logging and new hiking and skiing trails and access roads. The high-rez video feed revealed a cottage or two that had been grandfathered-in when the farsighted elders of Huntley concluded its purchase nearly 100 years ago. Old Wooster Road, on which the village beach was located, continued over the mountain and connected Huntley and Rte. 115 with Wooster. The pavement ended just after the beach. That's where all the mountain trails and roads had their terminus in a parking lot that, if memory served me right, was unpaved, too. Several small, stationary black dots could be seen in the middle of the lake. It looked like there was a pickup truck next to one.

Ice fishing shacks.

The drone began a slow swoop, descending as it traveled up the middle of the lake until the docks for New Albion's rowboat navy were visible. It followed an access road up the hill from there. Now, buildings and open spaces were more recognizable. I saw the square Bunkhouse that Chelsea identified, 30 Rock and the L-shaped Wren's Nest. I expected to see a couple of guys here and there doing chores. Instead, there were four squads with what looked like about ten militiamen each being drilled by a sergeant, moving in a large central area that had been well-plowed. There were numerous other men——all men, no women from what I could tell—moving to and fro. The leader of one squad called to his group and pointed at the drone. It started to ascend. The entire group began firing and other squads joined in and then the picture went black.

Someone in the department other than Dina Garrett needed to know the Fielding twins were being held by Miller and his crew. I mean, it made sense. They likely needed funding to feed the army and a successful ransom for $5 million would set them up pretty. But, it didn't make sense. This Breezy guy didn't fit the profile of a militia man. He was more like a pimp. If Dina was right, Celeste was telling us they were being moved within 24 hours. They'd agreed to give Honor until Friday—48 hours. Why would they risk moving them before then? And how could they move them with the Sheriff's office camped out at their front door?

I called Latch again. This time he picked up.

"Latch here."

"Sheriff, you got a moment?"

"Beckham. Thanks for the report. Looks like Stephen Fielding might not be our guy."

"Yeah, thanks. I think I know where the twins are."

"Okay . . .?"

"I think they're being held by Miller at Camp Wiki."

"What's Camp Wiki?"

"Miq-Maq, New Albion, Wiki," *Jesus, this was confusing*. "Whatever the hell you want to call it, I think they're being held by Miller where the Quakers got beat up."

"What makes you think that? This a "woman's intuition" or do you have something to back it up?"

I gave him the Cliff Notes version of my research including the triangulation of Breezy with the twins and Celeste's warning about being moved. I omitted the part about the possibility of Gill being dirty.

He was skeptical.

"Gill's been inside. He's former Military Intelligence and he didn't mention anything about any kids. Miller's more serious than I thought. I've got the FBI knocking on my door and they'll undoubtedly insert themselves into the mix."

I could tell this pissed him off. The FBI would shift the spotlight.

He continued. "Why would Miller muddy his waters by kidnapping kids? He's trying to establish his alternative reality with his base."

I was frustrated. "I'm not gonna pretend I know what Miller's thinking, but, sir, Chelsea Carpenter pointed out something specific she recognized from Wiki."

"Okay . . ." Latch said.

"Piglet in Wren's Nest."

Silence.

"Sir, it's not like it sounds. There's a patch . . ."

He interrupted. "Not like it sounds, Beckham? Oh good. I was worried there for a second. *Everything* will be okay now." His voice was building. "We don't have to worry about anything bad going down because, in just a minute, Tigger's gonna bounce in and save the fucking day! *Did I get it right, Beckham?!*"

I was quiet. I knew I'd be digging the hole deeper if I continued.

"*Man-oh-man,* am I relieved," he finally said. "Sure. An 18-year-old girl wants to please her new BFF so she "sees" something and *Voila!* We're invading New Albion? Not gonna happen, Beckham."

It was my turn.

"Look, Sheriff, we have got to get someone—I don't give a shit who—maybe it's Gill, maybe me, maybe it's *you*, but we have *got* to get someone in there and go building-to-building. Get the FBI, get the MSP, but get *someone* in there who can make sure these kids are safe."

"Are you kidding me Beckham? You are being incredibly naïve if you think Miller and his Nazis would allow anyone, for any reason, to waltz in and do a house-to-house. I was lucky to get Gill in and out in one piece. No, we'll do this my way or you can turn in your badge this afternoon."

"Well, what's your way? I found the twins. That was my assignment. Are we gonna just let Honor Fielding pay the ransom and hope—*hope*—she gets her kids back safely?" I could not let this go.

"You haven't found the twins. You don't know Miller has them for sure. I'm dealing with a powderkeg situation here. Miller's run up his flag and he's got guys streaming in from all over the northeast to be part of this. If this was Federal land we could stop 'em from entering but it's private so they can do whatever the hell they want back there. Go back to Fielding, tell her we think she should pay the ransom and that you'll be there when her kids are turned over. The main thing is to get them back safely, right?"

I let him know about my morning visit to the Landing. Or, lack of visit.

"Great. Just fucking great," he sighed. "Is there anyone you haven't alienated, Beckham? Let's see if you can follow directions one last time. Here's what I want you to do: Go back to Honor Fielding, in person, again—get back to South Prescott, go to The Landing and make nice—tell her whatever you need to, to get her on board. Engineer the ransom payment and collect the kids. We'll go after the kidnappers once we have them back safely. I'm trying to stop a Civil War." He was gone.

Twenty-four

The parking lot filled up during Latch's call. By now, there was a sea of buses, mini-vans, and cars with moms and dads reading or checking their cells and choking the space, awaiting dismissal. Standing for a moment, I stretched next to the cruiser as the "School's Out!" bell rang. Teens burst through the doors and began to disperse. I weighed the idea of throwing on lights and sirens and screaming out of the lot. Nope. The heat felt good sitting again and I cranked the Explorer and tried to be patient. This would give me a little time to reflect on what the hell I was going to do once I got to South Prescott. I slipped the Explorer into reverse and nodded at a Beemer who offered access to the flow.

Students', parents', and their friends' cars cruised through slowly, or just stopped-dead where clusters of kids gathered and generally held up traffic. Maybe it was my age, but I felt like there were a lot more students who owned cars than when I attended. The banked snow didn't make it easy to get a sense of the movement, or lack thereof. With the drifts, it was hard to see much beyond the perimeter of the lot and into the oncoming lane and I made mental note to complain to June. I was concentrating on finding a place in the queue when a boy/girl couple came out of nowhere and jumped in front with their hands up in mock horror. I hit the brakes hard. They banged the flat of their palms against the hood as if to stop my advance and then moved on, laughing. My cell started ringing. I was finally at the exit to Academy Hill Rd. and tapped the speakerphone button.

"Beckham here."

LuLu Charlevoix's accented voice filled the cruiser. "Deputy Beckham. Allie, is that you?"

What the hell did the M.E. want from me?

"Yes, Dr. Charlevoix. I'm kind of busy here. What can I do for you?" I pulled out of the lot and into the traffic that crawled in both directions. Kids darted across the road here and there, catching up with other friends who were walking home.

"Allie. Please. Just a moment of your time. I'm calling about the Fielding murder . . . well, not really about Fielding. That was open and shut. As you know . . ."

"Yes ma'am. Shot with a 9mm pistol. Close range."

"Yes, yes. You're correct. But that is not why I'm calling. I've been following the news of this group, you know."

Okay, you and most of the rest of Maine.

"Yes, ma'am."

"Having been at the crime scene when Eddie Miller tried to intervene . . ."

You're being very generous here . . .

"Uhh. Yes, ma'am."

"I have two things I need to tell you about him. They might not make a difference in the case but, in light of what has happened—that terrible beating that took place at the camp, my God Allie, the brutality . . ."

At this point, I was grasping for anything concrete, even if it was just background. I had a 25-minute drive ahead of me and LuLu was the only person actively reaching out.

"Sure, Doctor, go ahead."

"His father, he is the man who calls himself The Professor, yes? He and a brother were held overnight in the jail?"

"Yes, ma'am, you're correct. Eddie Miller's father is The Professor and his brother, Willy-Willy, was brought in with him and two other guys."

"You may have guessed, the other morning—it was not our first interaction."

"Oh?" I'd been surprised when she called him by name but nothing was said by her or Latch once the incident was over. I let her continue.

Her voice was hard. "*Non,* it was not." She paused. "I volunteer with Merc."

"I'm sorry, Doctor. Merc?"

"Excuse me. M-R-R-C-C. The Maine Refugee Resettlement Council of Churches. They work to give the assistance to refugees and to make sure they have proper food and housing. I have offered basic healthcare-checkups and work twice a week in the food pantry in Lewiston with them."

"Okay." I'd been away from Maine so long I didn't realize there was a refugee issue here. *El Paso, sure, but . . . Maine?*

"This fellow, this Eddie Miller. I would see him sometimes, hanging around the entry to the building at Merc. This was maybe two years ago, before all this New Albion. I am sure he was the man who roughed-up women as they walked home with their food."

"Did anyone ever report something like this to the Lewiston police?"

"*Non.* The women are too afraid. From where they come, the police, they are almost always on the side of the bad guys or require bribes to take action. *Non,* they told me that it happened, that they were scared, but that they didn't want to report it. I confronted him once. It did not end well. These are not good people, Allie."

"Have you told the sheriff?"

"After they were arrested I called but he did not answer. I left a message. So, *non.*"

"Thanks for this, Dr. Charlevoix." It was helpful information but I needed some time alone with my thoughts. She'd left her message. I reached for my cell.

She sensed the closure, "Allie, please, just a moment." She was insistent so I hesitated.

"Yes, Doctor?"

"Allie, please stop with the "Doctor" business. You and I, we have shared something; we are colleagues, yes? There is another piece to this that I must tell you. It is not something I am proud of, but . . ."

"Yes, LuLu?" It still didn't feel right to use her first name, but she needed to talk.

"I will make this brief. It was autumn, maybe 18 months past. There was a call for the paramedics to the Miller place, there, on Merry Hill Rd. Mabel Miller, The Professor's wife, was in distress. I was close-by and was the first person on-scene.

She was in cardiac arrest but, Allie, they wouldn't let me touch her. The men, they heaped abuse upon me while she died in front of my eyes. I was so angry I sank to their level and called them by appalling names. If EMTs hadn't arrived at that moment I'm not sure I would be talking to you. And then they blamed her death on my presence. There was a brief investigation. And yes, I admit to you, I received a discrete reprimand."

I was quiet. I felt the need to be supportive, but I also needed to figure out how I was going to get past the gatehouse at Fielding's Landing. LuLu was sharing. Well, I supposed I could share, too.

"That's tough, LuLu and it gives me some perspective on the situation with the Millers. Thank you for letting me know. Maybe you can help me with something else?"

"Yes, Allie, of course."

I quickly brought her up to speed on the past two days' investigation, the whole thing from top to bottom, including Latch's latest dictum.

"So, you need to talk to this Honor woman? From your story, perhaps his wife's parents are the key. They seem to hold some sway with their daughter."

She had a point. If I could get to one of the Chapmans, if they were the ones who answered my call, maybe Honor could be persuaded to let me back in. Frank might be the key.

"Thanks, LuLu. I'm sorry but I gotta go."

"Of course, good luck," I heard her say as I cut the call and pulled off the road at The Crooked Birch, a local grill and longtime watering hole. I Googled Frank Chapman Real Estate, Folkestone, Maine, hoping he still had a professional number.

"Chapman Real Estate." It was Frank. No secretary; he was in retirement mode.

"Mr. Chapman, Deputy Beckham."

"Yes, I know."

"Mr. Chapman, I know your daughter is angry—and you may be, too—and I apologize for Detective Gill's and my last visit. But all of us need to be working together to recover Trevor and Celeste. Presuming Honor is able to successfully negotiate their safe return, we want to find and prosecute whomever has done this to your family."

"My daughter is not boffing Kris Kringle," he replied. In any other context the line would have drawn a big laugh. I let it hang.

"What do you want from me, Deputy?"

"I'd like to meet with Honor today—I'm heading to South Prescott now—and discuss where she is with raising the money and any more communication she's had with the kidnappers." I didn't mention Kringle, but Frank wasn't stupid.

He calculated the downside. "Well, she's got nothing to hide." Then he paused.

"Allie, I like you," he finally continued. "And God knows I want to see my grandchildren again. Let me see what I can do. Come on down and go ahead and ring when you get to the gatehouse. If I answer, you'll know you're in. If it's Honor, well . . ."

"Thank you, Frank."

Back on the road, I called Barry Daniels at The Mountain to thank him for his message.

"Detective Beckham?" *Damn caller ID.*

"Hello, uh, Mr. Daniels." I wasn't sure which way to go with this. "It's *Deputy* Beckham, Mr. Daniels, but, please, call me Allie." I was feeling my way along here, not really sure where it was going.

"Allie! Thanks for calling. Did you get my message about the pictures okay?"

"Yeah, thanks. They were helpful."

"Good. Good. So, what can I do for you?"

"Look, I'm working on this case but I'm hoping to have it cleared by the weekend and I have Saturday off. Just wondering if the offer of a free pass was still good?" *And, there it was.*

"Sure! Absolutely. I can leave a pass at the desk, so yeah, sure. And think about saying "Hi" when you pick it up. Let me know if you'll be overnight. I can arrange a room for you."

"That sounds great. I'll do that. But, you know, Barry, it's been awhile—I was in Chicago until three weeks ago and I'm guessing you know there's not a lot of downhill skiing on the prairie. Maybe you could find someone to give me a refresher lesson?" *Jesus, men are dense.*

"We can do that!" he said. I could feel his smile.

"Okay, I'll let you know Saturday morning when I'll be up. Looking forward to my lesson."

"Great. Me too. Thanks for calling, Allie!"

I was at the gatehouse.

"Thanks for taking my call. I've gotta go."

I put the cellphone down. A date? What was I thinking? *"You need to be more optimistic."* was one of the last things Lt. Torres said to me before I left Illinois. I pressed the gatehouse call button.

"Yes?" It was Frank.

"Mr. Chapman, Deputy Beckham." Keeping it formal, just trying to get in.

"Deputy Beckham. What can I do for you?" Frank understood the game.

"I'd like to talk to Honor, if I may." I knew I was on speakerphone.

"Just a moment, Deputy Beckham." The line went quiet as he stepped away. I looked around. The snow from the day before and the blizzard over the weekend still hung in the trees. It would have been the picture-perfect holiday feel if it wasn't late-February.

The gate swung open.

I drove slowly to the compound. *Be honest. Well, try to* seem *honest.* The meadow opened to me. The tide was high and with the light breeze from the north, waves were kept to a minimum. The ocean was flat and true.

Frank was at the door.

"Come in, Deputy Beckham."

He took my coat as I stamped the snow off my boots. "Honor and Kris are in her office." All business. "I believe you know the way."

"Yes, thank you, Mr. Chapman." Mary sat in the living room, knitting. She didn't look up.

I was surprised to hear that Kringle was still there. His car wasn't in the driveway. I found my way through the dining room and up the stairs to Honor's office. She sat at her desk and he was standing at the windows when I knocked lightly.

"Allie."

"Honor. And Mr. Kringle. Hello, I didn't expect to see you here."

He turned. "Yeah, right." He looked at Honor, then me. "Cut the Mr. Kringle-formal-cop bullshit. Let me make something clear, Deputy Beckham. Yes, I love Honor, but not in that way." He turned his face to her again and she blushed and looked at the desk. He shifted his balance, "I loved Major, too. Our friendship was based on a common bond forged in our business and family relationships. It was deep and meant everything to me."

I stayed in the doorway.

"We were simpatico from the day he walked into B&C. I showed him the ropes and, yes, I should have listened to him in the run-up to '08, but we respected each other's strategies. Turned out he was right and I was wrong. Okay. But then, he stepped in to help when I stumbled. He knew what it was like to lose everything." He continued looking at Honor, whose eyes were now glassy and fixed on the large portrait of Major Fielding. She allowed a brief smile as she turned to Kringle's gaze and then cast her eyes downward again. She opened a drawer and pulled out a Kleenex and dabbed her eye. "He repaid me and Fran a hundred times over by getting me set up in Portland after the meltdown and throwing me clients that were too small for him to manage. Deputy Beckham, you've *got* to believe me. I would never, ever, do anything to harm Major, Honor, or the twins." It sounded genuine. He turned his back, leaned his shoulder against the floor-to-ceiling window frame and looked at the ocean.

"Why are you here?" It was Honor.

"Sheriff Latch has placed me exclusively in charge of the investigation. Lt. Gill has been pulled off this to work on the New Albion situation. I'm here to discuss where you are in the negotiations and to try to set up whatever you need to get Trevor and Celeste back home safely."

Kringle turned around.

It was Honor who responded.

"What? The Sheriff has left us with a rookie cop while he chases a bunch of fascist Minutemen in the woods?" She was angry but not out of control, yet. I started to say something but she cut me off. "Yeah, I know about you. You're here, what? maybe two weeks?—took over for that Martin guy who killed himself." *So much for Latch's attempt to tidy things up.*

Kringle's face opened and she sensed some recognition on his part. "Yeah, Kris—We met him a couple of years ago," Honor's eyes were boring in on me, but she continued to address him. "You remember that Christmas party the Sheriff hosted at the brewery, just after we opened? We had the kids with us that night—our annual Christmas dinner, remember? It was the last one with all of us together . . . it was early and there was that guy with the hooker wife—looked totally out of place and completely outta control?"

Kringle started to say something. Honor raised her hand. "Now *there* were a couple of sloppy drunks." She smiled ruefully. "Sheriff introduced us when he asked if there might be a separate room where they could wait for a ride? What he really wanted was to get them out of the 'public view.' Let's see . . . His name was Sam, right?" She asked it rhetorically. "Hers was . . . Kourtney. Oh—and she was insistent, the way drunks are, "Kourtney, *Initial C,* Considine-Martin. Ooh, so sophisticated with the hyphenated last name. And then she tried to get up all over you?" She nodded in Kringle's direction.

His eyes narrowed. "Right." He confirmed the memory. "And Fran was like, "What?" and would have pushed her to the floor if I hadn't caught her? Her boob almost came out of her dress . . ."

"Right—that night. Everything went to hell after that. Fran got into one of her moods and Major and I couldn't wait to get home. So, why's it *you,* Allie? Why are *you* working this case? Why's a Chicago beat-cop looking for my kids? Why don't we rate a local detective? Or the FBI? Why isn't that asshole Gill here?"

Something about Kourtney's name *pinged* with me. I put it on the back burner. I had answers for Honor Fielding but most of it was speculation. I was adrift.

"I'm what you've got, Honor," I said, simply. "I'm sorry if you think you're being shortchanged, but we can't get distracted from what's most important —getting Trevor and Celeste back."

Kringle walked to the desk and stood with Honor. Her eyes moved to the ocean view and she she searched the horizon.

"You know we've had another message from them?" she finally said, after considering. I suspected as much, but tried to hide my surprise. "You've seen it, right? It came in before dawn."

"No, I'm sorry, my plan was to go over any developments when I stopped by earlier." *If you'd let me in this morning . . .*

They looked at one another and an unspoken agreement passed between them. Honor continued.

"They still want the payment Friday and then, once that's confirmed, they agreed to delivery of the twins at a pre-determined site and time on Saturday."

"Can I see it?" I kicked myself for not checking the account Gill had set up.

Honor's mouth turned down at the corners and Kringle put his hand on her shoulder. Assuring. "Yeah," he said quietly, "Queue it up, Honor. Come over here, Deputy."

The monitor was black; then a cropped image of the kids laying prone filled the screen from left to right. Their backs were on the floor, chin to mid-thigh visible with about six inches separating them. The camera angle had been rigged from directly above. No sound, black and white. Someone must have noticed Celeste's gestures in the previous piece because their wrists were zip-tied together, hands lay flat at their waist, crossed over their bellies, and fingers were duct-taped. Frankly, they looked dead. Each wore a black turtleneck with a logo and sweatpants. The kids disappeared and a black screen with blocky, white text reading, "We know you called the police," flashed onto the screen and remained for a few seconds.

We jumped back to the twins. The toes of disembodied boots stepped into the left side of the frame straddling Celeste's head. Whoever it was squatted, and when they did, we could see it was a male wearing a gray hoodie. His face was covered by a black balaclava. He reached in with gloved hands to pull her arms up over her shoulders. She went rigid, resisting. He rocked back and slapped her so hard that her full face moved into the frame for a moment and we could see that her mouth and eyes were duct-taped, her braids were gone, and her hair was shorter than her brother's. Honor was crying and squeezing Kringle's hand at her shoulder. The guy was standing, then bent at the waist and used both hands to grasp the tail of her shirt and yank it roughly, so it pulled her head and shoulders off the floor. This time, her arms angled up and the shirt slid off her torso, exposing her breasts and tummy. He let her head bounce on the floor as he dropped her, leaving the shirt covering her face.

"Shit," I said, under my breath.

Mr. Hoodie stepped out of the frame. A shadow moved across the two of them. Celeste must have been instructed not to move because she remained with her arms over her head, face covered. Suddenly, her sweatpants were pulled out of the right side of the frame and she lay naked.

Black screen again.

"We can do anything," appeared.

Twins again. This time, Trevor's sweats were tugged down and he was exposed. He reached instinctively to cover himself but the gloved hand appeared and squeezed his genitals hard and Trevor's knees came into the frame as he reacted. A boot kicked him hard in the ribs and he straightened out, obviously in pain.

Blank screen. Then, "20% Penalty for contacting cops. Wire $6M to the following account Friday at precisely 12:07 pm." A screen with a series of numbers and letters followed, then, "Once transfer is confirmed, we will communicate delivery time and place." A final shot of the children laying exposed and trembling closed the piece. They were alive.

From my perspective, only eleven people knew the Fielding twins were missing. Five—me, delVecchio, Honor, Dina Garrett/Carpenter, and Chelsea—were above suspicion. I knew it wasn't me who'd told the kidnappers that the police were involved in this mess. It was implausible that Fran Kringle, her daughter Justine, or Becca Thompson were involved. Kris Kringle was looking more and more as though he was okay. Which left two, the Sheriff and Jack Gill.

Honor blew her nose, then reached for Kringle's hand and gave it one more squeeze. He gently pulled her from the chair and directed her to one of the loveseats, where they sat, anticipating.

"Well?" It was Honor.

I was at a loss, unsure of what the hell my next move should be.

"First of all, can you get the extra money?" I stalled while my mind went over the options.

"Yes, we have the $5 million and I can liquidate another millions-worth," Kringle said.

Must be nice.

Waiting.

To Kringle: "I'm guessing the numbers and letters were routing information?"

"Yes, Deputy. Undoubtedly somewhere offshore. I'm familiar with Swiss and Cayman codes—this didn't look like anything I've seen before. I can log-in and search where the account is located—would that help?"

Concerned.

"Sure," I said. Then, circling back to buy a little more time, "Tell me again, Mr. Kringle, how you came to leave B&C and open your own shop in Portland."

Twenty-five

"What does that have to do with getting my children back?" Honor asked.

Kringle sat up straight.

"I'd like to hear, in Mr. Kringle's words, a little more about his and Fran's return to Maine."

"C'mon Allie! We don't have time for this. My children's lives are on the line. I'm supposed to pay out six *million* dollars in 24 hours. What the hell? Fran bankrolled his shop. We're done."

Okay. Now, this might be interesting. I knew that Fran had inherited Cloutier Trucking about the same time they moved to Portland, which made sense. But I wanted to hear, in her husband's words, what the dynamic was. Maybe it was time to get more familiar.

"Honor, let Kris tell me."

Assertive. *Hey, I'm the cop here, guys . . .*

She crossed her arms and sat back, hard.

Kringle collected himself and began.

"The Recession was in full force. Justine was a baby. I was let go when B&C cratered. We were burning through the little cash we had. Fran took a call from a guy at the Penobscot county Sheriff's office asking whether she was Francine Cloutier Considine. I'd never heard the name before. To me, she'd always been Francesca Bianchi. When I'd asked about her mom and dad, she said they'd died in that airplane bombing that happened in Scotland."

No, not exactly, Kris. I needed to be delicate here. "So, how did you meet?" I was still trying to reconcile the Fran I knew with Kringle's mien.

He sighed and looked out the window. "It was a different world. Fran came to B&C as a Financial Assistant, right out of Business School. She was gorgeous and knew how to dress and knew what to say. She and I hit it off; she'd call me "Santa Baby" and somehow, when she joked about my name it was sexy, not a pain in the ass."

I thought about a lifetime of someone making fun of my name. It had to be tough.

"It was the '90s. The market was great and we were making lots of dough. We got married and the party continued. We killed in the Dot-Com bust. She and I were an amazing team." He dropped his head and slumped and he seemed to age before my eyes.

"Then 9/11 happened and, like a lot of our friends, we started to get serious. It took some convincing, but we finally decided to get pregnant. 2005 was a big year."

"Yes, it was." Honor took his hand.

"Major came to Bertram and Cohen and we met Honor. And then we all had our kids."

"And you know how it is, Allie," Honor was warmed, reflecting back to the time, "Even though she was a little older, Fran and I bonded over the kids. And they had so much fun! When we got together it was like the kids had the cousins I always wanted."

Kringle smiled and took his hand back. "Yes, the kids were—are—a joy. But Fran changed. After Justine was born, she wasn't the same. I mean, I know that happens to a lot of people. We ...I ... tried to find a way back. But she couldn't get back in shape, didn't even try. Wasn't interested. We didn't have the money for an au pair and so she wasn't my assistant anymore. B&C hired a new one, Tara, and that didn't go down well. Maybe you weren't aware, Honor, but she was spending a lot of her time with you and the kids because she wanted to make sure she knew where you were during the day."

Honor's face hardened.

"Then came the meltdown and, like I said, everything went to hell."

"Okay. But how did you end up back in Maine?"

"Well, Fran's father died in 2009, without a will. And you know, I thought he was long dead, I mean I thought he had died in 1988, so that was a big surprise."

"But, Allie, the truth is no less tragic," Honor offered, seeing my shift in expression. She looked at Kringle with sympathy.

Hmm, maybe Fran came clean after all.

Kris took a breath. "Yeah. Well, lots of us have issues with our parents, you know, and Fran's Dad. . . When I asked her about the airplane bombing, she admitted she had lied about it. She said she was hiding the truth—that she blamed her dad for her mother's death in a boating accident."

He nodded his head when he saw my reaction.

"They—Fran was with them when it happened."

Of course she was . . .

"They were far offshore when a gale came up unexpectedly from the north. They tried to tack back to land but, you know, they were only day sailors and the boat wasn't big. It capsized. Her mother was caught under the sail. No one had vests. I can't imagine how she must have felt, watching her mother drown as her dad held onto the boat for safety . . . But the particulars don't matter. The point is, she explained to me that she hadn't wanted to get into the messy details about her relationship with him when we were courting. So, she made up the story about Lockerbie—it took care of both her mom, who was dead from the accident, and her dad, who she had no relationship with. I never had a reason to question her about it; I was in love."

Kris Kringle, you'll never make a detective, that's for sure.

"So, do you know if she was talking to her dad before he died?" I felt like there was something there but couldn't tease it out.

"She said she hadn't spoken to him since she was 14," he replied.

"And you believed her?"

Maybe I was going at him a little hard. He stood and walked to the window again. Silent. "I apologize, Mr. Kringle. I know this time is difficult for you and your wife. Please continue . . ."

He turned, and with his hands behind his back, he leaned against the frame again.

"Her dad had this company, Cloutier Trucking, and she inherited it," he said, looking tired. "It was doing okay and for the first time since Justine was born, Fran was really committed. She's one of those people who has an intuitive business sense. She can see where the money is and she goes for it." He paused, reflecting. "Justine was getting to be old enough to start kindergarten; we needed a decent school system; Portland was really beginning to take off. It all seemed to make sense. So, we moved to Portland and she bankrolled my franchise with Regency Financial. And, with Major's help, it really took off." He was looking at Honor. She turned to him at the mention of her husband.

"He was more than happy to help," she said.

"Yes, thank God. So the market's been good again and we were able to buy the place at The Mountain. We don't hang out as much as we used to . . . that's over," he said, wistful and still looking at Honor. *Maybe, just a little bit of lust there . . . ?*

We were quiet.

I felt like Fran Kringle had some 'splainin' to do, but it wasn't my job to shatter his illusions. This was something they'd need to work out between themselves once this mess had passed and it didn't seem to bear on the situation at hand, anyway. I'd pretty much made up my mind.

"Thanks for sharing that," I said. "And thanks for your patience, Honor. This is what needs to happen."

I assured them that I was going to be following up on some possible leads and then laid out what I wanted done. It was pretty simple: respond positively to the video and make arrangements to wire the money. When they received instructions about delivery of the kids, we'd reassess. The main point was to get the twins home safe and in one piece. Latch would surely bring in the FBI to run the investigation once we had the kids. I was making that part up, but I needed to move on. Honor seemed relieved to have official endorsement of the direction she was most inclined to follow.

"Text me as things develop—you have my number, right?" I said as we closed our strategy session. Honor checked, and she did.

"Allie, I read about you and your sister," she said as the three of us stood in the doorway to the office.

I tried to hide my reaction.

"Yes, I know how to use the internet. I'm so sorry."

"Thanks. It happened a long time ago." Maybe she'd decided I could be trusted, after all.

Twenty-six

I PULLED OVER AT Pierce's to pick up a sandwich on my way through the village. It was midafternoon and lunch rush was done. The smell of aged grease, newsprint, and 75 years of fishing filled the air as I stepped to the counter. Two young men—fishermen by the look of their boots—were the only other customers and they were sitting at one of the three deuce-tables waiting for their order.

"Be right with you." A woman worked the grill. Her back was to me and floral tattoos covered well-defined arms and continued up and slipped under t-shirt sleeves that were rolled to her shoulders. Her left hand worked shaved steak with the edge of a long steel spatula as she used her right to squirt a short stream of oil from a clear squeeze-bottle. She leaned right, then expertly spatula-backhanded a mound of grilled onions onto the steak, topping the mess carefully with several squares of white American cheese.

"What can I do for you, Deputy?" she said, catching sight of the uniform when she turned. She grabbed an order pad and plucked a pen from an old Styrofoam cup filled with dirty rice. She looked up, expectant.

"Gimme a steak and cheese sandwich to go," I said, reviewing the backlighted Coca-Cola menu board as I reached for my wallet, "and I'll get a Diet Coke from the fridge. And a bag of chips." I began to move to the bank of coolers.

"Allie?"

I stopped and turned. I took off my sunglasses.

"Allie Beckham?"

"Janie? Janie Pierce?"

"Sonuvabitch—you're back in Maine? And a Deputy?"

The woman who stood before me was not the Janie Pierce of my childhood. She and my sister and I had been fast friends, but Janie and I had fallen away from each other after Hanna died. I recognized the freckles and the slight upturn to her nose, but the tats were new and so was the boob job.

"Yeah. It was the uniform, right?"

"Well, that, and your nametag," she said, smiling. She started to come around the counter, but thought the better of it. "I thought you were in Chicago—big scholarship to U of C and all. Never thought I'd see you around here again."

"Sometimes things don't work out . . . but how about you? Looks like you're 'workin' out.'"

"Yeah, thanks for noticing," she said, flexing her bicep. "After the kids came and Brandon left, I got pretty pudgy."

My eyes supplied the question.

"Brandon—Brandon W. Brewer . . . the *3rd*. Guy from away. Teen detour. Knocked me up a couple of times and hung around for awhile, fished with the Coughlan brothers, and then decided he'd head back to Connecticut and mom and dad. 'Least I got these out of the deal," she said, looking at her chest.

"Hey Janie, hate to interrupt the girl-talk but how 'bout our sandwiches?" The fishermen were hungry.

"Shut-the-fuck-up, Chip," she said, reaching and opening two sub buns with a single slash to each. She put the buns onto paperboard trays. My steaks hit the hot steel and sizzled as she whacked them around. She gave a final chop to her customers' mélange, tossed it onto the buns, and slapped them on the counter. "Come 'n get 'em, asshole." She wasn't in it for the tips.

Chip used the table to get up and stepped to the counter while his buddy set aside the paper he'd been reading. Under a headline about old people dying in Seattle there was a photo of the four guys at the Sheriff's office with a caption "Albion Four Go Free, Sheriff Feuds with MSP." Chip balanced the trays and delivered a sullen look before returning to the deuce and his buddy. I let it go.

"Wow. Kids, plural." I said. "What'd you get?"

"Two boys. Little hellions, they are. Mom watches them while I'm here. She and dad can't work the hours they used to. Mostly she does the books. You remember Dan, my brother?"

I remembered Dan a little. He was a pothead at the Academy and did some light dealing in weed.

"Dan did short time in the county jail about five years ago," she explained, "Straightened him out. He's married and has three kids. Mom and Dad are giving the store to him." She worked my sandwich contents some more as she bit her lip.

"Tell me about Chicago," Janie said, turning back and forcing a smile. "What made you come home? I see your dad once in awhile—if I'm here when he does his beer run." She rang up my order. "How's he doing?" There was a concern in her voice that touched me.

"Not sure. Been back for less than two weeks and most of that was the night shift. Haven't had a chance to check in on him yet." I paused a beat, considering which way to go. "Chicago was good. But I decided I wanted something a little more familiar."

She took the hint and carefully laid the steak, onions, and cheese on the bun. "You wanna put anything on here before I close it up?"

I applied ketchup liberally and then she cut it in half and piled it into a cardboard clamshell box. She stuffed the box, the chips, and a fistful of napkins into a paper bag. While she was packing me up, I pulled a bottle of water along with a Diet Coke from the promo cooler, and a couple of energy bars from the rack and tossed them on the counter.

"How much do I owe you?"

"Don't worry about it. S'on the house." She leaned down and wrote "COMP" across the order, tore it off the pad and impaled it onto the store's original order-spike with finality.

"You sure?"

She looked up, a little surprised. It was a fine line. She was an old friend, but I still didn't want to be the cop getting a favor.

"Sure, Dan can deal with it."

I jammed the water bottle into a jacket pocket, tossed the bars into the sack and picked up my Coke and the bag.

"Thanks, Janie. Good to see you."

"Yeah, likewise," she said, using a towel to wipe her hands. "Don't be a stranger. And . . . I know it's none of my business but . . ."

I stopped midway out the door.

"Your dad always mentions you when I see him."

Something caught in my throat.

"Janie, it really *is* good to see you," I said, moving past the moment. She smiled in agreement and turned to scrape the grill.

I overheard Chip's friend as I started to pull the door closed, "These guys are freedom fighters. Sheriff don't know what the fuck he's doing—and she's just window dressing."

I let that go, too.

◆

JANIE PIERCE HAD BEEN like family when Hanna and I were girls and her concern about my dad was genuine. I sat in the Explorer, pulled my cell, and keyed in the number I'd memorized when I was five years old. Straight to voicemail:

"Greg Beckham. Leave a message."

No need to worry him. Tapping the red button, I moved on.

Sure, it would have been neater sitting in Pierces, but I made do, laying napkins across my lap as best as I could and staging the sandwich, chips, and Diet Coke within easy reach. The drive to Huntley was going to take some time, especially since I'd need to take the Old Wooster Rd. over Two Spring Mountain and come in the back way. And I needed to keep moving.

Janie had been surprised to see me. I never expected to be back in South Prescott, either. She was comfortable with her story. I considered the past eight years. They'd nearly broken me.

◆

Yeah, I'd entered the University of Chicago with a full ride. John D. Rockefeller's penitential gift to the Midwest sits on Chicago's south side and the millions of dollars he poured into the Hyde Park campus and its educational structure had paid off. It was on a par with the great schools back east: Harvard, Yale, Penn, and had been the seat of the nuclear age, with the atom being split for the first time underneath its football stadium.

"Where fun goes to die." *is the badge of honor that U of C students subscribe to.*

The proud ethnic enclaves that rebuilt Chicago after the Great Fire were absent where I grew up on the Maine coast. We'd see diversity depicted on TV, we'd profess to believe in its worth, but as far as living among real, honest-to-God people of color—it just didn't happen. In our reality, diversity meant someone was from away or maybe The County. When I arrived in Hyde Park, the surrounding neighborhoods' pluralism—Black, LatinX, Asian, LGBTQ+, emphatically urban and hip—swept over me like a gentle comber at high tide. I loved it.

Where fun goes to die? *Not on my watch. Sure, I started out strong and discovered Art History. Made the Dean's list both semesters of my first year while I got the lay of the land. Took a full load during the summer while I worked at The Oriental Institute, U of C's home to near-eastern megalithic sculpture. But, by the time Christmas in my sophomore year rolled around, I was out of control. I needed to catch up on my social life. Besides, Hanna was the one who should've gotten the scholarship and I knew I was just faking it.*

Relationships didn't last. Most girls had a BFF. I had my own, starred, BFF system: Best For Fucking. Nothing lasted. I stayed in bed. I lost my work study job at the museum, and then two other outside jobs and when I stopped going to class I was notified I had to vacate my room. I wasn't going back to my dad. I lost weight. I needed cash. Hooking was out and I was too honest for dealing. I was booted from my dorm at the end of December and found my way to a rotating series of friends' places, a couple of guys and one girl I'd gotten close to, sort-of, during the worst of the Chicago winter. I crashed on their sofas until they said, "You gotta move . . ."

By the time March roared into view I was totally out on the street, homeless, jobless, broke. I'd made my way 26 blocks north to the Illinois Institute of Technology, where I got busted a couple of times for sleeping in the Student Activity Center. I was a white girl and when I cleaned myself up I looked like I might belong, but when they asked, I didn't have any ID.

It was dusk one Friday when I found a refrigerator box on a residential side street near Sox Stadium. It was still pretty much intact; the bottom panel had been cut off and stuffed inside. I dragged it back across the 35th Street overpass and searched for the source of some steam I'd noticed wafting and evaporating that morning.

I was exhausted from schlepping the Goddamn thing and it was dark when I finally found the steam grate—in the shadows, just outside the vehicle storage area of IIT's physical plant. Concertina wire topped a chain-link fence that separated trucks and university golf carts from the narrow strip of land that ran parallel to the exit ramp for the Dan Ryan expressway. The rush of jets taking off from Midway bled into the shriek and growl of elevated Red Line trains dividing the highway and only added to the city's dull roar. The grate probably provided some kind of access to coupling things for the university's HVAC system. It didn't matter to me.

Used lumber was scatter-stacked against the vehicle storage fence for future use. It felt like a good location: still technically on campus but away from any high pedestrian traffic areas and tucked into a slot among the two-bys and plywood like a kid's fort. Unkempt shrubbery loomed along another fenceline a few yards away, planted by the university to deaden train and traffic noise from the Dan Ryan. Fat chance—thousands of cars made their presence clear as they idled in Friday-night gridlock.

I centered the box up and took a final look around. All clear. One of the few things I'd kept with me was a forest green winter parka that I'd bought before I left Maine. I zipped it tight, lifted the hood and tightened it around my head so all I could see was a circle of fur, crawled into the box, pulled the loose bottom panel inside and wedged it so it was solid, and settled in.

I was dreaming about swimming with seals when someone tugged at the open end of my new home. With the weight of my body, it didn't budge. I didn't move.

"Gene, something's in it."

"Prob'ly just fuckin' garbage," Gene replied, kicking the box and hitting my back. "Hunh. Feels pretty solid. Check it out." My fists clenched reflexively. Gene's buddy tapped the loose panel with a 2x4 and it fell in. He leaned in and pulled the panel

away, dropping it and the wood to the side. I craned my neck to get a better view, but he was backlit and in silhouette. It wasn't a cop, or even an IIT worker-guy. He wrenched the box to his left. It spun easily on the fulcrum where my hip met the grate. The peachy glow from clustered lights on the Dan Ryan seeped around a lanky kid with a brown leather jacket and a black Sox knit cap pulled tight over his ears. He reached in and grabbed for the top of my hood, "It's our lucky night, Gene! It's a girl, wrapped in a box!"

"Leave me alone!" I yelled, batting his hand away. The thrum of traffic combined with the rumble of north and south trains to drown out my call. No one was around. No one was going to hear me.

Gene's smiling face appeared looking upside-down at the open end. He was missing his upper right canine incisor. It was not an attractive look.

"Well, well. Congratulations, Tracy. It looks like we found ourselves an early St. Paddy's Day present . . . a wee girlie leprechaun! Wrapped in green and ready to grant us a wish! Top o' the . . . evenin' to ya! Erin go Bragh! and all that."

"Heh-heh." Tracy's eyes grew and he literally licked his lips.

"Leave me the fuck alone!" I screamed. I kicked the back-end of my box but it was double-layered corrugated cardboard. I was trapped.

"God works in mysterious ways, Trey," Gene said, still upside down and looking deep into the box. "We come south to score some crank and he provides recreation." He gestured to Tracy to block the opening while he moved around for access. "Hallelujah! The Lord is Good," he called to the heavens, nudging his buddy aside.

He knelt and tilted his head one way and then the other. Finally, he inquired, "What's your name, little one?"

"Fuck you." I pushed myself back into the furthest reaches of my cell and got on my knees with my fists in front of my face.

"Happy to hear you're on board with the program," said Gene with a grin. He pushed Trey aside so the light was good. Where his buddy was skinny and sort-of emaciated looking—typical tweaker—Gene had more meat on him and was a good bit bigger than me. "Trey, keep an eye out while I negotiate my wish." He leaned forward, put his hand inside the box and began to crawl in.

Tracy shoved Gene at the shoulder and almost knocked him over, but caught him by the collar and yanked him back up so they were face-to-face.

"What the fuck, Dickhead? I found her! You said it was garbage!"

"Trey... Tracy, my man. You willing to take sloppy seconds? I'll front you the cash for a couple more hits. C'mon..."

The kid considered, but not for long. "Let's see the cash first." Caveat emptor.

I started screaming. I don't know what—I was making as much noise as possible and hopping up and down on my hands and knees and rocking the box side-to-side trying to make it look alive or roll it over or something to get someone's attention. I put my shoulder to the crease and it flopped to one side and I immediately realized I was even more vulnerable. I scrambled back to all fours. Gene paid off Tracy. They made sure to block my only way out.

"Okay, baby. Get ready for some fun." He unbuckled his belt and unbuttoned his pants. He began to crawl in.

"We've got all night long."

I waited until the right moment and then, using the back of the box, I launched myself toward him, nails out, searching for his face. He was quick and caught my leading wrist with both hands. He bent it back so fast and so hard my body dove uncontrollably to the ground. I tried a roundhouse with my left but the space was too tight and I couldn't get anything behind it and, besides, he'd raised his hand so it glanced off his shoulder anyhow. Close-up, his beard framed a wall of breath that would knock over an elephant. "That's right," he soothed. "You wanna be laying down for this." He drew me toward him.

I was shouting, screaming, swatting, as he groped for the tab at the bottom of my parka. He snagged it on the first try. He pulled and the Goddamn 'convenience zipper' opened the parka to him. My upper body strength, never great, was flagging. The heat of our struggle and his rank smell were stifling. I wanted to throw up, but nothing would come. With my jacket open, his right hand went for my left boob and gave it a hard squeeze, then slid to my crotch. I caught his wrist with my free hand, trying to stop him there, hoping to bend it back. He shook it off easily and dived into my jeans and inside my pants. His eyes closed for a moment and he smiled as he found what he was searching for. I clenched my legs together and drew my free hand back and started forward with it again, but it got snagged in my jacket pocket. He was stretched-out, facing me with his stomach flat on the ground. All his weight was on his left elbow and he locked on to my right wrist. I was pinned. He forced his hand between my thighs and four fingers pushed into me as he let out an audible, "Aaaaahhh." Now he used both hands to push against me and began to raise himself and, as he did, his hand pushed deeper. I wriggled as best as I could, trying to expel it and struggled to pull my left hand out of my pocket when it found a pen I'd lifted from a petition table at the IIT Student Union. I put everything I had into it and jammed it, hard as I could, straight into his right eye, then twisted it.

"Aaarrrgghh! Oh! Oh! Oh!" He released me immediately as both hands went to his face.

"You little CUNT! Oh my fucking God, my eye – My eye – My EYE!"

"You okay Gene?" Tracy stooped to look in from his informal lookout position. Blood streamed as Gene held his hand to his face and scuttled backwards out of the box.

This was my chance. The floor of the box was slick with red and I followed as closely as I dared.

"No I'm NOT fucking OK you fucking moron! She's put my fucking eye out. Kill the bitch, Tracy! Jesus fucking Christ what-am-I-gonna-do?!"

My face hit the cool of the outside air as Tracy turned in my direction. He was conflicted. He'd been counting on his share of pussy. I surprised him with the 2x4 that he'd dropped and swept his legs out from under him. He went down on Gene, who screamed bloody murder as he desperately tried to keep his eyeball from completely detaching. Hanging on to my club, I hopped up.

Tracy reached for me, grasping to catch hold of my ankle and I took the 2x4 and swung it like Big Papi. He shrieked as his arm went limp. These two weren't going anywhere and they sure as hell weren't going to follow me. I tossed the board well away and ran.

"You fucking cunt—I will hunt you down you bitch! Trey, get my phone and call 911, I'm gonna lose this eye—I will fucking find you!" Gene shouted after me.

I traveled west across the Ryan, then south, zig-zagging through the blocks and making sure I didn't double back. After I was well away from Gene and Tracy I slowed to a fast city-walk. I didn't want to attract too much attention. Hearing a siren that sounded like it was heading to IIT, I kept walking.

I found my way to railroad tracks that serviced Metra and CTA. There, the going was easy and I followed the tracks for a couple of miles, stumbling once or twice on crossties and scuffing my hands in the process. I finally crashed in a triangle of greenery where the tracks split south and west, sitting up against an abandoned switching station shack, exhausted and uncaring. I was alone.

Twenty-seven

I'D JUST CRAMMED THE last piece of sandwich into my mouth and was negotiating a wet-nap wrapper when my phone went off. My greasy finger got no response from the screen. I wiped it on my pants and hit speakerphone.

"Buffam hur."

"That you, Beckham?"

I dropped the wet-nap and swallowed hard.

"Yeshur. Jus-a-mint . . . Yes, sir. Beckham here"

"You okay?" Latch's voice was drawn tight.

"Yeah, yeah. I'm fine, sir."

"Look, Beckham, I'm bringing in Hodgkins to handle the Fielding case."

You can't be serious. Hodgkins?

"We need to show progress. You're getting nowhere. Hodgkins knows the background on the Fielding hit and you can bring him up to speed on the twins."

Okay, I get it. You want a happy ending. But Hodgkins? C'mon.

"Beckham. You there?"

"Yes. I'm here."

"—Thought maybe I lost you on the peninsula. Gill's inside Albion again. It looks like The Professor's put the word out to his buddies from across New England. Just a sec . . .," I could hear someone in the office with Latch. There was some rustling of paper. Latch's voice echoed in the room, "Here ya go, Red." Then he was back. "You still there?"

"Yes sir. You were saying about The Professor's call out?"

"Miller and his New Albion boys are organizing a march on Augusta for Saturday. They plan to make a statement. Full tactical gear. Gill's trying to short-circuit it. The FBI is sending a couple of agents from Boston. They'll be here tonight. Where are you on the kidnapping? Did you meet with Honor Fielding like I told you?"

"Yes sir. I met with Fielding and Kringle. The kidnappers bumped the ransom by 20% and Kringle is putting that together."

"Christ. Twenty-percent of five mil. What's your sense of Kringle? He our guy?"

"No, sir. I don't think so. He was at The Landing this afternoon and I'm pretty sure he's not involved. Not that way, anyway. There's been another video sent. Did Gill show it to you?"

"No, I told you, Gill's working exclusively on New Albion. What the hell, Beckham? Can't you think for yourself and take some initiative? What part of *"You're in charge."* do you not understand?"

My mistake—I must have confused "You're in charge." with "You're on your own."

"Sir, if you'd seen the video—"

"I don't give a shit about the video. They're alive, right?"

"Yessir."

"Okay. Do you have a schedule—are we getting them back?"

"She's agreeing to the six mil. She has the routing information. The cash drop will be scheduled for tomorrow. Once they confirm the deposit, they're supposed to let her know where they'll dump the kids Saturday."

"Goddammit. Saturday." Latch considered the timing. I leaned for the wet-nap, keeping my eyes on the road.

I wanted to get ahead of Latch. "Maybe Taylor or Farber," I said, offering two names from the morning shift, "or maybe McCann could surveil the drop site, you know, use a drone at a high altitude or something . . . We need to have a strategy for the next move once we've confirmed their safety."

"Jesus, Beckham, what the hell have you been doing the past two days? If you'd kept up with email you'd know we lost the drone. I can't spare any of the guys and I need you here. Hodgkins isn't much, but at least he knows how to make some decisions. What's your current status?"

"I'm almost in Folkest—"

"I want you in Gainsborough immediately to cover any emergency calls. Come directly here and check in with Red when you arrive. Wait for Hodgkins and don't make a move until you've explained the entire situation to him. Understand?"

Yeah, I understand. Captain Hodgkins, MSP, covers your ass.

"10-4, Sheriff."

"And Beckham . . ."

"Yessir?"

"Don't screw this up."

"No sir. I won't sir."

I had no intention of going to Gainsborough. Or conferring with Hodgkins. I snagged the wet-nap, peeled back the wrapper, unfolded it as I drove, and wiped the greasy mess off my hands.

◆

THERE WAS ABOUT AN hour of daylight left as I drove through Wooster, an 18th Century mill town. Dad drove this route with the family every summer on the way to Scotty's in Huntley via the Old Wooster Road. And every summer, he'd tell us the story of Jebidiah winning 500 acres from Evi Wood in a game of euchre at the tavern. Jebidiah Wooster built a series of mills along the banks of the Schilling River, which still rushes along the edge of the town whose name he changed from Woodston to Wooster. Ten generations later, his Neo-Classical home remains in the family and overlooks the green. Numerous ells and outbuildings illustrate the growth of the Wooster influence and fortune. Dad would always finish his story by saying, "If you're gonna gamble, be prepared to lose."

I crossed over the Schilling on the stone bridge that marked the end of downtown. The old Maine Central rail line runs with the river, crossing and re-crossing it as it heads north and south from the village. I slowed to a stop. Someone was fixing up the Wooster Station. A handmade sign with a fundraising thermometer was about three-quarters full toward the goal of $700,000. Even in the fading light of day, I could tell the bricks had been powerwashed and tuck-pointed. *They just might make it.*

I jogged right and drove about a hundred yards. In autumn, folks from away would heed the MeDoT sign emblazoned with colorful maple and other native leaves, and follow the picturesque brook that winds north to Bangor. In spring, bird watchers might head in the opposite direction where the river broadens and catches the watershed as it continues south to Gainsborough and its confluence with the Coaticook.

It was winter. The river was frozen. Work on the Station was at a standstill. I was heading up and over Two Spring Mountain and it was silhouetted by the western sky. I pulled up to the deeply rutted railroad crossing where the tracks mark the terminus of Old Wooster Rd. There were no gates. People were expected to be responsible. I looked both ways as my cruiser jounced this way, then that, negotiating the slight rise of the track bed.

◆

It had been a challenge, living on the streets. The morning after my attack I'd awakened to the squeal of a CTA train as it bit into the steel curve near my resting place. The early March sun delivered meager warmth through my parka. I cleaned up a little using some meltwater I came across in a nearby pile of tires and made my way to the street below. The spatters on my pants could be explained away as paint as long as I wasn't talking to a cop. After a brief reconnoiter, I realized I'd landed in the Bridgeport neighborhood, a district of old and newer factory and industrial buildings where I'd attended a few raves over the past 18 months. Pershing Avenue, part of Daniel Burnham's plan of Chicago, ran east and west one block north of me. It acted as a dividing line between new industry—trailer yards and mammoth warehouses that served the burgeoning over-the-road shipping business—and blocks of Chicago bungalows. I'd been told the neighborhood was Hispanic. One thing I'd learned during my brief time in the City of Big Shoulders was that, although it professed to be colorblind, the subtle outlines of its neighborhoods were strict and inviolable.

I established an informal rule not to go north of Pershing nor east of the Dan Ryan. There were no guarantees, but I didn't want to risk running into Gene or Tracey. It meant summer was stifling—no lakefront time for me. My perch over Halsted served me well and I figured out how to generate a little income. I tried hawking Streetwise, the local paper devoted to helping out homeless folks, but there was no Location Location Location that had real foot traffic and it's tough to make money when you accost folks by saying, "Buy my Goddamn newspaper!" I made money selling some plasma and gathering cans—there were a couple of places that actually saved their cans for me—Miss Congeniality and all—and I got lucky and scrounged some used camping equipment from a Goodwill store.

Someone told me that Katie was the girl's name that was most trusted, so I became Katie O'Shaughnessy. I wasn't homeless, just between homes, and occasionally I'd hang with other folks who were embracing this life. We were independent. We were striving for more and better, just like everyone else. There were those of us who had addiction issues, but somehow I was able to avoid the worst of that. We'd check in on one another but I never let anyone visit me or my fortress of solitude.

November arrived and I got rousted from my home by railroad workers conducting a walking inspection of the tracks. They'd been burned the previous winter by frozen switches and were trouble-shooting. What pissed me off is the crew walked through all nice and friendly, "Hey wow, cool place you got here . . . How long you been here? . . . Where's your garage? Hah-Hah." And then Metra Police arrived early one morning a couple of days later; blew through the wall of tires I'd carefully arranged to appear randomly stacked and took all my shit, just threw it on the sidewalk and said, "Move this stuff or lose it." It was already November. If they'd done this in August I could've found a place, but all the good spots were taken, and I didn't want to move into any of the encampments—much too much people.

Flurries were beginning to stick on the pavement and I sat on a retaining wall looking at what was left of my life. A woman walked a little white dog along the other side of the street. I'd seen the two of them before. Twenty minutes later, they came up my side. They stopped.

"So, what happened?" she asked. Her simple question, asked with genuine interest in a voice that was lightly accented, struck a chord and I broke down. What was

truly surprising is that she didn't leave. She stood and listened as I bawled. Her dog lay at my feet. She pulled a Kleenex out of her pocket and by the time I was done crying, a light coating of snow covered the sidewalk. She looked down at her dog who responded with an affirmative glance.

"If you want, you can spend the night at our place, get a shower, do your laundry. Tomorrow will be better," she said.

"Yes. Thank you." I hadn't realized how emotionally spent I was until that moment.

I gathered the most portable elements of my stuff and left the rest. We knew most of it would be gone the next day. My single night was extended to two, then a week, then two. Lt. Maria "Mama" Torres left me alone—somehow, she trusted me, something I hadn't encountered for a while. She worked in the 9th District office of the CPD. She apologized for what happened when I was rousted. Coming from her, it seemed real.

Over time, over coffee, over her hand-rolled tamales, we shared our stories. She had married late. She'd pulled over Hector Torres because his brake lights weren't working. When she said she was going to issue a citation, he began to argue with her, "How am I s'posed to know my brake lights aren't working? I don' see them when I'm driving!"

He'd contested the ticket and she'd appeared in court to defend the citation. When the bailiff announced Hector's case, he stood, thanked Maria, showed the receipt for the repaired lights, paid the fine, and asked her to dinner. The courtroom erupted in applause and after the judge regained order, she pointed her gavel to Torres and asked simply, "Well?" Torres was wary, but everyone in the courtroom expected her to say yes, so she agreed. He charmed her with stories of growing up in Chicago's Pilsen neighborhood and funny/touching songs he would compose on-the-spot and sing in an exquisite tenor as they said good-bye. There were weeks of dating before he kissed her and when he did, she melted.

Hector had served in the Army in his 20s and was teaching biology at a magnet science and fine arts school in Pilsen when he was called up in 2003 by the Illinois National Guard. He drove an unprotected Humvee that hit an IED early in the deployment. The three other soldiers recovered. Hector didn't. She and Hector hadn't gotten around to having kids. She took me in.

The Chicago Police Department's strained community relations, particularly on the South Side, have been widely acknowledged, but Maria Torres was a police officer who fully embraced the role of "Protect and Serve." To gain insight into her work, I'd go on ride-alongs with her whenever my schedule permitted, which meant my days off from my job as a go-fer at a warehouse were spent riding in a cruiser. I saw how hard she worked to earn the trust of everyone she encountered, from teens to the elderly, from gang-kid wannabes to hardcore gang-bangers, from cops to citizens. She understood that building mutual respect required picking her battles and being willing to let some things slide. Her approach was to give people a chance, even if they initially hated or mistrusted her. Maria recognized that beating someone five times wasn't the way to build helping-hands.

I once saw her skillfully de-escalate a tense situation involving Latino teens on the verge of a conflict with a rival gang over territory. Through active listening, good-natured banter, and genuine respect, she succeeded in getting them to abandon their bravado and express their concerns. It turned out they sought a safe route for girls traveling from school to a museum in the rival gang's territory. Leveraging her community contacts, she texted the rival gang boss and arranged a secure meeting between him and the indie-group's leader. Though I didn't attend, the lieutenant was content with the result: "No casualties. It's progress, Allie." Implicit was her awareness that, having facilitated the meeting, she knew all involved parties and their associates. This meant she could swiftly identify responsible individuals if anything went south.

I'd been living with her and Maestro, her Bichon Frise, for eight months when I announced I wanted to test for the Chicago Police Department. She was guarded in her response and questioned me like I was some kind of mope. I convinced her I was sincere. She offered to front me the cash for the application and tuition, but I told her I'd saved enough for that. She insisted I see a dentist—my teeth hadn't been worked on for five years and were killing me—and I said yes and she paid out of pocket for that. Once I started at CPD, I found a room on 57th Street and we got together at least twice a month. I owed her, literally and figuratively.

◆

I PAUSED THE EXPLORER after clearing the tracks. Old Wooster Rd. loomed just past my hood. Dispatching a plow to this monster was an afterthought for the county and it showed. No switchbacks in 1750—just up and over.

Here we go.

I hit the 4x4 low button and nosed onto the incline. It was like driving the wrong way on a ski jump. The gravel surface was rough before the blizzard and since then, the ice-pack had been compressed from snowmobilers and more adventurous motorists. Five deer darted into my headlights, coming over the stacked stone wall that lined both shoulders. They continued up the road, taking the path of least resistance. The deer had been gleaning leftovers from an ancient apple orchard on the right and their hooves dug easily into the glazed surface as they bounded away over the hill much faster than my cruiser could manage safely, even with studded tires on all four wheels.

I didn't have a plan. I knew from my conversation with Latch and earlier email and radio traffic that the FBI agents weren't expected to arrive until after midnight. Gill was back inside New Albion, trying to convince Miller Sr. that going to Augusta was a bad idea. Hodgkins hadn't arrived in Gainsborough yet.

The waxing-gibbous moon reflected large in the rearview mirror as the cruiser crested the mountain. I killed my lights. Powderhorn Lake opened to me as a pale white crescent that stretched to the north. I braked lightly and began my descent. About 200 yards down, I picked up some reflection from taillights off to my right and slowed. There was an unofficial pull-off where an early settler's cape once stood. Fifteen vehicles —SUVs and pickups—were parked haphazardly in the open space surrounding the stone slab foundation. I pulled off the road to check it out. There wasn't anyone around.

The northwest wind that came up and over the mountain made my eyes water as I waded into the informal parking area. There had been a lot of activity here and the snow mess revealed multiple occupants had departed from a number of the vehicles. Snowshoe tracks consolidated and moved away from the cluster in a rough line, crossed the field, then entered the woods heading downhill and, presumably, to New Albion. Reinforcements. A number of the tracks featured flattened, shallow U-shaped impressions that followed the footfalls—sled paths—that came together like tributaries at the trail leading downhill. This let me know the guys were bringing in . . . what? Canned goods? Artillery? I returned to the Explorer, popped the hatch, and checked my arsenal. I was supposed to have a Taser but Chuckles told Match, "I don't want Beckham to be issued a Taser until she's been trained and qualified." *So much for previous experience.* There was a box for a dozen flares, of which only two remained, and a pair of men's snowshoes and poles. Oh, and the snow shovel stationed in the shotgun rack. I got back in and positioned the cruiser to block any potential retreat, strapped on the snowshoes, jammed the flares into my back pocket and the energy bars into my jacket, took a deep pull from my water bottle, and followed the tracks into the woods.

The sleds had helped define the trail somewhat and, with the almost-full moon at my back, the going wasn't so bad, once I got used to the size of the 'shoes. It led me down, steeply at times, to an old logging road that probably came from the parking area near the beach. The road was groomed for cross-country skiing and ran along one of the ridges overlooking the lake. I could make out a couple of year-rounders' homes at Powderhorn's northwestern terminus throwing amber light through the open tree cover. They were close to a mile away. The only sound was my breathing and the *schupp-schupp, tick-tick* of the snowshoes and poles that documented my progress.

◆

IT'S TRUE THAT MAINE has one of the lowest crime rates—across the board—of any state in the U.S. and that was a big reason for my return home. Law enforcement should be easy—be honest, be fair, keep the peace, follow the law and stay within the regs—simple. Assigned to the Auburn Gresham district on Chicago's south side and armed with Mama's insight, I gradually learned to navigate the riptide of crime and corruption, social responsibility and enforcement that defines big-city policing. I wasn't too surprised when my first partner, John Kelly, was convicted for participating in a car-theft ring. He was arrested about nine months after we'd been thrown together. I was questioned. His last words to me were, "Hope yer happy, you fuckin' goody-two-shoes."

I had two kid-partners in quick succession—neither lasted more than a year. McCarrick and Trina were younger than me, just out of high-school. McCarrick quit and Trina, she moved to the 'burbs. One guy, Michel Dufas seemed to be a good cop. I don't know if he requested a transfer or whether it came down from above, but he moved north after about a year and a half and I lost track of him.

The vast majority of folks who live on the far south side of Chicago try to make it work: keep a decent roof over their heads; feed their kids; keep them in school and out of the gangs that permeate almost every aspect of their lives. Everyone is swimming upstream in one of the most expensive cities in the Midwest where an abandoned block with scattered architectural remnants might segue into well-maintained frame houses and then shift abruptly to broken-down mansions and buildings occupied only intermittently. Because of generations of willful neglect, there were relentless confrontations with residents who were angry about being underserved and sick of heavy-handed policing. And then there were the legitimately bad people who made their living completely outside the law.

Steve Doyle was the partner that had 'stuck'—we were together for almost four years. He was older and married with a couple of kids. His wife, Nancy, and I got along okay until we didn't. Doyle was one of those cops who was always pressuring for little favors—a taco here, free passport photos there. He berthed a big cabin-cruiser at Burnham Harbor. I wondered how he paid for that and the slip that went with it. In the end, it turned out he was using the boat to bang the Captain's wife. She worked for the Park District and had zeroed out his slip fees as part of their arrangement.

It was the week after Thanksgiving and too cold to snow. I'd taken and passed the Detective test and was waiting for something to open up—maybe Santa would be good to me. Doyle had committed us to babysit a holiday party at Alderman Tickman's place for overtime. I was a little pissed but, since I didn't really have a private life and needed the cash, went along with it. Tickman was a promising young pol who folks thought might go places. After Barack, anything was possible.

We turned on to his block and the first thing I saw were the extensive light displays set up on the two empty, well-maintained lots that flanked his three-story, contemporary greystone. Traffic was stop-and-go on the narrow street as couples dressed in fashionable holiday finery streamed up the stairs to Tickman's wreathed front door. Parking was at a premium. We cruised past a permanent No Parking zone the alderman had wrangled in front of the house and I commented on the Bergman's Glass Company van with mirrored windows directly across from the party. "Yeah, blends right in," observed Doyle with a smile. We circled the block and caught a break when an early departure opened a space on the alderman's side of the street, four slots up from the greystone. Doyle expertly parallel-parked our Explorer and we settled in. The vantage point offered a good look at the sidewalk and wide steps leading steeply up to the front door. We didn't have any responsibility, just your friendly CPD hangin' in the 'hood.

It was getting well-past 10 p.m. and the party was going strong. Da Bears were on track for another below .500 season so there wasn't much to talk about there. Doyle was droning on about how he'd gotten Nancy a new set of cookware for Christmas when eight carolers—two of whom I recognized from my time on the street—and Pastor Reggie from the Mt. Zion Missionary Baptist Church along with his wife Eileen, strolled down the block singing "Joy to the World." I'd heard about their music program for homeless adults when I was 'camping.' Reggie and Eileen dedicated themselves to making people whole again and the Lord's music was their vehicle.

I told Doyle to crack my window so we could hear better, which he did after grumbling that he was "too fucking cold already." The Alderman opened his door for a departing guest and then waved the rest of the party to the stoop. While they gathered, the singers got organized and launched into a soulful rendition of "Go Tell It on the Mountain." The carolers loved the genuine attention. They were beaming and sounded great. With their clouds of breath highlighted by the holiday lights flanking Tickman's house and on down the block, the scene was straight out of a Hallmark movie.

About that time, a hulking black GMC Yukon pulled up to the curb behind the choir. An expensively dressed couple emerged. The man, whose neck was heavily tattooed, helped his companion. She took a moment to adjust what little clothing she was wearing while he dismissed the driver and then they moved, hand-in-hand, to the curb and on to the steps. The babe was having a little difficulty negotiating the risers in 6-inch heels and her escort was being patient. Doyle moved reflexively upon seeing this guy and his doll. From there everything happened very fast.

The Yukon pulled away and turned the corner as the two continued up the stairs. I saw the Alderman's face go south for a moment, then he began to shoo his guests back inside. Simultaneously, there was other action on the street —a graphite-black Explorer with tinted windows two cars down and across from us began to move. Both its passenger windows dropped open. Gun barrels emerged and rested on the sills.

"Gun!" I shouted inside the car. No one outside heard me.

Doyle sat, frozen. Then quietly said, "Motherfucker," pulled his weapon and reached for the door handle.

The flashy couple was halfway up the stairs. Alderman Tickman didn't appear to be welcoming them. He pulled a final, reluctant guest inside and slammed the door shut.

"Police! Get DOWN!" I shouted as I burst from the car, weapon drawn. Bullets were already streaming indiscriminately. The party couple fell, bouncing and rolling down the steeply angled stairway to the pile of homeless people below. The shooting was over by the time I made it to Tickman's No Parking area. The SUV was gone. Tickman needn't have worried about entertaining his unwanted guests. They were dead. Doyle called it in as, sure enough, FBI guys jumped out of the Bergman Glass Co. van and helped with first aid. Pastor Reggie had been killed shielding Eileen. One of my two acquaintances in the group, we called him 'Sarge' but his real name was Tom Clark, died before the ambulance arrived. Several others were wounded. Doyle never got off a shot—there were too many people, he said in his statement, and that was the only true thing he said for the next two weeks. The Romeoville police found what they thought was the Explorer two days later, torched and in a heap near the Des Plaines River. There was an investigation that uncovered the boat, the banging, and a whole host of other infractions, major and minor, that Steve Doyle had racked up. I wasn't willing to stand with him and profess his limited innocence. I found a ripe, dead rat in my locker. Things went to hell

for him and Tickman, and I decided I'd had enough of Chicago. I was cleared by mid-January and as soon as that happened, I went to the library and Googled "Police Opportunities, Maine." Chamberlain County came up.

Kismet.

◆

I *SCHUPPED* ACROSS THE logging road and continued to follow broken snow that led to the shore where it disappeared into the deepening twilight. Lights, occasional mechanical sounds, and indistinct movement at New Albion meant there was plenty of activity going on. I needed a place to crash for a couple of hours. On my way down the mountain I'd noticed one or two rocky outcroppings that might provide some shelter, but no warmth. I looked across the lake to the camp again. Once I crossed, I couldn't hunker down and would need to keep moving. Now that I was at ice-level I could make out three blobs against the snow cover. The ice shacks. One had a pickup truck next to it. I wasn't going there. The second one was close to the truck shack. Buddies. If I was breaking and entering, I didn't want anybody to hear me. I ignored the snowshoe path and headed for the third that stood several hundred yards down the lake in the opposite direction.

I circled the shack at a distance. There was a quirky look about it. A single window was cut into the eastern-facing long side but that wasn't the quirky part. The structure itself was sort-of trapezoidally shaped on the short ends. If you threw a couple of candy canes on it, you would've had a dead-ringer for Cindy Lou Who's house, complete with rooftop snow-drifts.

When I got close enough, reflected light began to provide more detail. I could see wooden skid-skis were mounted fore and aft with an ingenious system of wheels – two to a side – that could be levered and locked into place and would raise the entire structure for the road. Split and cured firewood was cut to eight-inch lengths and was stacked in a tidy pile along one side.

Promising.

It was Thursday night. No one was home. A jigsaw cutout of a pickerel in typical trophy mid-jump was mounted above the door with a sign that said,

"Bite Me." It was cute. Not too many people lock their doors in rural Maine. They probably should. I undid the latch and, pulling my phone at half-flashlight power, stepped in.

The weak beam bounced back from stainless steel cladding in the far corner and silhouetted a shape that could have been Darth Vader's head chomping on a cigar. Rigid blue-foam insulation peeked from behind knotty-pine paneling and made the space a little tighter than expected. Kelly-green indoor-outdoor carpet—like you'd see at a putt-putt golf park—lined the floor. A bench occupying the long side, opposite the window, had well-organized storage cubbies underneath. I found a stack of the mini-firelogs, newspaper, and a box of strike-anywhere matches inside a zip-lock baggie stuffed with those little "dry packets" you get in pills and stuff. I needed to conserve my phone's battery and killed the flashlight and struck a match. In the flame's bloom I could see that Darth was actually a propane tank that had been brilliantly repurposed as a tiny woodstove. His cigar was a spiral of steel—a salvaged cooling coil from a welder's chipping hammer—and worked as the lever for the stove's door. Once the match died, I let my eyes adjust to whatever moonlight came from the window. I felt around on the floor and found a couple of tabs—three, actually—that opened trap doors to the ice and water. I pulled one and reached down into the black until my hand caught the wet. The cold felt good when I splashed some on my face. I continued exploring. There was a springloaded jumpseat that could be clipped down from the wall near the door and would accommodate a third person, and a hinged bunk that was pulled tight up against the ceiling. It would hang, cantilevered on chains, when in use.

I decided against lighting a fire. Even though it was unlikely anyone would notice the smoke rising from the chimney, its smell might alert the wrong person and I didn't want anyone snooping around my temporary home. I counted links and fastened the chains over the hooks on the outside corners of the extra bunk and lowered it carefully into place, figuring it would be better for me to have the high ground if someone decided to visit. I was pleased to discover blankets that had been thoughtfully folded and laid onto the thin mattress. I clambered up, confirmed that my phone was silenced and set it to buzz at 11:30, and settled in.

Almost like home.

Twenty-eight

"UUunhh!"

My forehead smacked against the roofline as I reacted to the phone buzzing in my chest pocket. I fumbled the damn thing and it tumbled to the floor, landing face-down and *zzz-zzz-zzz-ing*. Its faint outline was the only light inside the cabin.

Zzz-zzz-zzz.

It crawled across the fuzzy carpet like a bug. The moon's arc had taken it to the far side of the shack and whatever glimmer of light that had dusted the interior earlier was gone.

Zzz-zzz-zzz.

I sort-of oriented myself, turned and started to climb down but caught my boot on the lower bench and fell, landing hard on my back with the *zzz-zzz-zzz-ing* underneath. I rolled, wheezing, and silenced the phone. Then, for good measure, I turned it off completely. I didn't need Tommy delVecchio calling to chat about the weather.

I felt through my stuff while I sat on the bench eating an energy bar: cuffs, baton, H&K pistol—loaded, extra magazine, flares, all-purpose Leatherman tool—*Okay, I might need a screwdriver sometime*—pepper spray, hi-intensity flashlight—I held my hand over the end so it wouldn't throw light when I tested it. Check.

In Chicago, I'd packed a 9mm ankle backup. Mama suggested it and we found a sweet, "pre-owned" Ruger that she bought as a present for my first day at CPD. I pawned it for moving money when I left the city. No need for something like that in Chamberlain County.

Locating the blankets, I folded them, placed them back on the mattress, and used the pulley system to hoist the bunk back into place. There. I said goodbye to *Hotel Lago Vista*, strapped on my 'shoes, secured the door, and turned my eyes toward New Albion. It looked quiet. A few pole lights glowed in what I guessed were common areas. The shore was dark. I was careful to stay away from hummocks and black spots that radiated dark lines indicating soft or thin surfaces. When my path intersected the troops' snowshoe trail across the lake, I stopped to get my bearings. Their tracks probably led to the summer waterfront activity area. I continued in the direction I was already headed, planning to make land well south of the waterfront, in case lookouts were posted. It was cold as hell and my guess was that, if anyone was tasked with guarding from this direction, they'd probably said, *"To hell with this."* and found someplace warm. When I got about 25 feet from shore I slowed, testing with each step. The last thing I wanted was to go into this with wet feet.

After what felt like 15 minutes of approach/avoidance, I made land. The snow-shoes were helpful, but the brushy incline made progress difficult and without the reinforcements' groomed track through the woods, my progress was noticeably slower. I moved as quietly as I could, picking my way over downed trees and dodging branches and trying to keep an eye toward where I thought the road was. The moon was directly overhead. I came to a place where the worn, open width of a summertime shortcut reflected more brightly than the dense overgrowth edging it. The path made travel easier and I continued on, believing it would eventually intersect with the road.

I tried to imagine the map Chelsea and I had reviewed. I backtracked a little and moved off the path to the right. Twenty-five yards in, the terrain turned sharply steeper. I got on my hands and knees, which is not easy in snowshoes, then grabbed the base of an oak sapling and used it to inch my way up. I was at the road's shoulder. I peered over.

I found myself on the outside of the curve that wrapped around the bunkhouse. The dirt road was well-plowed—probably by the guy who gave me the finger a couple nights ago—and the raw hardscrabble reflected texture wherever the sun had reached through the ice. From my position, the road dropped right and to the lake, but leveled out and followed a gentle upslope left to the main buildings and common area. The bunkhouse space heater burned kerosene and the crisp air was marked with its exhaust. I thanked whoever winterized the building—with insulation and double-paned windows I couldn't hear the 30-50 guys snoring. And they couldn't hear me. I watched for a long time but nothing moved. I decided to use the road and hoped everyone's bladder would get them through the night. I unclipped the snowshoes and then, keeping low, scrambled up, stood, and moved quickly up the hill, trying to walk like a guy in case someone was watching.

The plan I'd come up with, such as it was, was to check Wren's Nest first for the twins and then move on to 30 Rock if they weren't there. In and out with no one the wiser. Beyond that, I wasn't sure. Ducking behind a tool shed, I inspected my pepper spray and shoved it into my jacket pocket. Chicago had taught me that it was too easy to shoot someone if the gun was in your hand. I decided to leave the snowshoes and poles. From what I could tell so far, most of the heavily-trafficked areas had been cleared and if I needed to make a getaway with the kids, well, snowshoes weren't exactly the fastest way to travel. I had a little time as long as no one discovered me, so I took a moment.

The area where the guys were marching when they opened fire on the drone—Chelsea called it "The Commons"—was at least another 30 yards up the slope. It was lit by a couple of vintage mercury vapor lights on telephone poles and they threw everything outside its perimeter into deep shadow. The broad front of 30 Rock began across the open area and to my right. Its darkened windows reflected a blank view of the well-lit Commons. I judged the space to be about 25 or 30 yards wide and extending maybe 50 yards from the Camp Office down to where the tree-line rimmed the hill above the lake. A couple of other service buildings stood in the shadow of 30 Rock.

Fluorescent fixtures inside the camp office accentuated the darkness on my left. Their light splashed onto a wide porch and I sensed someone, maybe multiple someones, were inside. I kept my eyes on its door as I stole back across the road again, then navigated from tree to tree and onward to the rear of the building. I was close enough to hear voices murmuring through the wall, but couldn't make anything out. I kept my body flat and tight against the fieldstone chimney that backed the structure as I moved in the darkness. Arriving at the corner, I knelt, using my right hand for balance against the rough-hewn stone foundation. Wren's Nest sat directly across a plowed single-lane roadway.

My session with Chelsea continued to be invaluable. She'd pointed out Wren's Nest's distinctive 90° L-shaped footprint. Chelsea said the folks at Camp Wiki had divided the L where the foot met the riser, so there were two spaces with a door between them. A light was on in the long section. A pull-shade was down on the double-wide window of what would be the 'foot.' The walkway from the lane to the front door wasn't shoveled, just dimpled lightly with a few footprints. So this was a space New Albionites weren't invited to.

The road before me led to The Commons and was mostly exposed to its illumination. I watched for movement, then took a breath and zipped across, finding my way to a corner that was in shadow. I knelt again and settled for a moment. I'd tried to glimpse what was inside as I scampered across. There was a bed—probably the bed they'd used for the twins' video—topped by a sleeping bag with someone in it. Beyond that, I had bupkis.

I crept around back and found a backdoor flanked by a pair of windows to the lighted section, confirming Chelsea's report. The snowcover was hard and slick from roofmelt that had refrozen. I moved to the far window in the corner, giving me a better overall view inside.

I squatted and gripped the sill, then pulled myself up. The new-ish wall dividing the two sections extended from where I stood to the opposite interior side. There was a door about three-quarters of the way down. It was closed. A broadcast-quality video camera sat on a pro-tripod that was pushed into the far corner, beyond the door. Unfinished sheetrock stopped halfway up the exterior wall and the aqua-blue of rigid foam insulation, inserted between vertical pine studs, set up a cool/warm visual rhythm. The Wiki folks had only gotten so far in their reno of this building—windows were the original nine-over-nine, double hung. It was as if they'd abandoned the project that afternoon. A pair of sawhorses topped by a plywood rectangle stood over an open five-gallon container of drywall compound. A hawk gooped with years'-old dried and cracked compound, brown with accumulated rust, leaned on the makeshift table, with nondescript hand tools scattered. Smears of drywall mud were left unsanded. I scanned back to the camera; a couple of equipment suitcases and a duffle for the tripod were splayed on the floor. A cheap ceramic heater, which I presumed was providing some warmth, sat near that stuff. Panning to the right again, Piglet poked his head above the bed. A round café table with three chairs and some leftover food on paper plates was hard up against the back door I had just crawled past.

Shifting my weight for a better look was a mistake. Both feet crunched through the snow and I dropped six inches, hitting my chin on the sill. I ducked and listened for any movement from inside. Nothing. I inched my way up again and tested my footing before fully exposing my face to the light. Feet seemed solid. I continued my inventory. A cooler had been drafted into service as a side-table and sat next to the bed. Light was supplied by a lone bulb hanging from a three-foot cord in the center of the room. A mounded-up, rusty-orange sleeping bag lay on the bed, its occupant's back facing my way. The cooler caught my attention again. There was a nine-millimeter pistol laying with the guy's wallet and keys. His coat and boots were strewn on the bare wood floor.

The foot of the "L" began to my left.

I crawled back and around the next corner. According to Chelsea, there would be a double-wide window at this end, matching the one I had seen from my surveillance behind the Office.

Bingo.

I found the sill and used it to stand slowly. My eyes were still adjusting from the brightness of the other space, but I was happy to see that since this window was on the rear, untrafficked, side of the building, it was uncovered.

The frigid glow emitted by the mercury vapor fixtures on The Commons filtered through and around the window-shade hanging at the opposite end. Two more, uncovered, windows along the left wall allowed incidental light and separated a trio of bunkbeds that jutted into the space. Dim illumination from the main room fanned out from under the door and threw a fourth bunk into silhouette. No tables. No chairs.

I examined the three bunkbeds. The vantage point of the window didn't give me much elevation—the floor of the cabin was raised over a crawlspace on stacked stone piers and the window sill was only about 18 inches above that—but there was an occupied sleeping bag on the bed nearest to me and, from what I could tell—or maybe it was wishful thinking—another in the next bunk.

Trevor and Celeste.

I reviewed my options. They weren't many. I could go in the front door, pepper-spray whoever was there, cuff 'em, hope there might something around to gag 'em with, and try to drag the kids out while the guy was banging around all over the place . . .

Or I could try the window and hope to get in, rouse the twins without making noise, leave via the window and make our escape.

My window was actually two nine-over-nines side-by-side that were split by a double jamb. I tried raising the left one, figuring it was closest to the bunks. No movement. Same with the other. Probably painted shut. I looked to the windows separating the bunk bed trio. Entering there would expose me to The Commons. I crept around the corner and stopped at the first one, noting that it was conveniently in the shadow of a mammoth, volunteer oak that had sprung up ages ago.

I pushed as gently as I could on one of the dividers that separated the panes horizontally. Soft splinters of dry-rotted wood crumbled with the upward pressure. I used my hip to dust off my glove and then peeled them both and jammed them into my jacket pockets. The snowcrust buckled but held as I shifted my stance. I shuffled my boots a little to make sure I was solid, reached, and pushed again on the second divider with my bare right hand. I felt a little give to the weight of the window and pushed a little harder. The window began to rise. I let it slide shut and looked down, hoping to find something in the snow to prop it open. I felt around blindly under the building's footprint, past the snowline, next to one of the piers. The back of my hand grazed something smooth. Here was a stout stick, no bark. Probably used as a prop for generations.

I raised the window and slipped it into the corner of the sill. A warm stink flowed over me as I used the pier to get a leg up. I boosted myself and—with a little awkward movement—was able to—mostly quietly—enter the room.

The thick smell of human waste made me heave, but I choked it back. The twins slept easily in their bags; they were used to it. Duct tape covered their eyes and mouth. Their bare arms were outside the bags and loosely zip-tied to the rails. Another ceramic heater chugged away in the far corner, offering a little heat and some white-noise cover. It was close to an unemptied 5-gallon shop bucket like you'd find at a big-box home supply store. I'd wake Trevor first, figuring he'd be likely to make a fuss and would need the most attention. As I bent over him, my foot grazed what I figured was a duffle stashed under the bed. Very gently, I placed my hand over the duct tape at his mouth.

The cold startled him and he immediately began squealing. I pushed harder on his mouth, and, as tenderly as possible, given his struggling, placed my other hand on his cheek. I whispered, "Shhhh. I'm here to help you." He quieted.

Celeste's head popped up from the mattress and turned toward the sound, but she was quiet.

I yanked the tape from Trevor's eyes, then Celeste's. They blinked and stared wide-eyed. I held my index finger to my lips, pointed to my badge, then mimed cutting the zip ties, getting dressed and exiting through the window. They nodded their understanding. I pulled the all-purpose tool and began to open the knife but heard the main door open roughly, followed by heavy footsteps.

I froze.

Someone kicked the cot in the other room. "Breezy, wake up!"

"Uh, whaaa?"

"Get your ass outta bed." Rustling, the sleeping bag being shaken.

"Ummm. Okay, okay. I'm awake! What's with the towels?"

"I need you to take the kids and get 'em showered and dressed. You're moving out at 1:30."

"Whaaa?" Confused.

"Yeah. Get yer ass in gear. Everything's set. C'mon, get dressed. And when was the last time you emptied that bucket? *Christ-all-fucking-mighty* it stinks in here!"

I heard the visitor move to one of the chairs, pull it away from the table and take a seat to wait for Breezy.

Jack Gill.

More rustling. Breezy's feet on the floor.

"Fuckin'-A, Jack. I was just dreaming about Celeste's tits. Have you seen them? They are *perfection*—"

"Yeah, yeah, nice tits. I don't give a Goddamn about Celeste's fuckin' tits. And neither do you. Got it?"

"I got it." Dejected.

My head was swimming. The twins were on their elbows staring at me in terror.

I mimed putting the duct tape over their eyes and then put my palms together next to my head and mimed sleeping. I had to get out of there—two guys were way too much for me to deal with, given the situation. Sure, I could come at them with the pepper spray but the 9mm on the cooler meant they were serious and there was no guarantee I'd get 'em both with my first shot. And with at least 40 ready-to-overthrow-the-government-right-wing-free-dom fighters less than 100 yards away, I didn't like my odds of getting out whole. Trevor was shaking and would have begged me to stay if he could have spoken. Celeste lay her head back down and closed her eyes. I replaced her tape. Trevor fought it but finally laid his head down. I managed to slip through the window and drop it just before someone came through the door.

The crawlspace. I flattened myself and rolled under. Leaves from who-knows-how-many-autumn seasons shifted and crinkled in my ear as I tried to compose myself. I hoped my body muffled their sound. Breezy and Gill's footfall sounded overhead. Their attention was elsewhere.

Light jumped through open spaces between some of the boards above me. "Wake up, kids!" *It's your best friend, Jack Gill!*

"We're gonna get you cleaned up, then go for a ride," Gill called. I was directly under him. This didn't jibe with a Saturday exchange.

He worked on cutting the zip ties. Soon I could hear general movement—beds creaking, mattresses compressing. The kids murmured as though they were just waking up.

"Sit up, both of you," Gill commanded.

"I'll get *him*," he directed. "You take *her*. C'mon, sit up Godammit!" to the twins. "We'll need to dress 'em decent after the shower. They're not coming back here. Hang on to their jackets. I don't want them getting any ideas."

"Christ I'm glad I don't have kids." Breezy.

Gill embraced his role as a foster dad. "C'mon, put your hands through the sleeves. Thaaaat's right. Jeezus, you'd think he was retarded." He stumbled and the bunk moved on the floor as he caught himself.

Slap!

Someone fell to the floor.

Trevor was sniffling. "Don't you ever, *ever*, hit me again, you little shit!" Gill hollered, then threatened, "You're lucky I don't cut your balls off."

I tried to imagine what it might be like to be dressed by a stranger, my mouth and eyes taped shut. Celeste was suddenly making guttural noises. She was upset.

"Goddammit Breezy—," Gill started across the room. "I'll chop your fucking hands off if—" and then he stopped. He took a couple of steps toward my wall and it got quiet.

Presently, I heard him rustle around in a bag—probably one of the duffles. "Give her to me. You finish with him—and don't think you can fuck with Breezy just because you know him," he said in an aside to Trevor. "Get 'im dressed. Here—." I heard someone stumble across the floor and I let out my breath. "I put some fresh underwear in this bag. It's got their jackets. Take it with you for after the shower."

"All work and no play makes Jack a dull boy," Breezy observed and laughed at his joke.

General movement.

"So, what's the program for Saturday?" Breezy asked. *Just two guys talkin' shop.*

"Latch and The Professor. What a pair. I've convinced Latch these guys are standing down and The Professor believes Latch has agreed to a march in Augusta. When they try to convoy outta here Saturday morning—guns and gear ready to go—it should be a shitshow.

"He's ready," Breezy said, finished with Trevor. "What about you?"

"I'll be ready. The Sheriff has already told Augusta that MSP should be on call for reinforcements if necessary. He'll never be elected again after this mess. You got the duffle? Don't forget this. Okay, let's go." I heard the kids stumble again as they were pushed to the door.

"You're coming, right?" Breezy asked.

"No, you take 'em. I've gotta update Latch. And keep your Goddamn hands off the girl."

They moved out of the bunk area and into the space where I'd first seen Breezy. They stopped in the vicinity of the bed. Breezy needed his jacket. I heard him scrabbling with stuff on the cooler. The front door opened and closed several times and then it was quiet. I was still under the floor.

Twenty-nine

THERE WAS ONLY ONE shower on campus that was winterized. They were heading to Angel Falls. I rolled from under the cabin and crawled back to where I'd first seen the twins through the double window. According to Chelsea, the showers could be accessed along a connecting path that led from my side of Wren's Nest, off to the right and past the back-end of 30 Rock, and on down to the new Dining Hall. Her cabin had been one of three located near the former Hobby Nook and she let me know the girls used the back path to race to breakfast after sleeping in. Breezy was taking the kids the easy way, across the plowed Commons where there was plenty of light.

I was tempted to follow them but, instead, made my way to the alternate path. Only heavily trafficked routes rated clearing in New Albion, so the secondary connecting paths lay untouched and, in some sections the blown snow was waist-deep. Keeping one eye on the Commons and the other on my direction, I tried to move across the frozen crust, actually sliding at times. Twice, my balance shifted and I plunged through the snow and fell sideways and got stuck in drifts to my hip. I wished I had brought a walking pole to help leverage my legs. Snow filtered into my boots and melted and wet my socks. There was a moment when I thought I'd be there when sun came up. The distance was less than a hundred yards, but it was slow going. A door shut in the direction I was heading, probably Breezy and the kids. Once I reached a spot where I could see a clearing and a structure that seemed to meet the dimensions I was looking for, I stole a moment behind a hemlock. The feathery branches, still weighted with snow, framed the view and provided cover at the same time.

This was the one building Chelsea had provided no detail about. When we talked, I didn't expect to be retrieving the twins from public-style showers. A long, forest green wall of vertically-lapped siding trimmed in white and topped by jalousie windows lining up under the eave faced my direction. A mini-split heat pump was working hard in the bitter cold. The short end of the building, nearest the Commons, had been halfway shoveled, maybe before the last snow, and the pole lights reflected off iced puddles and frozen footprints. Hard stuff. Steel cleats would have been handy. *Ah, well.* I made my way to the corner and listened in the shadow. A shower was running. Breezy was giving instructions that echoed slightly but were clear in the quiet of the sleeping camp.

" . . . not make any noise. Lemme get that tape."

The kids squealed when he yanked the tape from their mouths.

"Now strip and get in the shower and soap each other up. Yeah, *together*—you might as well get used to it. Get yer clothes off! Now! Oh, excuse me, girlie—feeling shy? Take yer pants down. C'mon now—," he cajoled, "Into the shower, like I said. I'm going to be watching so don't try anything. Understand?"

I heard Trevor begin to say something but Breezy cut him off, "Shut the fuck up! You wanted a date? You got one. Do not talk. If you understand, just nod your head." He waited a beat. "Okay. The water's hot. Here you go—"

The *schwing* of cheap metal shower-curtain rings and the bump of bodies against old tin walls let me know the kids were entering the stall together.

I needed something a little more convincing than pepper spray to encourage Breezy's cooperation so I pulled my gun. A glance toward The Commons revealed no motion. Gathering myself and being careful not to slip on the ice, I moved out of the shadow to face the door. *Shit.* There were two. A battered screen door provided ventilation during summer. It fronted a solid door that kept out winter's cold. I back-handed the screen door's brass handle with my left glove, pivoted and gently eased it back to hold it open with my right elbow, then shoulder. The pine frame was wobbly but the spring didn't make any noise. Decades of shower moisture had taken a toll on the wood of the solid door, causing it to become swollen and warped. It was loose in the jamb and probably hadn't closed tight without a good shove for years.

"That's good," Breezy said. "Soap her up good. All over." Then, more breathy, "Now, princess, on yer knees." Bumps and tussle. "On your *knees!* Suck his pecker. You know what I mean." More bumping, then only shower-sound. I grasped the handle of the interior door and turned it, just in case, even though I knew it wasn't latched, and swung it open as I raised my gun, hoping the hinges were well oiled. I didn't see Breezy. I relaxed a bit and stifled a sigh of relief. I slipped through and carefully pushed the door to.

My face immediately registered humidity from steam that was condensing to a damp fog. Hanging fluorescent lights shone hazily through clouds that billowed from the stall on my right. A scan revealed that the showers flanking the entry where I stood were matched by a pair at the opposite end. A galvanized sheet-metal trough—probably ten feet long—with a series of spigots used for collective washing-up and teeth-brushing bisected the space lengthwise. Five toilet stalls lined each of the two long walls. As with the rest of the camp, the dominant aesthetic was knotty pine. Johnny doors were held closed by screen-door springs. The door nearest their shower hung loose, probably a broken spring. The heat of the steam activated 80 years of camping perfume. It was rustic.

I planted my right foot, then swung around the corner of the stall with my gun up.

I had bet that Breezy would be otherwise occupied and I was right. *Couldn't get to that woodie fast enough, eh?* He was unzipped and stroking a hard-on of indeterminate size with one hand; his gun hung loose in the other, a skinny guy with a paunch whose longish blonde hair, soul-patch, and goatee reminded me of Shaggy from Scooby-Do. An expensive watch bobbed on his moving wrist. The twins were naked and in the shower. Celeste was on her knees with Trevor's erect penis in her mouth and her eyes shut tight. With the shower going I couldn't tell if Trevor was crying but he sure wasn't enjoying it. Breezy was fixated on Celeste. Trevor caught my movement as I entered the space and his eyes widened, registering my presence. Breezy paused.

No need to shout.

"Police, asshole."

I slammed the side of my H&K as hard as I could across the side of his head. He collapsed and his pistol clattered on the cement. I kicked it out of reach. Celeste dropped to the floor and her body was wracked by dry heaves. Trevor was wailing.

"Shut up!" I hissed. I didn't have time for Kum-bye-yah. They froze in place as the shower continued.

I kept my gun on Breezy, considering what to do with him. Wet clothes were heaped at the shower entry where he'd ordered them to strip. Towels, thoughtfully delivered by Gill to Wren's Nest, sat on a nearby bench. An open duffle waited under it. I grabbed Breezy's pistol and shoved it in my waistband, then reached into the stall and turned off the water and pulled the duffle to the shower entry. Silver-gray from a roll of duct tape caught my eye.

I tossed the towels to the kids. "Dry off."

Using one of their dirty t-shirts, I dried Breezy's face, then taped his mouth and eyes shut. *Payback is a motherfucker.*

I beckoned for them to step out.

"You two get dressed. We need to get the hell out of here."

Breezy began to stir. I liked the idea of cuffing him with his back against one of the trough's legs but I'd need help moving him. I knelt to get a good grip on his jacket collar and the back of his loosened pants so I could haul him across the floor.

The twins were finishing up with the towels. "Trevor! Give me a hand with his legs! *Now!*"

He froze, acknowledging his nakedness. Celeste dropped in front of Trevor, crouching and taking-hold of Breezy's boots. She adjusted her footing and was ready to move when she raised her head and shouted, ***"Look out!"***

A flash of camo registered in my peripheral vision from the direction of the open johnny door. Searing pain exploded across my upper back and shoulders, whiplashing my neck as brilliant sparkles filled my eyes. Whatever hit me had glanced off the trough before impact or it might have broken my back. Celeste and Trevor were screaming. Sensing the windup for a second strike and instinctively knowing there was nothing I could do to stop it, I cupped the back of my head with my hands. I was hit again and went down, flopping onto Breezy's chest.

Thirty

Water cascaded through my consciousness as molasses oozed behind my eye- *lids. Tympanic drumrolls of pain surged across my shoulders. Voices, conversation, tuned in and out like my grampa's old Bendix tube radio searching for the Redsox game on a summer night. Initially, it was just unintelligible baffle-gab.* Gradually, sound began to coalesce into parts of words, maybe.

" . . . ucking righ . . . er body is amazing."

My body is amazing?

I was yanked by my clothes and chucked aside like a sack of garbage. *Guess not.*

Dad pulled into the Transfer Station's drive-through dump, put the pickup in park and ordered me out. The rank of super-heated garbage rising from the com- pactor's well joined with late July's moist embrace and closed on me like a layer of warm lard. I wanted desperately to jump into a scalding shower but hoisted myself over the rear wheels and searched for footing in the crowded bed, grasping at a shifting mountain of bags ballooned with rot. Tossing them, heaving them, mustering Sisyphean effort, I worked to push the bloated sacks up and over the rail and into the gaping maw of the machine. And then, the bed was empty. I was alone and hovering, locked in place by an invisible force and peering into the pit, when Trevor and Celeste surfaced, clawing their way up through the rubbish. The walls sprang shower jets and they swam, shouting noiselessly and covered in muck and then the machine's crusher wheezed to life—

" . . . Breezy . . . u okay? Hey, wake up!" Echoes of recognition. I'd heard this man before.

I tried to open my eyes but the delicious molasses kept them shut. I wanted to lick it; I craved it.

The screen door to Gramps's house banged and he strolled, smiling his Grampa-smile, through a landscape that glowed in the warmth of a summer's afternoon. Just as I reached for a hug, his chipping hammer slashed the space between us and his face melted into rivers of ripened pus—

An old/new voice, different. ". . . ice job Eddie . . ."

In the Auburn Gresham station's interview room, I sat at a desk that seemed to be swallowed by the immense space around it. The floor spread before me like a football field, gridded with hashmarks every five yards. I sat, centered. The perimeter of the room was lined with knotty pine walls, each measuring 15 yards from midpoint to midpoint. Each wall was punctured by five doors. The scene before me was remarkably clear.

Suddenly, all the stalls swung open and twenty Trevors floated noiselessly forward. Dripping with entitlement, they found their footing and began closing in on me. The johnny-doors bounced and bounced again, as if protesting their closure. In response, multiple versions of Hanna—or perhaps it was twenty Hannas in identical flowing ball gowns—materialized out of thin air. They intercepted the advancing phantoms and together they all started waltzing to the pounding rhythm in my head.

"Take... belt an... isk her." More familiar. Commanding. "What the . . . reezy? . . . oing wi . . . ants down? Did he touch you?"

Silence.

The Trevors halted their advance and pulled the shoulders of the dresses down and the Hannas fought it but now I was naked, my arms shackled to the desk, which seemed to multiply before my eyes. The Hannas were thrown face-down across from the many versions of me seated at the multiple desks and the Trevors mounted the Hannas from behind, their cavernous mouths screaming silently as I watched, utterly helpless—

A couple of slaps. "Godda . . . an't keep your pec . . . your pants."

Dazed. "I didn't do nothing . . . *Nothin'*, I didn't *touch* . . ."

"Get yer Goddamn pants up."

Someone took the opportunity to violate me while he searched my pants pockets. Lashing out with elbows and knees didn't work.

Nothing moved.

My violator lifted and dropped me again, peeling my jacket and ripping off my flak vest. Palms flat on the puddled floor. The showers continued to run full-out, steam billowing forth and adding to the wet.

"Find anything?" The voices were beginning to make a little more sense. Pants were damp. I could feel that. It came to me that it wasn't summer.

The third voice, "—asics . . . uffs, pepper spray . . . ashlight, gun . . .flares, energy bar, keys to the cruiser, nightstick."

"Gimme the energy bar." The old/new voice was Gill. "I thought I'd be outta here hours ago."

Now I knew where I was.

"What're we gonna do with her?" Breezy.

"I'll take her." Third voice. "We got some unfinished business."

I willed my eyelids to flutter. I was close to the open toilet stall, sprawled with my left cheek on the floor. The cold from the cement flooded my ear like a wet finger. I shuddered. Three men surrounded me.

"You back with us Beckham?" It was Gill again. I felt his boot brush my ribs as he stepped over me from behind. I watched him, intermittently, through one eye. He turned and knelt. He was chewing the energy bar. He swallowed and followed that with a pull on my water bottle. He cleared his throat then grabbed a fistful of hair and pulled my head off the floor. I wanted to fix him in a *"You-touch-me-again-and-I'll-cut-your-fucking-arm-off"* glare but all I could manage was an eyelash-filtered, unfocused gaze. "Next time you come through a window, you need to wipe your feet a little better," he said, letting go.

Ouch.

"She's a problem." Breezy.

I yanked his legs out from under him and he pulled down the other two. Standing now, I drew Breezy's gun from my waistband and commanded them to stay-put while I radioed for help.

"No shit, asshole. Lemme take her," Third Voice urged while I tried using my elbow to raise from the floor. I must have been making some progress because he brought his boot down onto my shoulder and ground it into the concrete. *Nope, not gonna try that again.*

"Okay, here's what we're gonna do." It was Gill, standing and taking charge. I think he pointed toward the shower. "Get him some dry clothes. He's scheduled to meet Fran at Old Wooster Rd. Take Beckham and get him changed. I don't care how you do it, just get rid of her, then dump the cruiser. My bet is that she parked up on Old Wooster."

I smiled.

"Yeah, that's where it is. Funny how a good beating is like truth serum," Gill said. "I'm taking the kids to 30 Rock. Client wants one more look. Meet me at the production studio at zero one-thirty hours."

"Fran?" I managed to croak. Gill ignored me.

Mystery man lit a cigarette, leaned over and exhaled as he flipped me over. Eddie Miller. He grabbed an arm and, straightening, pulled me to a more-or-less standing position. My chin was on my chest. He nudged me with the business-end of an empty ax handle. I tried to make a fist with my left hand. Nothing but pain. Eddie stuck the ax handle between his knees to free one hand so he could push my sweater over my head. I twitched in a movement that was supposed to be a left hook. He stuck me hard in the ribs with his fist and completed his task and tossed the sweater in Breezy's direction. "You heard the man. You are *mine,* bitch," His Camel bounced at the edge of his mouth. "Breezy, you ready to go?"

I raised my head a bit and, seeing the twins holding hands, dressed and ready for something—I didn't know what—I realized how utterly I had failed them. I mouthed, "I'm sorry." Trevor welled up. Celeste didn't look at me. She was concentrating on Gill.

"You're sorry? You're *sorry?!*" Gill shouted, reading my lips. "You have no idea what sorry is, Beckham. Get her the fuck out of here. You two are coming with me," he said, motioning to the twins.

"What do we do with her stuff?" Eddie asked.

"Jesus-fucking-*Christ,*" Gill said, exasperated. "Take it with you in the duffle." He paused. I was still slumped with my head solidly on my chest. The room was pitching like a skiff in a lobsterman's wake. The only reason I was standing was because Eddie had me by the arm.

Miller piped up. "Breezy, get the fucking duffle," countering Gill's anger by asserting his command. He adjusted his grip.

"Hold on," Gill held up his hand, voice transformed to Mr. Agreeable. "You know what?"

Breezy was confused, not sure which way to jump.

"Nobody knows she's here. Change of plans. Breezy— go get some dry clothes. Eddie, you and Breezy take her down to the waterfront, whack her and put her under the ice. Make sure she doesn't come up. And make Goddamn sure you put all that shit back on her where it belongs. Here—," he stooped and gathered my outer clothes and service belt and pushed it all into the duffle Breezy held open for him. "—don't forget this . . . Confirmation she's a loose cannon who got in over her head." He smiled.

Eddie chuckled. I stirred. His hand clamped down hard on my bicep.

Gill stepped across and took my chin in one hand, lifted my face to his and squeezed my jaw so hard my lips puckered, "You shoulda learned in Chicago: 'Go along to get along.'" He dropped me, stepped back, paused, then to his boys, "Pickerel are hungry this time of year. Hey, Breezy, cuff her. You don't want any trouble." *Like I was a threat to anyone.*

Breezy did as he was told, making sure to yank my shoulders when he over-tightened the cuffs in back. *Okay, you've made your point.* I was still trying to figure out what was up with my hand. Eddie pulled me along and the three of us exited Angel Falls, followed by the double-bounce of the screen door as Gill shepherded the twins. I was shaking, probably as much from shock as the cold, and skidded on the ice. Eddie gallantly caught me and gave my shoulder an extra twist in the process. *Whatta guy!* My damp service blouse and sport bra didn't offer a whole lot of protection from the biting northerly. The wet pants didn't help either.

Gill and the kids moved on to 30 Rock. My escorts had me by my arms and made sure the traverse to Wren's Nest was as uncomfortable as possible. I stumbled along, wind penetrating up and down my clothes, delivering pin-pricks of frost by the time we reached the former hobby nook. We ran into one freedom fighter who was making his way to take a leak. He was cold and in a hurry and didn't bother to ask what was up. Otherwise, the guys were quiet and between their tugging and pulling, I tried hard to focus on the moment.

Breezy was first to the door at Wren's Nest. He let me go and entered, tossing the duffle with my shit onto the floor and immediately beginning to strip off his wet clothes. Eddie pushed me inside. The room was rank, but pleasantly warm, relatively speaking, and softly lit by the overhead lights on The Commons. Eddie casually pitched the ax handle onto the bed.

"Hey, Breeze—take her for a sec, willya? I don't wanna have to pull 'er back up from the floor."

Breezy was already down to his boxers. I had a feeling I'd missed something on the way from Angel Falls. He accepted the hand-off, assessed his prize, then unbuckled my belt and unzipped my pants.

Eddie had his jacket off and was working on his sweatshirt. Breezy got busy. He pushed me to the makeshift construction table and swung me around. Without clearing the tools, he shoved me face-down and put his weight across my shoulders with his left forearm and then worked his other hand past the cuffs, down the back of my pants, and between my legs. My nose was practically bent in half by some kind of cold metal handle.

"Whoa—Wait up, Breezy! Great minds think alike, my man." I had a sideways view of Eddie who was barechested. "Like I said before: The Deputy and I, we got some unfinished business, right, Deputy? Get 'er up and get 'er shirt off. I wanna see that rack. Gimme the key; we'll cuff her to the bed."

"Key's in my pants, right front pocket." Breezy withdrew his hand and tugged the collar of the blouse to pull me upright.

My back was to both of them and I could hear Eddie rifling through pockets. I flashed on Chicago and my cardboard box as Breezy swung me around to face him again and figured he'd get the party started. He pushed me backwards in the direction of the bed, a step or two away. The cuffs hurt—but that was good, because it meant that I was beginning to get some feeling back in my left hand. The edge of the makeshift worktable rubbed my thigh. I was a little more steady on my feet and going with it, shuffling and kind-of floppy, so he'd mostly have to hold me up. He paused and used one hand to begin unbuttoning my shirt from the bottom, looking for the big reveal. Eddie came with the key. I started to focus.

I felt Eddie's hard-on nudge my butt through his boxers just before he reached around and ripped the front of my shirt open—clearly he hadn't picked up on Gill's concept that it was supposed to look like I'd accidentally fallen through the ice— and Breezy slid his hand up under my bra. They were close, front and back, almost panting, stale breath and B.O. like a dose of smelling salts. I was standing okay now but, in their anticipation, they hadn't picked up on it. The wet shirt clung to my skin. I heard a *'click'* as Eddie tugged at the right 'cuff.

I caught a whiff of my scent when Breezy adjusted his grip on my boob. He slid the shirt-collar absently off my right shoulder with his free hand and with this other, he pinched my nipple, hard. Behind me, Eddie took over from Breezy and caught the top of the sleeve and jerked it down, hoping there'd be some pain as it cleared my hand and they'd be in business. He was right. It hurt like hell but I opened myself to the action and it slipped smoothly down and over my open hand, much easier than the boys thought it would.

"Here we go!" Breezy was exultant.

Both hands were free.

My right swept across the table and scooped the discarded broadknife whose handle had been jammed into my nose. The speed caught them both by surprise and I continued in a tight arc, bringing the tool's honed edge slashing across Breezy's neck. Momentum carried me forward and as it did, I pivoted and jammed my left heel down as hard as I could, catching Eddie's instep. Elementary self-defense. I came down so hard on his foot that I lost my balance.

"Oh you fucking motherfucking bitch—"

Breezy gurgled, wide-eyed. His free hand went to his throat and blood pulsed through his fingers. He began a slow crumple to the floor. His right was caught up under the sport bra and was pulling me down with him. I yanked it free. Eddie stumbled over him and went down, and as he did, I managed to twist backwards and land separated from the two of them. I took the brunt of the impact on my shoulders. *Big mistake.* Jolts of pain, as if they'd plugged my fingers into 220-volt electric sockets, rocketed down my arms and I involuntarily tossed the broadknife. It skittered across the floor and came to rest somewhere under the bed. *Shit.* Eddie and Breezy were heaped together. Breezy's final exhalation blew crimson bubbles at his neck and he was gone.

Somehow, I had the presence of mind to zip my pants. Unlike his pal, Eddie was in shape; I'd caught the shadow of rippled abs when Breezy turned me and now I needed to go on the offensive. He raised himself and began to crawl to the bed. Did he know the broadknife was under there? Or was it the ax handle he was going for? I reached to the duffle and pulled out the first hard thing my hand touched, then turned with my baton to see him with his hands on the mattress edge. His casual toss had landed the club at the far corner and he was having a hard time trying to stand. I doubted he could. Covering the distance that separated us faster than either of us thought I could, I delivered a roundhouse clip to the side of his head that resounded like a firecracker in the cabin. He dropped, but just for a moment. I realized, too late, that I'd gotten too close. He twisted and caught hold of my right thigh, drew his hand down behind my knee and jerked hard. I went down. My wrist whacked the steel upright on the cot and my baton slid across the floor, out of reach.

I landed on my knees between his legs, facing him with my hands at his side. Completely vulnerable. His back was propped on the bedframe. He smiled and began to go for my head. He was going to break my neck. My left hand was still at only 50%. I put everything I had into it and, as best as I could, grabbed his lats for leverage with both hands and butted my forehead into his face.

He tried to dodge but I caught him square on the mouth. There was a sickening crack and a four-tooth dental bridge dropped as I rocked off his lap. I felt a warm trickle along the right side of my nose.

Hockey player.

He covered his mouth with his left hand and lifted the bridge with his right, momentarily dazed. In a single movement, I wiped the blood that was getting in my sight, took his wrist, and used the flat of my dead hand to shove his shoulder forward. His torso separated from the bedframe and I slipped behind him on my knees and swung my right arm hard around his neck, locked onto my left bicep and pushed down on the back of his head with my left hand. Every one of my bones let me know it was not happy with this strategy—but I pushed through. Police choke-hold. I didn't really want to kill him, but I sure as hell wasn't gonna worry about it too much.

He might have rasped, *"You are so fucking dead."* as he struggled, trying to get hold of something, anything.

I was in trouble.

He was torquing and, on my knees, I sensed he might get free. I pulled extra tight and pushed off with my feet—the only body part that wasn't shredded—and, lifting him in a movement that was like something out of WWF, I was able to spring up and fling both legs around his waist. It was a gamble. We came down hard on the open floor with my boots between his legs.

"Uungghh!"

I found myself prone and face-up and under him, sucking desperately for air. The good news was that my heels slammed into his nuts on impact and his involuntary contraction gave me the chance lock my ankles and secure my legs tight at his waist. I pushed my boot advantage home, grinding the shit-kickers against his groin as I pulled back, hard, and arched like a yogi. It was all I could do to keep him in place as he continued to tear at my thighs—thrashing, twisting, pushing back—anything to gain some minor edge. I shoved even harder on his head and adjusted my elbow.

I flashed again on my Chicago box encounter and the feral energy of desperation—hungry, alone, violated —surged and I was ready to break the fucker's neck and be done with it. I pushed harder.

AC current rushed back and forth along my arms with every spasm. All I wanted was for my shoulders to unplug from my spine. I was back in Wren's Nest now. Eddie began to drop away, his legs kicking with less vigor, more of a twitch. Then he was unconscious. I held for a moment or two longer—I didn't want to be surprised. He was down for the count.

"Not yet, cocksucker."

Breezy knew how to follow orders. He'd made sure to gather everything from the floor in Angel Falls and had stuck back it in the duffle. After I cuffed and taped Eddie, I wiped my face with my shirttail, tossed the blouse aside—it was only going to get in the way—ripped a strip of duct tape and slapped it across my forehead. *Fashionable.* At least it would keep the blood out of my eyes. I threw on my sweater, vest, and jacket and replaced my stuff in the service belt. Eddie was still gone. I checked his pulse. He wasn't gonna feel good when he woke up, but he was better off than Breezy. It was time to get a move on.

Thirty-one

Gill's plan had problems. I wouldn't have my radio or phone—maybe he'd order the guys to leave them in the cruiser. But then, if I didn't have my keys when they put me under the ice . . . whatever. There wasn't time to worry about Gill's plans for me. I needed to find him and the twins. I checked Breezy's phone. It was 1:14. Gill would be expecting Breezy and Miller any minute.

But, Fran. I could have sworn Gill told Breezy to meet Fran. *"Perverted wickedness"* was her response to Justine's flirtation with pornography. Again, my job was finding the twins. Fran would have to wait.

The Nation of New Albion was dead quiet as I made the short trip from Wren's Nest to 30 Rock. I entered through the front door.

The glow from light poles filtered through the bank of windows and painted a grid on the wood plank floor. I stood in a single room which spanned the length of the building, probably 75 feet. Other than some circular tables stacked on low-slung rolling carts in the two front corners, it was empty. To the left was a well-used stone fireplace centered-up and occupying a full one-third of the unfinished wall. A new—well, new when it was built six or seven years ago—stage occupied the north wall. The space was easily 35 feet deep and faded to black as it receded. A beaten path emerged in the layers of accumulated dust, leading to what appeared to be swinging doors in the rear. The break between them glowed a dim red and threw their outline into gentle silhouette. Whoever walked this path knew exactly where they were going. The back-end of 30 Rock—where Chelsea said the video studios were—was through those doors. That's where I'd find Trevor and Celeste. There was no sound.

I took a moment. Gill was expecting Breezy to come pick up the kids. Breezy wouldn't skulk around, quiet-like, trying to sneak up on his buddy. No, he'd probably stomp his feet and *schlomp-clump* across the hollow floor and just open the door, boom, when he got to the studio. Gill might be more surprised if he *thought* it was Breezy coming through but I showed up instead. 'Course, I was betting he'd be alone. That was going to be a costly bet if I was wrong.

I pulled my weapon and chambered a round, then stomped my feet a couple of times and *schlumphed* across the floor with both hands holding the gun ready at my waist. When I got to the double-doors, I started to pull my flashlight but thought the better of it. Breezy wouldn't be using his; he'd know his way around. As I gently pressed against the left door, I could feel the two-way spring-hinge rocking backwards. They swung both ways. I sidled left, placed my palm flat in the center and pushed, cautiously, pistol fully extended in my right hand. The gun's weight made my arm a little wobbly as I stepped through, scanning the space. Chelsea had told me there was something like a waiting area where kids could hang out until a studio opened.

Check.

A pair of cheap loveseats arranged in a shallow "V" created a conversation nook that looked out one of three windows. Further on, there seemed to be another furniture cart, but this one was stacked with chairs instead of tables and sat under the back door's EXIT sign. A bare red bulb glowed next to Studio #1, nearest to me and farthest from any door that could take us out of the building. *Aww, c'mon. Why does everything have to be so fucking complicated?*

Neither light nor sound leaked from the studio. My guess was that, when I opened the door, all the interior space would flow to the right and south. *Think about it, Beckham. Don't shout unless it'll give you an advantage.*

The studio door was hung to swing in and to the left. There was a handle instead of a knob. I got tight to the face and gently put my weight against it as I pushed the handle down.

Pulsing electronic trance music flooded the waiting area, bass turned way up. I felt like I needed to lean harder into it just to push through. As expected, the room opened in two directions. A pair of walls and the ceiling were clad in expensive sound-deadening acoustic bricks. I had a rear three-quarter view of Gill. His attention was focused on the long wall opposite my position. It was brought alive by a close-up video projection of some vaguely foreign-looking guy whose hi-def baby-face filled the expanse. At this scale, his cratered complexion looked like the surface of the moon. Moss-green eyes leered at us and were framed by slick jet-black hair cut in a Prince Valiant bob. His lips moved but there was no sound. Gill was standing at a portable editing suite with a laptop to the side, tuned into the projection and wearing mic'd headphones. He had no idea I was there, no doubt waiting for Breezy to give him a friendly tap on the shoulder. I pulled the door closed. The volume was enough to wake the dead.

I did a second, quick, scan of the space. It wasn't deep, but wider than I expected with a subtle checkerboard of beige-y linoleum on the floor and a pair of heavy doors with an EXIT sign over them in the corner diagonally opposite. During its past life as a dining hall, this area had probably been the kitchen. If that was the case, it would make sense that the EXIT doors led to a loading dock. *So, maybe* not *so complicated.* There was a movable wall, like a stage set piece, standing haphazardly beyond Gill, an unmade, cheesy-looking brass bed and some other bedroom-type furniture scattered. Most of the stuff was on wheels. I found Trevor and Celeste sitting in profile to me on caned, ladder-back chairs with a pro-camera focused on them.   They were dressed and their attention was on the guy in the projection. They sat erect and still, ankles zip-tied to the legs of the chairs, hands free.

Celeste was closest to me. She caught my movement out of the corner of her eye and shifted her gaze enough for me to signal her with a finger to my lips and then point to the projection. She returned her focus to the wall.

Circling left in order to approach Gill from directly behind revealed the green-screen wall behind the twins. With the help of simple technical hacks, they appeared inside Pinterest's idea of a virtual 'Maine coastal cottage', complete with Scandinavian blue and white decor and a static view of the ocean through the window. A filtered flood provided ambient light which kinda-sorta worked with the camera's viewpoint. It was probably convincing, especially if you were paying more attention to the kids. Two thumbnail images floated at the top of Gill's screen: one was of Prince Valiant but the detective's shoulder kept obscuring the other.

He was pretty much shouting into the headset. The music drowned out most of it, but what I could make out sounded like he was replaying English in reverse. I glommed onto a phrase that might have had some meaning:

"Biz Kanadaga Koburn Gore o'tish joyidan kirib kelmoqdamiz va Monreal . . . aeroportiga soat to'qqiz o'ttiz dan kechiktirmay etib kelamiz."

The large screen responded something and leaned back, chuckling.

I could see more of the Prince. He was wearing an expensive blazer and shirt and there was an airplane porthole window with the shade pulled at his right. He adjusted his laptop to keep on screen and the interior of a private jet came into view. His expression shifted from lascivious to business-like. His lips moved. It appeared they were closing the meeting.

I raised my gun and took a step toward Gill. The client's face changed to alarm and he shouted something and I realized, too late, he'd caught sight of unexpected movement via Gill's laptop camera.

My plan was to shout, "Freeze, Gill!" but I only got out the "Free—" before he pivoted, swinging the editing cart with both hands and hammering its corner into my groin. I doubled over, *"OOooof!"* knees buckling. Wiring ripped from the wall and the room flashed to black when the flood's tripod upended and the bulb exploded on impact. I'd just about caught my balance stumbling backwards when, using the floor as a launching pad, he put his entire weight behind the cart and drove it in my direction. Even in the dark, his instincts were good. It rammed my left thigh and I went down, hard. He snagged the cart and was using it like a bulldozer now. Loose wires whipped my face and tangled my arms as it lumbered over my legs. He kept on. One boot grazed my hip and with his next step his heel was square on my chest, squeezing the air out of me before I clipped his ankle and he collapsed across me. I felt like I was being ripped apart.

I tried to bite his hand as he groped my face looking for something to grab on to, but missed it when he rolled, his wild punches catching my neck and then my ear. He must have used his other arm for leverage while my head was ringing because, in an instant, he was on his hands and knees, his shin planted squarely across one arm while he searched for my other and bounced his free knee on my chest—like I was getting CPR from King Kong. Once he found my wrist, he executed some kind of martial-arts move and my gun dropped, useless. He gathered it, stood, and then kicked me to make sure he knew where I was.

I gasped for breath.

"Jesus fucking Christ, what are *you* doing here?" he asked, clearly surprised.

"Good . . . good to see you too," I managed to wheeze.

He'd put the fear of God into the twins. They didn't make a sound. The only light in the room came from the laptop on battery power and the EXIT sign. Our eyes adjusted.

"Who's your buddy?"

"Doesn't matter."

"What the hell are you doing, Jack? It's one thing to look the other way but . . ."

"Give it a rest, Allie. You're so Goddamn clever? Big girl from Chicago, coming home to Maine? Oh, and you're gonna clean everything up, aren't you? Just like *all* the folks from away. I saw what you and Latch were up to when you walked in the door. Shut up and turn over and put your hands behind your back."

I turned onto my stomach. This was getting old.

"I don't know what you're talking about. Latch hired me to take over for Martin. End of story."

I heard him scrabble around on the editing cart, then *phuuwitt*, the sound of tape being pulled from a roll. Then quiet. He was in a quandary; he couldn't hold the gun on me and secure my hands simultaneously. Something dropped on my head and rolled across the floor. He stooped and felt for the flashlight on my belt, found it and clicked it on. He scanned me with the light.

"What's this?" he asked. "What's with you and the Goddamn flares? What're you planning to do, signal the cavalry?" He tossed them onto the cart. "Take off the belt and crawl over to the kids," he said, waving the flashlight in the direction of the twins.

When I pushed off so I could get to the buckle, he kicked me flat.

"I said *crawl* Beckham. On your belly."

I rolled, unclipped the belt and left it, then slithered as best as I could toward the kids. A glint of metal caught my eye and his toe flicked away a pair of scissors that must have fallen from the cart. I passed the roll of gaffer's tape on the way. He followed from behind, stooping and hooking the roll with two fingers of his flashlight hand. I stopped when I was a couple of yards from the kids' boots. It seemed close enough. I lifted my head.

"Closer."

I stayed low and moved until he said, "Okay, stop."

Gill shined his beam into Trevor's face, who winced in the spotlight. He dropped the tape at my feet and gathered the scissors.

"You," he said, signaling with a waggle of the light. "I'm gonna cut your ankles loose and I want you to tape her hands behind her back. Understand? Do not fuck with me or I will give you the beating of your life." He cut the zip-tie binding the boy's legs. Trevor took a moment and stamped his feet, just to loosen up.

"I told you to tape her hands!" Gill thundered. "Here. Take these, and then onto the floor." He handed the scissors to the boy, who was visibly trembling as he dropped to all fours.

Trevor scuttled across to the tape and then crawled to my side. He pulled a length. Gill moved closer, positioning himself behind me to monitor the situation. My cheek was flat on the linoleum, eyes in the shadow of my shoulder.

"Hold 'em together, Beckham." I did as I was told. "Okay, kid. C'mon, you can do it." He said it like he was talking to a baby taking his first steps. "Cut the tape and tie her hands. And make it tight."

Trevor must have been trying to figure out just how to do his. It wasn't exactly in the job description for a fourteen-year-old.

"Just fucking *do it!*" Gill exploded, stepping even closer. There was violent movement and a loud *SLAP!* followed by the tinny clatter of metal on hard lino. Trevor was laid out. I'll give the boy credit—he'd taken a jab at Gill's ankle.

"You fucking little *SHIT!*"

Gill kicked him in frustration.

The kid lay in a ball on his side, sobbing. Gill kept the gun on me as he knelt next to him. He knew what he was doing. *Two tours of Afghanistan in Army Intelligence, I guess you learn something.*

He leaned in close to Trevor's ear and rasped, "What did I tell you?"

Trevor sniffled. It must have been the wrong answer. Gill grabbed him by the shirt neck and rocked back, yanking him upright and then backhanding him before he could get settled.

*"What the fuck did I **tell** you?!"* he repeated.

"Not . . . not . . . Not to touch you again."

Gill stood.

"You want to play with scissors? Here's a game. Find 'em."

Lifting my head, I saw Trevor crawl to the pool of light. The scissors clicked on the linoleum as he picked them up.

"Back over here." The light waggled on the tiles between me and Celeste. Trevor dutifully obeyed. He found the space and turned, sitting flat with his empty hand nursing his side where Gill had kicked him.

"Pull your pants down."

"Please . . ." Trevor whispered.

"Pants *down!* I knew I should've cut your balls off."

Trevor laid the scissors down, undid his buckle, and unzipped. He lifted his butt and pushed his pants to his hip.

"The underwear, too." Gill waved the flashlight at the boy's privates.

"Further." Trevor lifted his knees and pushed his boxers to mid-calf. "Pick up the scissors." Trevor obeyed.

"Okay, open 'em up."

Trevor sat. He lifted the scissors so they were at his chest and opened the blades.

"Not the fucking scissors, asshole. Your legs. Spread 'em. Open 'em wide." Gill's calm made the request even more chilling.

Trevor lowered the scissors and opened his legs. With my chin hard against the floor I could see that his left hand was covering himself.

"That's right. Okay. Now—open the scissors and lift your scrotum."

Shaking, he lifted the tool and opened them a little. Tears streamed down his cheeks.

"Wide—I wanna see the blades!" Gill called, bumping the boy's nearest leg with his foot. Trevor's entire body jolted. Timidly, he opened the scissors to a broad "X."

Gill smiled.

"Okay Jack!" I yelled. "You made your point."

He chuckled. "Give me the scissors—handle first." He bent at the waist and collected them, then stepped in fast and kicked the boy three times in rapid succession. He pocketed the scissors. Trevor scrunched into a fetal position, catching his breath and blubbering.

Gill turned his attention to me.

"You look tired, Jack," I said over my shoulder.

"Shut up," he replied, and then, "You. Pants up. To the wall. Then do not move. I will kill you," to Trevor.

The boy did as he was told, then crawled on his hands and knees to his chair.

"No. Not there. Over here." Gill indicated with his light that he wanted Trevor to stay on the floor but up against the wall and in a line of sight with me. He complied.

"Okay. Let's try this again."

He cut Celeste's legs free. "Tape her hands."

"No."

Gill was stunned and wound up to hit her but caught himself.

"I won't tape her and you can't make me," Celeste pushed back, voice low and calm. "You won't because you need me. You can't deliver damaged goods."

"Don't bet on it, missy."

"Oh . . . so getting all up into Eddie's face after he hit me—that was just an act?"

"Celeste," I interjected. "I'm gonna get you outta here."

Gill grinned. Celeste's expression was blank. I hadn't exactly proven to be a reliable rescuer.

"That'd be comical, Beckham," Gill said, almost laughing. He continued, his voice laced with disdain, "if it weren't such a sad commentary on your abilities."

He turned his attention back to Celeste. "Tape her hands . . . ," he said, keeping my pistol pointed at my head as he stepped across to Trevor, ". . . or I'll break your brother's nose."

"Go ahead." Stone cold.

Gill switched the gun to his left hand and punched the kid, whose *"Aughhh!"* on impact sickened me. A stream of blood emerged and found its way to Trevor's mouth and then his chin. I couldn't tell if it was broken, but it sure looked bad.

"It'll be his front teeth next. Wanna try me?"

Celeste weighed the situation. She began to move. Trevor's tears were as much from the surprise of betrayal as the pain. He used his shirt to wipe his face. It was a mess.

I was still sprawled on the floor with my hands behind my back and trying to keep an eye on what the hell was happening. Gill had returned to his overview position at the rear limit of my peripheral vision. He checked his watch. "C'mon, hurry up." By now, Celeste was kneeling next to me and made a big deal of pulling a long length of tape and tearing it with her teeth. She stuck one end on my butt while she arranged my wrists before beginning to wrap them. I felt her forearms resting on my thigh as she folded to get closer. When I glanced over my shoulder she looked directly into my eyes. I could tell she was working hard to keep her body between me and Gill. My neck and shoulders kept reminding me how unhappy they were. I smelled something funky. So did Gill.

"What the hell is that?" he asked. Trevor began to cry again. "Oh, for Christ's sake. Did you shit yourself?"

"These aren't Taliban, Jack, they're just children," I said.

Gill raised his face to the ceiling, looking for relief.

"Oh, you have got to be fucking-*kidding* me. Come *ON!*" he screamed in frustration, dropping his gun arm to his side. At that moment I could feel Celeste's breath on my hands. Then she sat upright and used my butt to push herself away from my body.

"Okay?" she asked Gill, palms facing up and open like the girls on The Price Is Right.

Gill took a cursory look with his light.

"Tape her feet."

Celeste slid down and began to bind my ankles.

"I thought I heard something about Montreal when you were talking to your friend," I said, just to pass the time. "Heading to WinterFest?"

"Breezy's taking us to Canada," Celeste answered for Gill. It wasn't an endorsement.

"That's unlikely," I replied. "Breezy's dead."

Celeste paused. Gill was silent.

"Finish up," Gill ordered.

He was on to Plan B. He stretched and moved the cart closer and laid the flashlight butt-down, then pulled a burner phone, punched some buttons, and placed it on the table, exchanging it for the light. Celeste was still working on my ankles.

"Gill?" A voice on speakerphone filled the space.

"Hey, Professor. Yeah, look, we've hit a bit of a snag," Gill began. Celeste signaled for him to inspect the tape-job. He ignored the gesture and before The Professor could say anything, coolly asserted his authority, "Tell Willy-Willy to get over to Wren's Nest," he said while flashing the light at my feet for a moment. Satisfied with the ankles, he pointed the girl back to her chair. "Tell him to check on Eddie and Breezy. Yeah. Then have them all come to the studio."

"Everybody to the studio?" The Professor confirmed. *Okay, so that's why I was still alive. Gill was covering his ass—if everything went to hell, he wouldn't be responsible for the death of a police officer. It'd be the Miller boys.*

"Right." Gill's patience was getting shorter. "Tell 'em to hurry up. We're already late and Fran's gonna be pissed." The Professor's shout to Willy-Willy was cut short as Gill closed the call.

Efficient.

There she was again.

"What's with Fran?"

"Franesca Bianchi Cloutier Considine Kringle? She owns this rathole."

The scattered fragments of Fran's story began to coalesce for me.

"Yeah, smartass. Finally coming together, hunh?"

Condescending.

"I saw your report to Latch. A moving company working out of boo-foo Maine and making money? C'mon. You'd think a genius of your capacity could figure it out," he said, edging a little closer and shining the light on me. "Fran's dad recognized the market for U.S. kids is yuge, YUGE! And, like father, like daughter . . . it was easy for her to see the potential. Look at 'em. They're gorgeous. Moving our kids into Canada is *muuuch* easier than the other way 'round—*Eh?*" He waved the flashlight in the direction of the twins. "All-American, top-quality product. Even the runaways."

"Okay, Jack. But New Albion, Miq-Maq, Camp Wiki, wherever the fuck we are?"

"It takes vision to maximize profit, Allie. I caught Sam going at it with one of the girls. The bust at the Welcome Station? Eliminated the competition. Fran and Sam were moving, at the most, a couple dozen kids a year. Opportunity knocked when I heard about the camp. Fran got it for a song. We easily bumped our numbers to over a hundred, up and out."

"Plus porn," I said.

"Sure. Those satellite dishes? Not Dish-TV. Breezy runs production."

"But, New Albion. I mean, Jack . . ."

"Wake-up, Beckham. The United States that I fought so hard to protect—me, Willy-Willy, Eddie, so many of our patriots here—it's doomed. The so-called 'underserved'? Always whining with their hands out while they stab you in the back? What about *Americans*? You haven't fought for your country or seen it from the outside. It's so obvious."

I tried to calculate how long it had been since the phone call. It was going to take only a moment for Willy-Willy to get Eddie up to speed and I suspected ol' Eddie'd be eager to have another crack at me. I circled back to Fran. What the hell was she doing in this mix?

"But, Fran. And Sam . . ."

"Fran's a trip," Gill boasted. "She thinks she's helping these kids. She's convinced herself she's their savior."

I shuddered at the thought of the 'care' "her" kids might receive.

"Fran appreciated what her father passed on and everything changed for the better when she bought Wiki. But when she ran into Sam and Kourtney and made the connection, well . . . ," he seemed almost reflective, " . . . it all went downhill. If only I had known . . . When Fran recognized Kourtney and realized she had become everything she despised . . . it took time, but she recruited Tabby, and that pushed Sam over the edge."

"Did he kill himself, or did you?"

"No, Sam killed himself. He was at the end of his rope. His marriage was over and his daughter was dead. There was nothing for him."

"And these twins?" I asked. We were getting closer to the arrival of the Miller boys. Once they showed up, it'd be game over. I figured *What the hell?* at least I'd know why I'd gotten myself killed.

Gill sighed with longing and approached Celeste and Trevor. He examined Celeste with his light, as if caressing her. She straightened in her chair, uncomfortable with his gaze. "The twins were Breezy's plan. He saw their photo when they won the PenBay Cup and showed it to Husan . . ."

"Mr. Big-Stuff?" I asked.

"Go ahead and laugh, Beckham. Husan Karamova. Son of Rashid Karamova. Uzbek oligarch. Dad's the founder/owner of Megafon Wireless and Styx Metallurgy, among other major industries in picturesque Uzbekistan. These people have more money than God, Beckham—$20.5 billion with a 'B'. And Husan has an interest in kids. Twins like these Americans . . . "

"Uzbek?" I interrupted.

"Yeah—Uzbek. Pashto and Urdu. The Army has a helluva language school."

"So, you were never going to return them?"

His smile confirmed it but then the corners of his mouth turned down.

"Breezy fucked up. He got distracted and behind schedule. He had a million-dollar deposit he had to honor and ended up capping Fielding to take the kids. And he was greedy. $15 million was absurd."

I sensed movement through the floor. Maybe Willy-Willy and Eddie had entered the building.

Gill remained fixated on Celeste. The two of them were locked in a battle of will as she continued to resist his examination.

I'd be dead . . . or I'd be dead—either way I had nothing to lose. I jackknifed my body and Celeste's binding on my ankles acted like a sledge, catching Gill completely by surprise and sweeping his legs out from under him. The room pitched wildly as the flashlight fell. I wrenched at my wrists. What I'd hoped was true, Celeste had bitten through a portion of the tape and I ripped free. I didn't have time to undo my feet; I had to get to Gill before he recovered.

I needn't have worried. As soon as Gill began his topple, Celeste launched herself from the chair. He slipped on my service belt as he stumbled into the cart and she plucked the scissors from his back pocket. The table lurched and she fell with him, blindly jabbing with savage underhanded thrusts. When he hit, the impact drove the blades deep into his groin, all the way to her hand. He was shrieking. She kept on stabbing and grunting. When he tried to roll, she caught the femoral artery.

There wasn't time to consider first aid. It wouldn't have mattered anyway; he was done in seconds. I scooted across and watched him, face-up, twitching. He squeezed off a couple of rounds randomly, then nothing. He had my gun in a death grip. I pushed Celeste away and signaled, "On the floor, both of you!" with the flat of my palm, then reached across his chest and pulled his pistol from the shoulder holster and chambered a round.

The latch on the door clicked and the brothers Miller—I could tell it was Eddie in the lead from his limp, then Willy-Willy—alerted to danger and moving in a semi-crouch, kinda-sorta slid through with guns up, scanning the space from side-to-side. From my angle, the "Studio In Use" light reflected as a red puddle on the pale linoleum and threw them into perfect silhouette. I was prone, ankles shackled, Gill's pistol held in my right hand and resting on the palm of my left. The flashlight's fading beam threw a distracting shadow on the green wall. It was like being on the firing range. I put two in the chest of each brother and dropped them both. *Fuck that 'pepper spray' shit.*

Thirty-two

I took a breath—my record was four-for-four so far and I really didn't want to add any more to the body count. We needed to say farewell to New Albion. I didn't know what we'd find outside—for all I knew, the entire camp was up and preparing to repulse the invasion.

"Trevor, clean yourself up—pants down, boxers off. Use the clean side to wipe your ass and then get ready to go. Celeste . . ." She had raised herself and knelt next to Gill, scissors still in hand, face and front spattered with his blood. The dying flashlight delivered pale sepia uplighting. She remained motionless and our situation had the quality of that painting from art history class . . . Judith and *what's-his-name?* I shook that off and unwrapped my ankles, crawled around the body and hugged her. She put her head into my shoulder and her body was wracked with sobs.

I leaned back, putting some distance between us, then, as delicately as possible, touched my forehead to hers. Our eyes met.

"Celeste. We need to go." I said, wiping her nose with my sleeve. "Get your boots on." She nodded and moved to the wall and began.

I pried my gun from Gill's hand and slipped it into my holster, decided to leave the flashlight, then jammed his pistol into my waistband. By now, the kids were standing ready.

They followed when I found the double exit doors. Latched with a crash-bar, the right one pushed down easily and opened to a loading dock four steps up from grade. I welcomed the brittle air and noted we were in shadow on the Wren's Nest side of the building. I presumed the entire camp had been alerted by The Professor and the bunkhouse was probably in an uproar. The twins held hands—it would have been cute if we hadn't been so desperate—and I signaled them to halt.

I remembered catching sight of a large white lozenge-shaped form in the drone video, just before the image disappeared.

Taking Trevor's hand, the three of us scrambled down the steps to the snow below, where I pushed them up against the building.

"Wait here," I whispered.

They were terrified.

"Don't worry, I just need to go and get something I forgot," I reassured them and returned to the studio, leaving them huddled together. Searching for the fading screen of Gill's laptop, I located it, gathered the flares from the cart and started for the door, then stopped. I found Gill, flipped him over and checked his jacket for my cruiser's keys. Got 'em. *Thanks, Jack.*

"You okay?" I said to their nods as I rejoined them. "Stay on the wall and if there's any shooting, lay flat. Understand?" They nodded again.

This part of 30 Rock was indented, maybe five yards, from the former dining-hall room and we were relatively hidden. We began to move and I saw what I was looking for.

The folks from away had decided to update the heating when they took over and switched the system from oil to gas. There was a 1,000-gallon horizontal propane 'pig' positioned toward the rear-end of the building, separated by the requisite 20 feet. Elevated slightly, it looked like a submarine on stilts.

I licked my index finger and held it up and felt a faint breeze from the north. *Well alright! We're finally catching a break.* I pulled them to a huddle.

"Have you ever lit a flare?" I asked.

Blank.

I took one from my jacket pocket.

"You pull the cap off, like this," I said, demonstrating. "See this rough stuff here?" It was too dark to make out the texture. "Here, run your fingers across it," I said, pushing it into their faces. They felt the striking surface. "It's like a big match. You take the top of the long part and strike it like a match."

"I can do that," Trevor said. He was, after all, the guy in the group.

"Okay. But not until I signal you. And I'll signal you like this." I pumped my fist up and down like Hanna and I used to do when we wanted truckers to blow their horn. "When I do that, hold it out at arm's length and strike it. Once it lights, be careful to turn it sideways or it might drip on you. When you're sure it's going good, shove it into the snow with the burning side up. By that time, I should be back with you two and we'll head out. Got it?"

He nodded.

"Wait here."

The kids were nervous but scrunched hard up against the building. I made my way out of the shadow of 30 Rock to the pig.

An angular snow drift caught my eye. It was waist-high and looked out of place against the exterior wall of a nearby shed. I crept over. The residual smell of heating oil wafted from the ancient tank on the other side of the wall. I used my bare fingers on the mound, pulling away the snow and exposing a stack of bricks. The good news was that I could use one like a hammer and it wouldn't spark. The bad news was that they were frozen-solid like, well, like a brick. I felt for the Leatherman on my belt, opened it to the screwdriver and pried one free.

Making my way to the tank, I positioned myself on the twins' side and reached for the 'conning tower,' where the regulator was located. I knew when I started banging, the thing would chime like Big Ben. I was exposed—black uni against the white surface, but I needed to be able to get back to the kids as fast as possible. Even with my height, the position of the regulator, combined with the curve of the tank, made it hard to reach. By stretching on tippy-toes, I figured I could just about make it. I felt along the tower for the lip and realized I was on the hinge-side. This, I didn't like and moved to the opposite side.

A knob of refrozen snow had slid from the cover and onto the ground. The hump gave me a little elevation and as long as I was careful, I wouldn't slip. I flipped open the lid. My hands were stiff with the cold. I clutched the brick at one end and brought the other short-side hard against the regulator.

"CLANG!"

Nothing.

I took another swipe and the regulator held.

Third time—nothing.

I adjusted my stance and used the edge of the rim to set the brick at an angle and put everything I had into my next try.

"CLANG!—hisssssss"

We were in business.

By now, random voices were clamoring. No one saw me—the pig was between me and the Commons—but they could certainly follow the noise. The most direct way to the lake was straight across the middle of the Commons, past the bunkhouse, and down the road. But that would lead us directly into the militia.

I moved away from the tank and pumped my arm. Trevor, God-bless-him, was ready and struck the flare. Nothing. He hit it again and it bloomed. We needed to move, and fast.

"This way, *now!*" I shouted. New Albion was awake and looking for trouble. Trevor pushed the flare into a drift and they both ran at a crouch and caught up to me as I reached the rear corner of the building. We were going to circle around behind the crowd. Gill's gun was locked and loaded as I checked the way ahead. Empty and dark. We moved as fast as possible, occasionally crunching through the crusty surface.

My bet was that the propane would move out of the tank and drop to the snow in the cold. With the northerly breeze, it would carry to the flare and

*"Ka-**BOOOOOOM!!!**"*—a massive fireball erupted from the far side of 30 Rock. The windows on our side of the hall exploded outward. The flash turned the entire camp orange for a moment. We paused, reflexively bent for cover. I realized that I was holding Celeste's hand and she had Trevor's.

"Ka-Booom . . . "

" . . . ka-boom." The explosion echoed across the lake.

We were at the edge of the Commons, which was in chaos. Men were running half-dressed, arms halfway in jackets, tying boots that had been thrown on too quickly, and moving toward the site of the blast.

Red-hot sizzling shards of tank began to return to earth. I saw a guy catch one in the head. Wrong time, wrong place.

I tugged them along, keeping at the perimeter of the movement.

"Ka-BOOOOM!" Another explosion. Probably the old heating oil tank that had come to temperature.

I looked back. At least three buildings were in flames—30 Rock, Wren's Nest, and the office, likely some of the pines, too. We moved together into the shadow of the Bunkhouse. Everyone in camp was focused in the other direction so it was like we had a cloak of invisibility. Now we were negotiating heavy undergrowth and had to pick our way carefully since the terrain sloped abruptly downhill. A cruiser's *"whoop whoop"* raised above the din and I heard staccato bursts of gunfire. The cavalry.

The moon was at our backs and blocked by the hill, so we were navigating blind. We stayed in the woods, which continued to be hard going with branches, trees, and crunchy drifts. At one point, Celeste must have caught her foot under the crust and took a tumble, but got up and signalled, "Okay," and rejoined Trevor and me. The broad, matte-white surface of the lake came into focus and with it, the silhouette of the diving tower that marked the waterfront. Somewhere nearby was a path across Powderhorn.

At the edge of the road, I motioned them to stop. I checked in every direction. My tractor-friend had cleared the way to the shore. We ducked down alongside timbers that supported the porch of a log-building labelled "Memorial Lodge." The kids wore sweaters and knit caps. The adrenalin rush from the action at 30 Rock was wearing off after our slog downhill. They were shivering. I needed to give them a goal.

"We've got to cross the lake and climb that hill," I said, pointing in the direction of where my cruiser was waiting. "My car is parked up there and we can get you warmed up. You with me?"

They nodded. What was their option? There was a soft explosion between us and the sheriff's outpost in Huntley. It wasn't a firearm. Then another. The gunfire stopped. We started for the lake. *Whoop-whoops* began again and increased in volume as they edged in our general direction.

I had to keep the two of them moving, so we were jogging over the ice, using the millitia's track as a guide. Trevor led and I was acting as rear-guard. A little traction remained from the compacted snow so the pace was comfortable. Our long shadows created a sinuous line in the cool light. We were out from under New Albion's hill, past my ice-fishing shack, and about three-quarters of the way to the opposite shore. I smelled wood burning and turned to see the ridge that marked the location of Camp Miq-Maq/Wiki/Nation of New Albion alight in flames. Dusky peach billows of smoke rose and floated south on the increasing northerly breeze. No shooting. Multiple light-bars fanned out and drove at a crawl in several directions. A firetruck siren, then an ambulance asserted themselves in the distance. A sheriff's cruiser at the beach-end of Powderhorn clicked on its lights and raced in the direction of the camp entrance off 115.

A gentle, croaking, groan and a light splash caught my attention. I turned to see Celeste sliding into Trevor, who himself was sliding in slow motion, body flat to the ice, through a thin film of water that emerged from a growing crack in the icesheet. His lower torso disappeared into a hole that opened with his weight. Celeste was down, too, and used her boot to dig into the ice and spin around so she faced her brother as she came to rest. He was clawing at the edge.

"Hel.....Hel...Help me!" he called in a muted voice. "Celeste!"

"Hang on Trev!" she replied, abandoning any pretense of silence.

I ran to Celeste. I had at least 30 pounds on her; she would need to be the one to pull him out.

She was pushing her way through the deepening ice water.

"Stop, Celeste. Stop *NOW!*" I called.

She hesitated.

"P – P – Puh—Please! I can't— I can't hold on!" Trevor's hands slid three inches closer to the black hole. His head bobbed under and reappeared. I was on the ice sheet behind Celeste.

"Let me get your legs, Celeste."

I took hold of her ankles.

"Okay. Now inch in his direction. No pressure from your elbows. Try to keep as wide a profile on the ice as possible. Tell me when you can touch him."

She began to move, arms crabbing at the frozen surface.

My chin dripped ice-water as I raised my head for a view and heard a light splash.

"Okay, I've got him."

"Trevor, be patient. Do *not* pull. Just hang on, it won't be long now," I said, loud enough for him to hear and in as calm a voice as I could muster. "Celeste, be still and hold on. I need to do something."

"Okay but make it quick," she replied, shaky, "His grip isn't too great."

I hung on to her left ankle and used it for leverage to tuck and swing my butt around so I was sitting. *Okay, now what?* The multitool. I flipped it open and, trembling, searched until I found the awl and clicked it into place. The bottle-opener/carabiner-attachment-thingie slipped over the toe-end of my bootlace on the first try. *Whew.* Placing the Leatherman between my boots, I angled it to my lace, and the sole of my boot hooked on its fulcrum so the pointed tip of the awl was relatively vertical. Using both feet, I jammed the point into the ice as best I could. "Put your legs together Celeste!" I called and grabbed her other leg with my right hand.

"Trevor, all you have to do is hang on. *Do not pull!* Celeste—I'm gonna edge backwards and you need to hold tight to Trevor's wrists. Lock your arms and don't yank him. Trevor! Try to arch your body so you'll slide up onto the ice."

"Hurry, Allie! He's starting to let go!"

My heels dug in, and I kept my feet flat with the tool buried in the frozen surface and slowly began to push off. It actually worked and felt pretty good and I thought we were making progress until I realized that Celeste was just stretching out as I moved back. She was doing the right thing, but it started to get hard when there was some real tension.

"Hang on everybody. I need to move."

I slid my butt away from them about a half-body's length as I leaned forward and continued to hold Celeste. Then, once again, I wedged the tool between my feet into the icy surface and pulled while unfolding slowly backwards at the waist.

My effort paid off . Celeste was sliding on the ice and Trevor was gradually emerging. "Everybody hold! I need to move." I pushed away, dug in, and leaned back. Once I could see his knees on the ice, I stood, checked behind me for any issues, and then pulled them both to safety.

The temp was below 20 and the northerly made it feel like five degrees. I had to get these kids to some heat and fast. My shoulder was kicking in and I knew it wasn't going to be long before I'd have trouble doing anything besides walking.

"C'mon. It's not too far now," I lied.

We found the shoreline and pulled ourselves up and over onto some level ground. Trevor was soaked and his clothes were beginning to freeze. Celeste was wet on her entire front. My ass was numb. I made a quick calculation when we arrived at the first snowmobile trail. We could make our way up through the woods and avoid the possibility of discovery on the road, or we could take the more exposed route and walk to the parking area. We took the trail and a few minutes later arrived at a semi-plowed parking lot that was empty.

"I can't feel my hands or toes," Trevor said. He'd been walking like a robot, stiff-limbed and jerky.

Celeste answered. "Remember what dad says, "If your hands or feet are cold, concentrate on moving them, just keep them moving and that will bring the blood to them and they'll warm up."

"Yeah, but I can't feel them to move them, Celeste."

"Hang on," I said, catching up to them. We huddled so he was in between his sister and me. "Celeste, get as close as possible." I pulled her to me and reached down and took his hands. They were so cold it was as if mine were toasty. I rubbed them gently, trying to make some friction.

"Both of you, move your toes. Move 'em!"

We stayed like this for a few minutes, warming him marginally.

"We have a couple hundred yards to go, come on," I finally said, pushing them both in the direction of the hill.

On this side of the mountain, Old Wooster Rd. began with a gentle curve that circled a rocky promontory after the parking lot. No more woods. I got them walking at a cadence and as we came around the outcropping to where the roadway straightened and the angle increased sharply, I looked for my cruiser. We were at least a quarter-mile downhill and a white van was parked, blocking the Explorer. As we continued up, it flicked its lights two times, fast.

Fran?

I was spent. I tried again to manage a more masculine gait. There was no energy, strength, or even the will to take on another goon. Pushing the kids brusquely, I demonstrated to the occupants that I was "in charge."

"Hey, what was that for?" Trevor complained.

"Just keep walking. When we reach the van, I will signal you to sprint as fast as you can to the cruiser and hop in the back seat and lie down."

We were halfway there. An exhaust plume drifted from the rear of the vehicle. Whoever was in the vehicle knew there was a problem. They could see the shit going down across the lake. And by now, they probably knew something was amiss with the twins. I hoped, desperately, that the comfort inside would trump the need to inspect the kids. That, and the prospect that a combined $9 million payday was just within their reach.

"Celeste, I want you act like you're trying to run," I said, under my breath, then, "*Go for it!*"

She bolted to the left, but I caught her by the neck of her sweater and pulled her back in front of me. At the same time, I pulled the multitool again from my belt. *Jeez, I gotta write these guys a letter sometime . . .* I swung it behind my hip, searched for the awl with frozen fingers and locked the blade into place. I switched hands on her collar as I palmed the tool, then gave her a final shove. We were less than 20 feet from the van. She stumbled toward it. The driver's window began to lower.

"Okay, *now GO-GO-GO!*" I shouted.

The kids ran for both sides of the cruiser.

I reached into my jacket pocket and clicked the auto-unlock on the Explorer.

The lights went on the in the van's cab as the passenger, a true goon, opened his door.

Fran was in the driver's seat. She'd rolled up the window and was screaming frantically about the kids to her lackey. This guy wasn't too smart. Instead of running directly to the Explorer, he circled the door, then went around the front of the van. I wasn't exactly sprinting, but I was doing my best to beat him to the cruiser. His mistake gave me enough time to bury the awl with a loud *POP!* into the wall of the rear tire. I left it dangling. Celeste had thoughtfully clicked open my door on her way past. I dove in and hit the locks as I slipped the key into the ignition slot and gunned it. The guy slapped both hands against my window. He glanced over his shoulder and saw the rock wall and started for it.

Oh, no. This was *not* gonna happen.

I spun the wheel, slammed the idling cruiser into reverse and tromped the gas. Four studded tires dug in and we lurched to the right. I was happy to miss the goon who'd jumped out of the way and landed on all fours. He began heading for the stacked stones again. By now, I'd shifted into Drive.

Fran wanted us hemmed-in against the boulders, but even with the pedal floored, her flat tire and the icy surface of Old Wooster Rd. meant she was going nowhere. I punched the gas and the Explorer's reinforced bullbar creamed her rear end, sending the van spinning away. We came to a stop in the middle of the road, facing downhill. Fran wasn't as lucky. Her vehicle's front two wheels had dropped over the road's non-existent shoulder and gotten stuck. I shifted again and we were heading up the mountain in reverse at about 45. The goon chucked a stone the size of a basketball at us as we passed. It bounced off the hood. When we were out of range, I stomped on the brakes while simultaneously spinning the wheel. The car did a perfect 180.

"Holy shit!" It was Trevor.

Once I was heading in the right direction, I hammered it and we careened over the crest of the mountain and back toward Wooster.

Thirty-three

As soon as I confirmed Fran wasn't following me, I gently tapped the brakes. The last thing I needed was to flatten the tires on the rail crossing. We passed over the tracks without incident, navigated the dogleg transition from Old Wooster Road, and turned right for Gainsborough.

"Buckle up, kids." They were huddled close and Celeste was rubbing Trevor's arms. The heater was starting to kick-in pretty good and I directed the blowers to the back seat. All lights were flashing as we sped along, following the winding bank of the Schilling and surprising a few motorists headed in the opposite direction for an early meeting in Bangor. My fingers were tingling as they warmed on the steering wheel.

"Beckham to base."

"Al –! . . . Uh, Beckham, go ahead." It was Dina Garrett at the end of her extended shift. Ever the professional.

"Yeah, I have two minors in need of medical care. Proceeding to Macdonald Memorial Hospital."

"Roger that, Beckham. Does the Sheriff know your status?"

"No. My guess is he's pretty busy right now. We just came from New Albion."

"Roger that, Beckham. He wants all available personnel in Huntley."

"Not gonna happen."

Silence.

"Dina, I've gotta take care of these kids. Call ahead to the hospital. I've got two minors, probably both with hypothermia, maybe a broken nose, and dehydration. They each need a rape kit, just in case. Once I'm done with them, I'll call in and you can tell me I'm fired."

"Okay, Allie," she said, breaking character, then, "Are you okay?"

"I've been better. Make sure you tell Latch I have the twins. Oh, and Dina?"

"Yes, Allie?"

"Tell him to pick up Fran Kringle. She's driving a white, unmarked Chevy Express van, Maine license plate Golf-Hotel, dash, numbers seven, three, five, one: GH-7351." I'd had plenty of time to memorize it on the way up Old Wooster Rd.

Dina confirmed the plate.

"Beckham out."

I turned off my radio, not needing to hear chatter about finding bodies, putting out fires, etc. My future in law enforcement was in ashes. The Schilling River broadened and came together with the Coaticook. The eastern sky was beginning to lighten as I pulled into the Emergency Room parking.

Medical personnel were waiting with gurneys when we arrived. I waved off a nurse who tried to dress my forehead. Once the twins were checked in and being seen, I called Honor Fielding. I wanted to be the one to let her know they were okay; I'd certainly jacked her around with the investigation and it was the least I could do.

"Hello?" It was Honor. I was calling on the hospital phone and she had that, *"It's too early in the morning to be good news,"* tone of voice.

"Honor, Allie Beckham. I have the twins here at Macdonald Memorial. They're going to be okay."

She dissolved. Four days of anger, tension, and grief flooded out. She couldn't talk.

"They're going to be okay." I repeated, trying to comfort her as well as anyone can over the phone.

Eventually, she blew her nose and sniffled hard and managed a gentle, "Thank you, Allie."

"You should come here."

"Of course, of course, I'm on my way."

"Honor, they got a little beat-up but they were pretty amazing. The doctor said they must stay at least a day for observation and the Sheriff will have to question them. A lot has happened since we talked yesterday."

"Thank you, my God, thank you, Allie."

"Sure. Take care." I hung up. I didn't need to hang around to see the reunion. The kids still didn't realize their father was dead. I wasn't going to be the one to break that news. I left the hospital for 144 Cushing.

My parking space was taken so I put the cruiser down the street. I climbed two floors to the common bathroom and stripped. I was a mess.

Bruises bloomed up and over my breasts, made only more garish by the pair of vertical fluorescent vanity lights mounted on either side of the medicine cabinet mirror. My lower arms and hands looked like a road map of scratches from grasping twigs, branches, saplings, whatever would help get us through the woods. Face didn't look great either. I pulled the duct tape from my forehead. It was bruised and there was a slice where Miller's canine had caught me, but it would most likely heal okay. Holding on to the sink, I leaned forward a little, tilting my head to the side and guiding the deep auburn hair that mom had always made such a fuss over across my shoulder so it rested on my chest. I straightened. *Ouch.* Continuing to use the sink for stability, I swiveled from one side to the other to see if I could catch a glimpse of my back. Black and blue spread generously in two broad lines across my shoulders and neck where Eddie had battered me with the ax handle. I figured with clothes and makeup, I might almost pass for normal. I took a long, hot shower, wrapped myself in one of King's towels, and made my way to my room, where I collapsed.

Thirty-four

I BLINKED SLOWLY TO consciousness a little after nine. I could've slept another five hours, but dressed and found my way downstairs. King was in the kitchen; the TV was on and the final local news and weather update interrupted Good Morning America's coverage of the sickness in Seattle.

"Hey, I borrowed a towel last night, I'll wash it and get it back to you," I said, entering. He was in his chenille robe.

"Yeah, no problem." He'd dropped the whole *"Whoooo are you?"* bit, deciding I was okay. "Jesus, were you part of that raid they did on those militia guys?" he asked, picking delicately at the remains of a 3-minute egg, then pointed to the TV with his spoon.

"Sort of." I wasn't sure how much of this I wanted to own. "What's the news?"

"They found five dead: three burned beyond recognition, one stabbed and burned, one from some shrapnel. The reporter said the camp was like a war zone."

"You don't say?" I managed to make it not sound sarcastic.

"No, really, Allie—were you there?"

"Yeah. I'm heading to the station now. We'll probably have a chance to talk about it later."

I was hungry, but didn't feel up to eating. Stepping out into the morning, the air was marginally warmer. Weather had shifted west and the sky was a seamless shirt-cardboard gray. I drove to Gainsborough looking over the dent in the hood. There was no need for me to use the radio. What the hell—I'd park, give a statement, and collect the stuff from my locker.

Sarah Loundsberry was recording a follow-up to her overnight reporting when I pulled in. She'd positioned herself so anyone entering the station would come within camera range. I saw her watch me open the car door. I did the whole head-down, perp-walk-shuffle thing, hoping I could slip past her.

"Deputy Beckham! Deputy Beckham, would you care to make a statement?" Her new cameraman panned from her to me as I approached.

Shit.

"No, no. No comment," I said, holding the flat of my hand to shield my face from the camera.

"Deputy Beckham, we're told you were instrumental in the action that occurred last night," she called as I passed.

"No comment." I was at the door.

DeSimone was in the dispatcher's booth. She saw me and signalled what looked like it might have been a *thumb's-up* before she buzzed me through to the bullpen. There were a couple of disheveled suits I figured were FBI and one or two of the guys who'd gotten home and showered, otherwise, uniforms were sooty and most of the guys could have used about 24 hours sleep. Second-day shadows were the norm. As I approached my desk, McCann, Sr. and the Sheriff showed up, emerging from the hallway that connected to the rest of the building.

"Beckham!" Latch roared. "Where the *hell* have you been?"

Smirks appeared on several faces.

"Beckham, never before have I witnessed such a blatant disregard for orders, for the *law*, for ethics or even Goddamn standard operating procedures."

"Yes, sir." I wasn't going to apologize.

"You!" he said, pointing. "Follow me. Now!" He turned and then, over his shoulder, "DeSimone, hold my calls."

I followed Latch out of the room to suppressed laughter and heads shaking as he strode down the corridor, past the armory, up the steps, through the entry hall and into his office. I felt like a nine-year-old.

"Close the door," he commanded, standing behind his desk.

Shutting it carefully, I braced myself and stood at attention.

"First. Do you know what the hell happened to Gill? I haven't heard anything from him since last night about eight."

I pulled Gill's weapon from my jacket pocket and placed it carefully on the Sheriff's desk.

"Yessir. Lt. Gill is dead. Celeste Fielding killed him. His was one of the burned bodies."

Something flashed in his eyes.

"Oh." He seemed unsure where to go.

"Yes sir. I'm afraid he was part of the Albion operation, sir."

"Jesus."

He was looking in my direction but seemed to lose focus. He shook it off with some difficulty and began again, halting. "Beckham, I thought I'd be able to call you in here and tell you, privately, how proud I was of your accomplishment." His voice trailed off. "Now, I'm not so sure."

"Yessir? Proud, sir?"

"Well, yes. I'm proud of the initiative you demonstrated in bringing this to a close."

"But, sir, with Jack . . ." I was thinking of how Gill's involvement would reflect on Latch. Certainly, he would have gauged the up- and down-sides already.

"Yes." He pondered. "Jack." A beat. "That's going to be a problem. You showed *unprecedented* disregard for procedure and my authority and now . . . with this . . . That little girl killed Jack Gill? Well, we might be able to keep you out of jail." He seemed to rally.

"I'll never be able to admit this to anyone—this stays strictly between you and me." He coughed but caught himself. "Yeah," he said with a slight nod. There was some clarity forming. "I hoped all along you'd be able to run Gill to ground." He was back on track again. "Of course, I had no idea he would die in the process. Not Jack Gill. Not the Jack Gill I knew. But then again, I had no idea that what he was up to was this big."

"Sir, I'm not sure I understand."

"Have a seat. Coffee?"

"No, thank you," I said, continuing to stand.

He stood and poured himself a cup, sipped it and made a face. He put the mug down and turned to the window, clasping his hands behind his back.

"Look, Beckham. I will need you to make a formal statement about what happened last night. You remember I told you we had the Feds poking around? They arrived. Boston had been tipped that kids were being transported here from Mass but hadn't established a solid connection. They suspected a major porn operation but, again, because of routing and digital shit I don't understand, they couldn't confirm a physical source. You put it all together."

"I did, sir?"

"Yes, you did. I brought you back because I thought you were a good bet." He began to pick up some confidence here. "I needed someone from outside. There was stuff that didn't quite add up with Gill and Sam, and after Sam's death it grew more urgent." He coughed. "Sure, I figured it would take a little time. But you'd get to know Gill, gain his trust, and then you and I would talk." He started up with the coughing again but finally got it under control. He took a deep breath. It was wheezy.

"You okay, Sheriff?"

"Yeah, I'm fine. Just a tickle." He stood again and poured some water. "And then Major Fielding gets offed and his kids get taken and everything goes to hell. C'mon, have a seat," he said, gesturing to the unused chair after taking a couple of sips.

"No, thank you, sir. I'm okay." This was all news to me.

"Suit yourself. Between you and me, Allie, what happened last night?" he asked, sitting and leaning back. "We're off the record."

What's with the 'Allie?'

I hadn't begun to process what went down and standing seemed to help my perspective. I jumped in. Editing the events, I stuck to the highlights and added enough detail to justify my actions.

Latch interrupted my explanation about Gill's orders to meet at 1:30 and the assumption that the kids would leave afterward. "Shit, Beckham, this is why I emphasize procedure. Remind me what Gill said about their departure," he pressed. "What made you think they were going to Canada?"

I let him know that Celeste had told me the plan was to go to Canada and Gill confirmed it, if only obliquely.

"They were probably bound for Montreal," he interjected.

"Alright, maybe." I hesitated. "When he was talking to Karamova, the music was loud, and he was speaking Uzbek. I couldn't understand what he said, but yeah, I caught a word that sounded like Montreal. Not entirely sure, though."

Definitive.

"What time was it when you left Wooster?"

"It was a little before four when we rolled into the hospital. That'd make it about 3:15 when we left Wooster?" I guess-timated.

"Goddammit Beckham, we might still have a chance to prevent this Karamova guy from leaving!" he exclaimed, reaching for his desk phone.

Over the next half-hour, Latch made calls and coordinated with Chuckles, the Montreal Port Authority, an RCMP guy named Tremblay, and FBI Agent Rankin. They worked quickly and obtained an international warrant. What little detail I shared about MegaFon Wireless and Styx Metallurgy was passed on to Tremblay, who was expected to intervene and halt the departure of a private jet registered to Styx from Saint-Hubert Longueuil airport.

Finally, Latch turned his full attention back to me. "This . . . *this* is why I am so Goddamn angry. You should have called it—"

It was my turn to interrupt. "You're right, Sheriff. But I didn't call it in. I was too Goddamn tired and beat-up and I figured you had your hands full. You're right."

The air hung heavy in the following silence.

Finally, "Sir, what happened on your end? Why'd you come into the camp?"

He admitted he hadn't realized that Gill had been playing both sides against the middle. Gill had told me the truth; Latch had sent him to negotiate with The Professor and to get New Albion to stand down. Of course, Gill was never going to do that. He told Latch he'd gotten him "the best deal possible" and the militia was planning a peaceful march in Augusta. During overnight questioning, The Professor boasted the plan was to march to the state house, then defy orders to disperse and essentially, seize the city. He wasn't clear what would happen next.

"I mean, these guys' definition of patriotism must be pretty fluid . . . whatever suits them at the moment." His smile was more bitter than friendly, then he continued, "We were at the camp, monitoring any in-or-out traffic. But you know that already. I decided to leave the back door open, hoping we might be able to sweep up a few more of these guys that way. If they felt like they were getting away with something, you know, like kids sneaking around, it might encourage more guys to commit. It seemed to work."

He raised his coffee mug, took a sip, and made a face again.

"Something wrong, Sheriff?"

"Just the coffee . . . tastes 'off' today." He put the mug down with finality.

"When the propane tank went up, well, that was it. We had an excuse to enter—public safety and all that. We started in but ran into small arms fire at the bottleneck, it's a place—"

"Yeah," I interrupted. "The rocks. I saw it on the drone footage that, who? Was it McCann, Jr. who ran it?"

"Right, yeah, Chaz shot the drone stuff. Well, there were four guys there who had us pinned down. At least one had an AK; I haven't seen Randall's report yet. Match made sure we had those RPGs, just in case. So we sent a rocket into each rock face—*Boom!*" he smiled and gestured an explosion with his hands, "That was it. They took a hard fall—one guy broke his leg—and after that, we drove in."

"What else did you get from The Professor?" I asked.

"He shut up once Bradstreet relayed the news that his boys were dead. Claims he's gonna make certain you're prosecuted for Murder One. Said they didn't deserve to die that way. Says you had it out for them ever since the morning you found Fielding."

"He's a liar."

"Sure." Suddenly, he didn't sound so positive.

"What about Fran Kringle?" I asked.

"We've got a BOLO out and MSP's looking for her. We have the registration numbers on the Cloutier Moving vehicles and on her personal car. It won't be long. The Mister was in Portland. We picked him up this morning."

"I don't think Kris is involved."

"Don't tell me how to run my investigation, Beckham."

I stifled a chuckle. *"Your investigation?"*

"No sir."

"You seen a doctor yet? You look like shit."

"I'll be okay."

He assessed for a moment longer, then, after looking at the notes on his desk, he began to close the interview. The tone was distinctly less conversational.

"Beckham, you need to make your statement and you'll be put on administrative leave for a couple of weeks. You'll have full pay and benefits while we conduct a formal investigation. Keep your head down and don't talk to the press. Or anyone else for that matter. It wouldn't hurt to get a lawyer. Stay in Chamberlain County. Do not leave or I'll have to pick you up. Understand?"

"Yes sir."

"Okay. Dismissed."

I turned for the door.

"Beckham, I'll need your gun and badge."

"Right." I unclipped the H&K, laid it and my I/D next to Gill's pistol, and walked out.

Thirty-five

Randall drove me back to Folkestone.

We didn't talk.

After writing up my formal statement, I'd collected what little I had stored in the locker room. Kennedy and McCann, Jr. showed up and stood with their arms crossed at either end of the aisle as I stuffed a plastic shopping bag with my spare uniform and the framed photo of Hanna, my mom, and me I kept on the shelf.

I wanted to slam the door shut but closed it carefully, spun the dial on the locker, and looked at each of them in turn. "You got a problem?" I finally asked.

They boxed me in.

"You worthless bitch," spat Kennedy. They were as close as they could get without touching. I glanced up and was reassured to see the surveillance camera blinking. "Our own little Joan of Arc, waging her crusade for justice, hunh?" I was surprised he knew who Joan of Arc was. "Jack Gill was a veteran and a patriot. You best watch your back." The two of them held, hoping I would give them an excuse to hit me.

"Pardon me, gentlemen." They remained in place for several more seconds, then turned and left. I took a deep breath.

The bullpen went funereal when I walked in with my stuff.

"Let's go," I said to Randall. He, at least, had a little class and opened the door for me as we passed out of the room. DeSimone kept her head down.

King, and his boyfriend Reni, and I watched coverage of the press conference on the news that night while we ate some take-out. Sheriff Latch acknowledged Gill's death but was otherwise pretty tight-lipped, "Further investigation will be needed." He was going to try to bury it. He thanked the FBI and MSP for their help, thanked his deputies for their unflinching bravery, and let the public know I was on administrative leave as the inquiry continued. That was about it, and I was fine with that.

Latch told me to hang onto my laptop so I could keep up on Departmental communication. He recommended I copy him on any emails. I messaged Barry Daniels—didn't copy Latch on this one—saying I was tied up and wouldn't be able to make our date for skiing. He replied that he'd heard something about me on the news and suggested maybe, instead, we could do dinner sometime? *Persistent.*

Because I had attorney parents, I intuitively knew what to look for in a lawyer. I contacted Betsy Hardtack. She was a county institution—and had rightfully earned that reputation. Once I explained my situation, she took charge. She cautioned me about suing the department, not that I was ready to walk over that bed of hot coals. "Unwinnable," she said, and cited a Minneapolis case where the complainant alleged several officers were involved with porn, trafficking, and general lying. It was on course for the Supreme Court and unlikely that the plaintiff would win.

A couple of weeks of administrative leave turned into three, then a month. She was there for me every step of the way.

News about what happened filtered out from some of the New Albion guys. Hardtack insisted I get a personal phone and told me to refer any questions to her. I bought a burner. My inbox was flooded with requests for interviews and Loundsberry came to 144 Cushing and tried, once again, to shoot tape. The Professor shut up. At one point it looked like he might try to sue me for Civil Damages, but someone must have talked some sense, or at least suggested he wait until after his criminal trial. I kept my head down and read a lot. I called Mama Torres for the first time since I arrived in Maine and we had a long conversation. She offered to come to Folkestone if I thought it would help. I appreciated her sympathy, advice, and motherly love, but declined. I needed to ride this out on my own. I stayed away from the station.

There was a lot of time to kill. Getting in touch with my dad loomed large and there were a couple of times I screwed up the courage to call but couldn't bring myself to leave a message. The burner's number didn't merit a return on his end. I got close to King and Reni. We snuck down to Portland one night for King's show at the Sea Shanty, which was pretty good. He let me borrow his '07 Ion when I had to run errands.

❖

Lulu Charlevoix called. We met at the Crooked Birch for lunch and ended up sharing stories and discussing the case from more of a human-interest standpoint rather than the legal aspects. We were off the clock. We ordered wine.

She wanted to know about my family. I kept it short: twin sister died early, flunked out of U of C, some time at CPD, looking for quiet in my return to the Midcoast. In an effort to change the topic, I asked about her journey into medicine and how she ended up in Maine instead of Montreal. She took a moment and while she did, I observed the way the late afternoon light from the tavern window fell across the deep umber of her hand and its contrast with the polished maple surface of the table. Not "Maine."

She began her tale, "Bridget. Bridget is why I am committed to medicine." She went on to share a heartbreaking story about her high school girlfriend who mysteriously disappeared in Montreal. Her skirt and bra were found in the woods, but nothing else. There were no arrests. No one was charged. Lulu expressed her anger and frustration with the cruelty of some men and her unwavering dedication to bringing them to justice.

I was intrigued and couldn't help but ask, "But, what brought you to Maine then? It sounds like Montreal could use a good forensic physician."

Lulu lifted her glass, gazing into its depths before taking a sip. She assessed and then replied, "Yes, but Allie . . . you are one of the only people I trust to hear this. My family has a long history with the Pine Tree state."

My eyebrow raised and I leaned in, urging her to continue.

"Are you familiar with the story of Malaga Island?" she asked.

I'd heard of the place. Malaga Island was a settlement off the Midcoast in the 19th and early 20th century— a community of mixed-race families living together simply, until the locals deemed their existence unacceptable.

"Not Maine's finest hour," I remarked, acknowledging the unfortunate history.

Lulu agreed with a simple, *"Non."*

"But, how do you—how does your family—fit in?"

She looked at her hands, then past me to the curtained window as we sat in the quiet of the empty room. Jessie, the lone waitperson/bartender on duty, helped her afternoon regulars in the pub.

"We have no photos. I have never seen their faces. They were poor, eking out a living through subsistence farming and fishing. Malaga Island wasn't the only place suffering from poverty, but I believe it was the only mixed-race community in the state. They were good people, Allie."

I nodded, encouraging her to continue.

"My great-grandfather Ervin was likely the last child born on the island, in late 1910," Lulu explained. "He passed the story down to my grandfather Adam, and so forth. One day, his father—Ervin's father, Josiah—and his mother, Calpurnia, were on the mainland getting supplies. They had a friendly relationship with a husband and wife who ran a general store there. The wife pulled Calpurnia aside and shared her concerns. The newspapers were spreading wicked rumors about Malaga, and she worried for the community."

I interrupted. "So, my guess is that when they returned to the island, they voiced their concerns, but no one listened?"

Lulu sighed. "Yes, they were young, still in their teens. Living on an island off the mainland, nobody thought anything would happen. They were dismissed. But Calpurnia, thankfully, was worried about what would become of little Ervin if they stayed. In the fall of 1911, they left the community. It wasn't an easy journey, but they headed north and made their way to Canada, like the Acadians before them."

Feeling the weight of history, I asked, "What happened to the ones who remained?"

Lulu's voice dropped, "Many were institutionalized, deemed unfit for society. The others were dispersed, scattered like ashes in the wind."

She steepled her hands in front of her, smiled, and placed them flat on the table. Story over.

"So, this is why I am returned to Maine," she said, leaning in to it. "To be a presence. To honor my forebears. I suppose I am on a mission, and missionaries can be trouble." Her eyes crinkled at the edges with a smile that was a mix of bitterness and satisfaction overlaid with a past I could never appreciate. I thought back to the last time I'd sat with her, on Merry Hill Rd.

"Good trouble," I confirmed.

We were together, alone.

"So, now we know why we are both in Maine," Lulu finally said. And then, brightening, "Your father, he is around? You have seen him since you returned?" It was a fair question. I'd been prying into her past.

"No. Dad and I, we haven't been close for awhile," I said, looking away.

"Allie. You are a good woman but you are also a daughter. You should go see him. He is family and family is important."

Loud voices filtered into the space from the bar. Jessie stepped into the doorway and was surprised to see us sitting in the dark when she turned up the lights, "Ladies, can I get you anything else?" she asked gently.

"Not to worry, we're just getting ready to leave," I replied, hoping I could avoid Lulu's question.

"Allie."

I paused.

LuLu's smile was warm and supportive. She wasn't going to push it. "I'm so sorry for the fact that you were hurt." I looked at her and felt a deep connection. "Those men—they were bastards. In the end, they earned their reward. My family—I— have spent my life fighting to overcome that sort-of blind, unforgiving hatred."

I replied with a weary smile.

"Protect and serve," I said, and pushed back from the table.

◆

It was a month to the day when Latch called me in. King loaned me his Ion for the meeting and I drove to Gainsborough and climbed the steps to the courthouse entrance. McCann, Jr. was running the metal detector. He made a big deal trying to humiliate me, calling diSimone in to do a thorough frisking before giving me the okay. There were a couple of attorneys that came in behind me who, as always, were running late. McCann made sure they knew who it was that was holding them up. *What a prince!*

The door was open to Latch's office, but he was on the phone when I tapped lightly on the frame. He raised his hand as he closed the call, waved me in, and stood.

"Good morning, Beckham." He appraised me. "You look better than the last time I saw you."

"Thanks, Sheriff." *Always with the girl stuff.* "Are you feeling better, sir?"

The Seattle virus had made the leap from the west and suddenly everyone was talking about it.

"Yeah, I was down for a couple of days, no big deal. I heard the Guv's thinking of putting the state into lockdown, for Chrissake. Imagine the economic impact of something like that. Maybe the guys in New Albion had the right idea . . ." He drifted off for a moment, then was back with me. "I tell ya, just let people get it and get over it—no worse than the flu. Once the summer heat comes and folks are outside—I *guaran-damn-tee* it'll disappear. But thanks for asking. I'm okay now."

Affable.

"We're going to review our internal investigation this morning. Are you okay with that?"

What were my choices? I'd sat for a formal interview with an investigating panel and some of the officers had been closely questioned by Betsy Hardtack about what they'd found upon their arrival at MiqMaq/Wiki/Albion. She'd also had a couple of sessions with Trevor and Celeste, who at least corroborated my story. She couldn't—or wasn't willing—to let me know which way things would go.

"Yessir."

I'd tried not to make myself crazy by following stuff online. I watched the occasional evening news; read departmental email traffic that seemed relevant. It would be good to know the details of why I was getting fired. I continued to stand. Latch sat and folded his hands on the desk.

Formal.

"Have a seat." It was more than a suggestion. Once I had gotten comfortable, he began.

"How's the shoulder?"

Cursory.

"Doctor said I'll never be a volleyball star. But thank you for asking, sir. It's okay."

"First, I'm going to provide you with the results of our investigation into Fran Kringle, Jack Gill, and the Nation of New Albion. As you're probably aware, we picked up Fran as she was trying to cross into Canada at Coburn-Gore."

Official now.

"She and her bouncer-friend left the van on Old Wooster and boosted one of the militia SUVs. They traveled up to The Mountain where she must have stopped at the house, then jacked a Camry from the public lot. Not too bright—they left the stolen SUV next to it so we knew what they were driving as soon as it got reported. Some gal at the border crossing saw the description of the Camry come across the wire. She pulled the guy out of the car."

"Yeah. Is it true they found Fran in the back?"

"She was in the trunk, alright. Curled-up tight around a shopping bag with 120 gold Maple Leafs and $150,000 in cash. We're still not sure where they were headed. He'll talk, eventually."

He laid out the investigation's results in broad strokes, checking his notes now and again. There was information I already knew from LuLu and even Gill's rant at the camp, but Latch filled in some detail. Beginning in 2016, Gill and Sam Martin had threatened, then colluded with Fran Kringle to build on her child-trafficking operation. At first, they pushed kids through a run-down former car dealership garage in Hamilton that one of Martin's brothers' owned, but after they bought Camp Wiki, they moved the operation. "Breezy managed the housing arrangements and started video production at Wiki. He produced footage of kids performing a variety of unspeakable sexual acts with each other, adults, and in some cases, animals, and it was uploaded to a subscription site Gill assembled on the Dark Web."

Latch nodded as I acknowledged this last piece with a shake of my head. He went on.

"I tell ya, this was an honorable bunch. We ran across some insurance footage of Gill that Breezy must have shot . . . woulda made you puke. More 'mainstream' porn was uploaded directly to SkinFlix, where they got the standard advertising per-hit rate. SkinFlix, of course, denied any knowledge of the age of the kids or the provenance of the footage."

"Shocked, they were, I'm sure." I interjected. "No wonder Fran was so distraught when she saw Trevor's little video of Justine and Becca."

"Right. That happened right under her nose and suddenly, well, "What goes around . . .""

He continued. "Once Breezy was done with the kids, Fran would get 'em cleaned up and looking presentable as 'typical U.S. kids' and auction them via some digital finance system that Gill had found on the Dark Web. You ever heard of Bitte-Bit? She'd arrange for transport out of the U.S."

"Nossir, doesn't ring a bell. So, did they remain in Canada?"

"We're not certain, but we don't think so. We're pretty sure it was the clients' responsibility to make travel arrangements out. The Feds are coordinating with RCMP on that. With Longueuil and at least a half-dozen other private airports in the region, and then the St. Lawrence Seaway and all the potential for a marine departure—it wouldn't have been too tough to move a kid out of the country, or even multiples, for that matter. Where they were going, what they were going to be doing—they wouldn't need a passport."

We reflected for a moment on a future so grim. "What about the kids who were sold? Have you looked for them?"

"Not my job, Beckham." *Sounds about right.*

"What about Karamova? I haven't heard about any diplomatic kerfluffles. Did Tremblay stop the plane?"

"Short answer is no. When they went to Longueuil to serve the warrant, the plane was there, but the pilot told the Mountie that Husan had "gone to get a cup of coffee." He disappeared."

"So he hasn't shown up anywhere?"

"Tell you what, Beckham, I'll get my agents in Tashkent to check up on him." I smiled. *Whatever.*

"Fran and Jack." I was still trying to come to terms with how they could have been partners.

"That's a tough one." He was quiet. "Gill's dead and Fran hasn't been exactly forthcoming. From what I can tell, it was a complex relationship. She's a survivor."

I thought back to our call about Justine's video. She gave an Oscar-worthy performance when I'd told her Jack was in the room.

"Gill was Military Intelligence," he said, talking over my thoughts. "I'm no psychologist, but I think they were double and triple-crossing one another with financial chicanery and mind-games. Fran didn't trust love and is disgusted with sex—in the long run they've brought her nothing but pain. Gill had Marcie . . ."

"Marcie?" This was the first I'd heard of Marcie.

"Yeah, Marcie Langston. They've been dating, well, they *had* been dating a couple of years but that was more like a cover for him. He liked little girls and boys. Fran supplied them, for a price. The Bureau discovered Fran went through some pretty tough times between her murder trial and when she showed up at Bertram & Cohen. From my perspective, her relationship with Kringle looks purely political—a way to establish a toehold on financial security."

I was skeptical. It showed. "Yeah, but . . . " I interjected. What she had done to those kids was inexcusable.

"You may think it's a long way from the sexy secretary for a hot-shot trader to her final role in this business, but remember that Fran had been trafficked as a kid. She knew the ins-and-outs. And continuing the Cloutier's family tradition would deliver independent financial security. Her own money. And that was *her* weakness. You and I both know she needed to feel as though she was in control. On Jack's side, well, he was the only one in the group who understood and could manipulate the technology and maintain the Bitte-Bit account, which is where the big money was coming in. 'Course, he was skimming a percentage off the top that Fran wasn't aware of. How they each dealt with their cash was emblematic of who they were: Fran stashed hers here-and-there in hard currency, gold, and diamonds. We're pretty sure he had several offshore accounts, just haven't been able to locate them, yet."

"And Sam?"

Latch lowered his chin. "Sam." He swiveled in his chair to the window. When he turned back, he was composed.

"I hired Sam in 2005. He was a good cop and Beckham, it's true we all loved him. Everyone except Kourtney. Her contempt for him was painful to see. He couldn't possibly support her the way she wanted on his salary. The money Fran promised was too good to pass up. Then Tabby matured and there was the competition between her and her mom . . . it just killed him. No one knew of the connection between Kourtney and Fran. We're not sure if Tabby overdosed or was killed. Another ongoing RCMP investigation."

He glanced at his watch. "You seen Fielding?"

"We had dinner at the Brewery. She buried Major on the property, private service."

"Yeah, I figured." Latch was looking past me.

"I haven't seen the kids," I said, hoping to regain his attention. "They're both in therapy—she brought a shrink up from Yale who's staying at the Landing and giving them full-time access."

"Well, thanks to you she was able to hang onto another five million dollars," he said. "She can afford it."

"Six." I countered. He nodded, not thrilled about being corrected. "The kids are pretty messed up. Celeste not so much as Trevor. In the end, he'll probably be okay but he's got some issues to work through. Trevor feels like it's his fault that his dad's dead."

"They corroborated your account of what happened at the camp, at least what they saw and heard, and we don't see any reason to doubt what you said about Breezy. We're going to issue a formal reprimand for disobeying my orders."

I nodded.

"Beckham, you're in the clear."

Thirty-six

I THOUGHT I'D BE relieved.

Latch leaned forward.

"In the end, the department's gotten some decent press out of this cluster-fu . . . mess. Apparently, there are folks who see you as some kind of hero," he said with an almost imperceptible shake of the head. "Beckham . . . ," I met his gaze, ". . . I need a Detective. You ready to come back?"

He could see my surprise. It was silent in the office for a long beat.

"You're a good police officer, Beckham, despite the blow-back," he began again, filling the gap. "You're creative," he said, undercutting the compliment with air-quotes. "You have good instincts and you're willing to follow them. Surely you understand why I was so tough on you. I couldn't let Gill think I was favoring you or he'd close up shop."

"Yeah. I understand." But I didn't. I'd been hired to be a Deputy Sheriff, not a special investigator. I wondered whether this was just CYA bullshit or if he really brought me back to clean things up.

It didn't matter.

Suddenly, I was tired. Tired and angry. Tired of trying to make it work in another department that clearly wasn't ready for me. Tired of working for a sexist publicity-hound with one eye constantly on re-election. And angry that he'd used me like a stale mop.

"No thanks, Sheriff. I'll pass."

This time, it was his turn to be surprised.

Finally, "Beckham you sure about this? What're you gonna do for income?"

"Not your worry. Thank you, Sheriff. I'll find my way out."

Thirty-seven

I LEFT THE SHERIFF sitting at his desk, strode out of the courthouse without looking at McCann, Jr., found my way to the Ion, and sat.

The twins would be okay. Sure, Trevor had some issues he'd have to work through, but he'd make it. Honor would hire the best attorneys money could buy and he'd get off on the child porn stuff with a warning. Celeste remained as strong as ever. I'd try to check in with her mother once in awhile, to see how they were doing.

Dina Garrett let me know they'd cleared Kris Kringle. He'd had his head down, diligently trying to meet Major Fielding's expectations with the new business and, God bless him, he'd made an effort to make his marriage work.

Honor, Trevor, and Celeste. Who knew, maybe Fran's worst nightmare would come true and the young Mrs. Fielding and Kris would get together?

I was going to have some time on my hands. Latch had selfishly kept me out of jail. But who was I kidding? It was through Betsy Hardtack's lifetime of courtroom connections, hard work, and charm that she engineered my freedom. She earned her retainer. Now I had to figure out a way to pay her.

From my view in the parking lot, the broken, ice-choked, surface of the Coaticook moved south with all the urgency of a concrete pour. Rain, rather than snow, had been predicted, and by week's end we'd be in Mud Season. The Ion started on the first try. I nudged it into gear and crossed the river.

In my return to Maine, I'd been searching for positive change and perhaps a restored sense of belonging. I'd found neither. Making the turn in Folkestone, I headed south again on 145. Trees continued to reach, blank, into the sky. It was far too early for buds. Familiar fields passed in the flat light and glimpses of tidal water flashed black against the melting snow. After cresting Falk's Hill, I took a sharp left onto Bennett Lane as the downslope began. The Thibodeau place remained unchanged with its classic white trim on gray shakes. Cushing's Cottages looked like someone might finally be paying attention to their dilapidated state. The Ion bottomed out a couple of times, even though we were creeping along, trying to be careful, and I picked my way through the potholes that became more numerous on the unpaved gravel surface where the "Private Way" started after the DeRosa's saltbox home. Slowed to a crawl, we pushed through overlapping rosa rugosa bushes—invasive beach roses—that had been neglected to the point of blocking the road. There was a gentle *skree* of thorns scraping the paint on the Ion. King would be pissed.

After fording the dip where Campbell Creek spills over the roadway during a heavy rain, I revved up the hill. Debris littered an unkempt grassy knoll: a pair of worn winter tires here, a couple of rusted bikes there, wilting corrugated boxes—some empty, some full. To the left, a decaying carriage-house cum-garage with a blue tarp nailed to the roof stood behind an early model Prius. The car looked as if it might start but maybe hadn't been moved for a week. A trio of cats, summoned by the unfamiliar sound of the Ion, ambled in our direction. I'd probably known their parents. Bulging white kitchen garbage bags, many with holes gnawed and their contents spilling forth, formed part of a mother lode of trash which was stacked like a bulwark and filled the ell's step-back from the stoop to the window sill. The main building, an antique cape with peeling clapboards, sat wanly at the crown, a ragged crabapple tree clutching its southern end. I braked and pushed the shifter into Park, cracked the windows, and cut the engine.

My gaze followed the sound of lapping waves to the shore. The air was thick with the scent of low tide as rockweed draped and floated in gentle profusion along an exposed granite outcropping. Its broken outline framed a trio of lobster boats. They'd been slipped back into the water after winter refitting and awaited the new fishing season. Beyond them, South Prescott's tidy East Harbor opened to the bay and on to the Gulf, whose horizon lay as flat and hard as a sheet of battleship steel. I could just make out the first of The Triplets in silhouette in the middle distance, past Squirrel Point.

The view, if not the setting, was striking.

I unbuckled, left the Ion, and walked to the entry, softly kicking aside a paper bag of empty beer cans that *crankled* as they rolled on themselves. The front door stood within a frame of divided windows on either side and across the top, and I rubbed schmutz from one of the panes with the flat of my gloved hand, then shaded my face against the glass and peered through. Stairs on the left climbed steeply to the sleeping area. In the hallway, a pile of unopened mail sat on an antique side-table that was supported by delicately spiraled Jacobean legs. A framed photo hung above it. Blue light from a TV flickered at the rear.

As I opened the door, the accumulated sweet of rotting garbage pushed out of the house as if it was trying to escape from itself. I stepped through and propped it open with an old boot that happened to be handy. Breathing shallowly through my mouth, I started toward the back, pausing for a moment in the hallway to look at the photo of two girls playing in the crabapple tree.

The rear of the house expanded to an open-plan addition that might have once been described as 'contemporary.' The kitchen, if it could still be called that, was on the left. More garbage bags were piled haphazardly. The cooktop and the sink, while not clean, served as oases of open space in the overwhelming clutter. In front of me stood a sofa covered in nubbly fabric, its corners shredded to the stuffing by generations of cats. A courtroom reality show streamed on the TV. A man wearing a t-shirt and jeans sat, eyes unblinking. In his right hand was a can of Narragansett, tipped flat on the cushion, its contents leaving a dark stain.

He needed a shave and a haircut, but I recognized him. It was almost a minute before I understood why I was crying.

"Oh, Dad."

A Note to the Reader

I deeply admire the tireless efforts of our first responders—law enforcement, fire crews, EMTs, and others—who courageously navigate potential danger on a daily basis. In my county, our sheriff, unlike Chamberlain County's Jim Latch, has launched a volunteer "Citizens Advisory Committee" to provide a sounding board for Sheriff's Office public safety policy decisions and a communication channel between citizens and the Sheriff. He also cooperates with the local Restorative Justice Program as appropriate: two facets of how he and his entire department are working to transform lives and embody the essence of "serve and protect."

Regrettably, not all law enforcement agencies adhere to this standard. The narrative of *Bitter Passage* draws from real events, including the resignation of a Maine county sheriff in 2020 due to sexual misconduct and the recent conviction of a former gubernatorial candidate for possessing child pornography.

The National Center for Missing and Exploited Children conducts vital work in raising awareness about children in danger. While I champion freedom of expression, participants must be of an age and maturity level to make an informed choice. If you suspect child trafficking or exploitation, contact their hotline at 1800-THE-LOST (800-843-5678).

— G.B.

Acknowledgements

From the impenetrable forests and expansive potato fields of Aroostook County to the majesty of Acadia, from the forever wilderness of Baxter State Park and Mt. Katahdin to the bustle of Old Orchard, Wells, and Ogunquit beaches, from the snowy reaches of Carrabassett Valley to the rugged shores of the Midcoast region, Maine's natural beauty and warm and friendly people have sustained me for decades.

There are many to thank for their encouragement and help as the creation and publication of *Bitter Passage* unfolded. Thanks go to Bruce Robert Coffin, who encouraged me as I was getting started and to Matt Cost, a prolific Midcoast crime author, who generously critiqued writing samples.

Robin MacCready and Mort Castle, two friends who happen to be 'real' authors, deserve unbounded gratitude for agreeing to read, make comments about, and blurb the book. Larry Bennigson, another friend, delivered relevant and much appreciated observations about our county's Sheriff's department.

My early readers: Bethany Bates, Scott Belville, Barb Burt, and Bob Emmons all provided valuable feedback and I am sincerely grateful for their encouragement as Allie Beckham took shape on the page. Chris Bates, Asian martial arts expert extraordinaire and author in his own right, delivered important commentary on action scenes . . . thank you.

And finally, many thanks to my best friend, Susan, without whose clarity of insight, continuous encouragement, and love, I would be lost.

Geoffrey Bates

About the Author

A patchwork of moves beginning in his native New England and extending to the Deep South and the upper Midwest provides Geoffrey Bates with a rich palette of experience from which he shapes his narratives. Armed with degrees from the University of Georgia and Ohio University, he found a professional niche in arts administration and settled near Chicago. Today, he lives and writes on the coast of Maine where, in his spare time, he gardens, walks Bonnie the wonder pup, and enjoys ocean swims with Susan.